LIMITED EDITION

BONDED FATE

THE GUARDIANS OF THE MAIDEN

BECK MICHAELS

PLUMA PRESS

BONDED FATE Limited Edition © 2021 Beck Michaels
Bonded Fate bonus content © 2021 Beck Michaels
Shattered Souls content © 2021 Beck Michaels
Veron's Bonus Chapter © 2021 Beck Michaels
Map Copyright © 2021 Beck Michaels
Cassiel and Dyna artwork © 2021 Beck Michaels
Zev artwork © 2021 Beck Michaels
Lucenna and Rawn artwork © 2021 Beck Michaels
Cover © 2021 Pluma Press LLC
Map Illustration by Vanessa Garland
Character Artwork by Salome Totladze
Cover Art & Design by SeventhStar Art
and Whimsy Book Cover Graphics

PLUMA PRESS
P.O. BOX 341
Camby, IN 46113
Visit Us at PlumaPress.com

First Edition December 2021

Author: Michaels, Beck

Title: Bonded Fate / Beck Michaels

Series: The Guardians of the Maiden; 2

Genre: YA Fantasy Fiction

Summary: Dyna and her Guardians continue their journey across Azure as they face new
enemies, their inner darkness, and learn to trust each other.

Identifiers:
ISBN 978-1-956899-00-9 (Limited Edition softcover)
ISBN 978-1-7347639-8-0 (hardcover) | ISBN 978-1-7347639-7-3 (softcover)
ISBN 978-1-7347639-5-9 (ebook)

www.BeckMichaels.com

Printed in the United States of America

For my bonded—

*And for all the readers who hated me at the end of Divine Blood.
You might not be too happy with me at the end of this book either.*

The Seven Gates

Each soul passes through the gates at their beginning and their end.

HEAVEN'S GATE

LIFE'S GATE

SPATIAL GATE

TIME GATE

MORTAL GATE

NETHERWORLD GATE

DEATH'S GATE

Nine Years Ago

The window shattered like the shards of a nightmare. Dyna screamed, ducking protectively over her baby sister tucked in her arms. The blast threw her father back, and he collided into the door as glass rained down, scattering across the floor.

Outside, the snowstorm released a haunting howl, blowing icy wind and snow through her bedroom. Black smoke spilled across the windowsill and down the wall, crawling over the floorboards. Red eyes made of flame glowed in the darkness. Vicious. Hungry. The wispy shapes of horns took form in the moonlight, and then the shape of an inhumanly tall man with shadowed spikes jutting from his shoulders.

Fear gripped Dyna's racing heart, squeezing it so tight she couldn't breathe.

The Shadow had come.

Thane, trapped under the demon's spell, didn't move from where he sat on his bed beneath the windowsill. Her little brother stared blankly at the Shadow. Snowflakes clung to his lashes, red ringlets gleaming against his pale cheeks as his shallow breaths puffed in the chilly air.

Her father's hands flared green, but a gust of wind and smoke tossed him back as the Shadow snatched Thane from his bed through the window, lifting his body in the air.

Dyna stifled a scream, thrusting out a hand. Not her brother. Not Thane. She wanted to move. To save him. To do something. But panic locked her limbs in place.

Her father cried out, scrambling to his feet again, only for the demon to stretch open its jaws and swallow her brother whole. She covered her mouth, muffling her cries as the ground opened out from under her, throwing her into a pit of despair. A choked sob escaped her father's lips, and his knees hit the floor. Another wail followed from outside. Her mother, who'd gone out in the storm to search for Grandmother Leyla, cried out her brother's name.

"The Waning Amulets cloak all except sound," her father had said. The cloaking spell protecting her mother from the shadow demon had broken.

The Shadow dashed away, vanishing from view.

"Baden!" her mother screamed.

The call snapped her father into action. "Hide!" he told Dyna, then he dove through the broken window and disappeared into the freezing night.

The warmth of her baby sister, wrapped within her shawl, reminded Dyna of the precious weight in her arms. She scrambled to hide behind her bed as screams carried on the wind. Dyna clutched Lyra close and covered her ears. Tears streamed down her face as she rocked herself back and forth. Trembling uncontrollably, her breaths shuddered as she stared at the snow whipping past the window.

Mother and father are out there! Dyna couldn't leave them to face the Shadow alone, but what about her sister?

Lyra's cradle lay knocked over by the fireplace. Dyna pulled it to where they were hiding and lay her sister down, wrapping her in more blankets, making sure she wore the little amulet tucked within her swaddle. It would keep her safe. Lyra gurgled in her sleep, completely unaware of the horror outside.

Dyna kissed her sister's soft forehead with a whispered prayer to the God of Urn for protection and pushed the cradle out of sight behind her bed, then ran out of her room. The parlor was empty and quiet, carrying the herbal scent of medicine. Dyna ran past the table cluttered with tomes and dried herbs and went out the front door.

Her bare feet sank into the thick snow as she circled the cottage until she found her father's deep footprints and followed them toward the clamor coming from ahead. Burning torches lit the night. The frightened villagers of North Star clutched their children and ran in every direction to escape the demon at their backs. It moved like a wraith, tearing babes from their mother's arms and tossing them into its wide jaws, their screams vanishing into smoke and shadow. The demon eviscerated anyone in its path with its black claws, painting the white landscape into a crimson sea of death.

Dyna trembled, whimpers lodging in her throat.

"Blossom, what are you doing out here?" Grandmother Leyla was kneeling in the snow near the cottage. Blood and tears shone on the soft wrinkles of her face.

"Grandmother?" Dyna inched closer and saw who she held in her arms. Her world became a void as she took in her mother's blank eyes. She lay lifeless in a pool of red, her abdomen torn open.

"The demon..." her grandmother sobbed, holding her daughter close. "It cut her down."

"Mama?" Dyna dropped beside her. "Mama!" There was so much blood. She lifted her hands over the gaping wound, struggling to remember what her father taught her about healing. Her shaking palms sparked a faint green, only to sputter out. "Please work." She pressed on her mother's stomach and urged her power to come forth. "Work!"

"Blossom, she's gone," her grandmother said.

"No, I can save her."

"Dyna, please. She's already dead."

Dyna shook her head, pulling at her hair. "No, no, no!"

"We need to hide." Grandmother yanked her up, forcing her away from her mother's stiff body.

She sobbed, flailing to get loose. "I can heal her!"

"It's too late," her grandmother replied, her voice breaking. She tried to drag Dyna back to the cottage. "We can't be out here."

An array of brilliant light flashed below the hill. They stopped, watching as the village council members surrounded the Shadow.

The rare few who could wield magic threw out their hands, glowing with the color of their Essence. A volley of attacks forced the demon back from striking any more children. Her father hurled powerful spell after spell, lighting up the sky.

Lady Samira stood watching from a distance, gawking at the demon and the devastation it wrought. The powerful councilwoman had refused to believe the Shadow would come. Now she did nothing but stand there with her hands over her mouth, shaking her head as if this were not real.

Her father waved out his arms in a circle, and a roar of green fire exploded from him in a rising wave. It barreled into the demon, launching it across the field, but it rolled to its feet and released a piercing shriek of rage. Dyna slapped her hands over her ears, cowering against her grandmother.

The Shadow raked its razor-sharp claws through the air and black blades of smoke shot forth. Her father and the councilors threw up shields, but the blades sliced through those not quick enough to react. Dismembered body parts scattered like bloody puzzle pieces on the frozen ground. Grandmother Leyla covered Dyna's eyes from the carnage, but she could see through a slit in her shaking fingers.

Councilor Cairo turned and vomited. Councilor Pavin backed away, round cheeks bouncing as he shook his head, eyes wide with terror.

"Don't you dare!" Her father's shout reverberated over the village. Pavin ran away. The others moved back.

"Fight with me." He continued to throw spells. "I need you!"

Councilor Mathis shook his head. "We cannot defeat a demon." He cast an invisibility spell and disappeared from view. Ciro and Xibil did the same.

"Those inconceivable bastards," Grandmother Leyla hissed under her breath. Dyna didn't understand. They abandoned him.

"Samira!" her father bellowed at the councilwoman. "I need a containment dome."

His cry for help instantly snapped her free from the shock. Dyna gasped as Lady Samira's silhouette lit in a golden light, white hair flaring, as she raised her wooden staff and slammed it in the snow.

Gold light encircled the Shadow in a ring. It rapidly expanded and rose in a glowing dome, trapping the demon inside.

Furious, the Shadow clawed and beat against the dome with a monstrous roar. With each strike it cracked, and Dyna's fear grew as fractures spread across the surface. It wouldn't hold it for long.

Her father's entire profile glowed green as he chanted in a foreign tongue, startling her with the strange words. Her father didn't need to speak spells. But this ... this wasn't a normal spell. His Essence lost its color and filtered into a murky brown, bleeding to pitch black. Skin crawling, every hair on her neck stood on end.

Black magic.

Dyna pulled her grandmother's hands, gawking as a red line formed in the space between him and the demon. The light rose as he chanted, developing into pickets made of bone ending in sharp spindles. Once it reached a towering height, it blazed and solidified into the Netherworld Gate.

A miasma filled the air, twisting everything inside of her with terror. The gods created The Seven Gates with a power no mortal could withstand and by opening it, her father would sacrifice himself to cast the Shadow back to the realm of demons.

Pushing out of her grandmother's arms, Dyna sprinted toward him. Her grandmother cried out for her to return, but she couldn't lose him, too. She needed to stop this. She rammed into her father's side, and his chant cut off as they crashed into the snow. The Gate vanished, and the dome shattered in an explosion of light as Lady Samira collapsed.

Rising to its full height, the Shadow demon's attention snapped to Dyna. She immediately turned away, knowing if she looked into its red eyes, it would transfix her with its power. She held still and quiet. If she didn't make a sound, the demon wouldn't notice her.

"Dynalya," her father whispered. His wide gaze locked on the amulet laying a few feet away in the snow. She reached for her neck and found it empty of her protective charm.

The Shadow lunged. Her father hit it with a weak blast of Essence, but it barely made the demon stagger. Sweat shone on his pallid face, his breath heaving. He had no more power left. He'd drained himself when attempting to open the Gate.

Dyna stood on shaking legs and faced the Shadow. She called on her Essence. It sparked uselessly in her hands as she desperately tried to form a spell in her hands, tried to fight. But she didn't have any power or the means to save anyone.

The Shadow sprang. Her father pushed her out of the way of its claws and they caught him instead, spearing him through his chest.

"Papa!" she cried in a gasping sob.

He smiled at her sadly as blood dripped from his face. The single claw protruding from him swirled with smoke.

"Run, Dynalya," he begged her. When she didn't move, he shouted desperately, "GO!"

Dyna sprinted into the thick snowstorm. Her numb, bare feet sank in the icy hill, tears freezing on her cheeks as she headed for the glowing white tree in the mountains. She fled from the demon's roars and her father's screams. Away from the horror her actions caused. He urged her to run, his voice echoing over and over across the frozen valley.

Until he, too, fell silent.

CHAPTER 1

O ut of all the things Dyna could have expected to hear today, learning that she was married was not one of them. The icy wind swept over her, howling over the rocky cliff. She sat stiff and frozen on the ground, an incoherent hum echoing Cassiel's confession in her mind.

We are Blood Bonded.

He'd said many things to her during their journey. Some harsh, some arrogant, some surprisingly kind, but this jest fell flat.

An involuntary bark of laughter left her, anyway. "What?"

He must be jesting. If it were true, she supposed it would make sense why he would grow close to her, only to pull away. Not only that, but to marry someone without their consent and to keep it a secret...

Cassiel didn't laugh. His silver eyes were glassy and uncertain, lacking their usual steel edge. The lump in his throat bobbed repeatedly and sweat shone on his forehead. His black wings twitched behind him, betraying his lack of composure. Dyna's smile faded away.

He was serious.

Her vision tunneled, pulling her from reality. Cassiel said something, but the muffled words didn't connect in her head where everything had gone quiet again, overtaking her comprehension. The autumn breeze blew over the cliff where they sat together, slipping through the space between them. It brushed against her lips that were mere inches from his.

Dyna gasped softly and jerked away. Cassiel let her go. His hands slipped from hers, and his wings fell away, exposing her to the bitter chill. He wore a carefully indifferent expression, but a melee of his apprehension buzzed through her, squeezing her chest. She laid a hand over her heart, at last realizing what was different about it.

Since the night of the full moon, a connection had forged between her and Cassiel. Wherever he went, his presence, his touch, it hovered on her skin. And she developed the odd ability to sense what he was feeling. She thought it had all been her imagination.

"Dyna," Cassiel called tentatively. "Say something."

The sunrise highlighted the sharp planes of his jaw and glossy feathers. The unearthly glow exuding from his skin matched the one coming from hers. A recent change, she realized, appeared after that night.

"What should I say to this?" she asked incredulously.

"If you will give me leave to explain—"

"Then explain," she said, a tad sharply.

He exhaled and ran a hand through his ink-black hair, shaking his head. The wind nearly stole away his faint voice. "The Other ... you were gravely wounded, and I had no recourse but to heal you."

Reaching for her shoulder, flashes of the full moon night rushed through Dyna's memories: Zev turning into the Other, the horrid pain of his teeth crushing her collarbone and dragging her away. He had nearly torn her apart, but her skin was as soft as satin beneath her fingers. Rendered flawless by the power of Cassiel's divine blood.

"You used your blood to heal me..."

He swallowed, his throat bobbing again. "That was my intention, but in my rush to save you, we ... exchanged blood instead."

Exchanged blood.

That's when everything changed. Every touch of his left a tingle on her skin, a source of warmth and electrical energy. But she'd assumed it was because of his Soul Searching ability.

"Once a Celestial chooses a life-mate, they are wed with a binding of blood," King Yoel had explained when she first heard the term Blood Bond. *"It connects their souls eternally until they are torn from each other at death."*

God of Urn.

Warmth rushed to her cheeks. He had bonded them, then *kept* it from her all this time. Everything she felt toward him was bare for him to see—when she looked at him, thought of him, touched him. He must have known every silly pining she felt, because he could feel her emotions as she could feel his. Tears of humiliation rushed to her eyes.

Had everything between them also been a lie? Not a few minutes ago, he had held her in his arms, a breath away from kissing her. Had he only courted the idea because of the bond? When he purchased clothing and shoes for her, had it been out of obligation? Did he truly care for her at all?

"Why did you keep this from me?"

Cassiel's expression grew guarded, and he glanced away. "I never meant for this to happen," he said, avoiding the question. "If I could undo it, I would."

There was a twisting in her chest, as if her heart had withered and shriveled to nothing.

"Of course. Why would you want to be bonded with a stupid human?" She couldn't mask the hurt in her voice.

A tear escaped, and he watched it fall down her cheek. "Dyna—"

"No." She rose to her feet, too embarrassed, confused, and angry. Her voice fought to remain steady. "I cannot speak to you right now. I—"

His guilt hit her next, and her eyes welled further as anger grew into a tangled mass of frustration that she couldn't give words to. She couldn't make sense of all the emotions roiling inside of her. Some were hers, but others were his, tangled too tightly to understand every single one. She couldn't put her thoughts into words when she didn't know what to say to him.

Would they always feel each other now?

She needed a moment to process this. There was a deafening quiet in her mind, and it let nothing else in. She turned away and headed for the forest. Cassiel's emotions catapulted into her like a storm. Each raging and twisting, bombarding her too rapidly. Then there was nothing, as if he had snipped them away.

Dyna halted before the tree line. It reminded her of the first time they had met in Hilos when he warned her not to go into the dangerous woods. Those steps had led to a series of events that brought her here.

"Allow me some time to think," she said without turning around. "It's a lot to take to mind. But I will warn you. Say nothing of this to Zev, or he will surely kill you."

Cassiel didn't answer. All she heard was the soft rustle of wings. When she turned around, he was gone.

Dyna would have preferred to stay on the cliff a bit longer to watch the rising sun bathe the Kingdom of Azure in daylight. She needed more time to herself. More time to untangle her thoughts, but all she could do was stare at a pebble by her foot. A rustling in the trees made her tense with immediate alarm, but it faded when a large black wolf slinked out.

Dyna attempted a smile. "Good morrow, Zev."

Her werewolf cousin cocked his head, studying her intently with those yellow eyes. She held her breath, fearing he'd discovered the new secret she learned. Zev had heightened senses. He saw things differently when he was a wolf.

He huffed, tail lowering as his ears folded on his head. At sight of his mild but familiar annoyance, she relaxed. He must disapprove of her leaving the safety of the camp. Zev was overprotective at times, not that he didn't have a reason for it these days.

"Yes, I know. I shouldn't wander off, but I wasn't alone. I was with ..." Dyna paused, taken aback by the tightness in her throat at the thought of Cassiel. "Sorry to worry you." She held out a hand to him. "Did you come searching for me?"

The wolf sauntered over and pressed his forehead against her palm. His fur was coarse and thick, carrying the scents of pine and earth after a rainfall. Beneath it hovered the musk of something dangerous. Something vicious that thirsted to kill. But Zev would never hurt her—save for one day of the month. If she wasn't careful.

The wolf circled her, standing about as tall as she was. She could feel the heat coming off him, muscles shifting with a strength carefully contained. He nudged her toward the trees gently, indicating they should return.

"Must we?" Dyna asked uneasily. She wasn't quite ready to face Cassiel yet. Or anytime soon.

Zev bumped her elbow with his wet nose, chuffing. With a sigh, Dyna limped after him into the trees. Her ankle had nearly healed since she sprained it on the hills of Corron. The pain was mostly gone and would be completely well within a day or two.

Zev walked ahead of her, constantly sniffing the air, furry ears twitching as he listened beyond the natural chatter of the forest. Since the kidnapping attempt, he always remained on alert. They had stayed off the main road, traveling along the western slopes of the Zafiro Mountains into the wilderness to avoid the main roads.

"Tarn will not find us here," Dyna said.

Zev growled at the mention of the infamous leader of the Raiders. He had sent Commander Von to capture her. She shuddered, recalling how close he had almost succeeded. If Rawn hadn't aided Cassiel in the alley...

But why her? Why did all of this need to occur now?

So much had happened since she left the protection of North Star. Her secluded village was nestled deep within the mountains, peaceful and hidden from the outside world. She missed her home. She missed Lyra and her grandmother. What must they be doing now? Did her little sister resent her for leaving? Was her grandmother fraught with concern?

Dyna wrestled with her own worry. She had too much to accomplish in such little time. This matter of the Blood Bond was trivial compared to this new enemy she had to defeat.

"I won't let Tarn stand in my way," she told Zev. "It doesn't matter who he is. My only priority is the medallion. I need to find it before ..."

An icy chill sunk through her spine. Memories of the Shadow flooded her thoughts. Echoes of her father screaming for her to run haunted her. She'd woken in the morning to that awful dream, and the remnants of terror still clung to her skin. Dyna clenched her fists, squeezing her eyes shut.

Tarn may be a dangerous man, but he paled in comparison to the Shadow Demon. If she failed to reach Mount Ida and return home with the Sōl Medallion before the Winter Solstice next year, there would be no hope for her village at all.

But there were so many obstacles in her way. There was the risk of mages finding her, and now a man she didn't know hunted her. She couldn't afford this silly distraction with Cassiel. No matter the Blood Bond. All of it left her mind in knots. She didn't know what to do about that any more than she knew what to do about Tarn. Why had she ever thought she could defeat a Shadow Demon?

Dyna crouched and wrapped her arms tightly around her knees. Next year's impending winter hovered over her with the promise of what would happen to her little sister if she didn't reach Mount Ida.

Whining, the wolf licked the tears from her cheek. Dyna hugged him tightly, burying her face in his fur. "I can't fail, Zev. For Lyra and North Star, I have to do this."

As they made their way down the cliff, the memory of Thane falling into the Shadow's jaws replayed in her mind over and over, blinding her in darkness.

CHAPTER 2

Lucenna

Lucenna blinked drowsily as she studied the ugly, slithery creature with bulbous black eyes. The grindylow snarled at her from the page, baring its long, sharp teeth. Short rigid fins framed its bony face. It swam in the dark depths of a lake. Glowing blue scales coated its long body to its eel-like tail.

Steam billowed against Lucenna's cold nose as she sipped a cup of lilac tea. She flipped through the glossary of mystical beings with a frown. She had to get at least one of those scales.

A beat in her temple drew her from her thoughts. She glanced at the crystal orb resting on its stand beside the book. With a rhythmic pulse matching her temple, white fog swirled inside, beckoning her to answer. Lucenna rolled her eyes and tapped on the glass. The fog cleared away as she met her twin brother's lilac gaze.

"Good morrow, Lucenna. You appear particularly well-rested today," Lucien said with a quirk of his lips. The morning light spilling through his bedroom windows shone over his long white hair.

Lucenna rubbed her face with a heavy sigh and attempted to straighten her messy locks. "I don't appreciate the sarcasm, Lucien. You know I don't normally rise this early."

Her dear brother had taken it upon himself to wake her at dawn every day since her escape from Corron. She had to take advantage of every waking hour to put as much distance between her and the south of Azure. Unfortunately, she had attracted Enforcers. They hadn't been this close to catching her since...

She glanced across her tent to the small dining table with two chairs, and her chest swelled with emotion. Four years on the run, jeopardized because she stupidly exposed her magic. It had created a beacon to every nearby Enforcer in the country.

"Yes, pardon." Lucien's affable demeanor switched to concern, proving he had only been putting on a front for her. "Where are you now?"

"I'm making my way west through the wilderness behind the Zafiro Mountains. I've avoided the roads. Don't worry."

"How long until you reach the Port of Azure?"

"Perhaps another week."

"Make it less. You must take a boat out of Azure as soon as possible. They know it's you and are determined to capture you. From the last report I gathered at dawn, five Enforcers are on your tail. Father is waiting for leave from the Archmage before he makes his way there."

Lucenna swallowed thickly at the mention of her father. Five Enforcers shouldn't be a problem. She'd taken on as many before. But the thought of her father coming sent a shudder through her.

"How do they know it's me?" she asked.

Lucien searched her face, his brow tightening. "You tampered with the Time Gate, Lu."

The reminder drew her gaze back to the dining table.

"It sent such a strong ripple of power through the atmosphere that even I sensed it in the Magos Empire. It was simple deductive reasoning. No other sorceress could have expelled such a significant amount of power, nor would any in her right mind remain in Urn."

But she wasn't the only sorceress in Urn. Lucenna recalled the redheaded girl who had caused her to use magic in the first place. Where was Dyna now? Gods, Lucenna hoped she didn't run into the Enforcers first. A Celestial and a werewolf may accompany Dyna, but they would be no match for mages.

Lucenna shook her head. "I know. It was foolish."

"That it was."

No one knew where she was hiding until now.

She went behind the privacy screen to change out of her nightgown. "I plan to leave Azure, but I must make a stop first."

"Come again?" he demanded. "Did you not hear what I said? The Enforcers are gaining on you."

"I need to find the Moonstone, Lucien." The Lūna Medallion hanging around her neck was warm against her chest as she slipped on a black, form-fitting blouse with long sleeves. She tugged on a pair of black leather trousers next. "My mission will not end until I do."

"Lucenna, the Moonstone is on Mount Ida, and I don't believe you will find the hidden island in Azure."

"No, but I may know someone who knows where it is." She fastened on a black leather bodice over her blouse, then sat on her bed to slip on her heeled boots.

Lucien frowned. "Explain."

"In Corron, I overheard the mention of a fae seer in the Moors. I can ask him how to find Mount Ida." Lucenna rested her hand over the medallion, caressing the empty crevice where the Moonstone belonged.

With it, the Liberation would finally have the power to rise against the Archmage and end his reign of oppression. It was all they needed so the women of her kingdom could be free. Without the Moonstone, they were powerless.

"The Moors? Do you mean the *Phantasmic* Moors?" Lucien asked. "The fae will not give you this information willingly."

Of course, they wouldn't. The fae traded for things of value, like years of service, or deals sealed with a geas.

"Good thing I know exactly what to offer him." Lucenna returned to the desk and held up the book with the image of a creature that looked like a hybrid of a hairless siren and an eel. "The scales of a grindylow are highly valuable and incredibly hard to attain. It will be a good trade, and it so happens a nest of them lives in the Saxe Fjord. It's on my way to the port."

Lucien's eyes widened. "Lucenna, that will be highly dangerous. They are vicious creatures."

"If I can only get one scale, then I'll be able to get some answers."

"You mean to find the Moonstone."

"Yes, that's what I said."

He studied her face, arching an eyebrow. "It seems you had more you wanted to ask."

Lucenna bit back a curse, annoyed at her ever-perceptive brother.

"It's too much of a risk. You cannot afford to be in Azure any longer."

"But this may be the only chance we have," she insisted, her tone sharpening. "The women of Magos are depending on me. I need to find the stone and end the Mage Code. How can you live there, bear witness to their suffering, and tell me to run?"

Lucien pressed on his forehead. "I also want change, but not at the expense of your life. I'm searching for Mount Ida and any clues on the Moonstone from my end, but I cannot be at peace until I know you're safe. Promise me you will leave Azure."

She heaved a breath, lowering her gaze. "I will."

"Lu," he said, his tone firm. "I mean it."

"I'll leave, Lucien. Don't worry. Well, I must be on my way. I'll speak to you soon." Lucenna tapped on the orb before he could answer, and his image cleared away.

Looking around the tent, her heart grew heavy. Memories of her mother filled every inch, and were now a constant reminder of her absence.

Grabbing a waterskin off the dining table, Lucenna headed out into the morning chill in search of the stream nearby. As she crossed the threshold of the spell protecting her home, the illusion of a small, abandoned tent took its place. Dawn's gleam streamed from the branches overhead as she strolled through the forest.

A promise was a promise. She would leave Azure ... after she went to The Moors.

Once reaching the stream, Lucenna kneeled by the bank, plunging the waterskin into the icy water. Her determined reflection stared back. She had spent years wishing she could change the moment her mother died, to somehow prevent the mistake that had led to it and bring her back. The idea had been an impossibility until she learned how to enter the Time Gate. She could only stop time, but perhaps going back might not be impossible.

Something shifted in the air, and Lucenna stiffened as her Essence snapped to the surface of her skin. She jolted to her feet and stared into the trees, every instinct alerting her to the crackle of power in the air. Her breath caught as it grew frightfully prominent, closing in on her from every direction.

No.

They'd found her.

Lucien's cold splash of alarm hit her, and his urgent call pulsated in her temple. There was no time to answer or to retrieve her tent.

Lucenna bolted into the forest. Laughter and taunting voices slithered between the trees. Purple electricity coiled along her arms at the ready. Her legs pumped as she sprinted as fast as she could. There was only one place where she may have a chance out of this.

She burst from the trees into a vast clearing surrounded by the thick forest, making it to the center as ten figures emerged from the foliage. More than Lucien had originally told her. Mages under dark hooded cloaks circled her, each holding a staff with crystals of a different color. The force of their power choked the surrounding atmosphere, the haze warping the air like heat coming off stone. Their cloaks fluttered around them as the wind billowed over the field. Light coursed up their hands, and they slammed their staffs on the ground. The crystals and their eyes flared with their Essence. The triad symbol of the Magos Empire marked the right shoulders of their sleeves. Above it was another jagged symbol of their rank.

These mages were *Elite* Enforcers. Her heart raced as her power heated beneath her skin.

"There you are, little sorceress," one said as he stepped forward.

Lucenna recognized that voice. Ignatius pulled off his hood, revealing his long scarlet hair tied back in a series of braids. His amber eyes flamed as the sun fell over him. "We're taking you back where you belong."

"I'll die," she hissed as purple light flared in her palms and ran along her arms in winding trails, "before I surrender."

The mages tightened the circle and the crystals on their staffs glowed with the color of their Essence: indigo, deep crimsons, orange, black, yellow, light blue, and muddled green.

"It's daytime, Lucenna," Ignatius mocked as he lazily leaned on his staff. An onyx crystal woven in the wood at the top thrummed with power. He waved at the others, mages of the Sun and Earth Guilds. "In the middle of the forest. We're much stronger than you right now."

They were in their elements while her power was at its strongest at night.

"All you women are so stubborn and stupid," Ignatius continued. "I don't know how you escaped us for as long as you did, but you were always going to be caught. It's bad enough you think you have any genuine power. You're of the Lunar Guild, the weakest of them all."

"Weak." Lucenna laughed. "Yet my father sent ten of you to subdue me."

The moon may be the major element of her guild, but more than one element fed her power. She looked at the open sky. Electricity crackled in her palms as thunder rolled overhead at her call. Thick, dark clouds cloaked the sun, darkening the field. Pillars of lightning struck the ground with a violent crack, sending a powerful charge through her veins.

Lucenna gave the mages a harsh smile as her body blazed with purple light. "Let me show you how powerful a woman can be."

CHAPTER 3

Cassiel chased his shadow into the horizon, letting his wings carry him high in the morning sky. Pushing through the thin veil of clouds, he flew into the sun's glare and closed his eyes as the bitter wind stung his face. It numbed everything but the pang in his chest where Dyna's despair had settled.

When he saw the hurt in her emerald eyes, he didn't know what to say. Even with how kind and accepting she was of him, he expected her anger, but not her despair. Not the embarrassment or her need to run away from him. He would have preferred she scream at him or hit him, anything but wanting to escape him.

The air thinned as he pushed onward. His wings pumped harder, straining as he continued further than he should go. He wanted to leave the atmosphere and reach Heaven's Gate, even if it meant there would be no return.

When he reached the top of the world, Cassiel let go. He spread his arms, tucked in his wings, and let himself fall. He was weightless. For a moment, the heavy burden of his cursed existence lifted off his skin. His sullied half-breed blood seeped out of his pores. The fault of the bond. The guilt of killing humans. The hate of his kind. He left it behind in the skies as he plummeted back to earth.

Without it all, he was on his own. He had always been alone. Among the Celestials—among his kind in Hilos—he didn't belong. There wasn't anything for him in that place, not since his mother left. There was a reason why he followed Dyna.

How could he have forgotten?

Cassiel dropped through the clouds and snapped open his wings. He twisted sharply, righting himself again. Riding the wind idly, he looked toward the west, where he imagined the enchanted treasure island lay. He had disobeyed his father and risked the secrecy of Celestials to go on this mission. This infatuation with Dyna had gone far enough.

I will not repeat your mistakes, he had sworn to his father. A man was nothing if he couldn't keep his word.

When had he let himself become so disillusioned? Dyna was brave and hopeful, always striving to find the good in people. Every moment spent with her, he found himself forgetting what he was. The line between simple acquaintances had blurred. It was time he rectified that. Somehow.

Cassiel circled and flew back in the camp's direction. It wasn't safe to fly out during the day, lest he risk being seen by a passing traveler. A flash of lightning snapped him out of his thoughts. Thunder cracked and storm clouds rolled in out of nowhere, darkening the sky in a thick shroud. Before he could question it, he dodged a spear of lightning, missing him by a fraction. He cursed, wings banking right. He needed to return to land. If he got caught in the storm—

A flash of color came from the east. He frowned and focused on the canopy of trees on the horizon, and he saw it again. A brief flare of blue light, followed by a flare of red, then purple. More blazing lights came, accompanied by the distant sound of explosions. Another blast speared through the air. He arced sharply to the left, only for another to hit him with a brutal force, stealing every breath and thought.

Then he dropped out of the sky.

CHAPTER 4

Thunder boomed, making Dyna's heart jump in her chest. As she and Zev reached camp, dark clouds surged across the sky, concealing the sun. Lightning flashed, and a rumble followed.

"Strange," Rawn said, rising from where he had been sitting by the campfire. "There had been no sign of rain."

But a droplet splashed on Dyna's cheek, regardless.

"God of Urn, Cassiel is up there." She searched the skies. He flew through a pocket of clear blue before it was quickly snuffed out with storm clouds. Lightning cracked, and Cassiel deviated, scarcely evading the bolt. Dyna flinched and covered her mouth. His alarm flooded through her.

"What is he doing?" Rawn asked when Cassiel stopped to look at something in the distance.

Lightning streaked across the sky. He ducked nearly a fraction too late. Dyna gasped and jerked toward him.

"Get down from there!" she shouted, though he was too high to hear.

Thunder cracked through the air, followed by a streak of lightning. It struck Cassiel with a violent blow, and her entire body spasmed with a cry. He plummeted out of the sky. Dyna screamed his name as her mind raced for ways to save him, but she had no power. Her lungs heaved for air, the weight of terror crushing her chest. She could do nothing as his smoking form fell.

But Cassiel's wings broke open at the last moment, slowing his descent, and he slammed into the ground. They ran to him, and relief flooded through her to find him alive. Cassiel sucked in ragged breaths, his chest rapidly rising and falling. Smoke and the scent of burned skin rushed her nose. His clothing and wings were torn and scorched.

"Cassiel! Oh gods!" Dyna dropped by his side, not knowing what to touch first. Flesh charred black and red covered his chest and half of his face.

"I'm fine," he groaned. "I'm healing."

His skin began weaving new flesh through the burns. He would live.

She exhaled heavily and brushed his wet hair from his forehead as she checked his head and eyes. For now, she ignored everything else between them. "What happened?"

"I do not know," he said as the last of the wounds healed. His gaze focused on her as he searched her face. "Something hit me."

"Lightning hit you," Zev said, his voice caught between a growl as he shifted back to his human form.

Suddenly aware of how close she was to him, Dyna stepped back.

"No." Cassiel grimaced as he sat up. "It was something else."

The heavens shook with a forceful boom of thunder and released a torrent upon them. Rawn helped Cassiel to his feet and Zev yanked on a pair of trousers. They scattered, grabbing their packs, and ran toward the trees for cover. The rain beat down, seeping through her clothes. Water slid off Rawn's cloak, though. It must have been enchanted.

"Marvelous." Cassiel glowered under the feeble shelter of his wings. Without looking at her, he extended a wing above her head. He shifted his stance to face Zev, and his back took the brunt of the storm, blocking her from the assault of the wind and rain. "I assume you did not think to purchase a tent?"

Zev snorted. "No, but I made sure to buy your costly rice milk, Your Highness."

Dyna yelped when another boom rattled her skull. "Where did this storm come from?"

"This is not a natural occurrence, my lady," Rawn said as he studied the dark clouds.

Cassiel nodded. "I saw something beyond the forest. Lights. I'm not sure how else to explain," he added irritably when they all frowned at him in question.

The dark clouds spanned the sky. The eye of the storm was not too far from them. Streaks of lightning crashed on land beyond the forest as static prickled across Dyna's skin.

She raised a hand to the clouds, and sure enough, traces of power crackled in the air against her Essence. "You're right. I feel it. Someone has invoked the storm."

And the power felt familiar.

Cassiel frowned. "What—"

The sky exploded with blasts of green, purple, blue, black, and red. Their explosions shook the ground, vibrating through Dyna's legs. Her Essence hummed in response to the violent torrent of magic. It churned through Dyna's senses with several distinct traces.

Rawn's eyes widened. "This ... this is a battle of mages."

She could feel the immense depth of their power, whoever they were. But one of them was tremendous, and she had experienced the likes of it before.

From the sorceress she met in Corron.

"It's her," Dyna shouted over the noise. "The sorceress. But why would she risk using this much Essence?"

"Who?" Cassiel shouted back. "Do you mean the witch?"

"Why do you think it's her?" Zev yelled past another blast. "It could be anyone."

No, Dyna was sure of it. This power had the same potency as when the sorceress had trapped her in a rift in the Time Gate. And now her spells ripped through the air, violent and powerful, fueled by an intensity that only meant one thing. She was fighting for her life.

Dyna ran into the trees, and Cassiel muttered a curse.

"Wait!" Zev sprinted after her.

"We mustn't interfere in mage battles," Rawn said.

Zev caught her arm. "What are you doing?"

"She's in danger."

"How do you know it's her?"

"I know it's the sorceress, Zev. I've felt her magic before. If this is what I think it is, she will need our help," she said, and he tensed.

They were both taught the history of North Star and what women faced in Magos. The sorceress was a refugee. To be fighting like this meant Enforcers had found her. Dyna couldn't simply ignore that. Neither could he.

Zev inhaled a breath, growing serious. "If so, I'll help her, but you will stay back. They cannot see you."

She nodded, and they ran together for the sounds of the battle, the others following close behind.

The rain pattered loudly against the leaves, and an icy wind wailed. Flares of color and lightning lit the woods in split-second flashes, each a warning before a deafening explosion. Their boots squelched through leaves and mud as they followed the sporadic lights beyond the backdrop of convulsing, dark clouds.

They reached the end of the woods when a blue blaze came for them. Rawn ducked. Zev yanked Dyna out of the way. Cassiel dove over her, his wings splaying open to cover them. The spell smashed through a tree, splintering it to pieces. Burning debris hit him, and she winced at his pained grunt. Her back ached as if it had hit her instead. Cassiel shook off the splintered wood as he stood.

"This was a fine idea," he said stiffly. "When are you not seeking to get yourself killed?"

Dyna ignored his offered hand and got to her feet. "About as often as you seek to be so ill-tempered."

Zev motioned for them to be quiet and hide. She lowered behind a large boulder with him and peered out.

The sorceress stood in the center of a field with vivid purple light outlining her silhouette. Long white hair whipped around her in the raging tempest. Electricity radiated over her hands, up her arms, and neck. The power crackling in the air prickled against Dyna's senses. The glow in the sorceress's eyes brightened as rage transformed her delicate features.

The hooded figures surrounding her threw a volley of spells. Her angry screams rang amongst the blasts as she hurled spells in return.

They deflected her attacks and the earth burst where they hit, dirt blasting with ear-splitting explosions. Dyna choked on smoke and the magic strangling the atmosphere.

A mage lifted a staff with a light blue crystal, and three pillars of water formed in the air like volatile sea creatures that snaked for the sorceress. She threw out her hands and a blast of electricity pierced through the spirals of water and struck the mage. The attack launched his burning body across the field, his screams wailing overhead. He crashed by where they hid in a smoking heap, breaking his neck on impact, and the glow faded from his eyes. Two more bodies already lay on opposite sides of the field.

Dyna exchanged an awed look with Zev.

"She may not need our help," he said.

But seven mages remained. Their onslaught of water, fire, earth, and wind brutally attacked the sorceress at once. She strained under their force, holding out her trembling arms as she defended herself with her magic. Dyna read the exhaustion on her face. Power spilled from her in relentless droves. It was too much. Mages drew power from themselves, and there was a limit to how much they contained.

Dyna shook her head. "She won't last much longer at this rate, not against so many."

The sorceress reached for the sky and slammed down her fist, spearing a mage with a blade of lightning—another dead. Thunder boomed in the sky, and a barrage of lightning bolts struck the field. The mages leaped out of the way, some throwing shields, others returning an attack to counter. The sorceress stumbled, and her arms fell limp at her sides. Her wet hair clung to her face, shoulders heaving.

The mages closed in on her.

"There are too many," Dyna said. "She can't fight them all by herself."

Zev grabbed her when she tried to stand. *"Stay."*

"But—"

"We cannot fight against their power," Cassiel said on the other side of her.

"Be that as it may, I will not stand by while they outnumber her," Rawn said. He withdrew an arrow from his quiver and loaded his bow.

Zev nodded and peeled off his shirt. "We wait for an opening."

The sorceress's sudden manic laughter drew their attention back to the field. Her eyes were two glowing points of violet past her wet bangs. Lowering to her knees, she said something to the mages and stabbed her fingers into the dirt. The earth shook ferociously, and a crevice broke open beneath their feet. The mages scrambled out of the way, but one fell screaming through the hole.

Dyna watched in speechless amazement as the sorceress rose on her shaky legs and filled a hand with a blaze of fire and the other with a sphere of water.

"Impossible," Rawn whispered.

Mages were limited to elements of their guilds. Yet she had cracked open the earth and now wielded elements she shouldn't be able to.

"Not impossible, Lord Norrlen." Dyna grinned, knowing exactly what this meant. "It's merely improbable."

The sorceress hurled her attacks. The mages held up their staffs with two hands to ward off her power. A mage waved his staff in the air, and a tornado formed around her. She crossed her arms and snapped them open, blasting the spiraling wind away. The recoil pushed her back, but her arms were already rising for another attack. A mage blasted her with black mist, sending her crashing across the field. Dyna gasped, her smile fading. The storm broke, and the deluge reduced to a drizzle as the clouds parted. Shafts of sunlight illuminated the ravaged field.

The four remaining mages stalked for her. A red-haired mage raised his staff and hit the sorceress with a blow of black Essence, and it knocked her to the ground, pinning her hands and legs.

"Now," Zev growled.

Rawn raised his bow and aimed. The sorceress's screams of rage switched to frightened cries as the mage dropped on top of her and grasped her neck with glowing hands.

Dyna leaped to her feet. "Get off her, you filthy sod!"

Cassiel covered her mouth and yanked her down, but they had heard her. The mages spun around. Rawn released his arrow, and it pierced the red-haired mage through the throat. His eyes widened, blinking as though confused by the shaft through his neck. Blood poured from his mouth and his body swayed, toppling on top of the sorceress.

The others lifted their staffs; the crystals flaring. Zev shapeshifted and his black wolf tore across the field for the advancing mages.

"Stay with Lady Dyna," Rawn told Cassiel. He whistled for Fair and leaped on the saddle, riding away.

Left alone together, Dyna stiffened and Cassiel's jaw worked as he gripped the hilt of his sword. Neither of them looked at each other, tension filling the space between them. He probably would have preferred to fight than to stand guard with her.

Highly aware of his presence, she kept her gaze trained on the fight. The mages ran to meet Zev and Rawn, their crystals pulsing as they prepared to attack. But Lord Norrlen loaded his bow and shattered them. The startled mages dropped their staffs. Light flared up their arms as spells glowed in their hands.

Zev evaded a flying boulder and pivoted away from another detonating spell. Dyna's heart jolted, and she squeezed her fists. Magic filled the air, pressing into her with its might. Gods, these were powerful mages. She shouldn't have sent him out there.

"Zev will be fine," Cassiel told her calmly, though his face was tight with concern. His wide eyes followed the wolf sprint towards the barrage. "He is quick and—"

A sun mage raked his arms through the air and an enormous wave of fire roared through the field—coming right for Zev.

CHAPTER 5

Zev

Zev knew no matter how fast he ran, he wouldn't be able to avoid the immense wave of flames. He stopped in place, orange filling his vision. The shroud of fire blotted the sun as it crested over him. In the distance came Dyna's scream. But a strange sort of peace fell over him. He had only one thought.

At last.

The beat of hooves pounded into the earth. Rawn rode toward him—toward the fire. He armed his bow, lining his sight with the string. An arrow zipped over Zev's head and pierced the flames, dissipating them in a plume of smoke. Nothing remained but the scorched ground.

Fair leaped over him, and Rawn rode for the startled mages. Zev shook himself out of his shock and sprinted after them. He hadn't known Rawn could break spells, but he was reminded of the elf's abilities when he withdrew his enchanted sword.

The mages threw a barrage of attacks. The world shook, and the air crackled with their combined magic. Fair galloped through the explosions, well trained and swift in his movements. With a swipe of his blade, Rawn sliced through the spells, and they burst in puffs of smoke in his wake. Zev ran along his side, trusting him to cut through each one. Seeing they couldn't stop them, the mages ran for the sorceress.

Rawn leaped up on the saddle. *"Otla!"*

Fair jerked to a stop, launching him into the air. He spun mid arc and landed in front of the mages in a crouch. Zev tackled one, sinking his jaws into the mage's throat, ripping it free. Blood sprayed on the grass. Rawn faced off with the other two. They waved their arms and conjured a translucent shield between them. It was useless when Rawn could easily slash through it.

A mage with a mane of red hair and glowing amber eyes filled his hands with fire. "You killed my brother, blasted elf."

Rawn gritted his teeth. "A fitting death for one who resorts to such obscene deeds."

Zev growled his agreement, baring his teeth. If the mage were alive, Zev would have made sure he died next.

The sun mage scowled. His face shone with sweat as he studied them. "You have no business in our affairs. Go before we kill you."

"Believe me when I say the odds are not in your favor," Rawn said. "Stand down."

"It's you who should stand down!" said the other with dark hair and eyes—an earth mage, by the view of his bare feet buried in the grass.

Both bore the triad symbol of the Magos Empire on their robes, and another unfamiliar sigil on their shoulders.

"We serve the will of the Archmage, and therefore she is under our authority. She belongs to us."

Zev snapped his teeth, making them flinch a step back. Magic, hierarchy, guilds—he knew nothing about that. But injustice, misogyny, and the vile darkness of men—that's something he'd always fight against.

Noble beastie, the Madness whispered from the dark depths of his mind.

"She will not be going with you," Rawn said. "Leave her be, or you will force my hand."

The sun mage sneered. "This is a matter of the Magos Empire. Unless the Vale wishes for war, you will step aside."

Zev knew of the oppression sorceresses suffered in Magos, but who was she to merit an empire going to war? If the Archmage was truly involved, then this was far more serious than they thought.

"You know naught of what you're interfering with," the sun mage continued. "She is a princess of the Magos Empire."

Princess? Zev's growls faltered.

He met Dyna's beseeching eyes across the field, her hands clasped together. It didn't matter who these mages were and why they wanted the sorceress. They came for her power and her freedom. It wasn't their right to take.

"Our lady is extending her favor over this young woman," Rawn said. "Therefore, she will remain in our care."

The mages glanced right at Dyna. They cared nothing for Cassiel, or perhaps hadn't noticed him. At the sight of her, the initial surprise on their faces switched to satisfied sneers.

"Another sorceress is wandering free in Azure? What a turn of events this is," said the earth mage to his companion. "The Archmage will be pleased."

Cassiel drew out his sword and white flames burst along the blade. Zev snarled, crouching low. If they so much as moved a step toward his cousin, they were dead.

"Take any further action, and it will not end well for you," Rawn said. "Retreat. *Now.*"

The sun mage's eyes blazed orange, and he smiled as the world rumbled. The earth mage jerked his fists into the air, and chunks of rock shot out of the ground. One smashed into Zev, knocking him down. The sun mage released a barrage of fire. He and Rawn dove out of the way, searing heat blazing past them. Vines weaved through the grass like serpents hunting for prey. They ensnared Zev, and he keened under their thorny grasp, rapidly trapping him in a net. A thick tree root sprouted from the earth and slammed on Rawn before he could get back to his feet.

The earth mage cackled as he approached him. "It's you who will die here, elf."

Zev tore at the thorns, but they only tightened further. The vines tethered around his neck, squeezing so tight his vision swam.

Rawn wrenched an arm free, and a small, teal bulb of light formed in his hand. It was faint, barely a spark.

"Erb'mul," he muttered, and a petal of flame danced in his palm.

The sun mage laughed. "I thought the Elves were skilled in magic. Is that all you can muster?"

Rawn smiled. *"Eria."*

He blew into his hand, and a cyclone of fire hurtled through the screaming mages. It wrenched their bodies high into the air, and they landed as burning heaps on the other side of the field. The vines slackened, and Zev sucked in a breath. He shook off the loosened vines, and Rawn shoved the limp root away. They flopped back on the grass, staring blankly at the smoky sky as they got their bearings.

Cassiel landed beside them with Dyna in his arms.

"Are you all right?" She rushed to Zev and checked him over. "Are you hurt?"

He nuzzled her cheek. She worried too much.

Dyna huffed. "Don't give me that. You almost died."

And what would she think if she realized you were disappointed that you didn't? The Madness asked. Zev hadn't let himself think about it at the moment, but a part of him had felt robbed when Rawn broke the spell meant to end his life.

"Lord Norrlen?" Dyna turned to him.

He offered her a tired smile. "I am unscathed, my lady. All is well."

Cassiel removed a knife from his boot and cut the rest of the tangled vines off Zev's paws, then held out a hand to help Rawn to his feet. "Am I mistaken to say you *breathed* fire?"

"I combined a wind and fire spell," Rawn answered as he sheathed his sword. "It is the only offensive spell I have come to learn."

"The most useful one, it would seem," Zev said, his voice caught between growl and human as he shifted back on two legs. The thorns had peppered his body with gashes and punctures.

Cassiel handed him a pair of trousers. "I thought today was your last."

"Aye, so did I," Zev murmured, hugging Dyna when her expression broke. "But I'm fine."

"You're hurt."

"This is nothing." He nodded to the sorceress. "I think she's worse off."

Clutching her satchel, Dyna ran to her side. The sorceress lay motionless beneath the dead mage; her face covered under a damp curtain of silvery-white hair. Zev pushed the body off her.

"Look away, please," Dyna said. "I need to examine her."

They respectfully turned their backs and gave them some space. Rawn whistled at Fair to come to him, and they waited quietly to hear the verdict. Smoke rose from where the rain had put out scattered fires, and bodies riddled the destroyed field. Zev had never seen such power, let alone someone wielding spells outside of their Guild.

"Six," Zev said as he counted the bodies. "Out of ten mages, she took down six."

By the sigils on their arms, these mages were Enforcers. To kill as many as she had meant she was incredibly … dangerous.

Cassiel warily peered into the deep hole she had made in the earth. "Did she invoke the storm as well?"

"I would assume so," Rawn said.

No clouds dotted the sky now, as if it had never rained at all.

"She's unconscious, but she's all right," Dyna said after a few minutes. "You may turn around now." The sorceress lay in the grass with her clothes set properly. Her hair stuck to the perspiration on her pale face. Dyna gently brushed the white bangs from her forehead. "She spent a significant amount of Essence. She needs to recover."

Zev nodded. He'd seen it happen in Dyna frequently when she used too much power.

"Why did they want her?" Cassiel asked. He glared at the dead mage with an arrow through his throat. "Aside from the foul intentions of that one."

"They were not forthcoming with that information," Rawn said. "It seems they were under orders by the Archmage to capture her."

Dyna shared a look with Zev. They knew why the mages wanted her, but how could they explain it? The practices of the Magos Empire were a secret kept from the rest of Urn.

"We need to find a place to camp," she said, turning to the devastated. "Somewhere far from here."

Taking the form of his wolf again, Zev searched for a safe place to camp. The fading scent of the mages was everywhere. He paused every so often to sniff the wet soil as Dyna and the others followed close behind. Rawn guided Fair along with the unconscious sorceress laying on the horse's back while Cassiel flew overhead as a precaution to notify them of any further trouble.

When Zev reached a stream, he located the sorceress's scent and followed it through the forest, but it quickly faded until there was no scent at all. He couldn't smell the trees, the earth, or any of the normal scents that should be here. It threw off his senses and made his mind spin.

But there were small tracks in the mud that fit the size of a woman's. She must have passed through here. He ambled onward into a small clearing encircled by tall shrubs. Among the greenery was a feeble black tent, close to where the battle took place.

"You found shelter," Dyna said.

Zev shifted back into his naked form. He eyed the tent as he quickly dressed. "If I wasn't looking at it, I wouldn't know it was there."

"What does that mean?" Cassiel asked as he landed.

"It's as if the tent isn't there, but it is. I only found it because there is a slight disturbance of the vegetation in this area, but I didn't pick up a scent."

"That has the makings of a spell," Rawn said.

Zev listened for any movement within the tent, but there were none, and no footprints marked the undisturbed ground around it. The tent stood crooked, ragged and overtaken by the forest.

"It may not be currently inhabited," he said. "Or made to appear that way."

He would guess the latter. The footprints began right at the edge of the forest. He bet there were more hidden here.

Cassiel grunted. "It will have to do for now."

"The girls should take it," Zev said.

Rawn unsheathed his sword. "First, a precautionary measure."

He swept the blade through the air, and the atmosphere rippled with an iridescent sheen. Glamor, Zev realized. It peeled away like a veil, revealing a sturdy tent standing erect with footprints marking the ground.

"As I thought," Rawn said. "This place has been ensorcelled. I will scout first. Be ready."

Cassiel armed himself, and Zev extended his claws, both moving to flank Dyna. He cocked his head, listening again for movement.

"Your pardon," Rawn called. "Is anyone there?"

No one responded.

Lord Norrlen cautiously parted the tent flaps with his sword. He stared at something inside, his mouth falling slack. Zev stalked behind him and peered over his shoulder. The small tent didn't reflect the vast space inside. It was as large as a cottage, with a four-poster bed made of pale ash wood and elegant posts in one corner, draped in disheveled mauve bedding. An open chest with strewn clothing and dresses rested at its base.

Stacks of books scattered around the perimeter in small towers, and scrolls and more books littered a sturdy desk. Among the mess was a clear glass orb resting on a brass metal stand. A black folding screen concealed a wash area, and another corner held a makeshift kitchen with a hutch and a small dining table with two chairs. Candles throughout the space flickered with purple flames.

The same color that matched the sorceress's Essence.

Zev gawped. "What manner of magic is this?"

"God of Urn..." Dyna said next to him. Her wide eyes took in the space and they lit with wonder. "Stardust!"

CHAPTER 6

Von

The blade whirred through the air as it came for Von's head. He ducked and parried the blow, his knife clashing against Elon's sword. They jumped back and slowly circled each other. There were no tells in the elf's blank expression, but Von knew better than to underestimate this opponent. The Raiders who had gathered on the hill to watch the sparring match cheered and hollered.

"Get him, Commander!" Geon bellowed.

Von nearly snorted. As if he could defeat the elf, but he wouldn't lose face. Sweat beaded on his forehead, and he was already feeling the strain from the ache in his back. He was ready to end the fight. Elon dropped his guard, leaving an opening. Von shot forward, but a rapid thought reminded him the elf never left openings. Instinct seized, and he pivoted, scarcely dodging the blow of Elon's hilt that would have taken his jaw. Von slashed, his knife passing through the space the elf had occupied a second before. Elon spun and Von twisted. The sword caught the sun as it stopped inches from his neck.

Von grinned, the tip of his blade right at Elon's throat.

"Draw!" Geon announced. The Raiders erupted with boos and jeers. Money passed through hands to settle bets. Seeing the afternoon entertainment had ended, they returned to their daily duties.

Von chuckled. "You couldn't let me win?"

The stoic elf sheathed his weapon. "That would be an insult to your position, Commander."

"You humor me." He rolled his shoulders and carefully stretched the muscles of his stiff back. "Aye, your tonic worked wonders. I'm nearly healed. Thank you."

It should have taken weeks to recover from the whipping Tarn gave him, but Elon's elf medicine had reduced it to days.

The captain nodded. His expression was more pursed than usual.

"You disapprove?" Von asked as he gathered his scattered knives from the ground. "I told you, I don't trust Benton. He would no sooner curse me than heal me. The tonic will do fine."

"Benton removed the sorceress's spell," Elon reminded him.

Von touched his head. He didn't feel any different, but that didn't mean the old mage hadn't done something to him. "I would have preferred you to have done it."

"Impossible."

Von frowned at the curt answer. Sometimes it took a bit of prompting to get Elon to speak. They made their way up the hill back to the field where they camped. It was similar to the field Elon's magic had ravaged with blood and the bodies of the Azure Guard.

"I've seen you cleave through a cavalry of Rangers, yet breaking a comatose spell is impossible?"

"Mage magic and elf magic are not to be mixed, Commander," Elon said. "A spell on an object I could break. Not a spell on the mind. That which is most delicate should be unraveled by the same type of magic from which it was created, lest the mind shatter."

"Ah," Von said uneasily. "In that case, I pardon you. How does Len fare?"

"Her health has recovered."

"Good."

It was a miracle Len had survived her confrontation with the Guardians of the Maiden. If not for her enchanted armor, Rawn's arrow would've pierced her heart. Tarn kept the spelled arrowhead that nearly killed her on his desk. Von wasn't sure if it was to serve as a reminder of how quickly he almost lost one of his favored slaves, or if he was interested in the spell it held.

Pausing at the top of the hill, Von glanced at the edge of the forest where Len practiced archery. She drew her bow and winced, her arm trembling. The arrow flew and pierced a target about seventy yards away. She had missed the center by inches. Not at the caliber where her abilities normally were, but far more advanced than Von would have guessed for her condition.

"Len should be resting."

"She's eager," Elon said.

Von frowned at that. "If the mages healed her, why is she in pain?"

"Essence Healing only tends to the wound. Her body will be tender until natural recovery."

Tightness set her jaw, and another arrow flew. Len had been a determined girl since she was a child. At seventeen summers old, she was damn tenacious. She had come far from a life of slavery in Versai. The wind blew her long black hair away from her face, revealing the X scar on the dusky skin of her cheek. Len reached in the quiver at her feet and loaded more arrows, releasing them swiftly one after the other. Each struck the target with deadly precision.

Was she motivated by her need to please Tarn, or the need for revenge against Rawn Norrlen? If Elon cared that a Green Elf had nearly killed a spy under his command, he didn't show it. The scar on the back of his right hand had erased all signs of the Red Highland tattoo he once bore. How much loyalty could one have for a kingdom that exiled them?

"When are you heading out to track the Maiden?" Von asked him as they continued.

"Tonight."

"Who will you take with you?"

"No one this time."

Probably for the best. Elon was an excellent tracker, and he moved quicker alone. They needed to find Dyna's location first, before deciding on the next move.

"Very well. Report to me before you go."

They parted ways as they reached the camp. Rows of tents neatly circled the clearing where Tarn's great tent reigned. Raiders saluted respectfully as Von passed.

The sky rippled with an iridescent sheen, a sign that Benton's cloaking spell remained in place. Von worked his jaw, a simmer of anger hovering over him. The old bastard nearly got them caught by the Azure Guard. Breaking Benton's arm wasn't enough punishment for the fifty men they had lost because of it. He should have broken a few more bones. It would have been fine, as the mage's boys would have healed him quickly.

Benton's tent was set on the eastern point of the camp. Dalton and Clayton stood outside, the wind ruffling their long umber robes. Clayton's dark eyes hardened, a swirl of yellow flashing in them. Dalton looked away first, but his older brother held Von's stare. At sixteen and eighteen years old, they weren't boys anymore.

"Olssen," Von called to the tall, burly man brushing the horses.

The Raider stood at attention, his dreadlocks swishing around his head. "Aye, Commander."

"Put those two to work." Von motioned to the young mages. "Something to keep them busy and to teach them respect."

Olssen grinned and motioned grandly at the horse pen loaded with piles of dung. "I've got the perfect task."

"Good." Von continued on his way as he called over his shoulder. "And they are not to use magic."

The scent of something cooking filled the air as smoke wafted from the large tent on the north end of camp. He headed for it. Yavi's laughter and Geon's chatter greeted him before he went in. No one could have missed the huge Minotaur hacking away at slabs of bacon in the tent. Sorren towered over them at eight feet tall, his one horn nearly touching the ceiling.

"Come off it, you two," Sorren growled. "We've got work to do."

At his entrance, Yavi's face lit up. "Von, tell Sorren he needs to learn how to laugh. It won't kill him."

"See, I think it might," Geon retorted as he chopped some greens at a back table. He flashed Von a grin. "The bloke is incapable of good old fun."

Sorren threw a loaf of hard bread at the lad's head. Yavi pealed into wild laughter, and Von smiled at the sound, but it quickly dropped. She stood too close to the cauldron as she stirred it, and the flames licking around the base reached for her toes.

His heart nearly leaped in his throat.

Only whence she burns...

The words of warning from the Seer of Faery Hill blared in his head, and it took every ounce of calm for Von not to overreact.

He strolled to Yavi's side, casually pulling her further away from the fire as he pretended to peek inside the pot. "What's cooking?"

"Pottage, your favorite." She winked and tucked a lock of auburn hair behind her ear. Her hand dropped to her side, allowing their arms to discreetly touch. "Beans, leaks, and bacon."

Von wrinkled his nose.

"We can't all eat as posh as your master," Sorren grunted.

"It'll be good with some bread and cheese," Geon added. "Ale too."

"Is the master's meal ready?" Von asked.

The lad wiped his hands on his apron. "Aye, it is."

Von withheld a sigh as he watched Geon limp to another table. He regretted taking the lad with him to Corron. Now he would have a limp for the rest of his life. Geon might never have walked again if Dyna hadn't healed him—a fact Von had neglected to share with his master.

"Here's his dinner, Commander." Geon motioned to a silver tray with soft rolls, a roasted chicken stuffed with herbs, and venison adorned with pomegranate seeds and greens. He fidgeted with the dishes, wiping away any stray droplets of oil. "Sorren had me cook for the master today. Pray to the gods, he'll not whip me if he finds it lacking."

"He won't," Von said. Tarn hardly ate, and when he did, he had nothing to say about its quality. Von frowned at Sorren. "Unless he's meant to be displeased."

The Minotaur had found interesting ways to poison Tarn's meals when he'd first been made a slave. It nearly killed Von several times, since he had to taste everything first. That was his holy duty as a life-servant. Serve Tarn in everything asked. Even die for him, if need be. That was the life the fates chose for him. He'd learned a long time ago there was no escaping it.

Sorren's nose ring bounced with his snort. "I didn't touch it. You'll live."

"Thanks, mate." Von gathered the tray and headed for the exit.

Yavi subtly reached for him at the same time he did, and their fingertips grazed in a kiss of skin that was there and gone.

Later, the touch promised.

During the day, they were nothing more than superior and servant, but the night brought other liberties a man could afford his secret wife. Yavi's hazel eyes met his heated look full of wicked intent. Her pupils dilated as she flushed, teeth digging into the flesh of her bottom lip.

Aye, most certainly later.

Von made his way to Tarn's tent. He entered as the amethyst Forewarning Crystal on the ceiling finished announcing his arrival, and the dance of purple lights vanished. "I've brought your meal, Master."

Tarn sat at the head of his table in a grand chair. His lethargic, pale blue gaze stared into the flames of the brazier beside him. The firelight gleamed on his white-blond hair where it fell half over his face, partially covering the scar running diagonally along his right eyebrow to the left side of his jaw.

Placing the tray on the table, Von poured a cup of spiced wine into a goblet, bringing it to him. Tarn took out a small vial filled with a black substance from his coat. His hand slightly trembled as he poured six droplets into the wine, and the surface shimmered with silver light. Witch's Brew.

Tarn drank his enchanted wine in one gulp. Immediately, his gaze cleared and focused on Von. "Report."

"No Azure Guard sightings, Master. I'm awaiting Bouvier and Novo's return from Corron."

Von had sent them to place a sizable bounty on the Maiden and her Guardians with the Azure Warrant Authority. After their confrontation, they had vanished into the uncharted woodland, but eventually they would attempt to board a ship. The wanted notices should circulate to the Port of Azure by their arrival, if not sooner. Sending bounty hunters after Dyna and her companions would certainly hinder their journey. When the bounty hunters caught them, all Von had to do was bribe whichever jail held them captive.

But he had sent the spies five days ago.

"They should be back by now," Tarn said, voicing his thoughts.

"The delay must be a precaution, Master. We're making our way steadily to the north, but the Azure Guard now heavily patrols the roads."

They resorted to traveling around the mountains. Moving a camp of one-hundred-and-fifty men through the wilderness made for slow travel. With a reward of ten thousand gold pieces for his head, there was no shortage of bounty hunters aiming to claim it.

Tarn's finger tapped on the edge of his goblet, the ends of his mouth quirking. "It pleases me that after fifteen years, he remains as determined as ever to kill me."

"Only because the Azure King fears you will kill him first."

"Wise of him."

Von often wondered if Tarn regretted his actions that led to the warrant for his death. It had resulted in a life constantly on the run. But no, by the small smile hovering on the sharp edges of his mouth, Tarn harbored no regrets. Neither did Von, not about this. Tarn's plan was slowly coming together and once they had the Unending, he would go after the king next.

Von served himself morsels of every food item on the tray. He ate it all in one quick bite, savoring the rich flavors of venison and herbs. Geon had outdone himself. "Elon leaves to track the Maiden's whereabouts tonight."

"He is to take all the spies," Tarn said as Von placed a plate and silverware before him.

He paused, processing the unexpected command. Bouvier and Novo were up to the task, but Len hadn't fully recovered. "Elon planned to scout alone, Master. Rawn Norrlen is in their company now, and from what happened at the loch, we must learn his capabilities first."

"The Maiden has already gathered three Guardians. I want her caught before more arrive." Tarn eyed his meal with disinterest. "The sorceress may have already joined her."

"Perhaps not," Von said, his jaw working at the thought of facing her again. "If she has, then I will have another chance to bring you the Moonstone."

With it, they could open a portal to Mount Ida and avoid the dangerous voyage across the Leviathan Sea.

Tarn rested his chin against a fist. "The bounty will soon draw attention. Should Elon find the Maiden before she leaves the forest, order him to capture her and the stone if they have it." His icy eyes met his. "I don't care who he must kill. She has what I need to find the Unending."

Von sensed Tarn's patience was wearing thin. Everything he'd done over the years. Every life taken. Every item stolen. Every venture was in pursuit of the Unending—it was all for naught if he couldn't get the Maiden.

Dyna was the key to everything. Tarn wasn't about to let her slip through his fingers a second time. But the first attempt had resulted in the loss of twenty men.

Von glanced at the missives scattered on the table and caught a page with Tarn's elegant handwriting. The words of the Seer's divination. He had read and spoke them aloud so many times, Von had them memorized by heart.

Seek the Maiden with emeralds for sight and tresses of fire, for she holds the key to the Unending thou desires. Beware the Guardians who come to shield her from thee. She will be protected by one of divine blood and a dweller of the moon howling to break free. Thus follows a warrior bestowing his vow, and a sorceress grants her sorcery. A familiar face vies for vengeance, and a creature with the strength of ten eradicates the forgery. Great peril in the venture thou art pursuing. Be not swayed by love, lest it be thy undoing.

If they caught Dyna now, Tarn would succeed. But if he got his hands on the Unending...

Von suppressed a shudder at the chill in his veins. "Yes, Master. I'll pass on your command to the captain."

The Forewarning Crystal cast a dance of purple light in the tent as Elon and Len slipped inside, followed by Novo. Bouvier was nowhere in sight.

With the absence of the fourth spy and Elon's hard expression, Von had a sinking feeling. "What happened?"

Novo lowered the hood of his black cloak and the cloth mask that covered the bottom of his face. His messy, long brown curls were tied at his neck, windblown face haggard, and mouth ringed white with thirst. Shadows marked beneath his dark eyes from lack of sleep. He likely rode day and night to return.

"We couldn't enter Corron to place the bounty on the Maiden and her Guardians, Commander," Novo said. "It was swarming with Azure Guard. Too much of a risk."

Von clenched his fists, fearing what he would say next. "The Blue Capital was the nearest. I thought—"

"You thought going to the Azure King's city was a better option?" he shouted. "You should have returned here to report!"

Novo swallowed, the only sign of tension. "We placed the bounties, but there was trouble."

Von clenched his teeth, already guessing the worst. "Where is Bouvier?"

"Captured by the Azure Guard. They recognized him."

Von growled a curse. Since they'd stepped foot in Azure, everything that could have gone wrong had. Careful planning, stealth, simple missions. All of it was falling apart. As if the fates themselves were scheming against them. Everyone in Tarn's camp was wanted by some king or country. Bouvier had been a notorious thief in his past and had infuriated enough wealthy lords to earn himself a death warrant.

"Why did you not help him escape?"

"I attempted it, Commander." Novo's brow tightened. "But they guard the prison well. It's warded with spells and only the jailor carries the keys. He was my next target, but Bouvier ordered me to return."

Von cursed under his breath again, briefly closing his eyes. "You fool. They will eventually learn who he now serves."

Bouvier wouldn't talk, but Von had to assume the Azure Guard wasn't beneath torture. The spy knew valuable information that they couldn't risk reaching the Azure King. This called for a change of plans.

Von heaved a breath and faced Tarn. "Master, send me. I may have time to retrieve him."

Len stepped forward and bumped a fist over her heart, silently volunteering as well.

Tarn nodded before Von could protest, holding his gaze with those wintry blue eyes. "No loose ends."

They bowed and marched out of the tent.

"Len," Novo chided once they were outside. "You're not fully recovered for this mission. I'll go instead. Commander, take—"

Von snatched Novo's cloak. "You don't get to speak. Your rash choices have brought this about. Pray on your life that we can retrieve Bouvier. If I'm forced to kill him, it will be on your head."

But Von knew the weight of that death would fall only on him. As the commander, he was responsible for every life under his command. They had suffered fifty losses during the Azure Guard ambush, then more by the Guardians. Each loss was added to his ledger.

He was tired of losing men.

Len tugged on Von's fisted hold over Novo, her dark brown eyes narrowing.

"Get your horse ready. We leave now," Von snapped at her, then cut his glare back to Novo. "You will go with Elon."

The young spies didn't move. Though that probably had to do with the iron hold he kept on Novo. Len only watched him with a cold, silent fierceness. There was a challenge there that he would readily meet.

Elon's amber gaze landed on her, and she stiffened. Her hand slipped away, head lowering in respect to the elf. And maybe a little healthy dose of fear. No one challenged his authority.

"Go." Von released Novo. "Eat. Change. Then come brief me on everything that happened in the capital. We depart at sundown."

The spy backed a step, bowing his head. Then he and Len headed off together, moving swiftly through the camp. Elon stood silent like a pillar of stone, always steady and firm, when Von's foundation became unsettled. He heaved a breath and rubbed the stubble on his jaw.

Great peril in the venture thou art pursuing. Damn the Seer and her warnings. Of all the lines in the divination, that one worried him the most.

"Don't take any unnecessary risks," Von said. "Watch and learn. If you cannot find an opening to capture her, we will leave the bounties to do the rest."

The elf captain nodded and retreated.

Von secretly sent a plea to the God of Urn that Dyna had gotten far enough ahead to escape them. He'd once sent a similar plea fifteen years ago when they'd fled the Kingdom of Azure to escape from the one who hunted them. The Azure King was a powerful man. Someone to be feared.

The same could now be said of Tarn.

CHAPTER 7

Lucenna

Lucenna cursed and rolled over in bed, her temples insistently throbbing. Did Lucien have nothing better to occupy his time? Certainly, he had more pressing responsibilities than to worry about her wellbeing.

Let me sleep!

A sudden spark of light jolted her awake. Above her head hovered a torn piece of smoking parchment. It fluttered down and landed on her face, filling her nose with the smell of wet ink. She groaned and picked it off. Sporadic letters smeared and tore the paper where the quill had pressed so hard she could hardly read her brother's penmanship.

Please.

She blinked at it sleepily, her foggy mind too slow to understand what he meant. Lucien was the overprotective sort, but this urgency was odd. More slips of paper littered her bed. *Gods, why did he send so many?*

Creating messenger portals expelled a great deal of power, the type that was easily perceptible to others—like their father. She checked the other notes, and they were more pressing.

The Enforcers have your location. Flee now!

Sister, have you received my messages?

What's happened? I cannot sense you!

Are you all right? Have you escaped?

Lucenna, answer me. I beg you.

The most recent note now made sense. Lucien must be frightened. Her memory came back in spurts. Elite Enforcers had cornered her in a field. She fought, but there had been too many. Lucenna jerked up in bed. She was in her tent. How did she get here? Did the Enforcers bring her?

There were voices outside. *Male* voices.

Lucenna slipped out of bed onto her bare feet, only for her legs to give out. She went sprawling and collided with a stack of books. Her arms shook from the effort to rise on her knees. She had no strength in her bones, and a chill settled in her limbs. The familiar warmth of her churning power had dwindled to the faintest of embers.

Footsteps squelched in the mud outside, the sound growing nearer. She called on her Essence, but only a few purple sparks flashed at her fingertips. The battle had completely drained her. There had to be something to defend herself with. Lucenna looked about wildly as the footsteps neared. There were piles of heavy tomes to choose from, but she didn't want to damage her books. A brazier with an iron poker rested by her bed. She snatched the heavy weapon and faced the entrance on trembling legs, ready to skewer whoever walked through.

The tent flaps parted, and she sprang forward. But instead of an Enforcer, a familiar redheaded girl walked in. Lucenna tried to stop, but she stumbled and the momentum sent her crashing into Dyna, and they fell outside into the brisk chill.

"Oh." Dyna's wide eyes blinked at her. "You're awake."

Lucenna had her pinned on the ground—not that she had the strength to hold her there. The crackle of a campfire led her to spot three others who warily rose to their feet. She remembered them; they were Dyna's companions. The Celestial's silver eyes narrowed as he reached for the hilt of his sword. Cassiel, she recalled sluggishly. The elf was tall, but not as tall as the werewolf towering above them. His irises flashed yellow as he fixed on her intently, tension tightening every muscle of his strapping frame.

"My lady?" the elf asked, his gaze flickering from Dyna to the iron poker inches above her face.

"It's all right," Dyna said carefully.

Lucenna wasn't sure if she spoke to her or to the others who were ready to jump to her aid. Slowly, Dyna pushed the iron poker away. Lucenna scrambled back, breathing heavily, clammy sweat sprouting on her skin. She gripped the cold iron poker tightly, forcing herself not to shake.

How long had she been asleep? A shallow gasp slipped out of her as she remembered the last time someone had rendered her unconscious. But no one had taken her medallion this time. It hung safely in place around her neck.

"You slept for an entire day," Dyna told her, sitting up. "But I imagine you must be quite exhausted."

It went beyond that. Lucenna tested her magic, and Essence hummed weakly inside of her. She knew her father would send Enforcers after her again, but she hadn't expected Elite Enforcers. They normally traveled in pairs. Yet he'd sent ten after her. *Ten.* She had cast every spell she could, but it hadn't been enough.

"The Enforcers," she croaked, her throat dry. "Where are they?"

"You don't need to worry about them anymore," Dyna said.

Lucenna stared at her, incredulous. "What do you mean? *You* fought them?"

Dyna chuckled as she stood and headed for the campfire. "Oh, no, not me. Though I would have if I could."

The elf lifted a kettle resting beside the fire and handed it to her. He'd been with them on the hill outside of Corron, but Lucenna couldn't recall his name. She studied him and the others, not sure what to make of their presence. They shouldn't be here. How did they find her?

"Lord Norrlen and Zev came to your aid." Dyna motioned to the elf and werewolf.

Them?

"You fought the Enforcers and lived?" She hardly took down six, and it had cost every ounce of power she had.

Dyna poured the kettle's steaming contents into a cup and an herbal scent drifted toward Lucenna's nose, pulling at old, happy memories from a lifetime ago. She brought the cup to her. "Here, this will help."

Narrowing her eyes, Lucenna drew back. It smelled like rosemary, a special tea the mages used to revitalize their magic, but it could contain anything. Even if it didn't, why help her?

"You helped me once," Dyna said, reading the distrust on her face. "I want to return the favor."

Right. She had saved her from that man—Commander Von. The fool had stolen her medallion. She already planned to deal with him, but then he'd stolen Dyna too. Even if it had nothing to do with her, Lucenna had to intervene. She couldn't stand by and allow a man to hurt another woman.

Lowering the iron poker, Lucenna hesitantly accepted the wooden cup. Her stiff fingers soaked in the warmth of it, welcoming its heat seeping into her bones. Rosemary sprigs floated on the surface. The scent of it made a ball of emotion swell in her chest. Her mother used to make a similar tea for her after a long day of training.

The men silently watched her, waiting for her to drink, or perhaps out of caution. They were as uncertain of her as she was of them.

"Would you prefer I try it first?" Dyna asked.

Lucenna scowled and took a sip. It tasted mildly sweet with a bitter hint from the rosemary, some yarrow, and another earthy herb she couldn't quite place. The soothing, hot tea slid down her throat, settling in her empty stomach. Immediately, the muscles of her stiff body loosened, and her Essence stirred, the faint spark trickling through her veins. She eyed the cup in confusion. Not even her mother's tea worked this quickly. Normally, it took a couple of days before the tea fully restored her. But with one sip, her strength was steadily increasing. Lucenna took another drink. At this rate, she'd be back on her feet within the hour.

"What is this?"

Dyna smiled and held out a hand to help her stand. "An old tonic of Azeran's making."

Their fingers touched, sending a tingly jolt across Lucenna's palm and up her arm. A sign of their Essences meeting. There was little power in Dyna's, not nearly enough for a descendant of Azeran. Lucenna stood, holding the cup close to her chest. She didn't know what they wanted, or if they wanted anything. All she knew was that they meddled where they shouldn't.

"Why are you here?" she asked. "I don't take kindly to being followed."

Cassiel scoffed. "If she is well enough to accuse us, then we should go. I will have no dealings with a witch."

"And I'll have none with a Nephilim," Lucenna hissed.

It was quite an insult to call someone a witch who wasn't one. If he liked to delve out insults, so would she. For the Celestial with black hair and wings was no pure Celestial at all, but a half-breed. Not that she cared about that.

Red blotches colored his face, and his mouth curled over his teeth. "I wonder which form of yours is the true one. This or the old hag?"

Purple flames rushed into her hands at the flare of fury forming in her stomach. Lord Norrlen swiftly removed his sword as she threw a purple blast. In a rapid swing, he cut through the spell inches from Cassiel's face, and it disintegrated into a puff of smoke.

Lord Norrlen held out a hand to her, placating. "My lady, please, you are at your limits."

Lucenna blinked at him, her anger switching to bewilderment.

Cassiel's eyes widened with infuriated shock. "She nearly killed me."

"That discharge of Essence was not intended to slay," the elf told him. "Nonetheless, it certainly would have hurt and rendered you unconscious. Please refrain from offending her further."

Zev stifled a snort, and Cassiel cursed under his breath.

"How did you cut through my spell?" Lucenna asked, gawking at the sword. The blade glowed a dim blue before fading, and he sheathed it.

"My sword is enchanted to dissipate spells."

"I ... didn't know that was possible."

Lord Norrlen hesitated before saying, "It is a recent invention of the Vale."

Recent by elf standards, perhaps. Magos mustn't be aware the elves could disintegrate spells, or Lucien would have mentioned it. Though she couldn't fault them for keeping such powerful secrets when Red Highland and Greenwood were often at war. Every advantage counted.

"You must be famished," Dyna said. "I made dinner. If you don't mind, could we eat inside with you? It's a bit brisk outside."

Lucenna didn't know how to reply to this unusual situation. Never had she invited anyone into her tent before. Her stomach tightened with hunger, and whatever was cooking in the simmering pot hanging over the fire smelled good. There was plenty of space inside for all of them, but she wasn't inclined to have company. Not with men.

The longer she looked at Dyna's hopeful smile and her cheeks ruddy with cold, Lucenna's scowl wavered. An icy wind passed over them, making Lucenna shiver as it blew through her clothes. Well, the day was dreary outside. By the dark clouds overhead, it was ready to pour.

"Very well, you may come in. Except for that one." She pointed at Cassiel.

He stalked away toward the trees without a word.

"Are all Celestials this imperious?" Lucenna smirked.

Zev exchanged an uncertain frown with Dyna, no doubt uncomfortable by her question. She had touched on a delicate topic.

51

Lucenna rolled her eyes. "I have already seen him. Clearly, Celestials roam the earth. You have my word. I'll never speak of it. I have as much reason to hide as he does."

"Cassiel may not be much for manners, but he isn't as awful as he pretends to be," Zev said carefully.

Dyna lowered her gaze. They offered no more than that, neither confirming nor denying her earlier question.

"Your pardon, my lady," Rawn said. "Due to the Accords, we cannot speak on this matter any further."

With *her*, he meant.

Lucenna's temple throbbed again, interrupting her reply. She stifled a groan and went back inside her tent. The crystal orb on her desk pulsated with white light, fog swirling inside.

"It's been active since yesterday," Dyna said from behind her, having followed. "I didn't think it was my place to answer it."

"Nor could you," Lucenna said, a tad harsher than she meant to. She amended with a more level tone, "Orbs only respond to the embedded Essence. As this one is mine, no one else but I can answer."

Pushing Lucien's call away, she lowered her defenses so he could sense that she was all right. The pulsing in her temple eventually stopped, and the light faded. She could only do that for so long before he became angry at her for ignoring his calls, but they couldn't speak now.

With a snap of Lucenna's fingers, the objects strewn around the tent moved. The sheets rustled as the bed tended itself, the stacks of books straightened, the clothes folded, and the desk tidied up. The white crystals dangling across the ceiling post glowed, illuminating the space with soft light.

Dyna watched it all with her mouth slightly agape. "Incredible."

Gathering some fresh clothing from the open trunk by her bed, Lucenna stepped behind the folding screen to change. As she pulled on a black dress, her ring snagged on the lace. The sight of the pink gemstone drew the memory of slender hands taking hers and the scent of rosewood mingling with a voice she'd longed to hear. Sighing, she moved on to fasten the buttons.

By the time she finished dressing, Dyna had brought in a stack of wooden bowls and a loaf of bread. Lord Norrlen followed behind with their packs and made a spot in the middle of the tent. Zev carried in the pot but immediately froze in place, surprise crossing his features. His nostrils flared as his wide eyes found Lucenna.

Heat rushed to her cheeks. What? Did her tent stink?

He set down the pot at Dyna's prompting, and she served their meal, handing Lucenna a portion of bread and a steaming bowl. Dinner turned out to be soup. Stirring it with her spoon, Lucenna identified chopped mushrooms, potatoes, bits of onion, and herbs. Her mouth watered and her stomach growled. The others pretended not to hear it, but she was sure Zev and Lord Norrlen had. She waited for them to eat first before taking a tentative taste. The broth was full of rich earthy flavors, the potato dissolving on her tongue. Whether from hunger or the much-needed warmth, the food was delicious.

Lucenna ate quickly, using the bread to mop the broth. Thankfully, no one attempted conversation while they ate. The wind increased, rattling the crystals overhead. Soon, a gentle prattle of rain beat on the tent. Zev and the elf glanced at each other but continued to eat. Dyna kept watching the entryway, chewing on her bottom lip. Thunder rumbled in the distance before the sky opened and poured down.

Lucenna waited until she decided the Celestial had suffered long enough and said, "He may come in."

"Thank you." Dyna made a move to rise, but then she hesitated, uncertainty crossing her face. "Zev?"

His brow furrowed, and he cocked his head at her. She avoided his gaze, focusing on her bowl. With a frown, Zev walked outside. An awkward silence hovered while they waited. *Interesting lot*, Lucenna mused. Entirely different from one another. What had brought them together?

Soon she caught Cassiel's voice as they neared. "I do not care how warm it is. I will not go into the witch's den. The horse is better company."

Lucenna bit back a curse. Then he could freeze in the rain for all she cared.

"I told you, she's not a witch," came Zev's rumbling reply. "Have a care and show some respect."

He pushed Cassiel through the entrance. The Celestial angrily whirled around. Zev came in and crossed his arms over his broad chest, challenging him. A muscle jumped in Cassiel's jaw. His wet hair stuck to his forehead, and water dripped off the ends of his soaked clothes and wings, puddling by his boots. He turned away, conceding to the standoff.

By the gods, he had some sense, after all.

Cassiel sat beside Lord Norrlen and served himself. They continued eating, trying not to slurp in the awkward silence. Lucenna stole glances at them, taking their measure. In Corron, she'd met Cassiel and seen more of Zev's well-built body than she meant to. Lord Norrlen had been with them, too. He sat at the center of their group. The leader, perhaps.

He had an elegant beauty that only the elves possessed: agile, tall, with a vitality needed to wield his long war bow. Blond locks fell past his shoulders, braided in neat rows above his pointed ears. Stubble shadowed his striking face. He wore leather greaves and bracers, along with his Elvish armor, but his worn clothing was old and torn. Despite it, his speech was too eloquent for that of a penniless commoner. He wore no crests to represent his House, nor any visible insignia to identify which kingdom he pertained to within the Vale. A tattered evergreen cloak rested on his lean frame. Green Elf, maybe? It was a subjective guess.

She wondered if he was proficient in spells. Elves had access to limitless power since they drew Essence from nature, but their magic was much more difficult to learn, and it wore on their bodies. For mages, the degree of their power hovered on their person like heat from a fire, its intensity revealing how powerful they were. But with an elf, they revealed their level of power at the moment of attack.

Lord Norrlen's turquoise gaze caught her looking and lowered his spoon. "Forgive me. We have failed to properly introduce ourselves. I am Rawn Norrlen of Greenwood."

Ha, she'd been right.

"I'm Zev," the werewolf said, then he jerked a thumb at the Celestial. "His Royal Highness over there is Cassiel."

It sounded like a joke, but Cassiel had an arrogant air of nobility. It wouldn't surprise her if he were a prince.

Cassiel gave him a rude gesture. "We have already met."

Dyna beamed at her. "I'm Dynalya Astron, but please call me Dyna."

"Astron." Lucenna shook her head. "I find that rather hard to believe."

She fleetingly glanced at Cassiel from the corner of her eye. "I've been told that before."

According to the historical archives, Azeran didn't sire any children, and he perished during the War of the Guilds. However, the Magos Empire had written the history of the war. Only so much of it could be believed.

If anyone were to have access to the archive's records, it would be Lucien. But Lucenna hadn't told her brother about Dyna's claim to the Astron line. She didn't want to explain her encounter with Von, and how she had nearly lost the Lūna Medallion. Besides, she had assumed they wouldn't cross paths again. Yet by some strange fate they had.

"I do not believe we have been given your name, Princess," Rawn said.

"Princess?" she repeated coolly.

"The mages, they referred to you as so." He inclined his head respectfully. "They alleged to be following orders of the Archmage. Be he your ..."

"The Archmage is *not* my father," Lucenna said stiffly, annoyed by the assumption. She shared no blood with that monster. "And I'm not a princess."

Lord Norrlen inclined his head again. "Pardon. I did not intend to offend."

After an awkward pause, it compelled her to say, "My name is Lucenna."

They didn't need to know her family name or anything else about her. She shouldn't even be speaking to them. Where she came from, who she was, what she needed to do, were secrets she had to guard. Many depended on it, and many had died for it.

"Are you traveling unaccompanied?" Zev asked.

"It has nothing to do with you."

He raised his brows and returned to his meal. A miasma of disquiet hung too long in the air.

"If our stay here is burdensome, you need only say so," Dyna said quietly.

With a sharp sigh, Lucenna reined in her irritation. She couldn't help being suspicious. It's what kept her alive. But they had saved her from the Elite Enforcers. She disliked feeling indebted.

"You may stay for now. I should thank you for helping me, but help doesn't come without debts."

"We relieve you of your debt," Dyna said. "No one here will harm you. You have my word."

Lucenna observed the three men. An elf riddled with weapons who moved with unparalleled speed and could disintegrate magic. The werewolf layered in scars and muscle, frightfully strong and who, she suspected, wasn't a true werewolf when he could shift during the day. Then there was the Celestial, who'd turned his enemies to ash with his sword of divine fire. They all looked back at her impassively, but there was no doubt about how lethal they could be.

"That remains to be seen," Lucenna replied. Her manner wasn't that of a gracious host, but she didn't care. Their presence agitated her Essence. It hovered under her skin, instinctively ready to attack should she need to.

"Those crystals." Lord Norrlen glanced above him. "They have many uses, I imagine. One being a truth indicator. Have they notified you that we speak lies?"

She didn't reply, both of them knowing the crystals had done nothing but provide light so far. Even so, she would trust no one but Lucien.

But ... this lot held their own against Elites. Lucenna pursed her mouth as she studied them with new consideration. Perhaps they could be useful. She'd been headed to the fjord before all this. It would require more hands to get those grindylow scales safely.

"We were on our way to The Port of Azure when we heard your battle with the mages," Dyna said, glancing at Lucenna's bruised wrists she'd been absentmindedly rubbing.

Both were tender, her skin mottled from the enchanted bindings that Ignatius used to pin her. He was a gifted mage of the Sun Guild, who quickly worked his way into the Archmage's Royal Guard before becoming an Elite Enforcer. He wanted what every mage did. Power. She tentatively touched the tender bruises on her neck, and something cold sunk through her.

Lucenna lowered her head, her long hair curtaining her view of the others. She took several shallow breaths, trying to control the Essence heating in her veins. "I ask that you tell me what happened on that field," she said. "Exactly as you saw it."

They took turns speaking of the battle. When Rawn described her losing the fight, his expression tightened with sympathy. His tone became soft and careful as he described Ignatius laying on top of her. Lucenna's head rushed with a noise like screaming wind, and Lord Norrlen's voice faded beneath it in a dull hum. Ignatius's face marred her memory, and she could feel his hands on her body. He'd laughed in her face, enjoying her terror. *"I have come far for you, Lucenna. Before I take you back, I seek to transcend."*

Ignatius had grabbed her throat, and power peeled from her as he siphoned it away. Her chest heaved with a churning horror. *No.*

Lucenna searched inside and found a collapsed Essence Channel where he had stolen some of her magic. Stolen a piece of her. The loss ripped through her heart. From the tired depths of her body, magic flared to life and thrashed inside of her, ready to combust. She should calm herself before she attracted more Enforcers, but purple coils of electricity crackled around her body as she bent under its pressure.

She'd spent her life running from men as she fought to protect the one thing that was hers. Yet in the end, a mage held her down, took away her strength, and consumed her power for himself simply because he could. The violation coated every part of her, a degradation she couldn't see but keenly felt. He'd taken a part of her, and she could never recover it again.

A scream of rage tore out of her, and Essence burst free. Purple shot out, rushing across the ground like thunder clouds. A vortex of a raging whirlwind and lightning spiraled around her. Her hair whipped into her face as books, scrolls, and anything not anchored in place became a projectile.

Someone shouted at her to calm down, but she couldn't. Uncontrollable purple mist poured out of her, feeding on her pain. Rampant magic howled through the tent, threatening to tear it into the sky and take them all with it.

CHAPTER 8

Zev

Violent streams of electricity seared the air, burning Zev's skin. He shoved Dyna into Cassiel, and the prince shielded her with his body and wings. Leaping to his feet, Zev and Rawn made a wall in front of them, bracing against the raging wind. God of Urn. The sorceress would kill them all. Her eyes glowed vivid purple, light encasing her entire being. The storm of her power filled the air, bearing against them. Lightning struck and electricity bounced off the canvas like heated oil on water.

"You must calm yourself!" Rawn said above the magical storm. "Rein in your power!"

Lucenna gripped her head, squeezing her glowing eyes shut. The fierce sorceress Zev had seen in the field now folded into herself as if something had torn inside. He knew what that was like. Feeling so broken and afraid, you lost all form of control.

"Lucenna!" Dyna called out past Cassiel's arms. Determination rose on her face. "Lucenna, it's all right!"

"Stay here!" Cassiel held on to her when she attempted to wiggle out from him.

She scowled and rammed her knee into him. He jerked back with a grunt, releasing her.

"No, Dyna!" Zev lunged to grab her, but she ducked under him faster than he expected.

She ran towards the magical tempest, tackling Lucenna in an embrace. They fell in a heap, and the swath of purple vanished. Everything caught in the wind crashed to the ground as the tent went still. Soup dripped off the tent walls. The cauldron tossed over a pile of books. Zev breathed heavily where he crouched, his wolf ready to burst forth.

He heard nothing but the beating of racing hearts in the tent and the gentle pattering of rain outside. Slowly, he retracted his claws from the ground, and his fur receded into his arms. He inhaled deeply to calm his wolf, inadvertently breathing in more of Lucenna's scent. It was one hundred times more concentrated in this enclosed space than it had been in Corron, nearly overpowering everyone else's. She smelled of wild magic, like lightning cutting through the air. Beneath it were the traces of something else he hadn't noticed at their first meeting.

"Nothing happened," Dyna spoke faintly in Lucenna's ear, but not much could be hidden from Zev's hearing. "Lord Norrlen stopped the mage in time."

Lucenna covered her face, shuddering as she wept. Tears leaked through her fingers and trailed down her temples. "He took from me … he stole some of my magic…"

Dyna stilled and gave Zev a pained look. The mage. His hands were glowing when he grabbed Lucenna's throat.

He'd *siphoned* her.

They had assumed he intended something else, but this was no less foul. There was no telling how much the mage had stolen from Lucenna before Rawn put an arrow through his neck. Zev balled his fists, wishing he'd been the one to kill him. He couldn't imagine all that she'd endured as a refugee. Then for this to happen to her was simply unfair. When he'd seen her on that field, fighting with all her might for the freedom those mages intended to steal, he hadn't thought twice about defending her.

Admit it, you enjoyed the kill, the Madness hissed. *Their screams. The sweet crunch of their bones. The smell of their blood, so ripe and warm.*

Zev ground his teeth.

"Shall we give you a moment?" Lord Norrlen asked.

"I won't leave Dyna alone with her," Zev said. His wolf prowled inside of him restlessly, inhaling that familiar scent that wouldn't let him decide if the sorceress was friend or foe.

Cassiel got to his feet, clutching the hilt of his sword. "What was that?"

"I'm fine," Dyna told them. "And Lucenna is perfectly well. She's calm now."

The sorceress sat up, avoiding their gazes. Her pale cheeks reddened as she wiped them. "I ... sometimes my Essence is affected by my emotions."

"A significant amount of power has a tendency to go wayward," Rawn told her kindly.

Pain scattered across Lucenna's face, and she looked down at her hands. She must feel so robbed. She still had magic, but it couldn't quell the loss she must feel. Zev could only guess it must be like missing a finger or a limb.

Lucenna dropped her head in her hands as a light pulsed at the base of the bed where her orb fell. Someone was calling again.

"Forgive me if I was insensitive to you," Rawn said.

Lucenna sighed wearily and her wet lashes lowered. "Your concern is unnecessary."

"You don't need to be wary of my companions," Dyna told her gently. "Unlike the mages, they have no interest in siphoning you."

Lucenna stared at her in surprise. She must not have expected her to be so informed about the ways of the mages. Rawn and Cassiel frowned. They didn't know what Dyna referred to.

"You're not of the Magos Empire," Lucenna stated.

Dyna smiled. "No, I'm not."

"But how do you know the customs of the mages?"

"Our family history has been passed on to us." She glanced at Zev, and he nodded encouragingly. This encounter must mean a lot to her. Neither of them ever imagined they'd meet a sorceress from Magos, and a free one at that.

"Are you truly Azeran's descendant?" Lucenna asked her.

"Yes."

She glanced at a quartz crystal hanging among the others, painted with the horizontal, hourglass-shaped rune for truth. It would have glowed red with a lie.

"How can that be?" she said faintly. "Not only did he allegedly have no direct heirs, but the Astron line is of the Lunar Guild. Moon mages have white hair, and their eyes are purple, blue, or gray. You share none of those traits."

"Our bloodline isn't pure," Dyna said. "Azeran's descendants married humans. With each generation, the Lunar Guild traits receded, and Essence waned, but we didn't forget where we came from. Our family passed on his story over the generations. We have Azeran's account of the war. He kept several journals."

"You have his journals?" Lucenna asked, her eyes widening.

Zev tensed, alarmed at the turn of the conversation. He heard Cassiel grit his teeth, likely keeping himself from scolding Dyna for revealing that. They had one of Azeran's journals with them, and it was the most valuable thing they possessed. Catching Dyna's gaze, Zev gave her a silent warning. She discreetly nodded.

Lucenna stroked the silver pendant hanging from her neck, and her fingers rested over the large groove in the center where a missing jewel should be. Several diamonds adorned the circumference. "Do you have them with you?"

"They remain in North Star," Dyna lied without a shift in her expression, though her throat bobbed. "It's one of the sanctuary villages."

Lucenna gaped at her, and Cassiel's brow pinched at the reaction. Of course, this must all be odd to him. He didn't know mage history as they did.

"You mentioned this," Cassiel said to Zev, referring to the first conversation they had about Azeran. "You said he founded North Star for those who fled the War of the Guilds."

Zev nodded. "He enchanted the village to conceal them from the outside world."

"But Azeran was killed during the war," Cassiel said.

"And we explained that's a lie."

Lucenna stared at him as if he said the sky was red. Either from the tea or the meal, the color had returned to her cheeks, and her hands no longer trembled. That electrifying scent of hers had also grown stronger. Undoubtedly, after that display of magic, her Essence must have nearly replenished.

"The survival of Azeran and the existence of sanctuaries had only been folklore—nothing but a whispered legend," Lucenna said.

Rawn canted his head, his brow furrowing. "Was he not a wicked mage? Azeran began the civil war to dethrone the Archmage. He planned to dismantle the guilds, seeking to be the sole ruling power. Thousands perished by Azeran's doing before he was defeated."

"The history that you know of him is wrong," Dyna said.

Cassiel's silver eyes narrowed. "How can it be wrong?"

"It is," Zev argued when she didn't.

Something was going on with those two. He saw it in the way they looked at one another and didn't. Cassiel hadn't hesitated to protect her when needed, but now they stood a good ten feet from each other.

"Have you not noticed the Magos Empire allows no outsider within their kingdom?" Zev asked Cassiel. "Why do you think that is? They made it a priority to keep their secrets from the rest of the world. One of them sits before you now." He motioned to Lucenna. "There is a reason you assumed her to be a witch."

"She conjures magic."

Lucenna glared at him. "Oh, that makes me a witch, does it?"

"There is no mention that the women of Magos can cast spells," Cassiel replied tersely. "Nor is the term sorceress found in any texts. So forgive me if I question it."

Vivid purple strands of electricity crackled at Lucenna's fingertips as her eyes flashed purple. "You know nothing of the truth. Azeran tried to improve the Magos Empire for the better, to improve our way of life. He believed he could, and he almost did. But he lost the War of the Guilds because he was *betrayed*," she spat the word. "By someone he trusted."

Heavy silence filled the tent, buffered only by the sound of rain.

Lucenna got to her feet and stalked to her desk. "Get out. All of you."

They gathered their belongings and made their way outside without a word. Zev didn't fault her anger. The Magos Empire kept its secrets well. The rest of Urn was ignorant of their world and most likely would never know.

Zev followed his cousin through the forest, letting her pile his arms with sticks for tonight's campfire. After some delegation on Dyna's part, she convinced the sorceress to allow them to camp outside of her tent for the night. They would go their separate ways in the morning. It was too late to keep traveling for the day.

The rain had lifted, leaving behind a carpet of yellow and orange leaves on the sodden earth. He ground them under his boot, hating the color and everything that reminded him of that autumn night. But he could never forget how the leaves had floated in through the broken window of his home, landing on the glass scattered across the floor and sticking to the blood-splattered walls.

Blind beastie, the Madness whispered with cruel delight. *You look but do not see.*

But Zev did see—he saw the sins of his past and the end to his future.

Zev shoved the memory away. He didn't want to remember that or what he contained inside. But he was constantly reminded whenever he looked at himself.

You'll never be rid of us. You be us. We be you. We be bad, sad, mad.

The Madness had taken to eerie rhymes and odd phrasing; a stage Zev had been waiting for. The Pack immediately put down werewolves fallen into the Madness. Otherwise, it would advance, leaving them to become ... feral. If that was the case, it meant he wouldn't be able to resist giving in to his wolf's spirit much longer. When that happened, he'd be completely lost. Nothing more than a vicious, wild beast. It would force Cassiel or Rawn to kill him. He should care. He knew he should, but he was numb.

Death was less than what he deserved for what he did to his father.

Why delay the inevitable? The Madness curled in his mind, its voice like icy claws caressing his flesh. *Give in and forget what you've done. Forget it all.*

The gods knew Zev wanted what it offered. He craved the vast peace that promised to erase all of his sins. A warm blanket of solace fell over him, and he closed his eyes. The weight lifted off his chest, easing the pain he'd learned to live with.

"Zev."

He flinched, his eyes flying open. His breaths came in heavy at the jolt of his consciousness, snapping back to awareness. Blinking, his vision focused on the one who pulled him from the fog.

Dyna watched him anxiously, her hands on his cheeks. How long had she been calling his name?

"Don't leave," she said. "Promise me."

The sadness on her face sent a wash of cold guilt and shock through him. The Madness was getting stronger. It had lulled him so easily.

Zev sighed. "I'm not going anywhere."

Neither of them missed that a promise went unsaid. He couldn't promise that he wouldn't leave one day. Dyna was his anchor, the only thing keeping the Madness at bay. But the wolf instinct to protect family constantly warred with the rotten corners of himself that wanted no more of this life, and it was losing.

He lived to keep her safe, but he didn't know if that was needed anymore. The journey began with only the two of them until the prince joined, and now the elf. A guardian of divine blood and a guardian to guide her steps. Two capable warriors. He wasn't needed as a protector or a Guidelander anymore. They'd taken those roles from him. After nearly killing her twice, she had to understand he was better off dead.

"Whatever you're thinking," Dyna said, searching his face, "you're wrong."

The warped scars on his wrists where the silver cuffs had burned him so terribly had become waxy and discolored. The Other lurked inside of him too, waiting for the one night of the month the moon would set it free. Why keep fighting what he was?

Dyna laid a hand over the scars. "I know you can learn to control the Other. Uncle Belzev believed it possible."

Such a belief got his father killed. Grief welled heavily in Zev's chest. The back of his eyes burned as memories attacked his mind.

Blood seeping through the wooden planks of the floor. The broken window. His mother's screams.

Zev closed his eyes. Why had his father left him unchained? Why had he believed the Other would submit to him? Was there a trick he failed to learn? Who could he ask now? As far as he knew, he was the only one of his kind. Werewolves didn't rear half-breed pups.

"Don't lose hope, Zev."

Relying on hope was like kissing the edge of a knife and expecting not to be cut.

"I've long given up on that," Zev said as he added a log to the pile he carried. "This is who I am."

Dyna shook her head. "Well, I haven't. Neither should you."

He sighed, but didn't argue. They wandered through the forest as she continued gathering more kindling. Her usual humming and excited chatter were absent today. What caused this uncharacteristic silence? It couldn't be because of him. She'd not been her lively self since yesterday morning. Since she went in search of Cassiel.

Zev glanced through the trees, where he heard the prince grumble about something to Lord Norrlen. Where Dyna's cheer had reduced, Cassiel's unpleasantness had increased. His distant manner returned after the events of Corron.

It must have been hard on him, killing all of those Raiders for Dyna's sake. But this discord between them was new. Did he resent her for losing her divinity? King Yoel said the God of Urn damned Celestials who took human lives. Something Zev could sympathize with. Life had damned him a long time ago.

"Dyna?"

She stopped, facing a tree, and her back tensed.

What's wrong? He wanted to ask, but by her stiff shoulders, she dreaded the question. It only concerned him further. What had Cassiel done? He had a way with words, and most of them were unkind.

"What are we doing here?" Zev asked instead.

"We had to help her."

"Aye, but why are we still here?"

Zev was ready to move on. He didn't think it would be wise to linger around Lucenna much longer. After what had happened in the tent, it confirmed how dangerous she could be. If more Enforcers came searching for her, that would put Dyna at risk.

"Do you recognize the medallion she wears?" Dyna asked, turning around.

He shook his head.

"It's the Lūna Medallion." At his obvious confusion, she frowned. "It's the twin to the Sōl Medallion, do you not remember?"

It took him a moment to recall he had glimpsed it in Azeran's journal. Dyna was searching for the Sōl Medallion, a pendant made of gold with a Sunstone in the center. The stone contained the light of the sun. They needed it to obliterate the Shadow. There was a detailed illustration of it in the journal—and there had been another pendant drawn beside it.

"It's *Azeran's* medallion," she said. "But the Moonstone is missing."

Zev groaned and rubbed his forehead. "Let me guess. The Moonstone is also on Mount Ida?"

It wouldn't be much of a surprise. Mount Ida was home to innumerable treasures.

"It's possible," Dyna shrugged. "The Moonstone disappeared after the War of the Guilds. There was a rumor that Captain Roizen Ida stole it from Azeran himself, though he wrote nothing of it in his journals. The Sōl Medallion is on Mount Ida. Why not the Moonstone?"

"Let's say you're right. I'm waiting for you to explain what that has to do with us."

"I think she's searching for it, Zev. Even if I'm wrong, she's alone out here in the world. Shouldn't we ask her to join us?"

He inhaled a deep breath, smelling the fresh earth and crisp air, using it to keep calm. "Dyna, please don't tell her about the map."

The map to Mount Ida, tucked safely within Azeran's journal, was perhaps the most valuable thing in the world. That island was a place of legend, full of wondrous treasure many searched for. Most wouldn't hesitate to take it from them by force, and he would rather not have to fight a powerful sorceress.

"I won't," Dyna answered, much to his relief. "I knew not to do so without consulting you first."

But she said so while glancing at the trees toward Cassiel's voice. The setting sun streamed in through the branches, catching on her emerald eyes.

Zev patted Dyna's head, proud of her caution, even if it was done because she knew how the prince would react. "That was wise."

With a heavy sigh, guilt creased her features. "I could only hope for a little wisdom after the trouble I caused."

She hadn't meant to tell Commander Von about Mount Ida or the map, but neither of them knew he'd been spying on them in Landcaster. And now Von's master hunted her. Tarn. Infamous raider, thief, and cutthroat. Wanted dead or alive by the Azure King, for whatever reason. Whoever the man was, he wanted Dyna. If he ever got close again, Zev planned to tear the heart from his chest.

"How much longer must we hide?"

"Until we reach the port," Zev said as they made their way back. Once they boarded a ship out of the Azure Kingdom and put a thousand leagues between them and this new enemy, they could be at ease.

They arrived at the camp as Cassiel finished constructing the fire pit. Rawn spoke to Fair in soft Elvish while he brushed the horse's coat into a velvety white sheen. Fair snorted uneasily as Zev neared.

He tossed some firewood into the pit. "We have enough for the night."

With a murmur, Rawn conjured a flicker of flame in his palm. Soon the campfire was burning, and they were unrolling their sleeping mats.

Cassiel caught Zev's eye, arching an eyebrow in question as if to say, *well?*

"We leave at dawn," Zev announced. "We'll continue on our way to The Port of Azure."

"Good."

"But what about Lucenna?" Dyna asked quietly.

"Dyna, she cannot come with us," he whispered back. "You saw what she's capable of."

"But … what if more mages come after her?"

Zev sighed and kneaded his forehead. Lucenna was a sorceress constantly on the run. He wanted to help her, but Dyna's safety was more important to him than anyone else's. She was his priority.

"Whatever she is involved in has nothing to do with us," Cassiel said, also lowering his voice. "We have our own troubles and secrets we cannot afford to share."

Dyna sighed. "But what if we can help her?"

"I don't believe she wants our help," Zev said. The sorceress clearly wanted nothing to do with them. She didn't trust them, for good reason. Rawn nodded. "If our presence makes her uncomfortable, then we should not remain where we are unwanted."

"We're also short on time," Zev added, speaking at normal volume to signal the end of that discussion. "We can't have any more delays on our journey. How much further are we from the port?"

Removing Azeran's journal from his pack, Rawn turned his back to Lucenna's tent. "I believe we are about a week's travel from it."

He gently handled the black leather, careful not to disturb the cracked corners worn thin. A gold clasp kept the thick pages fastened shut. The fading sun shone over the embossed Astron family sigil on the cover. A crescent adorned with vines. Azeran had embedded a small part of his Essence in the journal, yet it was so powerful it hummed against Zev's skin like static. Rawn passed Dyna the journal so she could whisper the passphrase and she handed it back.

"Thank you, my lady. There is an old trade route north-east of here," he said to Zev as he turned the pages to the map. "It is steep terrain, not favorable for heavy caravans, and less likely we will meet other travelers there."

"Well, I found a quicker way to the port," Zev said

"Have you? I do not recall a shorter path in these lands."

Zev crouched beside him and pointed at a large body of water on the map, within the north of the range. "We can cross through the Saxe Fjord that cuts through the mountains. This way, we don't have to go around it and the route is secluded. It'll make up for lost time."

"Ah." Rawn rubbed his jaw. "I would not advise it. Allegedly, grindylows dwell within the fjord. They are carnivorous creatures that take pleasure in drowning their victims before consuming them."

"It's merely a rumor. Some say it's grindylows. Others say it's kelpies or selkies. Have you crossed the Saxe River or the Saxe Fjord before?"

Rawn frowned as he closed the journal. "I traversed the Saxe River whilst passing through the western peaks of the Zafiro Mountains to reach Landcaster."

"Did you see any grindylows?"

"I did not."

"Then it must only be rumors." Zev shrugged and took the journal so he could study the map tonight.

"It's not." Lucenna lurked in the shadow of her tent, watching them.

She had stood so motionless and quiet, neither of them had noticed her there until now. Zev inwardly groaned. How much had she heard?

"A nest of grindylows lie in the Saxe Fjord," she said.

"How do you know?" he asked, shifting his stance to hide the journal behind him.

"Because that is exactly where I'm headed. I need one of their scales."

"Whatever for?" Rawn asked.

The astonishment taking over his expression matched the one Zev felt on his face. What could she possibly want with that?

Lucenna crossed her arms, observing them each for a stretch of a moment, calculating something. Whatever she saw in them seemed to lead to a decision. "The scale isn't for me," she said, her mouth curling in a puckish smile. "It's for the Druid."

CHAPTER 9

Several questions rushed to the tip of Dyna's tongue, but she held them back, waiting for the sorceress to answer them on her own. Lucenna's silvery-white hair flowed around her as she cocked her head at their silence.

Cassiel broke the quiet first. "Should we know who you speak of?"

"You may not have heard of him," she said, shrugging. "The Druid of the Moors is a seer of sorts."

"You speak of Leoake," Rawn said.

"You know him?" Dyna asked.

Rawn nodded. "I have met him in passing. Interesting fellow. He lives in the Court of the Phantasmic Moors if memory serves. Home of the Wild Fae."

Dyna caught her cousin subtly handing Cassiel the journal before Lucenna noticed. He slid it behind his back, hidden by his wings.

Zev stood, drawing the sorceress's attention. "That's nearby."

"Precisely."

Rawn frowned. "Nevertheless, the fae do not bestow favors for free, my lady. Leoake, most of all."

"I'm aware," Lucenna said. "He will answer exactly three questions for rare items, which is why I'm headed for the fjord. I need grindylow scales to trade. They shine like blue pearls and glow in the dark. Priced nearly as much as jewels and are very difficult to get since the grindylows will eat anyone who gets too close."

"Why tell us this?" Cassiel asked, suspicion lacing his voice. "What do you want with the Druid?"

"That's my business." Lucenna crossed her arms. "I'm sharing this because the Druid can reveal great secrets, most hidden even from the world. I assume you lot need something as well, otherwise why be out here in the wilderness? Whatever you need, he'll have the knowledge—if we can get those scales."

"We?" Zev repeated, raising his brows.

"Are you saying you would like us to join you?" Dyna asked, intrigued by the whole thing.

Cassiel's mouth curled. "She means to use us again. You need us. Without our help, you will most likely die in the fjord."

Lucenna scoffed, her eyes glowing softly. "I don't need you or anyone else. After what you witnessed, I think my abilities are clear. However, having a team would certainly make the extraction easier." She raised her chin. "It's an offer. Each one of you must have questions you want to be answered. Give it some thought." Then the sorceress stalked back into her tent, leaving them to do exactly that.

Dyna spent all night staring at the stars in the clear night sky. Her mind wouldn't fall quiet, not after what the sorceress had revealed to them. She suspected the others were unsettled, too. Zev had shifted, leaving to wander the woods while Cassiel had flown into the skies as soon as night arrived, and Rawn fell into a restless sleep.

Dyna rubbed her tired, heavy eyes. The pink of early dawn streaked across the sky, and the canopy edge of the forest glimmered gold with the first rays of the sun.

Three questions. Only three? Dyna had so many. Too many to list them all. At the forefront, the ones who drew the most questions were the Shadow, Cassiel, and Tarn. The Shadow demon's arrival next winter was imminent, and the reminder brought a crawl to her skin.

Cassiel left a nervous apprehension in her chest. No, she couldn't think about him yet.

Tarn brought great uncertainty. She didn't know who the man was, only that he hunted her because the fae Seer of Faery Hill in Arthal had divined that she was the key to Mount Ida, likely alluding to the map. The Seer also mentioned she would have Guardians to protect her.

When Von and Geon first mentioned the divination, Dyna had been skeptical, then awed to think the fates had seen to her future. But the divination also annoyed her.

It referred to her as the Maiden accompanied by guardians. Zev, Cassiel, and Rawn were three of them, and there were three more out there. It took six to keep her safe since she clearly couldn't do it herself.

She didn't have Zev's strength, Cassiel's aptitude, or Rawn's skill. She couldn't even stand to be alone in the dark. That childish fear never faded, and it left her feeling pathetic. Even her Essence couldn't produce anything as fascinating or as powerful as the spells Lucenna cast. The sorceress had bent the elements to her will.

What was it like to wield that much power?

If only she could be useful and stand on her own feet. Zev and the others contributed so much already. Dyna wanted to give back. To help. To fight. The truth was, she'd always been weak.

"My lady?" Rawn called.

Dyna quickly wiped her wet cheeks before sitting up on her sleeping mat. "Yes?"

Lord Norrlen observed her, concern lining his expression. "Are you feeling unwell?"

"I'm all right." She stretched a smile on her face. "I simply didn't rest well."

"Nor did I."

He appeared as tired as she felt. What questions must have occupied his thoughts? She knew little about him other than his twenty-year search for a sword only found in Mount Ida. Without it, he couldn't return home.

Home.

The notion grappled at her heart. She missed her family and her cottage nestled within the rolling hills of North Star, missed the peace when it wasn't haunted by shadows. She'd never left home until now. If it weren't for the others, she wouldn't have gotten far, let alone survived the first day.

Her mind rattled off all the instances her life should have ended. The Watchers of Hilos. The cliff. The feral werewolf in Lykos Peak. The Ecru snake. The Other.

Dead.

Dead.

Dead.

Dead.

DEAD.

Dyna stifled a groan. As much as she wanted to deny it, the Guardians kept her alive. And if the fates sought to give her six, then she needed to find them all. They were her only hope of surviving long enough to reach Mount Ida.

"My lady, what is on your mind, if I may ask?" Rawn said as he relit the dying fire. "You seem troubled."

Dyna sighed and ran her fingers through her crimson locks, loosening the knots. A flush sunk in her cheeks. "There is much in the world I don't understand. I wish I could somehow learn all the answers."

"I, too, have wished for the same, but one must be careful what they wish for."

"Have you ever felt ... as though you were completely helpless?" She laughed weakly. "Sorry, that's a silly question. You're a warrior. You're the furthest thing from helpless." Dyna released her hair. "I know why I'm here and why I left home, but there are times I realize I'm a mouse in a field prowled by snakes and owls, where one wrong step will end me. I have no claws or fangs, no sword or bow, nothing but the determination to keep going. And I wonder, is that enough?"

"I must admit, there are days where I feel helpless," Rawn said, linking his hands on his lap. "A warrior's blade cannot defeat time. Nor can it bring me any closer to my family. I am at the mercy of my vow to find the Dragon's Fang for my kingdom, and I cannot return until I do. I nearly lost my life several times, but what kept me alive was determination. If I had given up, I would not have met you, and at last, found the correct path." She met Rawn's warm turquoise gaze. "To answer your question: yes, you are more than enough. We all start somewhere. I imagine this will be a journey of a lifetime, and there will be many things you must face. You may stumble, but the most important step is always the next one."

That's all she could do. Keep going. No matter what, for Lyra, she refused to give up. Some of the weight lifted off her shoulders.

"Thank you, Lord Norrlen."

"Of course, my lady."

The thrumming in her chest alerted her to Cassiel's presence. She heard the flutter of his wings before spotting him circling overhead. Zev slipped out of the forest in torn trousers. A smear of blood stained his lips from whatever game he'd caught. Cassiel landed beside him, and they exchanged greetings before coming over to join them.

"Good morrow," Rawn called.

"If only it were." Cassiel sat on his mat with his arm propped on his knee. The flight had left his silky hair windblown, his cheekbones and nose ruddy from the chill. "Well, I imagine all of you are considering her proposal," he said, referring to Lucenna. "Yesterday, she could not wait to be rid of us, but now she seeks our help? What does it serve her?"

Dyna frowned. If grindylows were as dangerous as believed, it would take more than one person to get those scales. "Even if Lucenna doesn't want to admit it, she needs a suitable team, and we're as good as any," she said with a shrug. "I admit, I'm curious about the Druid, but can we afford to delay our mission?"

Rawn shook his head. "Time is short, my lady. We must reach the ports as soon as possible. Once winter arrives, the Saxe Sea will freeze, and we cannot board a ship until the spring."

That wouldn't do. They needed to be on their way to Mount Ida, and the voyage alone would take months.

"The sea in Urn's Chip freezes, not the ocean," Cassiel said. "As long as we board the last ship out of the port by the end of the season, we should be fine."

"How far is the fjord?" Dyna asked.

"About three days away, my lady."

"It's on the way to the port," Zev added.

Then perhaps it was worth exploring.

"I understand the appeal," Rawn said. "However, I find this an unnecessary risk. We must avoid the fjord. It is far too dangerous."

Zev gazed at the fire. "The world is full of dangers, but nothing worth having is ever without risk."

"You want to go?" Cassiel asked him.

"I have questions that need answering."

The Other, Dyna guessed. He must want to ask about it. If Zev could learn how to control it, then he wouldn't need his chains. He wouldn't need to suffer so much anymore.

"I say we join her," she announced, deciding at that moment. "I think we can trust Lucenna."

Cassiel's jaw worked as his mouth thinned. Probably with the restraint it took not to call her a stupid human again.

"She helped us in Corron. Need I remind you?" Dyna said.

Fury burned in his gaze, as scorching as *Esh Zayin*'s divine fire. "I have more than paid that debt. My damned soul will never allow me to forget it."

His reaction squeezed her heart, twisting and hanging heavily like a weight she couldn't shake. He killed humans to save her. That would always be her fault.

Cassiel's remorse suddenly washed through their bond, and she stiffed at the unexpected sensation. His emotions had been absent after he left her alone on the cliff, but as they locked eyes, she saw the regret there. Cassiel had sensed her guilt. Heat rushed to her face, and she wanted to hide. Her emotions remained out there for him to read. When he had blocked himself from the bond, she assumed it worked both ways.

Dyna faced the others. "If we can afford the detour, then let's do it. I want to ask the Druid how to find the rest of my Guardians. It's a part of my journey. It has to be. I couldn't have made it this far without each of you."

While she wished she wasn't a frail maiden, if finding all of her Guardians meant she would defeat Tarn and the Shadow, then she would find them.

"Aye, but we don't know who the others are," Zev said. "Von withheld the rest of the divination."

"Therefore, we should consult the fae as Tarn did," she said. "All we need are grindylow scales. If we can each get one, then that is three questions for each of us. How bad could the grindylows be?"

"I think we can manage it," Zev said, his tone confident.

Cassiel exhaled heavily and waved a hand of resignation. "They are but overgrown eels with teeth."

He gave in rather easily. It could only mean he had questions for the Druid as well.

Rawn shook his head. "One, you may kill. Two, three, perhaps four. Nonetheless, grindylows swim in family groups. There will not be a mere few in those waters. There will be hundreds. It is unwise to venture there. I do not approve."

"Approve?" Zev growled. "Remind me. When have we needed your approval, Lord Norrlen?"

"Zev," Dyna chided, her eyes widening in disbelief.

That cold response was unlike him. Zev and Cassiel may have allowed Rawn to join them as their Guidelander, but they hadn't been exactly welcoming. Whenever Rawn attempted to guide them, Zev questioned every decision, arguing over which route of travel was best.

"It is all right, my lady." Rawn took out tea leaves from a pouch and sprinkled them into the kettle. "I suppose my approval is irrelevant."

Zev heaved a breath and ran a hand through his dark hair. "As you said, we have questions, Dyna. I'm willing to find the answers."

In the back of her mind, she hesitated to go against Rawn's warning. He was their Guidelander because he knew the land, but he also advised her to be determined. That's exactly what she aimed to do.

Cassiel crossed his arms. "Well, we have settled our differences with votes before. All in favor of the fjord?"

Three raised their hands.

CHAPTER 10

Dynalya

Dyna volunteered to speak to the sorceress about their decision. The others didn't like it, but they agreed Lucenna liked them a lot less. When the afternoon sun was high in the sky, and the sorceress hadn't left her tent, Dyna risked going in.

She found Lucenna at her desk, speaking angrily to no one in particular. "I told you I'm fine. I haven't been able to reply to you, as I had to recover after my confrontation with the Enforcers. Now stop sending me messages by portal. Father will sense it!"

Dyna took a step inside, and something crinkled beneath her foot. A piece of parchment with wet ink stuck to her boot. She picked it off, reading the smeared handwriting.

Contact me at once.

"I'm being careful," a smooth male voice with a Magos accent replied, startling Dyna. She took another step forward, spotting the white glow past Lucenna's shoulder. She was speaking to someone in the orb. "But I had to risk it. I feared the worst when you didn't answer me, Lu. I thought I had lost you as well."

Lucenna sighed and set her elbow on the desk, resting her chin in her palm. "I'm safe, Lucien."

"What happened after you defeated the Enforcers?" the voice from the orb said.

"Nothing."

She hadn't told him about them?

"Don't lie to me," he said. "I always know when you're lying. Why did you ignore my calls?"

"Because I'm not in the mood to talk," she snapped.

"My, you're in quite the snit. What happened? I felt a torrent of your Essence yesterday. But it was ... different."

Lucenna stiffened. "Nothing happened. Stop worrying about me."

"I'll always worry about you," Lucien said, the timbre of his words saddening.

Lucenna slumped in her chair, giving Dyna a better view of the glowing orb. Its once clear core was now cloudy with color. "I know. I'm sorry."

"What happened?" he repeated. "Tell me."

"I was thinking of mother."

Her mother? That's not what had caused the surge, but Dyna understood why Lucenna wouldn't want to tell him the truth.

"Don't torture yourself over it," Lucien said, believing the excuse. "Her death wasn't your fault."

"Let's not speak of it. I'll contact you once I reach the Port of Azure."

"Why do I sense you're not telling me everything, Lu?"

"Every lady has her secrets," she said. With a wave of her hand, the orb became clear again.

"Lucenna?" Dyna called.

Purple light sparked at Lucenna's fingertips as she whirled in her seat. Eyes glowed with a jolt of power that clashed against Dyna's Essence. Once she recognized her, the electrical feeling faded.

"Oh, you're here." Lucenna rubbed her forehead. Her hair fell in messy waves around her shoulders. She wore a black chemise, the thin straps dangling on her arms. "Were you listening?"

"Yes, sorry."

"I don't mean to lie to him," she said, shrugging. "I had to tell him something so he would stop pestering me. We can sense each other when our emotions are agitated. It happens with mage twins. I can't control it as well as Lucien can. He's aware of me most of the time. It's maddening."

Dyna tried not to think about how much that reminded her of her link with Cassiel.

Lucenna went to her bed, throwing herself over the rumpled bedding. She stretched like a lazy cat and nestled into her pillows, closing her eyes. "Is it morning?"

"It's midday," Dyna replied sheepishly.

The sorceress groaned. "If you need something, expect little from me today. I plan to lounge and enjoy some rest."

"I've come to say we decided to join you at the fjord."

"Hmm," she replied sleepily. "Splendid."

Dyna bit her lip. She wanted to ask about magic, and Magos, and other things she hadn't had the chance to ask. To meet a Lunar sorceress, she couldn't help but feel awestruck.

Taking in the tent, she observed the many books stacked on the floor and the crystals on the ceiling. Scrolls and other relics kept the orb company on Lucenna's desk. Beside it rested an item Dyna hadn't expected to find.

"It's his." Lucenna peeked at her through her long, white lashes. "Your Celestial's."

Your Celestial's.

Dyna stared at the silky black feather. With how defensive Cassiel was about his feathers, the sorceress couldn't have possibly found it. Did he give it to her? When? Why would he give such a thing to a stranger when he refused to let her get near them?

Lucenna sat on her bed. "It was a trade. He gave it to me in exchange for a tracking spell."

Dyna glanced at her questioningly.

"For when you'd been kidnapped in Corron."

Cassiel broke another law to save her. She hated that it had to be that way.

"How do you do it?" she asked her.

"Do what?"

Dyna met her gaze and rephrased her question. "How are you not afraid?"

Lucenna played with the ring on her finger. It was beautiful, with a pink gemstone set on a delicate gold band. Longing shadowed her delicate features. "I am. Every day."

Dyna didn't know what to make of that. The sorceress was fierce and powerful.

"No one is ever truly without fear. I remind myself every day why I'm here, what I lost, what I'm fighting for. And I keep those reasons close to my heart." Lucenna laid a hand over the Lūna Medallion, her lilac eyes glowing softly. "I will do anything to get it. Nothing and no one else matters."

Of course. How simple. Dyna already had her reason.

The distant chill of winter caressed her cheeks as screams echoed in her memories. For a moment, she returned to that snowy hill as the puddles of blood crystalized in the ice like a frozen rose.

"Why are you crying?"

Dyna exhaled sharply and wiped her eyes. "I've had enough of others protecting me."

"Then protect yourself."

She frowned. "Oh, that must be easy for you to say. When Von took me, I couldn't do more than kick and scream. But you disarmed him with a flick of your fingers. I'm not a fighter like you."

"Have you decided that or did someone say so?"

Dyna opened her mouth to argue, then closed it. No one had told her she couldn't fight. She simply accepted her abilities.

Lucenna evoked a small, purple sphere in her hand. It crackled with electricity. "You must know the women of Magos are not taught how to use their power. I refused to let that stop me. Don't allow others to place limitations on you." Her gaze hardened. "If you want to be a fighter, then be one."

Dyna sat on the edge of the bed. "If I could learn to wield spells as you do, I would. But I'm not capable."

"Have you passed through The Rising?"

"No, the Rising hasn't been seen in my village for nearly seventy-five years."

The Rising was when power first awakened in mage children. Their bodies levitated from their beds during sleep and their Essence enveloped them in a magical shield while they were at their most vulnerable. It was a rite of passage for mages while they learned how to control their power. While some of the people from her village had Essence, the power they could yield wasn't sufficient enough to experience it.

"Did you have a Guild Master?"

Dyna shook her head. A Guild Master was the most powerful mage in a guild who often took an apprentice. Lady Samira had been the head of the council and the last Guild Master of North Star before her passing, and her father the last teacher. The council had not bothered to replace him when no one had displayed any significant power.

"Magic is nearly lost in my village," she said.

Sad understanding settled on Lucenna's features. "How many spells have you learned?"

She cringed. "None."

"You didn't have a teacher?"

Dyna looked away. "No. My father passed away before he could teach me. It took me years to learn one thing on my own."

"And what was that?"

"Essence Healing."

Lucenna's eyes widened. "You know how to heal? Not even I have learned it. That's remarkable."

Dyna blushed from the praise. "It won't do me much good during a fight. I don't have true magic. I can't perform spells."

Lucenna smirked, shaking her head. "Essence Healing *is* a spell and a complex one at that. You're Azeran's descendant. Of course, you have magic. You're a sorceress, Dyna."

She didn't know how to respond to that. Never had she identified as a sorceress. Her human genealogy had washed out the magic from her bloodline. Essence was all she had left, and it was minimal. That made her human, didn't it?

"And you have wielded nothing else?"

Dyna glanced at the feather on the desk. "Only once. A wave of green fire that somehow burst out of me."

"Essence Blast," Lucenna said and motioned at the feather. "With that?"

"Yes."

Lucenna leaned over to pick up the black plume, and it lit up with golden light at her touch. "You know, like crystals, Celestial feathers heighten power." The sorceress tapped the feather on the back of Dyna's hand, and the hum of her Essence rose to the surface, reacting to the powerful charge.

Even if the feather had amplified her power enough to cause that spell, she wouldn't experience it again without another one. It's not as if she could ask Cassiel to supply them after his kind had been hunted and brutalized for their blood and feathers.

"Essence Healing is difficult for me," she admitted. "I struggle to wield the little power I have. I feel a barrier that keeps it from growing."

Lucenna searched her over. "I don't see a barrier. Do you?"

Dyna made a face. She didn't mean a literal one.

"Spells vary in complication by how much Essence and concentration is needed," Lucenna said. "Essence Healing is one of the most complicated spells there is. If you can do that, then surely you can do more."

Lucenna plucked one of the many books on her bedside table. It was thin with a leather blue covering. "Here. It's a book of preliminary spells."

An unexpected gift, one Dyna wasn't sure she should accept. "Oh no, I couldn't, possibly."

"Don't be silly. It's rude to refuse."

She hesitantly took it. "Thank you."

"Start with levitation. That was the first spell I learned."

"Levitation?" Dyna gaped. "That sounds too grand for me."

"Nonsense. It's easy." Lucenna went to her desk and rummaged through the missives, returning with a wooden ball the size of an egg, and put it in Dyna's hand. "Practice with this. I'll teach you."

The moon sigil of the Lunar Guild was engraved on the polished surface. Dyna traced the groove with her thumb, a ball of emotion swelling in her chest. She, at last, had someone to train her.

She swallowed, blinking away her tears. "You're far too kind. I don't know what to say."

Lucenna nodded, her expression softening. "There are many like us who don't know how to fight, but the power to do so is inside. You only need to find it." She stood and gathered some clothing from a trunk at the foot of her bed. "May as well begin now."

"Now? But wouldn't we attract more Enforcers?"

Lucenna slipped behind the privacy screen. "I will cast a veil over the camp. It's much more proficient than a cloaking spell, and it will hide our presence in the mortal world. Though I don't think we will have a problem. If you were a full-blooded sorceress, training this late in age would be dangerous. But your Essence is minimal, so it should be fine."

Dyna curled her hands on her lap. If she didn't have enough power to be dangerous, then any spell she cast wouldn't amount to much.

"Mage children need to learn control of their Essence early, or it erupts with every tantrum. I, unfortunately, learned later than I was able." Lucenna stepped out in a flowing black dress with transparent sleeves. "For what you've done for me, this is my debt repaid. Until the day we part, I'll be sure that you learn more than one spell."

Dyna grinned, excitement stirring in her. She caressed the embossed floral designs decorating the frame of the book. There must have been hundreds piled around the tent. Sorceresses weren't allowed to read or write, let alone learn magic. It must have cost Lucenna a great deal to get these books. She was brave to go against the laws of her kingdom. Dyna wanted that, too. The bravery to defend herself and the strength to protect others.

In a year's time, she would face the inevitable. The Shadow was coming, and she had to be ready.

CHAPTER 11

Cassiel

There was one thing Cassiel knew for certain, and it was not to trust a witch. He crossed his arms as he watched the tent steadily. Dyna had been in there for a while now. What were they doing? Had the witch done something to her? No, he would have sensed it. Instead, something new passed through the bond. A warmth like the rays of sunlight. Dyna was happy.

Relief flooded through him. His confession had left something heavy on her, and it had weighed on his body as if he'd been buried beneath it. He shouldn't have told her about the bond. It was foolish to have dared for some inkling of acceptance, to have contemplated such a notion. Even from a girl with a kind heart.

Blood Bonds didn't instill any sort of affection, let alone love. He knew many bonded mates who cared nothing for one another. Celestials didn't come to love easily, but when they did, he heard it was unyielding. Not the fickle love of humans, but an all-consuming, immeasurable sort of devotion he couldn't begin to understand. That love was perhaps almost as rare as True Bonded mates.

His grandparents, King Rael and Queen Sapphira, were True Bonded—bound in mind, body, and soul. Two parts of a soul, as the fates determined, or so he was told. As far as he knew, it wasn't a good thing.

Rael had experienced Sapphira's pain when the humans tortured her. He heard her cries in his mind. Felt it when her soul was ripped from his. The agony brought Rael to his knees as he screamed and screamed. Then he unleashed his divine fire and burned all those who harmed her, decimating an entire city until it was nothing but ash. But Rael perished soon after, not able to withstand the pain of living without his mate.

"Losing a True Bonded is the worst agony a Celestial can endure," his father had said. *"For when the bond breaks, they are losing half of themselves."*

Cassiel shuddered. Thank *Elyōn* that sort of vile thing rarely happened.

He needed to free Dyna from him. It was the right thing to do. Yet, Blood Bonds were a perpetual pact. Bound eternally in the Mortal Realm until death doth they part. But if this Druid was truly all knowledgeable, he may know another way to break the bond that didn't involve either of them dying.

Cassiel glanced up when Dyna strolled out of the tent. A brilliant smile shone on her face, as bright as the morning light reflecting on her scarlet locks. Her emerald eyes nearly danced with joy as she clutched a book close to her chest and rushed to sit by Zev.

"What have you got there?" her cousin asked.

"It's a spellbook." She showed it to him, nearly bouncing in her seat. "Lucenna offered to teach me."

She wanted to learn magic from a witch? Cassiel kept his retort to himself. He doubted anything he said would be taken well.

Zev didn't appear bothered. "Did she, now?"

"Isn't it magnificent? I'll have a teacher."

Zev smiled. "I'm glad."

"Of course, I'll never be as powerful as her, but to learn more spells and from another sorceress? I couldn't ever have imagined this." The rapid words poured out of Dyna with her excitement. "We're starting today. She's going to teach me levitation first."

Rawn chuckled. "That is wonderful, my lady."

Cassiel couldn't even be annoyed about it when her happiness washed through him so strongly.

Dyna's smile faded, and she squared her shoulders. "There is something I would like to ask of each of you". She drew in a breath and said, "I want to learn how to fight."

Silence filled their campsite.

"If I may request, I would like for each of you to teach me. To truly teach me." She looked at Zev. "Not only how to hit, but to wield a blade and a bow."

While unexpected, it wasn't surprising. Cassiel had already attempted to teach her how to at least throw a punch before circumstances interrupted their lessons. Now was a prime time to continue.

Zev crossed his arms. "Dyna."

"I can't protect myself, Zev. I'm..." She made a face. "I'm a damsel."

"That is not true, my lady."

Dyna frowned at Rawn. "Lord Norrlen, simply by that honorific, I know you see me as a delicate lady. Zev sees me as helpless. Prince Cassiel sees me as reckless."

Prince. The title sat on his head like a crown of thorns. She had returned to being formal with him.

She met each of their gazes. "If it's not true, then deny it now."

None of them did.

Dyna's aggravation prickled on his skin. Their silence had offended her. He wanted to disagree to ease the sting, but it would be a lie. She left her village with no experience, or training, or even a proper plan. She was soft, clumsy, easily breakable, and yes, occasionally reckless.

She tightly clutched the book. "I don't wish to be that way any longer."

"Very well," Cassiel said.

Dyna's emerald gaze snapped to him, her surprise hammering through the bond.

"The most lethal Watchers of the Four Celestial Realms are women," he said, removing a knife from his boot.

Her eyes locked on the handle of black opal and widened with recognition. "That's ..."

It was the knife she had admired in the Corron market, one of a pair. Its twin tucked in his other boot was constructed with a handle of white opal. He had always intended them for her. Cassiel offered the knife to Dyna, but when she reached for it, Zev snatched it away.

"No weapons."

"But—"

"No, Dyna." He stood. "Magic is enough."

She visibly wilted like a small flower trampled on the road, squashed before having a chance to bloom. Cassiel glared at Zev, but his eyes flashed yellow in warning. He stalked away to the forest, and his tall frame vanished into the bushes.

"What did I tell you?" a sharp voice hissed. Lucenna stood outside of her tent with her arms crossed. "If you want to learn, then learn. Don't ask *men* for permission."

Dyna bit her lip, toeing the ground. "He means well."

Lucenna snorted. "Anyone who would force their will upon you doesn't mean well."

"Your opinion is irrelevant in this matter," Cassiel said stridently in defense. "Zev only cares for her safety."

Lucenna completely ignored him. "Lord Norrlen, I imagine you have no qualms with teaching her how to use a bow?"

Rawn smiled at Dyna kindly and nodded. "With pleasure, I shall endeavor to do so forthwith."

A small smile returned to her lips. "I haven't troubled you with my request, Lord Norrlen?"

"It is no trouble at all, my lady."

"Good, now that's settled." Lucenna clapped once. "I hear you will also join me at the fjord. That gives me more time to properly plan now that the advantage is greater." She nodded to Dyna. "It will require both of our power to succeed. I'll need three days to prepare you. Now come along. Your first lesson begins now."

Dyna readily followed her to the creek in the distance.

"Well, I best go in search of the proper materials to fletch a dozen new arrows for Lady Dyna," Rawn said as he put out the fire. "Though, I am hesitant to go against Zev's wishes."

"Never mind that. I will speak with him." Cassiel stood and went into the woods.

The quiet trees clustered close together, a mix of pine, oak, and ash. Most of the branches hung bare. A carpet of yellow leaves layered the ground, preventing any tracks, but he soon found Zev in a small clearing. He stood there, staring blankly at the knife.

The leaves crunched underfoot as Cassiel approached. "Zev?"

He whirled around with a snarl. "I'll not argue about this with you."

"I thought the role of sullen, intolerable arse fell to me," Cassiel said dully. "Care to explain why your manner has been more feral as of late?"

Zev grimaced, and Cassiel immediately regretted his thoughtless words. He had shortly forgotten about Zev's struggle with the Madness.

"Do you hear the whispers?" he brought himself to ask.

"Always." The faint confession faded into the forest.

He really was an insensitive idiot.

Zev roughly rubbed his face as if to get rid of the mad voice that haunted him. "I know what you came to say. My answer won't change."

"Why?"

"Why?" Zev repeated angrily. "Killing is the worst sin one can commit. You know this as well as I do."

Yes, a lesson Cassiel was forced to learn. "Training with a blade and striking someone with it are two different things."

"Then what is the purpose of learning how to handle weapons if not to take lives with them?"

"To defend herself. To feel capable. Safer. Would you rather she be completely helpless? What if, by some unfortunate happening, she is taken from us again?" His chest tightened at the thought. He didn't want to ever feel the way he did when she was taken. What if next time he couldn't save her?

Zev started pacing. "I won't let that happen."

Cassiel scowled. "Neither of us wanted it to happen, but it did. It is foolish to be unprepared for all possibilities. When misfortune comes for her, be it through an enemy or circumstance, it will devour her in an instant. Misfortune always comes. Right now, she is defenseless. I will not leave her to be."

Zev's eyes flashed yellow when he whipped around, a growl his only response.

"Be angry with me if you must, but she asked this of us, and I will help her."

"She doesn't need to learn how to use weapons," Zev rumbled. "She has us for that."

At the wildness sharpening his features and his growing fangs, and it dawned on Cassiel that Zev's wolf only surfaced when he was angry—or threatened. Damn. The witch hadn't been far off the mark.

"This is not about Dyna, is it?"

Zev turned away, and it was answer enough. He didn't want her to learn how to defend herself with a weapon because he saw himself as one. As a weapon to be wielded for her sake. A werewolf's instinct to protect their family prevailed over all else. It was the only thing keeping him sane.

"Do you believe if she learns how to protect herself, she will not have need of you anymore?" Cassiel asked.

Halting in place, Madness swirled in Zev's yellow eyes. Claws extended from his fingers, and fur spread across his shoulders and neck. Cassiel quickly stepped back, his heartbeat quickening. It was overtaking him. Dyna hadn't told him what to do if this happened.

"Zev?" he called warily. "Do you hear me?"

Fur continued sprouting all over his body as he shook. It was too late.

He was sinking.

Before Cassiel could think it through, before this could go any further, he swung. The punch snapped Zev's face back, and he stumbled against a tree with a curse.

A menacing growl rumbled deep in Zev's throat as he bared his teeth. "Did you hit me?"

Cassiel flexed his fist, testing the bones for breaks. Punching him was like punching a rock. "Do not expect an apology. You are, however, free to thank me."

Zev snorted half-heartedly. His fangs slowly retracted as the fur along his arms gave away to skin. He closed his red-rimmed eyes and dropped his head against the trunk. It may have been treated as a jest, but Cassiel meant it. He hadn't known what else to do. By some dumb luck, striking him had been enough to snap him back to his senses.

"I'm losing reasons to be here," Zev said. "Dyna's changing. Growing. She's advancing in life, and I ..."

"Feel stagnant?" That's what Cassiel's life had been like. Unchanging and insignificant like the sediment at the bottom of a lake. Well, it had until she came bumbling along, stirring up the waters.

"No," Zev rasped. "I've fallen from the branch, left to rot in the mud."

Cassiel followed his empty stare to the yellow leaves at his feet. Some were already browning. They would desiccate and crumble piece by piece until they were nothing but skeletons of what they once were.

A chill of trepidation crept through him. Zev was unraveling. It hovered on his trembling form, and in the shadows of his lost gaze. The Madness fed on his grief and self-hate. It consumed him, and it would keep consuming him until there was nothing left.

CHAPTER 12

The wooden ball hardly weighed anything. It was small and inconsequential, yet it was the biggest obstacle in Dyna's way. She concentrated on the green mist in her palm, cradling the ball. She tried to visualize its energy, to give it form and substance.

Move!

The ball lifted a mere inch into the air. She willed it to go higher, but it stayed right where it was.

"Push the energy outward," Lucenna instructed beside her.

"I am," Dyna said, not able to hide the frustration that seeped into her tone.

Lord Norrlen sat on a fallen log by the campfire, working on carving arrow shafts. Beside him, Cassiel sharpened knives on a whetstone. She could feel them watching in the distance, and her face warmed under the audience. Zev had wandered off somewhere when she'd made no more progress.

How could she convince him of her capabilities if she couldn't even do this? She'd been training since yesterday morning and hadn't made it go any higher.

"You're not concentrating," Lucenna chided. "If you were, you would have levitated the ball."

Groaning, Dyna released her Essence and dropped her arm. "I don't think I can do it."

"No, the matter is you're *not* doing it." Lucenna took the ball, and it floated freely above her palm. "Listen to your instincts. Focus on your intent and direct it. That is the first lesson they teach the children of Magos. It's vital. For without it, your magic will go nowhere. Levitation is the easiest spell there is, and the most flexible." She flicked her fingers, and the ball arced over her head into her other palm, hovering above it. "The Guilds possess certain spells that pertain solely to them, but levitation is wielded by all classes. With it, you can carry, push, throw, or lift."

The wooden ball shot from her hand and bounced off a tree. Then it flew back into her waiting palm.

"Is that how you broke the boy's bones?" Dyna asked, thinking of Geon.

With a twirl of her finger, Lucenna had tossed him about and snapped his limbs.

Lucenna paused. "That is a more complicated spell. Levitation can be used to attack either by moving your opponent or moving an object against them." She waved her hand, and a large boulder crashed across the meadow. Fair, who'd been grazing nearby, galloped away with a startled neigh. "The force behind it is related to the strength of your Essence. The greater it is, the heavier the objects you can move."

How would she ever lift something that big? She could barely lift the ball. Maybe this was beyond her. She may not be able to do more than heal.

Lucenna crossed her arms. "Why are you here?"

Dyna blinked, surprised by the question. "What?"

"You're a sorceress. Why did you leave the safety of your village?"

"But I'm not a—"

"You knew it would be dangerous, and yet, something required you to leave." Lucenna glanced past her. "Though, you need not tell me the reason. I have a feeling they don't want you to."

Dyna glanced at the others to find them watching her warily. Cassiel's stare bore into her, and a feeling of warning passed through the bond. She could almost hear his voice in her mind. *Do not dare tell her.*

Which only made her want to tell Lucenna about Mount Ida and the map simply to spite him.

"I want you to remember why you're on this journey," Lucenna continued. "Lock it in your mind, write it down, or repeat it to yourself every morning, if you must. That is your weapon. Your motivation." She tossed her the ball. "Now go practice. As soon as you can levitate the ball, I'll teach you how to levitate people."

"People?" Dyna repeated, widening her eyes.

"That is our goal," Lucenna said as she headed for the camp. "You will need to learn that so we can get the scales."

"Wait, where are you going?"

"I have taught you what you need to know. Now apply it."

"I can't do it alone."

The sorceress turned and fixed her with glowing lilac eyes. "You must learn how to stand on your own feet, Dyna. There will come a day where you will be alone, and you will have no one to count on but yourself."

Chest tightening, Dyna inhaled a deep breath and nodded. She had to figure it out. This was how she eliminated her helplessness. She couldn't strengthen herself without putting in the work.

"What are the three theories of magic?" Lucenna asked.

"Essence is the life-force energy of the elements," Dyna recited. "Magic is life-force energy manifested. Spells are magic directed by the will."

"Will is the matter at hand. If you don't *will* the ball to move, it won't." And with that, Lucenna strode for her tent.

Was it really so easy? Well, if the sorceress said she could do it, then it had to be possible, right? Accomplishing this meant she would meet the Druid, and meeting him meant she would find her Guardians. There was no time for self-doubt. Dyna bit her lip and stared at the ball.

Lyra was her reason. Saving her and the children. Defeating the Shadow. She repeated it in her mind like a chant.

Lyra. Children. Shadow.

The ball floated an inch above Dyna's hand, then one more. But her smile fell when it went no higher. Why wasn't it working?

"If you focus any harder, you will rupture a vein."

Dyna yelped. The ball fell between their boots, and heat flared in her cheeks. So lost in what she was doing, Cassiel's approach had gone unnoticed until he stood in front of her. The gentle wind picked at his black jacket, fluttering the ends. His divine sword didn't hang from his hip. He must have left *Esh Zayin* back at camp.

She took a step back, putting much-needed space between them. They would have to speak eventually, but she wasn't ready. What could she say? A nervous tingling rushed through her chest. What was there to say when she could only think of one thing in his presence?

He was her—*God of Urn.*

Thinking about it sent another wash of heat through her face and churned a multitude of emotions inside of her that she couldn't sort through yet. The only one that made sense was anger. She could handle anger.

Drawing in a shallow breath, Dyna made herself meet his silvery gaze and said coolly, "Yes, you're probably right."

Her head was throbbing, and she felt mentally drained.

"If you would like a distraction, I thought I might offer a new lesson," Cassiel said.

His eyes roved over her face, taking in the tension of her features and the firm set of her lips. Wherever he looked, Dyna felt the featherlight impression of his touch, exploring her the way he'd done on the cliff.

"A knife and bow are but tools—the true weapon is the one who wields them." Cassiel withdrew a knife from his boot and flipped it in his hand, presenting it to her hilt first.

The black handle shone with an iridescent swirl of blue and green, sunlight gracing the beautifully etched design on the blade. He held her gaze, his silver eyes full of grueling promises and something unknown that should have frightened her, but Dyna's pulse rushed with nervous anticipation, wanting whatever he was offering. The corner of Cassiel's mouth curled in a subtle smirk that scattered her thoughts as it had the first time she'd seen it.

"If you wish to learn how to fight, then brace yourself, Dynalya," he said, his voice low and dark. "For when I'm finished, you will know exactly where and how to cut."

The way he gazed at her sent a rush of thrill along her skin. "You'll teach me?"

"Is that not what you asked?"

It was. Though she'd half expected him to change his mind.

Dyna carefully accepted the knife and glanced at the trees. "Yes, but Zev will not approve."

"I have already spoken to him. I'm merely teaching you with the purpose of defense, not how to kill."

Zev was worried about that? She couldn't imagine ever killing someone.

Cassiel reached in his jacket and removed a thin leather belt. From it dangled an empty sheath. "This is yours."

He took a step, then hesitated, waiting for her reaction. When she didn't move, his arms came around her waist, and she held her breath. A tremble sank through her spine, and her chest tightened with the conflicting need to escape him—or to get closer.

But he was careful, barely touching her as he fastened the belt on her waist. Once it was buckled in place, with the scabbard resting on her hip, Cassiel stepped back.

He observed her, dragging a thumb along his bottom lip. "It is certainly ... becoming."

The knife was hefty in her hand, its presence too conspicuous. She sheathed it, finding the knife fit perfectly, then slowly drew it, admiring the beveled blade.

"If you hold it like that, you will cut yourself. A knife is not a stick. Treat it with respect."

She nearly dropped it, taken aback by his strict tone.

"Before you can learn to use it, you must first learn how to hold it." He carefully took her hand, eliciting a current of tingles rushing up her arm. His fingertips grazed her skin as he adjusted her hold on the hilt, so the edge pointed away from her body. "This is a short-edged blade. Meant for close range. It will cut, lacerate and puncture. Let us begin with the three basic techniques."

Cassiel stepped back several feet and withdrew another matching knife. The handle was made of white opal with a brass pommel. He spread his feet apart, and she copied his stance. He raised the knife above his right shoulder and cut the air diagonally to his left hip, then left shoulder to right hip. Next, he slashed diagonally in a straight line, left and right. And finally, sliced up and down from head to waist. He moved slowly and deliberately, showing her exactly each angle. She repeated the motions.

"Once you have learned these techniques, they will come easy to you."

Dyna watched as he combined every motion with a rapid, calculated sweep of the knife. His skill undoubtedly saved him in Corron, but slaying all those Raiders had done something to him.

Cassiel's jaw flexed, his gaze hardening as if he sensed where her thoughts wandered. "Now repeat until you cannot raise your arms."

Dyna watched him go through the positions once more. Then she joined him. Cut, slash, slice. Left, right, up, down. Repeated in an endless loop. She didn't move as gracefully as him, but she managed to awkwardly follow along. The sun crawled across the sky as the hours passed. Her arms screamed for respite, and sweat sprouted on her brow, but she enjoyed it. After so many turns, she didn't have to think of the movements.

It was dark when Cassiel at last straightened from his stance and handed her a waterskin to drink. She could hardly hold it without it slipping through her numb fingers. Her exhaustion might not have been the only reason for her trembling hands. Now that the lesson was over, there was no buffer between them but the windy silence and the loud buzz in her head. As much as the cowardly part of her itched to go back to camp, she didn't leave. She wanted to give him a chance. *Them* a chance—to sort through the tangled knots they'd found themselves in.

"Perhaps we should start with strengthening your limbs first," he said, frowning at her gangly arms.

After hours of silence, that's what he chose to say?

Dyna frowned at the wooden ball nestled in the grass at her feet, making it the focus of her contempt. Power rushed through her veins, static dancing on her skin. She shouldn't have expected anything.

There were more important things to do than to worry about what was or wasn't between them. Why had she thought Cassiel might try to talk to her? He was arrogant, rude, and a *liar*.

The ball shot up and whacked him on the chin.

Cassiel flinched back, glowering at her incredulously as he rubbed the welt. *"Ow."*

"I'm sorry!" She covered her chin, wincing. By the sharp sound the ball made when it hit him, she could almost feel his pain. Her mouth fell open. "I-I moved it. I levitated the ball."

"Yes, clearly." His idle voice carried no more than annoyed sarcasm.

"Sorry." Dyna grabbed it and tried again. She may as well have tried to lift the world. No matter how much she willed it, the ball only floated a few inches above her palm. "What had I done differently?"

"Anger," he said.

"What?"

Cassiel sighed. "I felt your anger before you attacked me."

Dyna quickly looked away, knowing her face had gone as red as her hair. She hadn't meant to attack him, but she was angry and—

Oh.

Emotions agitated Essence and expelled it wildly. Hers had surfaced when her attention focused on him, and therefore, so did her power. No wonder she hadn't been able to levitate the ball before. She hadn't concentrated on her power, as Lucenna said. She had been concentrating on the ball itself.

Dyna drew on her Essence, and it surfaced instantly. She focused on that, building the energy, and commanded it to rise around the training ball. It lifted higher in the air and continued further than she thought possible. She held the ball in the sky in speechless amazement.

Nearly whooping with joy, she pushed that energy outward and aimed it at a tree. The ball whizzed past and bounced off the trunk. The ball moved with each invisible pull or push of her power. Lucenna was right. It was so simple.

Fatigue soon crept through her aching limbs from a long day of training and from the little magic she already expelled. It served to remind her she hardly had any. But strengthening Essence worked essentially like growing muscle. It would take daily practice to grow her stamina. If she had any hope of defeating the Shadow, she had to push herself harder.

Dyna wrapped a green mist around the ball, drew it back, and caught it out of the air. Cassiel had been of some help, after all. "Thank you."

The edge of his mouth hitched. "Glad to be of service."

That playful smirk stalled her reply. How easily he scattered her thoughts. Something crossed his face, and she knew whatever she was feeling had revealed itself to him. It wasn't fair. She was so exposed.

"How do I keep you from feeling me?" Dyna asked.

"You cannot."

"Then why can't I feel you?" She glowered. His emotions had been so clear to her before he'd confessed about what he'd done. "You're lying to me again."

He dragged a hand through his inky hair as his frustration washed through her. "I'm not. I'm shielding myself, but it takes a great deal of concentration, and it is not infallible."

It had to be true, because some of his emotions occasionally slipped through.

"How do I do that, then?" she asked. "How do I make a shield?"

"Construct a wall in your mind. Make it solid and fortify it."

"That will block the ... bond?"

He exhaled a heavy breath. "No. Emotions, perhaps—but I will always know where you are."

Dyna bit her lip. That part didn't need explaining. The moment the bond formed, something inside of her linked with Cassiel, tying her to him in a way she didn't fully comprehend. Wherever he went, she simply knew the direction. His presence was like a pinpoint on the map of her soul. If ever they were separated, she knew the bond would lead her to him.

The autumn gust passed over them, coursing through the meadow. A small black feather slipped from his wings and caught in the grass by her boots. She hesitated to take it, remembering how he had reacted the last time she tried to. Cassiel watched her steadily as he came closer, close enough to buffer the cold. His warmth pressed into her, and she inhaled the ambrosial scent she was convinced only his kind had. He picked up the sleek plume and tucked it into his jacket.

"You gave her a feather," Dyna stated evenly, and an unexpected twinge of jealousy passed through her. She didn't know the feeling had been buried in her heart until she mentioned it.

Cassiel's brow furrowed as he searched her face, then he glanced away. "I hesitated."

His meaning wasn't lost on her. He had hesitated to trade it to save her.

"I understand why you would. But what I don't understand is why you would freely give your feather to a stranger."

To someone he believed to be a witch when he couldn't stand for her to touch them. She didn't want to know the answer.

Dyna turned to leave. Cassiel's hand clamped on her arm, and a fiery bolt of the bond's energy zapped them both—stronger than it ever had before. He swung her around so hard the momentum sent her sprawling against his firm chest. A scowl etched his mouth as his heated eyes met hers.

"You do not understand why I would not abandon you to your fate?" Cassiel asked, his voice low and harsh. His fury and another emotion that tasted of despair swarmed through Dyna, draining the air from her lungs. "At the moment, my fear of losing you was greater than my fear of the law. I was so far beyond myself I would have given my blood to save you."

Any words she could have said caught in Dyna's throat, and her heart thudded behind her ribs. He would have given his divine blood? That was the most vital thing to a Celestial, the thing more sacred and protected by his kind.

"Are you ashamed of that?" Cassiel asked, sensing her again.

"No, I'm ashamed of myself," she admitted, her vision blurring. Her inability to protect herself constantly put him at risk. "I'm truly so helpless it's pathetic."

"Why should that be of surprise?"

She suspected he thought of her as weak, but to hear it spoken aloud, he may as well have crushed her heart in his fist. This was why she wanted to be stronger, so she wouldn't feel inadequate. So he wouldn't think of her as a stupid human.

"That was a poor choice of words. What I mean to say is, you have not had the same training as us," Cassiel amended quickly, but she didn't need him to soften the blow for her sake.

He wouldn't dare say the same about Lucenna. If he did, the sorceress wouldn't take it kindly, nor should she. Dyna's Essence burst in a brief gust, shoving off his grasp. Surprise flashed across his face. Cassiel stared at her as if he'd never seen her before.

"No, I have not trained as you have," she said. "A fault I am well aware of."

"I did not say it was a fault."

"It certainly seemed that way."

He groaned and pressed on his forehead, muttering under his breath. "Why do I have the sense that no matter what I say, none of it will be taken well? Your emotions are such a complicated mass that it is beyond bewildering."

Dyna clenched her fists. "If it's so bothersome, simply ignore them."

"I would if you did not shout your every whim at me. It nearly seems intentional, mind you. As though I need reminding that you are angry with me."

She scoffed. "Do you not understand why I'm angry?"

Cassiel's jaw worked, his mouth tightening in a thin line. "Oh, no, I understand your contempt quite clearly, but I will not have you accuse me."

"Accuse you?" she repeated in disbelief. "I have not once accused you."

He barked a dry laugh, shaking his head. "I feel it, and I see it in your eyes. Do not deny it. The bond was an accident, Dynalya." Cassiel stepped closer, holding her in place with that cold silver gaze. "Done while saving your life, once again, I might add. Since Hilos, all I have done has been for your sake. Breaking every law. Spilling my blood. Shedding my feathers. *For you.* Yet you despise me for it."

Tears rushed to her eyes. He was wrong. That wasn't it. She was angry that he lied. Angry that he touched her heart when she thought he'd opened his for her. Angry to find the only thing between them was this bond. That he may not have found her remotely interesting without it.

Cassiel's irritation ensnared her, but there was something else there. A deep well of sadness. The hardness faded from his expression, and he exhaled heavily. "Am I so repulsive that you cannot stand the thought of being tied to me?"

The question was so startling, all words left her. He thought she found him repulsive? He did. It was there on his face. The lies his people fed him fortified his belief that he was a worthless half-breed. But how could she answer his question without exposing more of herself? She couldn't.

"This isn't about that," she said instead, avoiding the question. "You lied to me."

Cassiel straightened as his mask slipped back in place. His wall slammed between them so violently she stumbled a step back. "The world is full of liars. You will do well to accept that."

There was an accusation in there that made her sick to her stomach. He thought her acceptance of him had been a lie, that her friendship had been false. She shook her head. "Cass—"

"How quickly you forget we are both trapped in this net."

Trapped.

The back of her eyes burned at the sting of his words. He considered himself imprisoned by the bond. What else would he feel about being married to a common human? He was a prince that should have married a princess she couldn't ever compare to.

"I never asked for this." Dyna hated that her voice broke. Hated that every emotion was clear for him to see. She constructed a wall around her mind and her heart. Layered it with steel and fire. Built in an instant before she could admit what she wasn't ready to.

His wings twitched, betraying his cool demeanor. Her wall had blocked him.

Cassiel gave his back to her. "I expect nothing of you, Dynalya. I free you of any obligations you may have feared of a union with me. Rest on that. Should I find a way to break the Blood Bond, you have my sworn word, I will break it."

Her lips parted in a sharp intake of air. That's why he readily agreed to meet the Druid. He wanted to seek the one who may know how to free him of his new prison.

Cassiel headed for camp. Her vision blurred with every step he took as he walked away. Her heart ached. It cried out, demanding she stop him and explain, but she let him go. The bond fell silent between them as the doors closed on both ends. She imagined it would feel like this when he severed their link forever. It was for the best, Dyna told herself.

So why did it hurt so much?

CHAPTER 13

Cassiel stood knee-deep in the icy stream, wearing only trousers rolled to his knees, as he washed his clothes. After traveling under the rain yesterday, not a cloud appeared in the crisp blue sky, and the sun offered some warmth. Leaves covered the ground in a carpet of red, orange, and yellow. The stream carried them along, some sticking to his legs.

He tried to keep his focus on what he was doing instead of on Dyna. But his gaze kept drawing to her. She stood further along the bank of the creek, directing the wooden ball in the air and making it spiral around her, per Lucenna's instruction.

Where there was once a constant bombardment of emotions flooding through the bond, now there was nothing. Cassiel thought he would have welcomed it, but it left a vacancy behind. Like an empty cavern that only echoed back silence. It shouldn't bother him, but it did. They hadn't been bonded long enough to feel her absence so keenly. It didn't matter. As soon as they found the Druid, she would be free of him.

He met Zev's stare where he idled in the creek beside him.

"What?" Cassiel dunked the clothing he'd been washing back in the water.

"I was about to ask you the same," Zev said, wringing out a white tunic and draping it on his shoulder. Water sluiced down his bare chest, following the paths of the chain scars that marked him. "You both keep stealing glances at each other. Is there something I should know?"

Only that he'd accidentally married his cousin and now she loathed him.

"Her new ability merely impressed me. She learns quickly."

They watched Dyna lift a stone in the air next to the ball, and they spun around each other.

"How is she doing with her other training?" Zev asked.

"She is doing well," Cassiel said carefully.

Even after their argument, Dyna awaited him that morning with her knife to continue with the next lesson. It was the moment he could truly put everything else aside and focus on nothing but the blade swiping through the air between them.

"We attempted archery, but my longbow is a bit much for her," Rawn said where he sat by the bank with Fair, his washing already finished. He chiseled away at a small piece of wood and curled shavings floated to his lap as he worked. "Lady Dyna requires one for her size."

"Then we will get her one," Zev said, surprising Cassiel. He waded out of the water and hung his shirt to dry on a line of rope they'd tied between two trees. It swayed in the gentle breeze like a white flag of surrender. Was he coming to terms with Dyna's training?

Cassiel headed out and hung his wet clothes next to Zev's. He slipped on a dry tunic and his mother's ring caught on a loose thread. Gently, he tugged the chain free. It dangled from his neck, the sun catching on the sapphire stone.

"What are you carving?" Zev asked.

Rawn blew on the piece of wood, scattering the dust. It was taking the rough shape of a wolf. "A gift for my son. I will send it home along with the letters for my wife by portal. There is a mage courier's office in the Port of Azure."

"Is your son not twenty years old now?" Cassiel said as he buttoned his tunic. "He is much too old for toys."

"I suppose you are right," Rawn said with a sigh. "But it brings me comfort all the same. It is my way to show that I think of him. I know not what else he may prefer." Rawn lowered the chisel. "Perhaps he wouldn't care for such things and find them a nuisance."

Cassiel scratched his neck. He shouldn't have said anything. Rawn cared about his son, and while Cassiel didn't know what that was like, a small part of him wished he did.

"I don't believe he would find it a nuisance," Zev muttered so faintly he hardly heard him. "Not when they come from his father."

There was a dejection on his face that Cassiel rather not let linger. "What is the plan for the fjord?" he asked Rawn to change the subject.

With all of them gathered, they should discuss how they planned to gather the scales. They would reach the Saxe Fjord tomorrow. Some instinct warned against it, but the indifference on Dyna's face fortified his reason for going.

Unease crossed Lord Norrlen's expression. "Ah well, I remain against the task, but I take it Lady Lucenna has a plan."

"I do," Lucenna commented, coming to join them with Dyna. She crossed her arms as she studied them. "I'm sorting out the details. We'll discuss the plan tonight."

"There is nothing you wish to ask the Druid, Lord Norrlen?" Dyna asked.

Rawn gathered his belongings and returned them to the saddlebag strapped to Fair. "I admit, I am intrigued by the idea of asking Leoake about the well-being of my family. When we briefly met some years ago, it had not occurred to me to ask. However, I do not believe risking our lives is the way to do it."

"You risk your life every day," Zev pointed out. "Or is it the grindylows you're nervous about?"

"I do not doubt my abilities, but precaution kept me alive for the past twenty years." Rawn gave them a bleak look. "I have little hope for that tomorrow."

"If we die, at least we'll feed them," Zev retorted.

It was a sarcastic comment, but they stared at him. Not only was it unusually rude of Zev, Cassiel didn't think it was a joke.

"My, you're a grim lot," Lucenna said.

"And you are the pleasant one?" Cassiel shot back.

"I'm about as pleasant as you are, Celestial." A smirk curled her mouth. "I know you don't like me, but I don't care. If you're bemoaning over what happened in Corron, I don't care about that either."

Something ugly curdled in his stomach. She had used him to distract the Raiders, and now whatever sanctity he had was gone. He didn't know if his divine blood even worked anymore.

"You did what you must, and you shouldn't feel guilty for it," Lucenna said. "I won't. I've resolved to fight with all my strength and to harm those who would see me harmed. I feel no guilt for removing anyone who stands in my way."

Cassiel clenched his teeth. "No, a witch would not."

Purple sparked at her fingertips. "Careful."

"Or what?"

"Enough, both of you," Zev growled, his eyes flashing yellow. "Your bickering is setting me on edge."

"You're the one setting me on edge," Lucenna replied, her gaze flitting over his chest.

Zev stiffened. "Sorry to have offended you with the sight."

"You misunderstand. I find nothing wrong with scars. They are a testament of our past."

The look that crossed his face was anything but comforted. He headed for camp.

"Zev." Dyna hurried after him.

"I need a moment," he said, walking away.

"You should not speak of things you know nothing about," Cassiel said sharply to Lucenna.

She grimaced. "I didn't mean to offend him."

At least she cared about that.

Dyna shook her head, rubbing her face. "I need to go for a walk."

"I shall accompany you, my lady."

"I will go," Cassiel said as he put on his boots.

"I prefer to be alone."

He tried to ignore how she wouldn't look at him as he buckled on his scabbard. "You know you cannot be alone."

Dyna sighed heavily. Well, she clearly didn't want to be around him anymore.

"Gods, I'll accompany her." Lucenna hooked her arm through Dyna's. She held up a hand when he took a step to follow. "You're not welcome. Unless you wish to hear us discuss the woes of our courses. I think my monthly bleed is about due."

Cassiel stopped short, and his face heated. It shouldn't have embarrassed him, but she caught him off guard.

"Yes, I should think not." Lucenna led Dyna away into the woods with a satisfied snicker.

A curse left his tongue. He hesitated at the edge of the woods, his fists clenching. Leaving Dyna out of his sight didn't sit well. Avoiding him shouldn't take precedence over her safety.

"*Osom'reh,*" Rawn called Fair's name in his native tongue. "*Evy alanap'moca, Dynalya. Emasiva is asap ogla.*"

Nickering in response, Fair trotted into the woods after Dyna.

"There, that will do," he said. "Fair will notify me if there's trouble."

Cassiel snorted. Well, now she was *perfectly* guarded.

He followed the creek further downstream, but he didn't go far. His tie to Dyna was too strong to leave her out of his reach. He sat on a boulder on a lower ridge of the bank and kneaded his forehead, letting his wings hang limp.

The stubborn part of him wanted to go after them, but Lucenna was a reminder of what he lost. She was right. He didn't like her. He blamed her for what happened because it was easier. Whether she was there to put him on that path or not, Tarn would have come for Dyna. One way or another, Cassiel would've had to kill those Raiders.

Sometimes he could smell the ash of their charred corpses as though it were trapped under his fingernails or in the pores of his skin.

Humans had died at his hands.

He would never cross through Heaven's Gate.

Cassiel pointed his face at the clear sky, closing his eyes against the morning sunlight as he absorbed its gentle warmth. Another passing gust ruffled his hair and feathers. Maybe it didn't matter that he'd killed them. He was a Nephilim. His kind wasn't permitted in *Elyōn's* presence, whether he led a righteous life or not.

"Prince Cassiel."

He flinched, and his eyes flew open with a mixture of surprise and aggravation.

"Pardon, I did not intend to startle you." Rawn kneeled beside him and removed the stopper from his waterskin before plunging it into the current to fill.

"How can you slink upon others without making so much as a sound?" Cassiel asked in annoyance.

"Stealth has been ingrained in me. I do it unawares now."

"Is that what they teach you in the army?"

"The training elves must surpass to enlist in the army is quite arduous. My father strictly raised me in all aspects of becoming an able-bodied soldier." Rawn met and held his gaze. "Yet there was one thing he could not prepare me for."

"And what is that?"

"The burden of taking lives."

Cassiel's smirk dropped. "Do not make the mistake of thinking you know me." He dipped his hand in the stream, letting the current run between his fingers. "I had to kill those Raiders. You fight, or you die. I chose not to die."

But even he heard faint disquiet in his voice. He was trying to convince himself, trying to justify what he had done. Because if it was wrong, then where did that leave him?

"You are a general, Lord Norrlen. Surely you must have fought during the last war between Greenwood and Red Highland. A soldier's livelihood goes hand in hand with defending and killing."

Rawn nodded. "It is a double-edged sword I know all too well."

"The world was never meant to be full of death. There was none in time beyond the First Age until the God of Shadows unleashed wickedness in the Mortal Realm, along with his demons." Cassiel brushed his fingers over the single sapphire decorating *Esh Zayin's* langet and traced the golden crossguard honed into the shape of open wings. The crest of Hilos glinted on the pommel. "*Elyōn* created the Seraphim to protect the worlds of men. The Celestials must also abide by this holy law. By spilling human blood, I have gone against the natural order he established."

"You did what you must," Rawn said. "Accept that. The remorse you feel stems from taking that which was given, but you did not take with ill intent."

"Ill intent." Cassiel laughed sardonically. "You were there. You witnessed the slaughter, yet you believe I had no ill intent? At that moment, rage outweighed the fear for my own life. They stole Dyna from me, and I could not forgive them for that. I was content to cut them down, even if I did not get what I wanted. The worst of it is, if given the choice again, I would resort to watching them all burn. What does that say of me?"

That was the question that haunted him. In his rage, he lost himself in the divine fire as he slew each one, rendering them into nothing but clouds of ash. His only focus was reaching Dyna, and it didn't matter how many he killed or tortured to do it. The need to protect her was far greater, even if it sullied his soul.

"I say many would share the same sentiment." Rawn rose to his feet. "Should it have been my wife and son in danger, nothing would have stopped me either."

Wife.

That's what Dyna was, even if he didn't want to admit it. Well, not for much longer, the fates willing. Her life wouldn't be sullied, too. He would find a way to free her of him.

"There is darkness in all of our hearts, Prince Cassiel. It only consumes us if we allow it."

He nearly laughed at that. "My heart is already black and rotten, Lord Norrlen. I'm surprised it beats at all."

The useless thing died inside of him a long time ago, and he was better off for it.

"Where's Dyna?" Zev asked as he approached.

"Lady Dyna and Lady Lucenna have gone into the woods."

Zev turned to Cassiel angrily. "You allowed them to go?"

"I tried to stop her, but she demanded to go alone. In case it may have escaped your attention, Dyna can be stubborn." Cassiel crossed his arms and added, "Worry not. She is escorted by the witch—and a *horse.*"

"I trust they are capable," Rawn said.

"She can levitate a ball, so that is enough to defend herself?" Zev growled, his eyes flashing yellow.

The animalistic sound had Cassiel warily standing. Zev had been prickly with Rawn, be it from his agreement to teach Dyna how to shoot a bow or another reason entirely.

"You both know what is at risk," Zev said. "Tarn could find us at any moment. Dyna isn't safe until we get her on a boat away from Azure."

They weren't too far from the port now. They might leave the kingdom before the man found them again.

"I think it will be all right, Zev. Lord Norrlen made the right call to go through the wilderness. Tarn will not find her here—"

Something shifted inside of Cassiel, bursting the bond wide. Dyna's fear rammed him in the chest, stealing his breath. Then came Fair's neighing cry.

They ran.

CHAPTER 14

Gentle sunlight streamed in through the treetops, bathing the woodland in soft warmth. The chitter of critters in the bushes hummed around them. Dyna inhaled a breath, taking in the scents of the forest. It eased some of the tension from her chest. It was silly, really. She should talk to Cassiel instead of avoiding him.

"All right, what's bothering you?" Lucenna said, crossing her arms. "You've been in a mood all day. You and the others."

Dyna sighed, and Fair nudged the back of her neck, nuzzling her hair. She petted his velvety muzzle. "Nothing is the matter."

"Even I know that's a lie. Is it the pompous lord? I take it you fancy him. Few could resist such a face."

She frowned at her.

"I'm not prone to his countenance, so you need not worry." The pink diamond on Lucenna's ring glinted as she brushed her white hair over her shoulder.

"Why do you provoke him?" Dyna asked as they continued into the woods. What did she get out of making Cassiel angry?

Lucenna rolled her eyes. "I have no patience for his self-pity. When it comes between me and my enemies, I've long decided I'll be the one to walk away. I will feel no shame in fighting for my life. Neither should he."

Taking a life held far more meaning to him than the sorceress could understand.

"How far were you planning to walk?"

"Not far." Dyna kneeled beside a batch of weeds. "I only wanted to clear my mind. I also need to gather some fennel."

"What for?"

"To relieve you of any pain you may have during your courses."

Lucenna snickered. "I said that to keep your Celestial at bay. It seemed you didn't want him near."

Your Celestial. She wished Lucenna would stop calling him that. He wasn't hers.

"Well, I'll pick some for myself then," Dyna said.

"Is yours coming soon?"

"It began this morning. The aches are awful."

"The afflictions of a woman." Lucenna leaned against a tree, watching her pull up plants by the roots.

The scent of dirt and herbs drifted in her nose as she tied a batch of wild fennel with twine.

"I hadn't thought to ask until now, but why did that man kidnap you in Corron?"

"I don't know," Dyna mumbled, not daring to meet Lucenna's gaze.

It was partially true. She didn't know Tarn's intentions. He sent Von to kidnap her because he wanted her map, but it was simply a means to get what he truly sought. Mount Ida held an unknowable amount of treasure, but Tarn didn't care for jewels or gold. What did he want?

"I assume it's another thing your guardians don't wish you to say."

Dyna stilled, but from Lucenna's nonchalant expression, she only called them that as a jeer at their overprotectiveness.

"Why did those mages attempt to take you?" Dyna countered.

Lucenna narrowed her eyes, clearly not wanting to divulge the answer to that either. Dyna arched an eyebrow at her in return. The sorceress had secrets of her own she needed to keep. There was a reason Lucenna was trekking through Azure alone. Dyna sensed it had something to do with the Lūna Medallion and the missing

Moonstone. Lucenna had nearly killed Von for trying to steal it from her.

With neither of them wanting to discuss their business, they fell quiet.

Dyna moved on to another thicket and searched through the growth, picking out some dark blue leaves. Raising her head, she noticed the white trunks and indigo canopy she'd once seen in Hilos.

"Blue trees ..." she whispered in awe.

"There used to be many all across Azure," Lucenna told her. "It's said this land was once completely frozen as part of the Everfrost."

The Everfrost was a tundra in the north of Azure that remained frozen all year round, Dyna recalled.

"During the First Age, the trees were white with leaves like blue gemstones, and the animals were blue too," Lucenna said. "The land was ruled by the Ice Phoenix. No other could ever oppose his power—until he fell in love with a human. It's an elaborate love story. I have the book somewhere in my tent. I'll lend it to you sometime."

Dyna picked up a blue leaf from the ground, running its smooth surface through her fingers. She'd heard the tale before. It was one of many her mother used to tell her before bed. "I would like that."

"Who knows if the fairy tale is true, but these trees gave Azure its name before the kingdom gained its wealth from mining sapphires and other precious stones." Lucenna gazed at the indigo canopy. "Now they are rare and too far in between. They only grow in mystic areas. We must be close to the Moors."

She motioned with her chin, and Dyna noticed a cluster of leaves fluttering about the forest on an unseen wind, moving in spinning arcs. A few dived to Dyna and spiraled around her face. They weren't dancing leaves but tiny little creatures with translucent dragonfly wings. Their beady eyes peered at her curiously. Long pointed ears protruded from their bright green hair, their thin limbs resembling leaves as if they were born of the trees themselves.

Dyna smiled as they fluttered around her hair, chirping in high-bell tones. "Fairies."

"These are forest sprites," Lucenna said. "While mages need Essence to live, most of the smaller fae rely on nature's magic.

Enchanted streams, fairy blooms, trees, and the like. If this tree were to be cut down, for example, these fairies would most likely perish."

Fair then proceeded to chomp on a low-hanging branch.

"Don't eat the magical trees," Lucenna scolded, smacking his rump.

The Elvish stallion whinnied, startling the fairies away. He swatted her face with his tail and trotted away with a dignified snort.

Dyna giggled. "He let you know exactly what he thought of that, didn't he?"

Rawn often spoke to Fair as if the horse understood him, and she had half a mind to believe he truly did. She heard Elvish horses were an intelligent breed.

"I'll go get the willful brute." Lucenna rolled her eyes and went after Fair, disappearing past a wall of shrubs.

'Willful brute' better described someone else Dyna knew. God of Urn, what was she to do after yesterday? Everything was in pieces, and she didn't know how to put them back together. The thought of Cassiel made her chest ache. He was always on her mind, like a scar on her heart that would never fade.

Things had changed since they had nearly kissed on the cliff. But that day had been nothing more than a mingled breath stolen in a moment.

Dyna wiped the tear that escaped and continued picking wild herbs. Worse was she couldn't speak of it to anyone, least of all Zev. Not simply because he wouldn't hesitate to kill Cassiel, but because he was struggling. The Madness hovered around him like a black cloud. He was drowning, and she didn't know how to help him. It scared her that he was going to give in to the Madness. If there was a way to help him, the Druid would know.

She had to find him.

A high-pitched, mewling cry interrupted her thoughts. The keening yowl came again, followed by a rustle of leaves. Dyna leaned to peek past the tree and found what was causing all the fuss. A small fox was stuck in a thorny bush. Its beautiful, aqua blue coat shone in the sun as its three fluffy tails swished back and forth, desperately tugging on one of its hind paws caught in the thorns. It keened again, rattling the bush as it struggled violently to break free.

"Hello, sweet one," Dyna cooed in awe as she scooted closer.

The fox startled at the sight of her and growled, baring its sharp little teeth. It had a diamond-shaped patch in a deeper shade of blue on its forehead and vibrant aqua blue eyes. The fox's fur expanded as it tried its best to appear fearsome, but it was only frightened.

"Shhh, I'll set you free." she cooed again. It snapped its teeth when she neared. "It's all right."

It fought harder, yowling as the thorns dug into its flesh with each tug. The little creature was barely a juvenile pup. If she didn't free it, the fox would lose the use of its leg. Dyna inhaled a breath, then stuck out her hand. Those tiny, sharp teeth clamped on her fingers, and she held in a yelp. Quickly, she untangled its hind leg from the thorns while it was preoccupied with her other hand. As soon as it was free, the fox scampered away. But it stumbled on its injured leg and flopped on the ground, sides caving in against its ribs with every heaving breath.

Dyna wrapped her hand in a cloth she took from her bag. As she approached the little fox, it gave her a weak growl. "You're hurt, sweet one. Let me help."

She slowly reached for its back leg, making soothing noises. Green light glowed within her palm at her call. The fox lowered its ears, but no longer growled. Dyna hovered her hand above its leg and sent her power forth, enveloping it around the fracture inside. Carefully, she mended the tiny bone, tendons, then wove its shredded flesh. A pink scar formed between its fur. Fully healed, the fox leaped to its feet. Dyna smiled and slumped as exhaustion settled over her. It was a minor wound compared to the others she'd healed on their journey. She wouldn't faint this time.

The creature scampered away, but paused and peered at her with those vivid eyes. It cocked its head and sniffed the air.

"My name is Dynalya, though most call me Dyna." She grinned, feeling a little silly to introducing herself, but perhaps it understood.

Holding out a hand, she beckoned the fox closer. But its long ears perked up and twitched as it peered into the forest, alerting to something.

"What's wrong ..." It dashed away into the bush. She frowned after the fox, not sure what spooked it. Then she noticed the quiet.

It was too quiet.

Nature's symphony of birdsong and the chatter in the underbrush had fallen dreadfully silent. Dyna heard the ever-faint crunch of light feet on dry leaves that would have otherwise been muted. She turned and found two men in black cloaks watching her. Their faces were shadowed under hoods, black masks covering the bottom halves of their faces. One may have had dark eyes, but it was hard to tell. The other removed his hood, revealing eyes the color of amber. From his crop of dark brown hair were two pointed ears.

Zev had said that if not for Rawn, Tarn's elf would have killed them at the Kazer Bluffs.

A sharp gasp caught in her throat. With a trembling hand, Dyna covertly reached for the knife at her waist. She couldn't fight them both, but maybe stabbing one of them through the foot would give her time to run. Cassiel's alarm washed through her when he sensed her fear, and she couldn't help her overwhelming relief.

He was coming.

"Has anyone ever told you it's not safe for a girl to be alone out in the woods," the brown-eyed one said, his northern Azure accent muffled behind his mask.

"She's not alone." Lucenna appeared from the trees, her eyes glowing vivid purple. Her power filled the air, and static crawled along Dyna's skin like a thousand ants. The sorceress pulled her up and shoved her towards Fair.

"Stay behind me," Lucenna said, her attention fixed on the men who slid into defensive positions. "Should I even bother to ask who you are?"

The man withdrew two knives with serrated edges, and the elf unsheathed his sword.

The sorceress smiled coldly. "Men of few words. Perfect."

A purple hue painted the forest as light spidered up Lucenna's arms in response, and Fair released a loud neigh. The elf muttered an Elvish command, calling on a blue light that flared around his blade.

Dyna's heart thundered in her ears as his power pressed into her, a forceful charge clashing with Lucenna's. It was different from mage magic, as if it lived in the air.

Lucenna snapped open her arms, and the air exploded with a surge of electricity. Diving back, they scarcely dodged the attack. The knife-wielder spun away from another volt and threw his knives, one after the other. Lucenna tossed them aside with a wave of her hand. With a swipe of his blade, the elf cast a wave of blue rays. Lucenna thrust out her hands, and a curved shield formed in an instant before the blast hit. The concussive force threw Dyna against a tree and she fell in a heap, her vision spinning.

"Dyna!" Lucenna called, throwing more spells left and right to keep the men at bay.

"I'm fine." Dyna forced herself to stand, ignoring her body wincing in protest. She couldn't simply stand around. Withdrawing her weapon, she lined up behind Lucenna. She could at least protect her back.

The elf motioned with two fingers, and the knife-wielder nodded. They moved into another formation.

"*Ot'neiv.*" The elf swept his hand, and a powerful gust of wind tossed Dyna across the clearing. He headed for Lucenna, chanting another incantation. "*Az'reuf ed erb'mul, et'neirroc ed auga, ojulf ed otneiv, esab ed arreit—ranib'moc neyurt'sed.*"

Blue blazed in his eyes, and a swirl of Essence erupted from his palm, solidifying into a hexagonal light rimmed with symbols. Dyna recognized the Elvish runes for fire, water, wind, and earth, but not the spiky one in the center that flared the brightest. Lucenna gasped as her eyes widened. Dyna scrambled to her feet. Her heart thundered in her ears as his power filled the air, pressing into her with its weight.

"Run, Dyna!" Lucenna quickly formed a shield, layered it with another and another. "Go!"

An echo of her father's voice shouting at her to run rang in her head.

Grinning, the knife-wielder backed away. "You're dead now, witch."

The elf raised his blazing hand. An arrow flew through the trees, piercing the hexagon, and it vanished in a puff of smoke. Zev bounded out with a vicious snarl and charged after the knife-wielder. Cassiel landed by Dyna. His wings snapped wide as he drew *Esh Zayin* free. White flames burst to life along the blade, the roots a vivid blue. Her legs gave out from utter relief. Cassiel wrapped an arm around her waist, holding her close to his chest. He stayed with her instead of jumping in the fight, and she quickly saw why. Together, the others were more than enough of a match for the two men.

The knife-wielder slashed and dodged, struggling to keep Zev at bay. He was fast, light on his feet, but not fast enough. His legs and arms bled where teeth or claws had caught him. Rawn and Lucenna teamed up against the elf, simultaneously attacking with sword and magic. Their exploding spells lit the forest, the underbrush catching fire.

Tarn's men began retreating. They wouldn't win this fight. The wolf lunged for their retreating backs. The man slashed, catching him in his face. Zev whined, shaking his snout as blood leaked into his eyes. Dyna moved to help him, but Cassiel gripped her tightly.

With a wave of his hand, the elf knocked Rawn's sword away. He chanted another spell and a new hexagon formed. This one had two rings spiraling around it.

"Shield!" Rawn shouted at Lucenna.

She cursed and thrust up a fist. A crackling dome of light arched over them, covering a wide berth that included the blue tree. The spell exploded, and the clash of purple and blue blasted them off their feet. Lucenna's shield shattered. The explosion ricocheted, hitting a formation of rock, and it came crashing down.

Tarn's men dashed into the woods for their escape. Rawn darted back, and Cassiel yanked Dyna out of range. A boulder came tumbling down for Lucenna. Dyna screamed for her to run, but the sorceress froze beneath its shadow. Zev rammed into her, and they fell out of the way as it smashed into the ground behind them. Thick smoke and debris choked the air. The knife-wielder slinked out of the smog. There was a flash of silver, then a cry as Rawn stumbled.

"Rawn!" Dyna struggled against Cassiel to get to him.

Lord Norrlen held his bleeding shoulder as he chanted, *"Orum ed erb'mul."*

A wall of flames blazed between them and Tarn's men, forcing them back.

"You're lucky I missed, elf," the knife-wielder snarled with a venom that sounded personal. "Next time we meet, I'll put one in your chest."

Then he and the elf vanished into the forest.

Rawn dropped his fire and Lucenna waved her arms outward, casting them in another golden shield that formed like a round hut with them inside.

"Containment dome," she told them. "It will serve as an impregnable shield until we're certain they're gone."

Cassiel continued holding on to Dyna so tight it hurt. He was shaking.

"Cassiel," Dyna laid her palm over his hand clamped on her waist. "It's all right. I'm safe."

"I told you not to go without me," he said tightly. "This is what happens when you do not listen. What if I had not—"

He cut off, and she followed his wary gaze to the others.

What if I had not felt your fear? He didn't say it, but she sensed the question somehow. The bond was their unspoken secret they both agreed others couldn't know of yet, if ever. Especially Zev.

"I'm sorry," Dyna murmured. It was a peace offering and an apology for last night. She didn't want to fight anymore.

Cassiel searched her face, seeming to understand. His thumb brushed over the scrape on her temple, and she winced. It must have happened when she crashed into the tree.

"They hurt you," he said, his mouth bracketing.

"I'm all right."

He searched her over, her skin tingling as his hand grazed her arm. "Are you injured anywhere else?"

She shook her head, muted by the concern in his eyes. His fingers found the bruise on her arm, and his nostrils flared. A stream of his anger slipped through the bond. It doubled when he spotted her bleeding shin.

"It's nothing," Dyna reassured him. "Barely a scratch."

"I could—"

"No, it's fine." She drew back, and he nodded stiffly, his hold slipping away.

After everything he had done for her, she couldn't ask him for more blood to heal such a tiny cut.

Dyna went to her cousin. The wolf whined as she lifted his head to peer at the lesion along his face. It had barely missed his eyes. "You will let me heal that." She gave Zev a stern frown before turning to Rawn. "Lord Norrlen, please allow me to tend to your wound."

"Thank you, Lady Dyna."

Pressing her hand over the injury, she called on her Essence once more. She'd been fortunate Lucenna had followed her into the woods, but she needed to be more careful with her safety. Tarn wouldn't cease until he captured her. He was getting too close.

"Would any of you care to explain what that was about?" Lucenna crossed her arms. "Why did they want you?"

"It wasn't me they wanted," Dyna said. "The hilt of the elf's sword, it was red."

She'd barely paid attention to that detail, but she was grasping. Lucenna cocked an eyebrow.

"I ... I believe he was a Red Highland assassin." Dyna shot Rawn a sheepish look. He subtly nodded, approving of the lie.

"Lord Norrlen is a wanted elf," Cassiel commented casually as he sheathed his sword, extinguishing the flames. "Red Highland seeks to take his head."

"Then why attack us first?"

In a puff of receding fur, Zev shifted. "Easy prey," he offered, squinting through his bloodied eye.

The sorceress glowered at them. "If that's your story, fine. Whatever it is, see that I don't get involved. I have enough people after me. Once we have the scales, we will go our separate ways."

Cassiel sneered. "Gladly."

But Dyna didn't want them to separate. If what happened today proved anything, they were stronger together.

CHAPTER 15

Von

The Blue Capital could be seen for miles. Von frowned at the city from where he and Len watched on a distant cliff. The royal castle rose like a white mountain with blue spires so high in the sky as though it hoped to reach the Heavens. It had taken them two days to get here, two days too long. Coal nickered uneasily, sensing his impatience. Von patted the horse's dark gray neck absentmindedly, as if that would ease him, too.

The sprawling city was built into a hill with an immense wall of stone surrounding the entire circumference. Azure Guards manned the watchtowers on each corner. The only way in was through the gated entrance on the central road. There would be no ferryman to smuggle them into the city this time, and going through the main gate was too risky.

"The archers would take us out if we attempted to scale the wall," Von said.

Len didn't offer any response. Not that he expected one.

Tarn took the Versai native into his service when she was only a small, starved child. Von had never even heard her voice. Perhaps she didn't have one anymore for reasons he could only imagine with the gruesome scar of an X burned on her cheek.

She sat straight on her chestnut horse. Dressed in all black leathers, Len had come fully equipped with a utility belt around her waist, black karambit knives strapped to her thighs, a bow and quiver slung on her shoulder. The sun shone on her long black hair braided from her tanned face. Len had been honed and sharpened, like the many weapons hidden on her body.

Tarn had made sure of that.

Von dismounted, and Len followed suit. They ate a quick meal of dried meat, cheese, and stale bread as they continued to observe the city. There had to be another way in. It wasn't until he went behind a tree to relieve himself that an idea came to him. Von buttoned his trousers and hurried back to the cliff's edge.

"The sewer tunnels." He pointed at the large gateways that spilled water and sewage from the walls into the Liath River that passed by the northern end of the city. "There."

Len nodded her wordless agreement. Good. They found an entry point.

"Weapons check," Von ordered.

Tightening her leather straps, Len secured her blades in their sheaths. He double-checked the crossed bandolier loaded with throwing knives strapped to his chest and adjusted the weight of his belt. They didn't know exactly what to expect on this mission, so they'd been sure to arm themselves well. Their arsenal included poison and explosives, but the latter was a last resort. Von wanted to slip in and out as quickly as possible, unseen and unheard.

He needed to return to Yavi. There were too many chances of her getting burned in the camp. Not being around to protect her gnawed at him.

They rode down the hill, keeping to the forest. Once they got close enough, they tied the reins to a tree at the edge of the tree line, and Von removed his cloak from his pack. Len had already donned hers. She tapped on the concealment rune embroidered on the inside, and the black cloth changed color with every movement, camouflaging her to their surroundings. Von slipped on his cloak and did the same. Static prickled along his skin, signaling the activated spell.

Pulling up their hoods, they made their way across the vast valley to the city. They kept to the tall grass and boulders, trusting their cloaks to keep them hidden, but also cautious of the Azure Guard archers who manned the wall. It was early afternoon by the time they made it to the river. They continued walking along the bank, watching the city walls until they reached a large, gated culvert that drained sewage into the river. Von chose a shallow end laden with wide boulders, sleek with moss. Carefully, they made their way across and headed for the culvert. A rusted inlet gate sealed it shut. The water and air stank of human waste and other revolting things he'd rather not give too much thought to.

Len removed a garrote from the many compartments on her utility belt. It was a tool he'd seen her take pleasure in using when strangling her targets. For now, it would make do. The sharp diamond wire glinted as she passed him the garrote and took out an extra one for herself. They got to work. Sparks scattered to their feet with each slice of wire against metal. He was soon drenched in sweat. The sun hung low in the sky, and his forearms ached by the time enough bars had at last been removed for them to slip through.

They drew masks up over their noses to stifle the stench before making their way into the dark, wet drain. Von had selected a culvert with a shallow current. He secretly thanked the God of Urn it didn't reach their ankles. The light at their backs faded as they went deeper into the bowels of the city, the echoing drip of water their only companion. He took out two enchanted quartz crystals knotted to a line of leather cord. The *sōwilō* rune was engraved on their polished surfaces.

"*Lux,*" Von said, speaking the mage word for light.

The crystals glowed white, casting a soft light on the damp, curved walls. Handing one to Len, they secured the crystals to their belts with the cord. He drew a knife, and the curved black blade of Len's karambit glinted as she armed herself. There was no telling what might live in these drains if anything did, but he wouldn't be caught unprepared.

They continued into the thick darkness. Alert and listening. There was the skitter of small claws, and the squeak of rats as their oily forms drifted in and out of view. The dark tunnel settled on Von with a chill. It eventually narrowed, forcing him to take point with Len in the rear. The further they went, the more he had the sense they were walking through an endless black void that nearly swallowed the light from their crystals. Elon had trained Len so well that he couldn't even hear her breathing, giving him the sense she wasn't there at all. The only solid proof of reality was the horrid stench and the slosh of water beneath his boots.

It wasn't before long that Von heard the sounds of life in the city, much to his relief. The distant call of voices, the clomping of hooves, and the creak of wheels echoed off the walls of the tunnels. The light ahead marked the first sign of a drain cover. It opened to the main street, so they kept going until they found a quiet one. Von climbed the slippery rungs and peered out, finding the drain led to a shadowed alley. He checked for any witnesses before climbing out, closely followed by Len.

The dank alley was full of rubbish. Broken crates and barrels were strewn everywhere, the air stale with filth and urine. Von stepped on a weathered old paper and picked it off his boot. The ink was smeared, but he could barely read the letters.

BY ORDER OF THE KING

SLAVERY IS ABOLISHED IN AZURE. MASTERS MUST FREE ALL LIFE-SERVANTS AND PAY THEM FULL WAGES FOR THEIR YEARS OF SERVICE. ANY CRIMES COMMITTED DURING THE PERIOD OF INDENTURED SERVITUDE IS CHARGED AGAINST THE MASTER. THOSE WHO REFUSE TO RELEASE THEIR LIFE SERVANTS WILL BE SUBJECTED TO WARRANTS OF ARREST.

THIS LAW IS HEREBY DECREED BY THE KING OF AZURE. EFFECTIVE IMMEDIATELY.

Von stared at the page for so long the words blurred together. Slavery abolished? That ... that couldn't be right. He stamped down the faint feeling of something in his chest he wouldn't dare acknowledge. This was a matter of the holy law, not the law of man. The King of Azure had no say against it.

No one did.

There were dire consequences for it, and Von wouldn't make that mistake again.

He crumpled the paper into a ball and tossed it behind him. The only one who could release him from servitude was Tarn, and Von wasn't foolish enough to believe that would ever happen.

Not until one of them closed their eyes for the last time.

They sheathed their weapons and removed their masks, turning off the concealment rune of their cloaks. They headed for the sunlight and came out onto a busy street. People streamed by the hundreds as they went about their daily lives. Fair-haired elves in Greenwood livery walked by. Mages in brown, red, and white robes with staffs holding colorful crystals drew awestruck stares.

White stone fortified every structure, the roofs painted blue in honor of the kingdom. Navy blue banners hung from posts on every street corner, flying the king's colors and Azure's sigil: a gold, interwoven seven-pointed star. One point for each of the Seven Gates.

The castle rose over everything as a white peak. It was as imposing as it was resplendent, its pillars glinting with blue and gold. Platforms rising hundreds of feet high extended from the south and north ends of the castle like wings, where waterfalls poured in glittering streams. Von imagined the rulers of Azure liked to stand there as they gazed at their vast kingdom.

This was only one of the king's castles. Another had been built in Crown's Harbor by the eastern sea. Now that was a true castle, not this gaudy thing that was merely a show of wealth. The third castle lay in Old Tanzanite Keep, claimed by the Azure King once Lord Morken had died. The reminder churned Von's stomach.

"Make way for the King!"

Von pulled Len back, and they blended into the edges of the crowded street. Men in blue armor marched by, carrying matching scutum shields, their navy capes flaring behind them. The kingdom's golden sigil gleamed on their breastplates.

Azure Knights.

The sight of them brought back memories Von would rather not remember. Life in the barracks, the long days of training, the code of honor, and oaths sworn to lord and land. He was once a knight of Old Tanzanite Keep in the service of Lord Morken. He remembered the weight of that armor, along with the pride he once bore. But that was a lifetime ago.

Now, all it gave him was a bitter taste in his mouth.

A herald in posh cerulean garb announced, "King Lenneus graces you with his presence! Bow before His Majesty!"

Behind the procession came a luxurious carriage pulled by six white horses, with fluffy plumes bouncing on their halters. Nearly every angle of the carriage was obnoxiously gilded in gold and encrusted with enough sapphires to feed a quarter of the city. Sharp spindles jutted from each corner of the carriage, flying navy flags with the gold sigil of the kingdom.

The curtains were drawn, refusing to give the people a glimpse of their ruler. Yet the citizens of the Blue Capital bowed, either by deference or from the cold glares of the knights passing by. King Lenneus' personal Royal Guard was also present, identified by their cobalt armor and their breastplates embossed with the silver sigil of the king's family crest: a magnificent white bird in mid-flight.

The Ice Phoenix of the Everfrost.

It was a symbol of power. Only granted to the rightful rulers of the land as decreed by the ancient powers that be—or so the legend said.

The Royal Guard rode on fine horses that flanked the carriage, and another sat with the driver, a second with the footman, and two more crouched on the carriage roof with crossbows. Von wagered there were another two inside as well. They eyed the crowd with sharp gazes, searching for any signs of a threat. Searching—Von suspected—for Tarn.

The news of his return had spread to all of Azure, and there had been no shortage of Azure Guards scouring the land for him. Rangers scouted the central roads, and now the Azure Knights had arrived. The king was certainly taking all precautions.

The vile old man must keep Royal Guards in his chambers, guarding him even when he shat and slept, too afraid of every creak and thump.

Von retreated further into the shadow of an alley, with Len at his side. Dark eyes narrowing beneath her hood, she watched the carriage pass with cold calculation. Her gaze flicked from the surrounding rooftops to the knights and Royal Guards, taking in all variables. With her bow, Von knew how lethal she could be.

But they weren't here for the Azure King.

"His life isn't yours to take," Von warned quietly beneath the hum of the city. "It belongs to the master alone."

The only sign of Len's resignation against any plan she may have been brewing was the settling of her gaze on the crowd.

"Come. Step lively. Every hour hastens Bouvier's death."

Von and Len made their way through the alleys until they reached the sordid part of the city, where all manner of depravity reigned. The Azure King liked to boast of his peaceful and wealthy kingdom, but every kingdom held those shady, hidden corners where people liked to … indulge.

The streets grew darker with the descent of the sun. They kept to the shadows as they moved through the silent cobblestone streets lined with shoddy taverns, gambling houses, and brothels, if the passionate moans and grunts coming from the darker alleys were any indication. The air reeked of filth and sin.

Len's profile grew taut, like the string of her bow. A flash of steel slipped in her hand.

Ahead, Von's gaze immediately drew to a building painted all red. It stood proud and defiant in the twilight, alluring passersby with a series of small dangling lanterns. The sign above the door read *The Night's Ruby* in swirling gold paint. It was the brothel Novo said the jailor frequented. Von was almost surprised it wasn't called some other dowdy name meaning blue. Nearly everything in Azure honored the color by some unspoken mandate.

Von nodded for Len to follow him into the tavern across the street from *The Night's Ruby*. It was loud inside with laughter, music, and a din of voices, the air thick with smoke. He headed for a table by the window with a view of the brothel. The two men already sitting there glanced up from their drinks.

Von jerked his chin. "Move."

They scoffed, grunting curses and giving him foul gestures. Their glassy eyes turned hungry when they got a look at Len.

The man on his left leered. "Hello, love. Why don't you forget about this bloke and have a seat with us instead? My lap is free for the taking."

She tossed her knife, and it pierced the tabletop in the sliver of space between the man's fingers.

"The next one goes through your prick," Von said.

"Right, off we go." The man and his friend gathered their belongings, giving them a wide berth as they moved to the far end of the tavern.

Von and Len took their seats. A barmaid came by to offer them food and drink. Might as well eat while they waited. After placing an order, they resumed watch over the brothel as people came and went. With any luck, the jailor was already inside or would soon appear. Once he headed home, sated and drunk off his wits, lifting the key wouldn't be a problem. They needed it to break into the warded prison.

If the laws of extradition hadn't changed, they would transfer Bouvier to the beholder of his warrant within a month, if not sooner. The Blue Capital was a center of commerce and diplomacy. There was bound to be a representative of the United Crown here—the kingdom in the northwest which had a warrant for Bouvier's head. A death warrant was precedent and would be dealt with quickly.

It went unsaid, but Tarn's order had been clear. If they couldn't retrieve Bouvier, Von had to kill the spy to protect his master's anonymity. They had to get him out by tomorrow's nightfall, at the latest. As far as the Azure Guard knew, Bouvier was a petty thief who stole from the wrong people. The longer he was in their custody, the sooner they would discover who he now served.

"Tarn is no one," a voice declared.

Len stiffened across from him. They maintained their attention on the brothel while focusing on the conversation being held at the table beside them. From the filthy glass surface, Von distinguished the reflections of four men drinking and playing cards.

"All this fuss over one man," the same voice said, belonging to a reedy fellow with greasy brown hair. "It's ridiculous. He's nothing but a murdering bastard."

Len bared her teeth. Von nudged her foot, silently warning her not to draw attention.

"A *dangerous*, murdering bastard," corrected the dark-skinned man seated next to him.

Another, with a round belly and bald head, grunted. "He may not even be here."

The men guffawed at that.

"Aye, and my mother's a fertility goddess," the first one mocked. "No other man could have defeated an entire cavalry of Rangers and three units of Azure Guards. Tarn's Raiders took them out. Dead. To the last man."

Von dully frowned at his reflection in the window. They had nearly died that night and most likely would have, if not for Elon's magic.

"That's why King Lenneus has dispatched the Azure Knights," said another.

"Old man must be pissing in his britches, then."

"Enough to hire The Skulls, too."

Von's next breath stalled in his lungs, and a curse rang in his head. Len's hand on the table clenched into a fist.

The Skelling Mercenaries, better known as The Skulls, were infamous swords for hire who bowed to no one and nothing but gold. They served no king unless heavily paid to do so. Given their name, they were rumored to adorn the saddles of their horses with the skulls of their victims like grisly trophies.

That they should come here was unusual. They worked in the west end of Urn or overseas. But Tarn was worth a king's ransom. The bounty on his head, in addition to whatever the Azure King had promised, must have been tempting enough to draw them here. To have hired them went to prove how far Tarn's notorious reputation went.

Von had to complete his mission and return to the master to report this recent development. Last he heard, The Skulls had been in the country of Carthage across the Glacial Ocean, fighting in some other monarch's war. With any luck, they were still there. The voyage across those icy waters back to Urn would take them months.

The dark-skinned drunk shuddered as he took a drink. "If the man's smart, he'll leave Azure."

"I rather he stays. Should the fates allow it, the last sound he will hear is the rattle of bones before they take his head," the stout man said.

"I don't think Tarn is one to relinquish his head so easily." The quietest one of the four men adjusted the spectacles on his thin nose. "I heard King Lenneus had hired the head of the Huáng Clan to assassinate him ten years ago. They called him Guǐ, the Wraith, for you'd never knew he was coming until your soul passed through The Gates."

Von exchanged a look with Len at the mention of the Xián Jīng assassin.

"And?" the others pressed when their companion fell quiet. "What happened?"

A small conspiratorial smile rose on the man's face as he took a drink from his mug. "Well, Tarn is still alive, isn't he?"

By some luck. The assassin had been soundless and quick, exactly like a wraith. They hadn't known Guǐ was hunting them until Von saw the swipe of his blade catch the moonlight at the last second.

"So, let me ask you this," the man continued as he dealt a new round of cards. "If he truly is another murdering bastard, why go to so much trouble to kill him?"

Why, indeed.

A fight broke out at the other end of the tavern, drowning out their responses. It drew cheers from the patrons and shouts from the tavern keeper. The barmaid returned with their mugs of ale and two bowls of stew, muttering something about drunken fools.

Len dug into her food. She always ate as if she hadn't eaten in days. Before Von could reach for his bowl, he noticed two men walking casually down the street outside the window. It wasn't the fact that they were headed toward the brothel that caught his attention. It was the way they moved with a swift and confident gait he recognized in soldiers. The walk of trained killers. They wore long, dark coats, the bottom halves of their faces covered in black masks, laden with leather armor and weapons. When they faced the door, the low moonlight shone on the white emblem of a bird's skull on their backs.

The Skelling Mercenaries.

Summoned like another cruel jest of the fates.

Von had a sinking feeling they weren't visiting *The Night's Ruby* for pleasure. He and Len didn't have until tomorrow to break Bouvier from jail.

They had until dawn.

CHAPTER 16

Von

There would be nothing covert about this plan. It wasn't how Von liked to do things, but the time for stealth was over. When the Skelling Mercenaries had walked out of the brothel with the drunk jailor in tow, the chance to grab the key was gone.

He and Len watched silently where they crouched on a roof on the outskirts of the city. Across from them loomed the prison. It was a plain stone building, three stories high, with watchtowers on each corner. Two Azure Guards manned each one, and more patrolled the perimeter below. There was most likely another group inside. There wasn't much around the building besides the barracks and a stable for the horses. Outside rested a wagon piled high with hay. A transparent dome shimmered around the prison itself, iridescent like a soap bubble beneath the moonlight.

An electrical hum of power hovered in the air, prickling against Von's skin. The spell Benton had placed around the camp was made to keep unwanted people out. The Azure Guard spelled the prison to keep people and all manner of mystical beings inside. They would have spared no expense in hiring the most powerful mage they could find to put it in place.

No spells would break Bouvier free, but there was one ultimate weapon Von knew could completely thwart a mage.

He pulled out a special knife strapped to the back of his belt. The amber bead studded on the pommel glinted. Encased inside was a black clover. The only thing that could absorb magic. Von hadn't used it on a direct spell before. It might not work, but it was worth the attempt. If it didn't, well, they would only have moments to escape the city.

Len moved to the chimney of the roof, slipping into its shadow. She took out a small candle from one of her many pockets and lit the wick, laying it by her boot. Removing her bow, she loaded it with an arrow that had a cloth wrapped tightly around the arrowhead. The potent scent of ale drifted in the wind. She gave him a nod, signaling she was ready.

They paused, waiting for the exact moment the guards in the watchtowers faced the opposite direction, then Von signaled. Len lit the arrow and drew back her arm with perfect form. No sign of any pain. The flaming arrow flew and pierced the bale of hay below. It quickly burst into flames. Azure Guards shouted in alarm, and a watchtower guard rang the brass bell hanging from the rafters. The commotion drew a swarm of men in blue from the prison. They ran with buckets and dunked them into the water trough to put it out. The commotion had all of their attention now.

Von hurled the black clover knife at the dome. The blade went through, and the amber bead flared. An electrical pulse rippled through the air and the dome vanished. His knife clattered to the courtyard below.

Gods. It worked.

The watchtower guards immediately spotted Von. A guard's shout cut off as an arrow severed his gullet. In rapid succession, Len took out the guard in the left tower with an arrow straight through the eye. Then she targeted the right tower. The arrows zipped, taking them out one by one, sending their bodies tumbling over the ledge. The remaining guards fell before they realized what was happening.

Von hung a roll of rope on his shoulder and armed himself with two more knives from the many others strapped to the bandolier on his chest. "Cover me."

He moved to the far end of the roof, then he sprinted and dove off the edge for the prison. Gravity clawed at him as he fell. He swung his arms with all his might, and his knives pierced the prison building as his body smacked against the cold stone with a grunt. The trajectory had landed him on the second floor. Tightening his grip on the knives, Von climbed. According to Novo, Bouvier was on the third floor, the fourth window from the left.

Von reached it and peered through the bars. "Bouvier?"

From the shadows, a form moved. "Commander?"

"Aye."

"Thank the gods." Bouvier's tanned face slipped out of the dark. The moonlight fell over the silvery strands of his short hair, and his mustache curled with a smile. "I expected to be left for dead."

"Don't thank them yet." Taking hold of the bars, Von handed Bouvier his weapons. He unhooked a small wooden container off his belt provided by Tarn's arsenal. "A little *huyao* from Xián Jīng. Carefully dump it on the windowsill and back up as far as you can. Quickly now."

Bouvier popped open the lid and piled the black powder on the stone ledge. He moved to the furthest corner of the room, fading into the dark. Von climbed to the roof and signaled at Len. She lit another fire arrow. He ran to the far edge and ducked. A deafening *boom* rattled his skull as the explosion shook the entire building. Even the King of Azure must have heard that. The guards most certainly did.

Von rapidly tied two lines of rope to a tower post and rappelled down the side of the prison. The third floor now had a gaping hole, as if a giant had punched through it. Hacking a cough, Bouvier rose from the rubble, his face covered in soot.

Von grinned and tossed him a line of rope. "Now you can thank them."

Bouvier dove outside as two guards burst in through the cell door. They rapidly scaled the wall to the courtyard, only to find a group of armed Azure Guards waiting. Their rapiers gleamed in the firelight.

"Halt," one ordered. "Or we will cut you down."

Von glanced at Bouvier, and they shared a dark smile. Without hesitation, they ran to meet them.

Von darted, evading the swipe of a blade whizzing past his head. He parried the guard's next swing and slashed through his chest. The fallen guard's rapier skittered across the ground to Bouvier. With a flick of his foot, he kicked it up and caught the hilt. He moved with a graceful swiftness, gliding like water between opponents in an elegant dance only known in the Misty Isles. Blood spurted as his blade lacerated through flesh.

Five Azure Guards charged at Von. He let his knives fly. They found their targets and impaled them through their hearts. Two bodies hit the ground. He faced the other three. An arrow pierced the left guard's neck, and another went through the right guard's eye.

The third guard wildly searched the dark roofs. "Archer!" he shouted in warning to the others.

Von shot forward and swept his knife through his neck. Red sprayed the air. They fought their way through the courtyard, and the clang of steel merged with the cries of those they killed. Arrows flew past them as Len took out Azure Guards from her perch. As a team, they cut their way through the unit one by one. Blood pooled in the cobblestone beneath the bodies they left behind.

Bouvier plunged his sword through the stomach of the last guard standing. The fall of his body revealed two men watching them from a short distance. Von immediately knew they were not part of the Azure Guard. They were dressed in long, dark blue coats, with the bottom halves of their faces covered in black masks. The fire glinted over the metal plates of the pauldron on their shoulders, and on their bracers and greaves. The steel emblem of a bird's skull was pinned to the baldrics strapped to their chests.

Von drew in a ragged breath and forced himself to slow his heart. Unless more Skelling Mercenaries were coming, these might be the only two sent to investigate before the others arrived in Urn—or so he hoped. But two was more than enough.

"The Skulls," Von warned under his breath, wiping the sweat from his brow.

Bouvier stiffened and muttered a curse.

The mercenaries prowled forward and the sound of their footsteps echoed through the quiet courtyard. They split, each picking a target. The slightly taller of the two chose Von. Firelight haloed the waves of his blond hair in orange, the flames flickering in his cold blue eyes.

The other had dark brown hair with an eyepatch over his left eye. His good eye, a piercing gray, remained fixed on Bouvier. He reached in his coat, and his gloved hand came out with a series of throwing stars tucked between his fingers. The other mercenary reached for the crossed sheaths on his back and withdrew two short swords. The blue pommels were shaped like grinning skulls, the curved edges flaring with two serrated points.

They weren't bothering to call out orders of surrender. Bouvier's warrant was for dead or alive.

So was Von's.

He flipped two knives in his hands and said to Bouvier, "Should you fall?"

"March through the Gates," the blue-eyed mercenary replied in a brogue accent, his gaze taunting.

His companion circled Bouvier. "Go with your God."

"But I doubt he will receive you, mate," continued the other.

Von stared at them as every muscle in his body chilled. That prayer. The mercenary had altered the last line, but it was something he'd taught his men to say before every true battle. As it had been taught to him years ago when he served as a knight for Lord Morken.

These men were of Azure.

The one-eyed mercenary flung his throwing stars—right at Len. She fell out of view, and Von heard the thud of her body hitting the roof, then nothing after. He growled a curse.

The blond mercenary came fast and vicious, matching Von with each strike of his blade. The heavy clash of steel against steel vibrated up his arms. Within seconds, he knew these men fought at an advanced level. For every rapid slice of his knife, his opponent countered with his own.

Von aimed for his throat, and the mercenary blocked his arm. He released his knife and caught it with his other hand, slashing for the stomach. The mercenary knocked the knife out of his hand with a swipe of his weapon. Von quickly grabbed another. Their blades clashed with every strike, an exact mirror of each other as they fought for an advantage.

The rapid dual blades left him reeling. It was a technique Von had seen before. The mercenary snapped out a kick and threw him against the prison. The blow left Von's vision spinning. Before he could get his bearings, the mercenary leaped and rammed his knees into Von's chest, knocking him back into the wall. Wheezing, he sank to the ground.

The other mercenary threw Bouvier over his shoulder and he hit the ground hard. His rapier clattered away, out of reach. The spy raggedly groaned, clutching his bleeding side.

Damn it all.

There would be no surrendering here. The thought of returning to Yavi had Von gritting his teeth. He armed himself with another knife and forced his lungs to recover the air stolen from him. If they couldn't stand, they were dead.

He was hit with overwhelming relief when Len silently slipped out of the smog. She stalked behind the one-eyed mercenary, taking advantage of his blind spot. Blood leaked from the gash on her cheek. Teeth bared, she withdrew a karambit and launched at him. He noticed her a fraction too late. Len's curved blade slashed through his back, and he dropped under her weight.

The blond mercenary whipped around. "Eagon!"

Von tackled him to the ground. He brought his knife down, but the mercenary caught his wrist, bringing the point to a stop above his eye. A throwing star knocked the knife from Von's hand. Eagon was still alive and locked in a fight with Len. With a twist of her body, she leaped and wrapped her legs around his neck, tossing him on the ground. He rolled to his feet, and they came at each other with vicious kicks.

Von's opponent rammed a fist into his face. They traded blows, each hit more brutal than the last. It loosened the mask and Von ripped it off, revealing a face layered with a cropped beard. The firelight blazed in the mercenary's eyes, turning them a piercing white-blue.

He kneed Von in the gut and snaked his legs around him in a rapid move, throwing him on his back. His short sword stopped at Von's neck. "Where's Tarn?"

He glared silently back.

"The king abolished slavery for all Azure citizens, Von. You don't have to serve him anymore."

He froze at the sound of his name and the information the mercenary knew. It mattered not. He would never betray Tarn. It was his duty as a life-servant to always protect his master.

Seeing his defiance, the mercenary's mouth twisted with an icy smile. "Aye, if you'll not speak, I have other much more interesting ways of making you sing, mate."

Von narrowed his eyes at the brogue voice. "What part of Azure do you hail from?"

Sneer sharpening, the mercenary's sword faintly grazed Von's jugular. The warmth of blood leaked down his throat. "I'm offended you haven't guessed yet."

His accent was northern, and he knew the prayer. He fought with moves that were strangely familiar.

"You're of Old Tanzanite Keep," Von said.

The mercenary's smile grew vicious.

Before Von could respond, Bouvier struck the back of the man's head with his rapier's hilt. He fell limp. Von shoved him off and crouched over the mercenary. Now that he wasn't trying to kill him, he appeared a lot younger than expected for The Skulls.

There was something about his face.

A throwing star sliced through the edge of Von's ear. He leaped away with a curse. Eagon fought Len off and now had his fury set on Von. Red leaked from the edges of his coat, splattering on his black boots. His fingers gripped more of those sharp-pointed weapons.

A gallop of charging horses thundered in the distance. Reinforcements were coming. Called by the explosion that had rattled the city awake. Smoke from the wagon fire spiraled like a signal in the sky.

"Get away from him," Eagon snarled.

Von twirled a knife in his hand, contemplating. It wouldn't take more than a flex of his fingers to end the man's life.

Eagon jerked a step forward. "Harm him, and I'll kill you."

Von nodded to Len, who had another knife ready to fly. "Aye, then she would kill you. And I give you my word, she won't miss. I'd rather we make a deal, Eagon. I don't touch your captain, and you stand down."

The man's one gray eye burned, and Von knew he'd guessed their ranks right. He had the leader of The Skulls at his mercy. Eagon's hard gaze flickered between Von and the captain, lying unconscious at his feet. Len and Bouvier flanked him as they awaited the mercenary's response.

"Go," came Eagon's guttural growl.

Von took a careful step back. The others shadowed him while watching the mercenary. He watched them too, taking a step toward his captain with each one they retreated until they reached the alley.

"Von." Eagon lowered his mask, revealing another young bearded face. Scars coursed down his cheek from beneath his eyepatch. "Let your master know we're coming for him."

By that look of pure loathing, Von had no doubt The Skulls would. They withdrew into the dark alleyway and ran into the night.

CHAPTER 17

Zev

The earth felt cool beneath Zev's paws as the wind passed over the forest, undulating his fur. His perked ears twitched, listening beyond the chatter of wildlife as he sniffed the crisp night air for any uncommon scents. The sky glimmered with a dash of stars, the half-moon glowing softly among the wispy clouds.

Dyna and Lucenna's conversation about the classes of magic blended with the scuff of their shoes where they walked ahead of him. Beside them, Lord Norrlen rode Fair. His keen sight remained on the surrounding trees, also on alert. Cassiel's flying form was but a shadow in the night. Lucenna maintained small purple spheres of spectral light to guide their way. Nothing was amiss, but after what happened, Zev wouldn't lower his guard.

Tarn had found them a lot sooner than expected.

"Spies," Rawn told him and Cassiel when they had a moment to discuss it. "Sent ahead to scout information on our position and strength. They were testing our abilities."

That was Tarn's way. Otherwise, there would have been more men. They must have been watching, and when another opportunity to take Dyna presented itself, they attempted it. Captain Elon had come this time and the spry one who'd nearly taken out his eye. Zev regretted not ripping off a few limbs before he escaped.

At the sound of his growl, Rawn pulled on the reins, and Lucenna's eyes immediately ignited with her power as electricity sparked at her fingertips.

"Zev?" Dyna whispered, rushing to his side. She searched their surroundings. "What is it?"

He shook his head, huffing. It was nothing. He hadn't meant to startle them.

She frowned and ran her fingers through his fur. "All right?"

Yes. No.

There were too many things wrong to answer that question. One of them being her. It became glaringly clear each time he looked at her with the eyes of his wolf. Dyna glowed like she was filled with starlight. An odd trait she'd gained ever since Cassiel healed her with his divine blood. It changed her somehow. Changed her smell and Cassiel's, too. Their scents carried a trace of one another, as if their spirit had imprinted on each other.

After so many days, Zev worried the change was permanent. Cassiel owed him an answer, and he wouldn't let the prince use his blood on her again until he had it.

Sauntering behind Rawn's horse, Zev shifted. His body briefly ached as it reformed itself and fur gave away to skin. Rising to his feet, he pulled out a pair of trousers from his pack strapped to Fair's saddle.

"Sorry," Zev said as he slipped them on, then returned to Dyna. "Nothing is the matter. I was aggravated."

She searched his face and gently squeezed his hand. "I'm safe."

He rubbed his forehead. "I know."

Lucenna's gaze traveled over the ugly indentations on his chest and arms, then quickly away. Zev slipped on a shirt.

"We have traveled far enough," Rawn said as he dismounted. "Here is as good a place as any to camp for the night."

They had arrived at a small glade by a stream, closed in by a tall formation of rock that blocked the bitter wind. Cassiel landed on top of it and looked at him questioningly.

"We're camping," Zev called.

He nodded and flew down to join them. Lucenna waved her hand and from her satchel came out a miniature replica of her tent. It spun in the air, flashing with a golden powder as it expanded and grew until it was large again. It floated away and landed on the ground a good distance from their campfire.

Rawn and Cassiel went to walk around the tent, studying it. Dyna ran her fingers through the glittering gold remnants hovering in the air.

"How did you do that?" Zev asked.

Lucenna shrugged. "It's a simple spell made with pixie dust. While Stardust creates limitless space, pixie dust changes the size of an object."

"And the inside of your tent is enchanted with Stardust."

She nodded. "My satchel, too. I'm able to carry a limitless number of items."

Which was mind-boggling. Her satchel was hardly bigger than his foot. What else did she have in there?

"It's very useful," Lucenna said.

"I imagine so."

She eyed the bulging pack at his feet. "That must be heavy."

"It is." But the chains hardly weighed much to him.

"Here." She produced a purple velvet pouch. "I'll apply stardust to your baggage. Remove your belongings first."

Curious, Zev complied and dumped everything out. His clothes, packs of food, and the silver chains fell to the ground. Lucenna stared at them for a moment. From the velvet pouch, she took out a pinch of shimmering silver powder and sprinkled it inside his bag.

"There. Return your belongings."

He nudged the chains back inside with his foot, and they vanished inside. The bag remained flat, as if there was nothing in it at all. When Zev lifted it, the bag weighed nothing, and made no sound.

"You can now carry as many items as you wish."

"Thank you," he said, truly grateful. Now he no longer needed to hear the constant clank of his chains, counting the days to his next change. It was a couple weeks away.

The moon rose above the clouds, spreading a silvery hue over the clearing. It tugged at his skin, calling to his wolf with the urge to shift. Lucenna pointed her face at the night sky and briefly closed her eyes, inhaling a deep breath. The Guilds drew strength from their elements, as did the beast inside of him.

"When I was a little girl, I used to send my wishes to the moon," she said.

Zev rubbed the waxy tissue circling his wrists. "If I were to make a wish, I would make it to the sun, for the moon has never been kind to me."

Her lilac eyes caught the moonlight as they flickered to him, then to his scars again. Questions crossed her face. He waited for her to ask, deciding he wouldn't hide what he was.

"Why did you save me?" Lucenna asked.

He cocked his head, not expecting that question. At first, he thought she meant against the mages, but then Zev recalled he had pulled her out of the way in the forest when a boulder came crashing down. It wasn't something he had given a second thought to. Pulling her to safety had been instinct.

"That's what wolves do," Zev said. "Protect family."

She followed his line of sight to the others, where Dyna was explaining how pixie dust worked to Cassiel and Rawn.

Lucenna's face softened for a moment, but then her expression cooled. "I'm not a part of your family. We're only traveling together while our interests coincide, then we will go separate ways."

With that, she stalked away, her scent drifting to him. Zev hid a smile.

Lucenna offered Stardust to Rawn and Dyna, sprinkling more shimmery powder in their packs. "You need only think of the item you want and it will appear."

"Thank you, my lady," Rawn said as he fastened his pack to Fair's saddle. "You are too kind."

"Yes, thank you." Dyna laughed as she played with placing and removing several items from her satchel.

Zev peered inside the endless pit of his pack. He reached in and thought of his chains. Once the shackle appeared in his palm, he quickly let go at the sharp sting of a burn.

The sorceress arched an eyebrow at Cassiel, who ignored them as he gathered firewood. "For you, it will cost another feather."

"I'm not for trade."

"Suit yourself." Lucenna turned away and waved her hand in the air.

The energy of her power pressed against Zev as she cast a veil spell around their camp. She did it every time they moved to a new area. If he stepped outside of its perimeter, he couldn't see, smell, or hear the camp. The veil was as cool as the surface of a pond, cold and slippery, spreading ripples that revealed the shape of the dome.

With another flick of her fingers, Lucenna carried over a large log from the edge of the forest and laid it by the gathered kindling. "Bring the other one, Dyna."

Dyna's eyes flickered over the others. Zev sensed her nervous unease. She aimed both hands at the smaller log and her palms glowed. The log groaned as it slowly loosened from the earth.

"Feed more Essence into it," Lucenna instructed. "Focus on your intent."

Biting her lip, Dyna flexed her fingers. The log wobbled into the air and continued its shaky approach. Zev backed out of the way. It lined parallel with the other log on the other side of the fire, then plunked on the ground. Dyna winced, her face flushing as she slumped back from the toll it took from her.

"Well done." Zev patted her back, and she gave him a bright smile.

Dyna never ceased to amaze him. He should have praised her as soon as she levitated the ball. Here they thought she couldn't do more than heal, but after a few lessons with Lucenna, she had learned new spells. Dyna wanted to learn more. He could see it. The hunger to grow and live. To fly far beyond what the world offered and reach the stars. Zev knew she would one day.

They were quick to get a campfire going. While he set up their mats, Dyna knelt in the grass and took out vegetables from their pack for a stew. A potato rolled away from her and bumped into Cassiel's foot. Picking it up, he lowered to one knee and offered it to her. Slowly, she reached for the potato as they held each other's gaze. Zev glanced back and forth between them, not sure what to make of the odd exchange. Something unsaid passed between them before Cassiel stood.

Zev caught Dyna's eye. She ducked her head, resuming her work. Cassiel moved to sit at the end of the log closest to her, but Zev bumped him aside with his hip, using enough force to send him sprawling to the other end.

Cassiel glowered at him. "Do you mind?"

"I do, in fact, *mind*." Zev bared his fangs in a feral grin. "Your Highness."

Cassiel backed away and righted himself on the far end of the log without further complaint. Zev placed a basket of carrots between them and they worked on peeling and cutting.

Rawn cleared his throat, drawing all their attention. "We have yet to discuss the matter concerning the course of our journey. Tomorrow we will arrive at the fjord."

Lucenna crossed her arms. "If you're having second thoughts, now is the time to voice them. The mission will be dangerous. Truth be told, the longer you remain in my company, the more you're also at risk. Enforcers are constantly hunting me."

"What are Enforcers?" Cassiel asked.

"They are a specialty military unit of mages, powerful enough to sense even the most minuscule traces of Essence in the air. I'm constantly on the run. I only risk entering cities and towns when I run out of food and need to earn coin."

"Leading to your trade as a fortune teller." Dyna arched an eyebrow at her playfully. "When we met, you put a spell on me."

"Yes, I cloaked you. A mage was tracking your Essence with a location spell."

"What?" Zev growled.

Cassiel's wings expanded like an angry hawk. "Who was tracking her?"

"Most likely a mage that wanted to report Dyna as a refugee." Lucenna shrugged. "She was fortunate. If the mage had been an Enforcer, he would have captured her right away and taken her to Magos. She wouldn't have stood a chance against him. With my cloaking spell in place, I'm the only one who can magically track her."

"Thank you." Zev sighed. "I wonder when that could have happened."

"At some point, Dyna met a mage, and he sensed her magic," Lucenna said. "With a simple thing as a touch, one could lock onto another's Essence and use it to locate them."

Dyna's eyes widened, and she met Zev's gaze as Cassiel stiffened beside him. She had told them about Dalton, the young mage in Landcaster that accused her of being a sorceress. He was a Raider under Von's command, both of whom were slaves to their master's every whim. That's how they had followed them to Corron. It hadn't been an Enforcer tracking her—it was Tarn.

"But I hardly have any power," Dyna said, feigning ignorance.

Lucenna narrowed her eyes as they flashed. "It matters not. You could have merely a drop, and the mages wouldn't hesitate to steal it from you." She nodded at the others. "You all have a little magic in you."

"I have magic?" Zev asked.

"You have the supernatural ability to shift into a wolf," she told him, then glanced at Cassiel. "I figured out immediately that you were a Celestial from the power of your divine blood. Lord Norrlen, you have Essence as well."

"Yes, my lady. However, I only know a few elementary spells. Not much use they would have tomorrow."

Zev met his stern stare. Dyna may have asked Rawn to be their Guidelander, but Zev had already mapped the trail they would take to the Port of Azure. He had guided them along fine until now, without Rawn's interference.

"You remain against the Saxe Fjord," Zev stated.

"Why?" Dyna asked.

Rawn sighed. "I would not advise it, my lady. Grindylows seem like simple-minded creatures, but in a large group, they are far more dangerous than the nymphs of Naiads Mere."

"What are grindylows exactly?" she asked them.

"They are Dark Fae," Cassiel answered. "Amphibious creatures, similar to sirens, but hairless and hideous, with a single fin. There are stories of them living in the Saxe Fjord where they devour whoever should cross it. But you should not believe half of what you hear," he added at her frightened expression.

"There is far worse fae out there." Lucenna shrugged. "Fae that eat your soul or drink your blood. Have you heard of nightwalkers? Should you ever meet with one of those, you may as well invite death."

Dyna paled further, and Zev frowned at the sorceress. This wasn't helping.

"Crossing the fjord will shorten our journey. We have lost a lot of time moving off-road," he said. "If we follow this stream, it should lead us to the fjord."

Dyna glanced between him and Rawn. "How are we to cross? Are we going to swim?"

"No, my lady. You mustn't swim there."

"I have a boat," Lucenna said.

Cassiel smirked. "Of course, you do."

Rawn pressed on his forehead. "I am against this matter, regardless. This decision is foolhardy. Herein lays risk."

"But we need the scales to trade with the Druid," Dyna said. "Are we willing to risk the danger to get our questions answered?"

Everyone nodded except Rawn.

"That settles it," Zev said, and he motioned to Lucenna. "Let's hear your plan."

"You have me training with levitation and now Essence Blast," Dyna said. "I'm assuming there is a purpose behind that."

The sorceress nodded. "I have pondered over it since our reunion and considered each of your abilities. Lord Norrlen and Cassiel are best served as air support." She glanced at Rawn. "Should you care to be involved, we could use your bow as protection from above, same with Cassiel, should he be so inclined."

Cassiel leaned forward as he rested his elbows on his knees, but didn't disagree.

"As for Zev." Her lilac eyes met his across the fire. "Are you a good diver?"

He curled one end of his mouth in a small smirk. "I'm an excellent diver."

His lungs could withhold more air than a human's, and the enhanced strength of his body gave him the ability to swim fast.

"Good. We will need you to dive deep to retrieve the scales."

Dyna gasped. "What?"

"I can do it," Zev said. "And where does that leave you and Dyna?"

Lucenna eyed each of them, and Zev knew he wouldn't like the answer. "We will serve as bait."

"No," he growled.

"Only over my stiff corpse will I allow that to happen," Cassiel said at the same time.

Rawn shook his head. "My lady, that is not—"

Lucenna rolled her eyes. "Gods, hear me out first. We will stand by the bank to draw the grindylows away from their nest so Zev may retrieve the scales. I'm not concerned about the grindylows. You have seen my power. It's enough to protect me and Dyna. With Rawn and Cassiel covering us from overhead, nothing will touch her." Lucenna nodded to Dyna. "Your task is simple and the most important. You will be the one to lift Zev out of the water in the slight chance he's not able to swim back to the surface."

She stiffened. "Me? But—"

"My task will be to keep the creatures at bay. You can do it, Dyna. You have mastered levitation."

She shook her head. "I could barely lift the log."

"Your execution needs a bit more refinement, but I'm confident in your abilities. I have sensed an increase in your Essence." Lucenna smiled. "You're growing stronger."

Joy lit Dyna's face. "I am?"

"Yes. I trust you can do this." Lucenna lifted her eyebrows at them inquiringly. "Well? Agreed?"

Zev crossed his arms. He didn't like it, but the plan made sense and Lucenna was powerful enough to keep Dyna safe. She practically glowed with confidence now. He didn't want to snuff it out.

"She stays on dry land," he said.

"Far away from the water," Cassiel added.

Rawn released a long sigh and dragged a hand down his face. "May the God of Urn have mercy on us all."

"Good." Lucenna rubbed her hands. A mischievous smile crossed her lips as she glanced at Zev. "Come, Dyna. While our meal is cooking, now is the time to train some more. Instead of lifting a log in the air, you will lift Zev."

He chuckled nervously. Well, this may be a long night.

CHAPTER 18

D
yna woke with a tired smile. Once Lucenna had taught her how to latch on to the Essence of another, she spent hours lifting Zev in the air. He had been nervous at first, but once she stopped dropping him, he enjoyed himself. Then Dyna left the men to sleep while she and Lucenna had stayed up late discussing which spell to learn next.

It was a dream really, being able to achieve not only one but two new spells and soon a third, as Lucenna promised. They were small preliminary spells mage children learned, but it made all the difference to Dyna when she'd thought she couldn't do more than heal. Her power may not be as substantial as Lucenna's, but she hadn't reached her limit yet. She was growing stronger. That had to mean she could do so much more. Dyna's body was heavy and achy, exhausted from all the power she had used last night. But she was a step above faint, and with some of Azeran's tea, she would regain her strength within hours.

She stretched out on Lucenna's enormous bed. The sounds of Zev's soft snores from outside the tent reached her, the dim gray light of the dawn trickling in through the entryway flaps. Candles burned on the desk, providing soft light. Lucenna lay on the other side of the bed beneath a mound of blankets and books as if she had fallen asleep reading. Dyna sat up. From her chest, slid an open tome. On the page was a beautiful illustration of a massive ice blue bird in a snowy landscape looming before a woman with pale blond hair dressed in furs and holding a spear.

She closed it and embossed on the cover in silver was the title: *Lord of the Everfrost.* Beneath it was the sigil of the Ice Phoenix. The fairytale of Jökull and Sunnëva. Their union was said to have set the foundation of the Azure Kingdom. Anyone born with fair features claimed to have some ancestry connected, even if it was a mere drop of blood. The royal family were direct descendants and by law, only they could fly the phoenix crest.

Whether the story was true begged the question. But who was Dyna to say when she was also searching for fairytales?

With a tired sigh, she prepared to warm up before Cassiel rose for their daily training. Even if they were at odds, he had kept his word about teaching her. Dyna had to admit she enjoyed this part of the day the most. It was the only time they could be in each other's presence, where nothing mattered but the blade.

She stood and stretched through a yawn, then grabbed her pack and went behind the privacy screen to change and use Lucenna's enchanted chamber pot. The sorceress had also spelled it with a dash of Stardust, so it never had to be emptied.

Dyna muffled her giggles. *Ingenious.*

What else had Lucenna enchanted? She pulled on a pair of brown pants made of a thin but warm cloth that clung to her legs. Much easier to move in when sparring.

"Dyna?" came Lucenna's confused, sleepy voice. "Is that you snickering? If not, then I should be worried."

"It's me." Dyna briefly peeked out from behind the screen, flashing her a grin. She removed her chemise for a cream-colored shirt with fluffy sleeves, the hem falling mid-thigh, with four corners ending in tapered points in the front, back, and sides.

"Why were you laughing?"

"I simply thought your idle ways were clever." After slipping on the straps, Dyna laced the leather bodice and buckled on her belt. Then stepped out and tugged on her boots. "How did you come up with the idea to enchant your chamber pot?"

Lucenna smirked. "I have many grand ideas." She rolled over to face Dyna, her face softening as she gazed at the second chair tucked in the small dining table made for two. "It's all due to my mother. She made sure I learned one thing: the lack of strength is overcome with intelligence. Whatever challenge you may face, the advantage of your opponent doesn't matter. Be smarter than them, and you will win."

Dyna smiled. "She sounds like a wise woman."

"That she was. I applied the lesson to everything I came across, including the chamber pot."

Dyna laughed and went to Lucenna's bureau, where a basin rested with several bottles of oils and soaps. After pouring in water from an ewer, she washed her hands and face, then used a minty solution to rinse out her mouth.

"What was your mother like?"

It was a careful question, for Dyna sensed Lucenna's mother was no longer alive. She'd come to recognize people touched by loss.

Lucenna continued gazing at the chair. "My mother was patient and kind. Brave." Her voice hitched, her facing contorting. "She was everything I'm not."

Dyna returned to sit on the bed beside her. "Now that I don't agree with. You intervened on my behalf and saved me from Von. You accepted me as your apprentice when you didn't have to. Whatever your reason is to be out here alone in the world, it's tremendously brave."

The sorceress lowered her head, her hair falling like a silken white curtain around her. "And you? What was your mother like?"

Dyna leaned back on her hands as she observed the crystals and charms hanging from the tent ceiling. "My mother loved to tell me stories. She liked to laugh and sing and work in her garden. She always smelled like lavender. My father—" Dyna shoved aside the image of his bloody face and replaced it with one of light and warmth. "He always listened to me when I wanted to talk, no matter how silly. He could be strict but patient, and he always took the time to teach me and Thane."

"Thane?"

She inhaled a shallow breath. "My little brother."

Lucenna's expression creased with sympathy. "How long ago did they pass away?"

"Nine years ago."

"I'm sorry." The sorceress squeezed her hand.

They sat in a moment of silence and in support of what they had lost. Dyna didn't ask how Lucenna's mother died, and the sorceress didn't ask about her family either. Perhaps because she understood how much it hurt to speak of.

"Do you have more family?" Dyna asked after a moment.

"Lucien. He's my twin brother and the only one I count." Lucenna answered after a pause, and she rolled her eyes. "He is, occasionally, a nosy nuisance."

Dyna had yet to meet Lucien, though she imagined he must be similar to Lucenna. His elegant voice was all she knew of him since Lucenna took his calls on the orb in private. But from the little she had overheard, they had a close relationship. Lucien pestered Lucenna because he cared. It made her wonder what her relationship with Thane would have been like if he had lived.

The Shadow slashed through her memories like broken glass piercing her skin. She saw Thane's form in the moonlight and heard her father screaming at her to run.

A white light pulsated in Lucenna's orb with an incoming call, pulling her from the memory.

Dyna stood. "I'll leave you to speak to him."

It surprised her when Lucenna asked, "Would you like to meet him?"

"I thought you didn't want him to know about us."

"It's more like I don't know how to explain who you are without him bombarding me with so many questions. But he knows I'm hiding something, and I'm tired of lying to him." Lucenna shrugged, giving her a mischievous smile. "I'm sure he would love to meet you."

She went behind the privacy screen to handle her business and change. The orb stopped flashing, most likely from the lack of response. Lucenna emerged wearing black leather pants and a matching redingote jacket.

"Come." Lucenna went to her desk where the glass orb rested on its iron stand.

Dyna joined her, and the sorceress twirled a hand in a semi-circle around them. An electric force pressed against her skin with the power of Lucenna's Essence. Golden sparks flashed on the ground, and they encircled the desk in a glowing ring with them inside. From the ring, a hue of golden light rose until it curved over their heads to meet in the center, surrounding them in a translucent dome. Dyna hesitantly touched the surface and found it solid, though their surroundings remained visible.

"A containment dome?" Dyna had first seen one when Lady Samira invoked one, and recently when Lucenna used it to protect them from Elon's spell.

"It's a powerful shield," Lucenna explained. "Domes have many uses, from entrapment, offenses, and defenses. It also mutes sound from inside out. This way, we can speak freely without waking the others."

"Oh." Dyna frowned, not sure why that was necessary.

"You will soon see why we need it." Lucenna pulled her orb forward and set the stand on top of a stack of books. She stared at it, her eyebrows pinching together in concentration. A haze formed into a swirl inside of the crystal sphere, illuminating with white light. It cleared away like steam on water, and the image of a man appeared.

The vantage point of Lucien was off, with a view of his face and neck from below. Dark fabric shrouded the edges of the image. From the angle, Dyna realized he was holding his orb in the crook of his arm.

Sunlight shone over his long white hair that flowed to his chest and the dark blue robes he wore. Lucien stood by a bookshelf. His slender hand pulled on the spines before returning them in place.

"Good morrow," Lucien said, analyzing the cover of a book he was considering. "Pardon if I disturbed you. I was calling merely to wake you. I didn't expect you to answer."

"Normally, I wouldn't. I thought I'd have a conversation with my brother, but it seems he is much too preoccupied now," Lucenna said with false sadness.

In response, his mouth curved. "I have some time before the morning assembly."

"What are you searching for?"

He frowned at a book and put it back. "A reference tome on horology magic."

"Venturing into the advanced arts, I see. Wasn't it you who said not to meddle with time?"

"I'm not meddling. Horology is the subject of today's lecture," Lucien said as he reached for another thick volume. "Are you doing well?"

"Yes, thank you." Lucenna took a breath and said with sudden seriousness. "I have a confession, Lucien. You're right. I have been keeping things from you. Once you see, I'm sure you will understand."

Lucien's playful smirk fell when he glanced at them, spotting Dyna right away. Pushing the book back on the shelf, he raised the orb. He was as striking as his sister, but his jaw was more angular, his cheekbones more prominent. Lucien kept his white hair neat and pulled away from his face. A knot formed between the brows above his clear, lilac eyes as he studied her in surprise.

Dyna gave him a shy curtsy.

He nodded politely. "Lucenna, will you do me the kindness of explaining?"

She grinned. "Dear brother, it's a pleasure to present to you a sorceress born of one of the fabled sanctuaries. This is Dynalya Astron, a direct descendent of Azeran Astron."

Lucien's eyes grew wide before his image fell out of view. There was a loud smash of glass, and the dark image shattered before Lucenna's orb became clear. She dropped her face in her hands, and her whole body shook with boisterous laughter. Now Dyna understood the reason for the dome. The commotion would have woken the others.

"What happened?"

"He dropped his orb!" Lucenna wheezed, smacking the desk. She laughed a good while before she composed herself. Her face was red as she wiped the tears from her eyes. "For once, I got the better of my ever-poised brother. He must be excited."

"Excited?"

"According to our history, Azeran died in the war. People like us who hope for change wondered if the legend that he escaped was true. Lucien was one of those believers. He greatly admires Azeran, so to know that you exist is a dream come true."

Dyna blushed. "I see, but he broke his orb. How will he communicate with you now?"

"Lucien has several." She laughed. "He's broken his fair share of orbs. I'm sure he is simply regaining his composure before he contacts me again." No sooner had Lucenna said it, her orb pulsated with light. She tapped it, and Lucien's image appeared. He'd moved to a new spot now, sitting in front of a window with the morning light shining on his face.

Lucien openly stared at Dyna, observing her in awe for a long stretch of quiet. They began speaking at the same time, then awkwardly laughed.

Clearing his throat, he tipped his head. "It's a great honor to meet a sorceress from Azeran's line and one so beautiful."

Lucenna snickered behind her hand.

Dyna bit her lip, her cheeks heating. How could he call her beautiful when he looked like an artist had sculpted his face?

"Oh, thank you," she said, surprised by his immediate acceptance. "You're the first to believe the claim."

Lucien smiled. "I have seen paintings of Helia of House Fuego, Azeran's wife. You have the same features and the same coloring, down to the eyes. One look at you is enough to dispel any doubt."

A splash of surprise washed through Dyna. She'd thought the features of white hair and purple eyes faded in her family because her ancestors married humans. She had Sun Guild ancestry as well? Azeran had taken Helia for his wife but he hadn't written of having any children with her before she passed.

Lucenna gawked at her. "Good gods, I see it now too."

"You're a legend in the Magos Empire. I-I mean, the stories of Azeran surviving and building sanctuaries are a legend," Lucien amended, his face reddening. "If I could ask, what is your life like in your sanctuary? What kind of magic dominates there?"

"Oh well, um ..." Dyna didn't know how to tell him the truth. He was so overjoyed she was reluctant to crush his imagination.

Lucenna broke the news. "Essence is nearly lost in the sanctuary. They have joined with humans."

"Oh ... I see."

"But the women of the village are free," Dyna offered. "We achieved the freedom that Azeran fought for."

A warm smile lit Lucien's face. "Well, then that is all that matters."

"Dyna has a bit of magic." Lucenna winked at her. "She can perform Essence Healing."

His excitement returned. "That is an impressive spell, and it's not easily mastered. Azeran had perfected it."

Dyna chewed her lip, feeling unworthy of the praise. "I tend to faint when I use it."

"That is normal. The level of our Essence limits our power. Using too much can exhaust you to the point of unconsciousness, and Essence Healing exerts a substantial amount of energy. The more you practice, the stronger your magic will become. One day you will find you hardly feel faint."

Dyna smiled. "Should fate allow it."

"How did you learn that spell? Did you have a Guild Master?"

She relayed the history of her family and her village. Lucien listened intently, patient for her to pause to ask questions. He asked his sister how they met, and Lucenna reluctantly told him about Corron and Dyna told him about the Enforcers.

"This is incredible." Lucien began pacing, working his thoughts aloud. "It's such a small world for you to not only meet Azeran's descendant, but you helped her, and she appeared exactly when you needed aid. It must be the fates who have brought you together."

"I have never seen him so lively," Lucenna whispered to Dyna, making her giggle.

"You two need to be much more careful now. Two sorceresses together are bound to capture attention." Lucien trailed off into a quick lesson in cloaking spells.

Lucenna rolled her eyes playfully. "Lucien thinks of himself as my warden."

"He is your brother. He cares for your well-being."

There was a faint thudding behind them. Cassiel stood outside the dome, his mouth set in a thin line. He said something indiscernible and motioned for Dyna to come out, probably to remind her it was time to train. His wings furled and unfurled repeatedly, reflecting his irritation passing through her, along with his worry and his distrust of Lucenna. He didn't like that the sorceress had her trapped inside.

"I'm all right," Dyna said, but he couldn't hear her.

Reaching for the quill in an inkpot, Lucenna scribbled on a piece of parchment and held it up for Cassiel to read. His silver eyes zipped across the page. His face grew taut and a muscle popped in his clenched jaw. He stalked back outside. Lucenna set down the page with a satisfied smirk.

Confused, Dyna peeked at it.

Dyna is speaking with my brother. They are having a lovely conversation, and I think they would make a perfect match. So be a dear and don't interrupt.

"I'm jesting," Lucenna whispered when Dyna gaped at her.

Completely oblivious to what had occurred, Lucien stopped pacing. "Oh, forgive me! I seem to have lost my sense of etiquette." He swept into a bow. "I am Lucien of House Astron, heir of Galveston Astron, ascent head of the Lunar Guild in the Magos Empire."

Dyna's mind reeled at the long introduction. She blinked slowly, repeating what he said in her head. "I am Dynalya Astron, daughter of Baden Astron, born of North Star. I have no titles to speak of."

Lucien gave her a kind smile. "My lady, you're the progeny of Azeran himself, and thus, you are a noble." There was no sarcasm in the statement, only genuine welcome. "It was a pleasure to meet another addition to the family, but alas, I must now depart. I'm late for the assembly. I bid you both farewell until we can speak again. Be safe."

Lucien waved, and the orb cleared.

Dyna slowly faced the sorceress. "You … are an Astron?"

Lucenna sighed, tangling a lock of white hair around her finger, her lilac gaze meeting hers unsurely. She should have known. The sorceress not only had the same features as Azeran, but his Lūna Medallion also hung from her neck.

"Well, before I explain, can I ask that we keep it between us?"

Dyna nodded.

Lucenna stood. She took a deep breath and dipped in an elegant curtsey. "I am Lucenna of House Astron, daughter of Galveston Astron, sorceress of the Lunar Guild." She lowered her eyes. "I am a descendant of Andrez Astron. He was Azeran's only brother ... and the one who betrayed him."

Dyna was at a loss for words. There was another soft thud on the dome. Zev frowned at them from the other side, motioning at it questioningly. Training would have to wait. She was glad that Lucenna had placed them inside of the dome. They were going to need privacy for this conversation.

CHAPTER 19

Zev

Zev caught the faint voices drifting from the tent as he worked on stretching the tight muscles in his back. They must have finished their private conversation within the golden fortress. Cassiel was miffed about it. He'd grumbled about mages and inappropriate advances to himself most of the morning. All Zev could get out of him was that Dyna had met Lucien through Lucenna's orb. To introduce them must mean the sorceress had taken a liking to her.

A bitter gust passed through the forest, rattling the trees. The morning sun glimmered over the layer of frost coating the ground and grass. Cassiel trained with his sword, his breaths swirling in the chilly air. Sitting by the fire, Rawn worked on fletching more arrows.

Zev pulled his arms taut in front of him and rolled his neck, every muscle tightening. How deep would he have to dive? A jitter of anticipation went through him. Yellow leaves fluttered past, brushing his cheek. The water must be cold, but he would hardly feel it with the heat of his wolf.

A sensation of broken glass crunched beneath his feet.

He could hold his breath for possibly five minutes and get enough scales for them. It shouldn't be too difficult.

Blood dripped from the walls.

How dark were those waters?

His mother's scream tore through his ears. The stench of rotting flesh flooded his nose.

Stop! Zev shouted in his head.

The bombardment of bloody memories ceased. Zev froze. He had never spoken to the Madness before. He simply ignored it and learned to live with it.

I know what you're planning, beastie, it whispered.

Zev grit his teeth and moved on to stretching his legs, feeling his aching muscles pull taut. Dyna had done a number on him when she practiced levitating him in the air.

Rest, the Madness said. It prowled around him, its claws caressing his mind. *Be at peace.*

There would be no peace for him until—

One moment he was in the woods, and in the next, he was inside his home in Lykos Peak. No blood stained the walls. No smell of death lingered. The sunset streamed in through the window, lighting the ash trees swaying outside. His father stood before him, smiling with so much love as he clapped a hand on Zev's shoulder. He inhaled a sharp breath at the touch. It was warm and solid, like this was real. The scent of the forest, of home, of his father, all hit him. And the scent of silver. The mound of chains his father held hit the floor when he let them drop to his feet.

"It's time," his father said, exactly as he had in the past. "You don't need these chains anymore, Zev."

He shook his head, fear tearing through him. "I do, Father. Please put them on."

"You're strong. You're in control."

The moon pulled at him as the last of the sunset faded. The Other's bloodthirsty excitement rose to the surface. It pushed against his skin with a strength that threatened to shred him apart. Zev learned far too late that he had never been in control.

Screams ripped from his throat as his body cracked and twisted, breaking into a new form. He tried to fight, tried to hold it at bay, but any semblance of control faded as the dark creature of nightmares took his place. His father's face paled as he backed away.

Don't show me this! Zev squeezed his eyes shut and gripped his head. *Please!*

The memory faded, but the horror ravaging him remained. He had long known since the day he woke to find his hands drenched in his father's blood that there was only one way it would end.

You're weak and pitiful, the Madness growled, taking a new tone he hadn't heard before. *Blind wretch.*

Zev didn't remember the Other's memories. The Madness having access to them left a sick feeling in his stomach. If refusing to witness himself kill his father made him a pitiful, blind wretch, then he would gladly wear those titles. Seeing the aftermath had been enough.

But the Madness was evolving somehow. For once, instead of coaxing, it sounded angry, manic, and it was forcing memories on him. That wasn't normal. Well, if anything could be normal about having a sentient being speak to you. Its presence was far more tangible than it had been before, moving around him like the caress of the wind. As if all it needed to step outside of him was a body. Either that was a sign the Madness would soon take over completely, or it already had. Maybe these were his thoughts now, and he had truly gone mad.

His body chilled. He forced a slow breath through his nostrils. He couldn't let that happen. Not yet.

"Zev?" He opened his eyes to find Cassiel watching him. Damp black hair stuck to his forehead, his white tunic clinging to the sweat on his arms. "All right?"

"No." For once, he wanted to expose the bitter pit of despair that had carved its way inside of him.

But the girls came out of the tent, drawing their attention. Dyna walked confidently with her knife at her hip. A black leather hugged Lucenna's lithe frame, and the gentle breeze swept through her long white hair. They walked with their arms linked and smiling as if they shared a secret.

"Ready?" Dyna asked as she slipped on her capelet, face shining with giddy excitement.

Zev forced a smile. "Aye, time to kill some grindylows."

They gathered their belongings and put out the campfire. Rawn secured his pack to Fair's saddle and slung his quiver full of arrows on his shoulder. He'd been quiet since last night and had woken before dawn to prepare his weapons in solemn silence. Perhaps he was angry at being forced to take part in this venture. Their gazes met, but he had nothing to say, it seemed. Zev nodded for them to move out.

Cassiel took off into the sky and flew above them. Rawn walked ahead with Lucenna as she rode Fair side-saddle, guiding the horse along the stream. Before Zev could follow them, Dyna grabbed his hand and signaled for him to wait. She guided him closer to the stream, letting the others move further ahead.

"Why do you impede Rawn's decisions?" Dyna whispered, attempting to hide her voice from the elf's keen hearing with the burble of running water. "He's doing his best to lead us, but you two seem to constantly argue."

Zev glowered at the woodland. "I'm attempting to guide us to the Port of Azure as soon as possible. It may take months to reach Mount Ida, and we need to return to North Star before next winter."

The truth was, he was reluctant to give Lord Norrlen the reins of their journey. Leading them had been Zev's role in their makeshift pack before he showed up.

"You've met Lucien, I hear," Zev said, changing the subject.

"I did." A shy smile rose to her lips, and she fidgeted with her sleeves. "He's quite charming. Not at all like the mages we have heard about."

Zev wiggled his brows. "You seem fond of him. Shall I ask Lucenna to make a match?"

"Stop it." Dyna laughed. "I'm not taken with him in the manner you're suggesting." Her green eyes flickered to the sky, then at her feet. She chewed on her lip as her face flushed.

"What is it? Is there someone in the village who has caught your fancy?"

"Oh no, of course not. Come off it, Zev!" She tried to shove him with little success.

Zev chuckled, but let it be. Although he liked to tease Dyna about it, he had mixed feelings about her having a love-mate. It worried him that someone would take advantage of her kind and naïve nature. He had little else to care for other than keeping her safe. Once someone else filled that role, she wouldn't need him anymore.

"Lucien is glad his sister has company," Dyna said. "He worries for her wellbeing."

"I'd be worried about you too if you were venturing through the world on your own."

"I'm glad to have you with me."

"As am I." Zev wrapped an arm around Dyna's shoulders. "And you haven't told her anything about..." He glanced at her satchel.

Dyna's smile faded. "No, but—"

"Good," Zev cut her off. He knew what she was going to say, but they couldn't risk telling Lucenna about their journey to Mount Ida. "How is your training?"

Dyna shrugged, her cheeks reddening further. Her fingers grazed the black hilt of the knife. "As well as it could be, I suppose. He says I must carry it at all times."

Zev hated that she needed a weapon, but it was unfair to hold Dyna back. She should learn to fight, if that's what she desired. She deserved to have everything, no matter if he couldn't be the one to give it to her. The knife sheathed at her waist, the ability to protect herself—that wasn't his to take from her.

Even if it left him without purpose.

They continued through the forest after the others, listening to the trickle of water. The stream widened as they hiked for several miles along the muddy bank. Yellow ash leaves carpeted the ground, sticking to the soles of Zev's boots. He tried to ignore it, but the color was everywhere, reminding him of things he didn't want to remember.

"I detest this time of the year," Zev muttered to himself. He rubbed the tension forming on the back of his neck. "It's the leaves and the smell in the air. I wish I could hibernate like the bears and not wake until spring."

Dyna hugged his arm. "There is only a month left of Autumn. Once it passes, you will feel better."

Until next year. But Zev didn't want to repeat the same cycle. He was sick of feeling it year after year. It was suffering he hated, and it wouldn't ever let him go.

CHAPTER 20

Zev

The pine trees thinned as Zev led Dyna through the forest to reunite with the others. Once he heard the gentle churn of water, he knew they were near. He pushed through a gap in the hedgerow, and they came up behind Rawn and Lucenna. The Zafiro Mountains rose above them like a silent behemoth resting on the spine of land. The iced peaks capped the high rise of the west, descending towards the east. A soft crash of water came from thin waterfalls spilling over a ridge. Pine trees carpeted the lower passes as far as the eye could see. And set between two immense cliffs were the dark waters of the Saxe Fjord.

It looked so vast and tranquil he almost couldn't believe there were carnivorous creatures within it. A thin layer of ice coated the edges of the bank, and the air was much colder here. The surface reflected the afternoon sun and Cassiel's form, where he flew overhead. A small rocky island rose in the center of the fjord. Zev closed his eyes and breathed in the salty scent of the sea.

"We've arrived," Dyna said, her breath clouding in the icy air.

Lucenna dismounted Fair and opened her satchel. Throwing out her hands, the air rolled with the crack of thunder as they watched her construct a gold shroud over the sky. Her brow tightened, and her arms strained as it grew and rounded over the mountains in an enormous, translucent dome, thicker than the veil she usually used.

"This will contain any sound and traces of magic we may expel," Lucenna said, panting.

With a flick of her fingers, purple light swirled with golden dust as it carried out the figure of a boat from her satchel. In the air, it expanded until it took the shape of a wooden rowboat. It landed on the bank with a hollow thump, two oars rattling inside.

"You really do have a boat," Dyna said, rubbing her hands for warmth. "Where did you get it?"

Lucenna gave them an impish smirk. "I bought it for a bag of gold."

Zev wasn't sure if she was joking. He cupped Dyna's icy hands in his, passing on his natural heat, and she gave him a grateful smile. "How many things do you have in there?" he asked Lucenna.

She simpered coyly. "You may never know."

Rawn removed Fair's saddle and bridle as he said in soft Elvish, *"Ayav, Osom'reh. Son somerart'nocne nifal aled anat'nom."*

The white stallion neighed and galloped away.

"Where is he going?" Dyna asked worriedly as the stallion disappeared into the forest.

Rawn placed the horse tack in his pack. "Fair isn't fond of deep water, my lady. He will take the long road around the fjord and rejoin us in a few days."

"I hope he will be all right."

"Fret not. Fair is capable," Rawn said nonchalantly as Cassiel landed.

But Zev sensed he sent the horse away to keep him out of danger, rather than his dislike for swimming.

Rawn took a breath and faced them. "See the inner point that is the furthest from the shores?" He pointed at the center of the fjord, where it was the darkest. "The deepest point is where Grindylows make their nest. That is where their scales will have gathered. I will climb to that high ledge and cover you." He motioned to a section of rock jutting out of the cliffside. "Cassiel will provide extra coverage on all fronts. Lady Lucenna and Lady Dyna will remain here on land to draw the grindylows away."

Rawn met Zev's gaze. "Take the boat and circle the shore until you are east of us to row to the nest. Go slow and do as little as possible to disturb the water. Do not draw their attention. Once you reach the center and the nest is clear, dive. Be swift and leave as soon as you have attained the scales." He watched them all with grave seriousness. "Arm yourselves and keep your wits about you. Grindylows are fast and their claws are as sharp as any blade. Once they smell blood, they do not stop hunting."

Cassiel crossed his arms. "Any more advice, Lord Norrlen?"

"Aim for the head," he deadpanned.

The lack of optimism was making Zev uneasy.

"God of Urn be with you all," Rawn said and began climbing the cliffside.

Zev straightened and exchanged a nod with Cassiel. "We do this and we get those scales. Be careful out there."

The prince smirked. "I'm not concerned about overgrown eels."

Cassiel glanced at Dyna. His mouth parted to say something, but he turned away and soared into the sky.

"May I borrow your knife?" Lucenna asked her.

Dyna handed it over. The sorceress winced as she ran it across her palm and held her hand over the bank's edge. The scent of her blood tickled Zev's nose as red droplets plinked into the water.

"There, that will lure them out," Lucenna said and nodded to Zev. "Go."

Ignoring his sudden bout of nerves, Zev gave Dyna an encouraging smile. Now that he was about to leave her side, tension gripped him. The danger would come in her direction instead of his. He wrapped her in a hug. "Be safe."

But she saw right through him. "Don't worry. I'll bring you out if anything happens."

"Even if you don't, I'll forgive you." His answer came out less playful than he intended, and her smile faded. "Everything will be fine," he assured her. "I believe in you."

Zev gave her a wink and lifted the boat, easily carrying it above his head. He walked away as Dyna took Lucenna's injured hand in her glowing palms.

He hiked over the uneven shore, careful where he stepped. After a good trek, he made it to the east end of the shore, far enough that the girls standing within the trees were visible. Rawn crouched on a low ledge overlooking the fjord, and Cassiel circled overhead. Carefully setting the boat onto the water, Zev leaped in and used the oar to push away from the bank's slope.

He rowed, his movements slow and careful not to disturb the water beyond what was necessary. Everyone kept still and quiet as they watched his progress. But as he crossed the fjord, nothing appeared or moved. The surface was as still as a darkened mirror. A breeze rustled through the pine trees, softly rippling the water. Maybe they were on the wrong side of the fjord. Either the nest was further west, or the rumors were wrong. Maybe there were no grindylows here at all.

Zev sighed. He had to get those scales. Dyna needed them, and if he was being honest, so did he. Ever since Lucenna mentioned the Druid, he'd tried to suppress any thoughts of what he could find out from it. But if he could ask the Druid only one question, he would ask—

A flash of movement in the water snapped his drifting thoughts back to attention. He had reached the midway point at the deep end. A current of adrenaline ran down Zev's spine, and his muscles tensed in response to the threat. His vision sharpened with the change of his wolf eyes as he searched for the cause of his alarm. Nothing stirred.

Cautiously, Zev peered over the lip of the boat. The dark waters were bottomless, another world on the edge of their own.

Cassiel whistled and motioned at the water. Zev tensed, his claws growing at his fingertips. On the ledge, Rawn aimed his bow at the fjord. Lucenna invoked two spheres of electricity, and Dyna formed a small ball of green fire between her hands. They held unmoving, each studying their quiet surroundings.

Zev's heart lurched in his chest when he met a creature peeking at him over the edge of the boat's frame with bulbous eyes, slick and black as oil. Its face was narrow and flat without a nose or lips. It rose further, revealing its pale gray-blue skin stretched across a gaunt frame. Twitching fins attached to the side of its head extended out as if to catch the merest whisper of sound.

Zev tried not to gag at the potent stench of spoiled fish.

Cocking its head, the grindylow studied Zev in return. Webbed hands curled over the frame's ledge and its long black talons tapped against the wood in a contemplative rhythm. The gills on its neck constricted with a breath and the creature smiled, revealing rows of sharp teeth. It let out an ear-piercing screech that rang in the fjord. The baser side of Zev's instincts recognized the meaning in that sound.

It was announcing a hunt, and he was the prey.

The grindylow lunged. Zev dodged the rake of its talons and slashed with his own. It dove back into the water with an angry shriek. He searched where it went, only for the creature to spring out from behind him. Zev threw himself back as it arced above him. An arrow pierced the creature's skull. It hit the water with a wet flop and floated motionless on the surface. From its back jutted a rigid dorsal fin ending in a thick eel-like tail. A pattern of vivid blue scales coursed down its body.

Zev exhaled a breath. Well, that went a lot easier than he thought. He reached for the scales, but clawed hands snatched the dead grindylow and dragged it into the deep. Blood clouded the surface like spilled paint.

Gods. They were cannibalistic.

The water burbled all across the fjord as a mass of grindylows rose above the surface. They released a howling shriek and swam for Dyna and Lucenna in a swarm of slithering bodies. Lucenna's electricity crackled over the fjord in blinding flashes. Streaks of lightning hit the creatures. Their screams pierced Zev's ears, and the stink of their flesh overwhelmed his nose. The scorched bodies were thrown back, the scales rendered useless. But the creatures kept coming. Rawn's arrows rained as he and Cassiel strafed the fjord.

"There are more of them than we thought!" Cassiel yelled at Zev as he raced through the sky for the girls. "Get to land!"

"No, get the scales!" Lucenna called to him.

He hesitated when his first instinct was to protect them. But Dyna stood sure as she threw green blast after blast, taking down grindylows one by one.

"Zev, hurry!" she said.

Now wasn't the time to watch proudly. Zev grabbed the oars and rowed quickly for the nest. Grindylows came for him and were quickly killed by swift arrows.

Cassiel reached the shore and drew out his divine sword. He decapitated one after another with a torrent of flames. A grindylow sprung out of the lake and whacked him with its large tail, nearly knocking him out of the air. More leaped out of the water and grabbed onto his legs. They clung to him with their teeth and claws, dragging him down.

Rawn aimed at Cassiel. "Be still!"

The arrows whistled through the air and hit their marks. The dead creatures plummeted into the water. Lucenna sent streaks of lightning, hitting the remaining grindylows clinging to him.

That freed Cassiel, and he flew higher into the air. He looked at Zev, and his eyes widened. "Zev!"

More rose out of the water. So many more. They were all around him, filling the fjord. Hundreds of black, glistening eyes fixed on him as they bared their teeth. Zev's breath stalled and for once, his veins ran cold. The multitude attacked the boat and the shore. Their claws cut into his limbs, and they yanked him towards the water. He tore into their eyes, snapping their necks, thrusting his claws into their chests, but more kept coming. The creatures were endless.

Dyna's scream rang through the fjord. He tore a grindylow in half and whipped his head toward her. She and Lucenna backed away from the shore as grindylows slithered across the ground for them, climbing over each other with a vicious hunger.

God of Urn. They could go on dry land.

Electricity stormed in every direction, a sporadic flash of green following. Arrows and fire rained from above, but it wasn't enough.

"Get them out of there!" Zev roared at anyone who could listen as he cut through another grindylow.

Rawn began scaling down from the ledge. Zev rowed for them, but the sea creatures wrenched the oars from his hands. They lunged for him. Slashing and biting, trying to drag him off the boat with unexpected strength. He tried to keep an eye on Dyna, but he couldn't see past the claws swiping at his face and biting his flesh. Tearing them off him, he snapped their slimy necks and shredded through them with his claws. He hardly noticed his wounds, desperate to keep his view on the shoreline. His fist slammed into another creature's head and its skull caved in like an egg.

The onslaught suddenly stopped. The grindylows moved away from the boat and bared their teeth, watching him cautiously.

Zev snarled back and raised his bloodied claws. He was not easy prey. They hissed angrily, then dove back into the water.

Their shadows swam beneath the surface in the direction of the shore, right for the girls. He grabbed a broken oar and tried to row back, cutting down any grindylow that attempted to attack him. He scoured the land, spotting a flash of green. Dyna threw spells left and right, but she stumbled and the Essence in her hands sputtered. Claws yanked on her ankle and she fell, disappearing under the mass of writhing bodies.

"No!" Zev cried.

Cassiel dove into the throng and ripped her free. Rawn threw a knife, impaling the creature springing for them.

"Go. Take her!" Lucenna told Cassiel as she hit another with a blast of electricity.

He lifted Dyna in his arms and flew her away from the shore. Zev watched with relief as he brought her to the rocky island in the fjord, far from the shore. It rose high from the water with a narrow base and wide flat top. Cassiel checked on her briefly, then went back and grabbed the sorceress.

Leaving Rawn to face the mass alone.

He whipped out his sword and sliced through them as rapidly as he was able, throwing out flares of fire. They came from all directions, forcing him across the clearing. Right for the shore. They were herding him.

Zev shouted his name. Two grindylows vaulted out of the water and tackled Rawn. His sword hit the mud as he vanished into the fjord. With their victim, the throng dove in after him, and the water eerily stilled once more.

"Rawn!" Dyna jerked to the edge of the island.

"Don't," Zev ordered from the boat.

Cassiel pulled her back. "They will kill you before you can reach him."

"But we have to save him. Lucenna, send another volt!"

The sorceress shook her head, her eyes wide. "I can't. If I electrify the water, it will kill him too."

"Levitation then," Zev said. "Lift him out."

"We only practiced with you, Zev. I don't have a lock on Lord Norrlen's Essence."

Nausea churned in his stomach. This was his fault. Rawn tried to tell him. He refused to listen. Now Rawn would die because of him, same as his father.

"Is this it then?" Dyna said, gripping her hair. "We can't let them have him!"

"We won't. I'll go." Zev stood. "No matter what happens, stay with Cassiel. Promise me, Dyna."

"I promise," she said shakily. "And promise me you will come back."

Zev held her gaze for a moment, his chest tightening.

Her eyes widened at his silence. "Zev?"

He inhaled a deep breath and dove off the boat. The icy water slammed his senses, making him almost release the breath he held. It was so damn cold even his wolf shuddered. Once he stopped flailing, the dark depths cleared. His wolf eyes focused on the cloud of blood among the bioluminescent lights at the bottom of the fjord. It was coming from the swarm of grindylows. Their fins and the patterns on their backs glowed vivid blue in the dark. Zev swam towards them as fast as he could, his powerful arms and legs giving him speed.

Rawn was there, desperately fighting off the creatures with his knives. Zev tore off the one chewing on Rawn's arm and stabbed another in the gills with his claws. They were too fast and too many. Their teeth tore into his flesh. Blood filled the water, hindering his sight. Zev slashed blindly, his claws tearing into soft tissue as they tore into him.

An abrupt eruption in the water startled the creatures into scattering away. It cleared enough of the blood to reveal Cassiel swimming towards them. Rawn went limp as his eyes rolled closed, having lost all his air. Zev caught him and motioned at Cassiel to take him. Grabbing Rawn, he swam for the surface. Zev watched them go, relieved they would survive.

But he didn't follow.

Within the deep dark depths of the fjord was the nest. It was filled with bones of all creatures and humans alike. Skulls of children laid with them. Entire families devoured. They had killed so many. And among the white bones, thousands of blue scales glowed. The waters became brighter as the grindylows returned.

Zev faced them with resolve.

Perhaps it was the season, the end of his perseverance, or the guilt of leading his friends to their death—but he was tired. There was no way out. For years, he fought the Madness—fought for control, for emotional independence, the need for separation, for silence, and peace. He was so damn tired. He was tired of carrying the weight of his father's death. Tired of living.

What purpose was there to it?

He had to see his father again, even if it meant following him through the Seven Gates.

The grindylows surrounded him, cutting off all escape. Their sharp teeth flashed in the light of their glowing fins. His throat burned for oxygen. A momentary sense of panic filled him when his lungs constricted in agony, but it soon passed. He chose this. He chose the end of his road.

Coward, the Madness shouted. *If you will not fight, then give in!*

He was done fighting himself and his mad thoughts. If he could, he would have laughed at the irony. He had torn his father apart. It was only fitting that he perished in the same way.

Zev extended his claws and bared his teeth. He wouldn't go down until he killed as many of those wretched beasts as possible.

CHAPTER 21

Dyna was out of magic. Nothing but pure adrenaline drove her now. The grindylows had figured out how to climb the island. Their talons dug into the stone as they swarmed them. She slashed and gutted with her knife, as Cassiel had taught her. Lucenna threw spell after spell, protecting the rear.

Where were they? They had been gone too long. *What if—what if—*

Cassiel burst out of the water, and she gasped a sob of relief. But it died when she saw he only carried Rawn.

"Where's Zev?" she asked when he landed

"He's right behind me," Cassiel said as he lay Rawn on the island. He was unconscious and covered in so much blood. Red leaked from countless lacerations.

Dyna rushed to him and checked his pulse. "He's not breathing."

"He was down there too long."

"Move," Lucenna said.

She threw a blast of electricity behind her for good measure, then knelt by Rawn. Her hand hovered over his chest, and she closed her eyes. Lucenna flexed her fingers as if grabbing something, then swept her hand toward his neck. A globe of water left Rawn's mouth, and he coughed violently. Dyna rolled him over as he spewed, beating his back.

"Thank the God of Urn," she said. "You'll be all right now, Lord Norrlen."

More grindylows clawed over the ledge. Lucenna cast out fire, and Cassiel's sword blazed as it severed heads.

Dyna stared at the water, her heart clenching. "Zev isn't coming out."

Cassiel searched with her, and his expression grew worried. "But he was right behind me. He had time to escape. Why didn't he come?"

A horrible sinking feeling twisted through her. No. He wouldn't do that. He wouldn't. But as much as she hated to think of it, deep in her heart, she knew Zev had always been waiting for a way out—and he had found it.

"No," she cried, shaking her head. "No."

"We practiced this," Lucenna told her as she continued to fight back the creatures. "You need to get him out."

"But I used all of my magic!"

"Don't feed into the panic. Close your eyes and find his Essence. Feel it."

Dyna searched inside and called on her magic, begging it to come forth. But it had faded like a snuffed candle melted to the wick.

She stared at her trembling hands. Her vision spun as her lungs struggled for air. "I don't have enough power."

"You can do this, Dyna," Cassiel said, striking another grindylow. "You have to, or he dies!"

Zev's Essence was there, a mere wisp against hers, and it was fading. She gritted her teeth, and her body shuddered with the power she tried to wrench out of herself. But her magic was locked behind an impenetrable wall.

"I can't." She gasped for air, hyperventilating. "I can't. I can't. I can't!"

She wasn't enough to save Zev.

Defeat crushed her under its weight, stealing the icy air from her lungs. Dyna tumbled through the cracks of her mind as reality caved in. He would die here because of her. Lucenna shouted something, but it was lost to the ringing in her ears. She couldn't breathe. Her heart hammered against her ribs, threatening to pitter out.

She wasn't enough.

Hands came over her face, and she met Cassiel's silver eyes.

"Ett haor sheli," he said in the language of the Heavens, his voice so soft it was almost a whisper. Even in the raging chaos around her, the shrieks of the sea creatures, and the explosions of spells, she heard him loud and clear. "From the first day we met, you have proven to me time and again that you are capable of far more than I could ever have imagined. I believe you can do this. I know you can."

The softest of smiles tugged at his lips, and the bond glowed. His presence filled her from the pit of her soul to the weavings of her heart. She was full of him, and only him.

His voice seemed to flutter across her mind. *Now show me.*

Without so much as a flinch, Cassiel yanked a handful of black feathers and shoved them in her hand. They blazed with gold light, and something shifted inside of her. The barrier that contained her power dropped. An abundance of Essence rushed to the surface and barreled through her veins. The feathers disintegrated to gold dust, absorbing into her palms.

Her body throbbed as power filled every crevice of her being. The Essence of everyone around her pulsed in Dyna's mind, and including the one fading in the fjord's pit. Anger and determination flushed out her terror. Zev may have wanted to give up, but she wouldn't let him. She raised a hand and snatched his Essence with her own, ripping him out of the water with the grindylows clinging to his flesh. His body hurled through the sky, and she guided it to the island, where he landed in a bloody mess. Cassiel and Rawn quickly killed the creatures on him. Lucenna drew the water from his lungs, but Zev still didn't move—

Dyna cried out at the talons stabbing her knee. *Esh Zayin* cleaved through the creature, turning it to ash. She stumbled back and applied pressure to the wound. Blood gushed through her fingers. Lucenna, Rawn, and Cassiel continued fighting, but they were exhausted. Soon, they would be overpowered. Endless grindylows climbed over the edge, surrounding them from all sides. The vicious things were everywhere.

So many. Too many.

Death's presence lurked in the chaos, waiting for them to die. And they would, right on this lump of rock. Their journey would end with such a foolish mistake. Choking on the metallic scent of blood and burned fish, Dyna couldn't do more than close her eyes.

Her father had faced certain death, and he fought until the end. So would she.

She pictured him on that snowy night, pictured his stance and the spells he formed to keep the Shadow at bay. None of those she knew except how to make her Essence burn like fire.

Dyna inhaled a deep breath, gathering all of her power, and aimed both hands at the raging grindylows. Her palms lit with a spiraling green light that raced up her arms. She opened all Essence Channels, and power shot through her veins, burning through her being in a way it never had before. Her magic flared brighter as it reached her shoulders, brighter as it crawled over her neck, and brighter until an effervescent glow lit her body. Her vision filled with blinding green light that faded all reality, even the solidity of the ground.

Her every nerve was on fire. It was too much. Trapped within her, and it had nowhere to go—but out.

The atmosphere pulsed. Dyna screamed as green fire exploded out of her into a blazing ring. The inferno bathed everything in a scorching wave. It crested over the entire swarm of creatures in a wave of green flame, continuing through the fjord with a roar. The earth shook, and the air shattered like glass. Cracks fractured through the cliffs, releasing massive segments that crashed to shore.

The burning faded and left behind the flimsy shell of her being. She had a moment to realize she was floating off the ground, then all the feeling left her. Her vision swayed, and she dropped. She landed on something firm and arms adjusted around her as Cassiel's startled face came into view.

He brushed the hair from her face. "Dyna, are you all right?"

"Bring me to him," she said faintly, her skin buzzing.

Cassiel carried her to Zev's side. Blood soaked through his shredded clothing; dark red trails seeped from the deep lacerations all over his face and chest.

But not dead. Not yet.

Dyna kneeled beside him, hot tears rolling down her cheeks. "You will not do this to me, do you hear? I won't allow it."

She raised her hands over him and called on her Essence once more. It was spent, but she had enough. She would make it enough. Green light reappeared in her palms, throbbing through her with a strength that wasn't her own.

Dyna closed her eyes and gathered it like a blanket; letting it fall over every wound she could feel. Her power sunk into skin, weaving through the crevices of muscle and tendon. She took in the pain, as it in turn took from her. Power leached from her life force, mending cuts and broken bones. She guided every strand of torn flesh and wove them piece by piece.

Her body bowed from the strain. She grew numb and heavy as weakness found her once more. The light behind her eyelids faded, leaving pain radiating all over her body. An arm wrapped around her when she slumped and pulled her close. *Cassiel.* His fear faded with a sense of wonder and shock. Dyna let him gather her against his chest, too exhausted to move or care.

Lucenna gasped, and Lord Norrlen murmured in his language.

"Look," Cassiel said in quiet awe. "Look at what you did."

It took every ounce of will to force her bleary eyes open. Zev's wounds had healed into fresh scars. His chest rose and fell with steady breaths, and his pulse was strong where his wrist rested beneath her fingertips. Rawn and Lucenna were also healed. Both stared at her with wide eyes, their shocked expressions splattered with blood. Then they glanced past her.

The fjord was completely black. For a moment, she thought it had been destroyed, that the water had evaporated into nothing but an ashy bed. But it was hundreds of grindylow corpses, burned to charred husks. The few left alive peered out from the surface, only their glistening eyes visible, as if they didn't dare to reveal more than that.

Lucenna conjured electricity in her hands. "Unless you want to become fried fish, I suggest you retreat."

They hissed and sunk back into the water.

Dyna's vision dimmed. "The scales..."

It's what they came for and nearly died for. Had it all been for nothing? By the grim expressions of her companions, she knew the answer.

Lucenna raised her hand, and the forgotten rowboat lifted in the air by a cloud of gold pixie dust. It was the last thing Dyna saw as her eyes closed. She let sleep take her before the sense of failure could.

It was frightfully cold. Ice crystallized in Dyna's veins where there had once been fire. It bit into her skin as snow whipped past her face. The wind howled over the hill where she stood, barefoot and completely alone in the night. Only the full moon overhead bore any light.

Her breaths shot out in rapid spurts to find herself in this place. In the distance came a familiar roar, and her heart quivered.

"No." The faint cry shook on her lips. She didn't want to relive this dream. She didn't want to experience the crushing weight of it all.

Something ran past her. A child. His red ringlets bounced in the moonlight as his tiny body ran across the hill for the dark forest in nothing but his nightgown.

"Thane!" Dyna ran after him. She must keep her brother safe. The Shadow was coming.

The snow numbed her feet. No matter how fast she ran, her brother fell further out of her reach.

"Thane!" Her scream echoed in the snowstorm, clashing against the barren trees. "Come back!"

He stopped by the forest edge and peered at her over his shoulder. The wind swept through his hair, exposing his face. But he had no face. It was nothing but a black, mangled hole.

She lost her footing and collapsed in the snow. When she looked again, her brother was gone. He had long left the world of the living, and Dyna sensed she'd reached the threshold of the dead.

"Why are you here?"

Dyna spun around.

Lucenna stood on the hill, watching her impassively, wearing only a thin black dress. The storm beat against her, though it didn't seem to bother her. "Why did you leave North Star?"

She shook her head. "I cannot tell you."

The sorceress cocked her head. In a blink, she changed into the image of her father.

Dyna gasped and shut her eyes. "Please, not his face."

His image blurred and took on Lucenna's face once more. Whoever Dyna spoke to now, it wasn't the sorceress or her father.

"Why are you here?" she—it—repeated.

Dyna searched the frozen landscape, surrounded by darkness. It didn't mean this place. She stood on her shaky feet. "I'm here to save my sister."

"Why are you going to Mount Ida?" Lucenna pressed as she circled her. "Why did you leave your safe village and risk the unknown?"

Dyna frowned. She had already answered those questions. "I left to save my sister."

A cold smile touched the sorceress's lips as she leaned in close and hissed in her ear. *"Liar."*

A crackling growl sounded within the forest. Two red eyes blazed in the darkness, watching her from the trees. Dyna lurched and fell. Her heart thrashed in her chest, crushing the air in her lungs. She crawled backwards on her hands and feet through the snow. Terror seized her as the dark form approached in wisps of smoke and shadow, horns extending from its head. It rose to its full height and veiled the moonlight. Its molten stare held her prisoner, turning her to ice as tears froze on her cheeks. She had died this death a hundred times. What was a hundred more?

The Shadow sprang for her in a burst of black, swallowing her screams.

CHAPTER 22

Cassiel gripped his head as Dyna's cries rang in the night, passing over the clearing in a haunting wail. The sound echoed in his mind, and her terror wrenched through his chest. She had been trapped in her nightmares for two days without him there to ease her free. If he could only hold her hand, he could guide her out of it. He had done it before.

Cassiel whirled around with mad rage. "Let me go to her!"

The wolf standing guard in front of Lucenna's tent snarled, baring its fangs. Cassiel moved, but it lowered in a threatening crouch, claws digging into the ground. Zev would attack him if he took another step.

"What is the matter with you?" Cassiel snapped.

The wolf growled low and deep, his fur expanding. Zev had woken in a feral mood. As soon as he realized what happened at the fjord, he shifted and refused to speak to anyone.

"Her fever has gotten worse, Zev. She needs my blood. Let me heal her."

"Why did Lady Dyna not heal herself?" Rawn asked.

Cassiel rubbed the tension from his brow. "She can only use it to heal others, not herself."

And now the wounds she'd gained by those wretched creatures had become infected. The gash in her knee oozed with foul-smelling puss, the skin around it swelling mottled red and purple.

Lucenna wasn't knowledgeable in healing magic, and Rawn had already used the last of the Dynalya flower to help her. Cassiel felt like a fool for hesitating to give her his blood, not wanting to cross any further boundaries that she may despise him for. When her health became worse, Zev refused to let him go near her. He allowed no one inside the tent but Lucenna.

"Is my blood not good enough for her anymore?" Maybe it wasn't. He didn't know if he still had the ability to heal others. "You thanked me the last time it saved her life," Cassiel said. "If she dies, the blame will fall with you."

The wolf snapped its teeth, vibrating with an undeserved fury.

"There, Prince Cassiel." Rawn took his arm. "Come sit while we wait."

He allowed the elf to guide him away to the campfire where Fair rested. The Elvish horse had reunited with them yesterday.

Cassiel sat on a log by the fire and placed his shaking fists on his lap. The flames burned high, but it did nothing to warm his bones. He was so cold—and afraid. Gooseflesh prickled his arms as if the shadow of Death stalked him. No, it hovered over his bond with Dyna.

It was thin and frail.

Everything had gone so completely wrong. He never should have agreed to this stupid detour. But when he had been presented with a chance to right his wrongs, he blindly grasped onto it. All he wanted was to ask the Druid how to free Dyna from their Blood Bond. He thought getting the scales was the answer.

Whatever the reason, it was all for nothing. There were no scales found within the charred corpses left in the fjord, and the ones hidden within those depths were not worth another attempt. Not when his bonded's screams continued to beat against his skull. A phantom pain lingered deep in his right knee. The sensation had been with him since the grindylows attacked her, but he refused to think about that now.

Cassiel ground his teeth. Overgrown eels, he'd called them. He'd been an arrogant idiot. Those creatures had been vicious monsters, and in such numbers, they never had a chance. Without Dyna, some of them would have died, if not all of them.

Dyna had panicked when she thought Zev was gone. She couldn't invoke the magic he had seen her practice so much with, and it slipped through her fingers. He'd felt the fractures in her soul break further when she thought Zev would die.

"Give her a feather!" the sorceress had desperately screamed at him.

So he had. Cassiel hadn't stopped to think or count how many he gave her. When he put them in her hand, Dyna burst with light as if she had become the sun itself.

Her power had lit the bond and pressed against him with an invisible heat. Then, defying all reason, she rose into the air as debris spiraled at her feet. She had floated. *Floated.* And her eyes. Her beautiful eyes had turned into green flares as light streamed up her arms. She somehow pulled Zev from the water, then released a cataclysmic explosion that took out nearly every grindylow in the fjord.

The sight of her at that moment had been frightening and … magnificent.

All of that power.

A shiver crawled over him.

That was inside of her? Or had his feathers amplified a gentle breeze into a storm?

Dyna's screams quieted to mournful sobs. Rawn shifted in his seat as he and Zev looked at the tent. Both tilted their heads in a way that let Cassiel know they were listening.

"What is it?"

"Lady Lucenna is speaking with her brother."

He straightened. "What is he saying?"

"She is describing Lady Dyna's condition. Lucien is questioning her on what has occurred and what exactly attacked her so he may instruct her on what potion to make."

Cassiel scowled. They didn't need the mage when his blood could end the infection in seconds. "She now thought to ask him after Dyna has suffered for so long?"

"We are all at our wit's end, Prince Cassiel. It had not occurred to me to inquire of him either." Relief crossed Rawn's face. "Alas, we have an answer."

Lucenna threw open the flaps. "I need a branch of Thornwood, fairyweed, and blue maidencane. Enough of each. Do you know what they look like?"

Rawn stood. "I do, my lady."

"Good."

"But—"

"I know." She waved him off, sighing heavily. "I know. Find it and bring it as soon as possible. If this fever doesn't break by morning ..." The sorceress heaved another breath. "Find it."

She went back inside.

Zev barked at Rawn.

"Thornwood is a red prickly bush found near a hedgerow," he told him. "You will recognize it by its truffle fragrance."

The wolf chuffed and gave Cassiel a low growl. He wouldn't leave until he did.

Cassiel scowled. "You would rather we hunt for weeds while she stands at Death's Gate than to allow me to heal her?"

Zev's lips pulled over his teeth.

He shook his head and said to Rawn. "How do we find the others?"

"Blue maidencane grows by the edge of the water."

"Like the fjord. And the other?"

Rawn rubbed his jaw, his expression tensing. "Fairyweed is a multi-branched forb with white flowers. It grows only within high, rocky peaks."

"Why do you look worried?"

"I'm afraid it may be past its season. Fairyweed is a summer plant."

Cassiel eyed the mountainous range enclosing them. He had to try. "I will go."

Rawn nodded and mounted Fair. "A word of caution. The fjord is the border of the Moors. We are now on fae land. Careful where you step and whom you offend. I wish you luck."

Cassiel's wings unfurled, catching the wind once again. He soared into the night sky, praying for exactly that.

As the fates would have it, there was no luck to be had. Cassiel flew high and low, searching the highest peak of the mountains for fairyweed, and found nothing. The sky's darkness faded, signaling that time was over. A sudden pang hit his chest, knocking the air out of him. The bond. It was weakening. He raced back to camp. Whatever put the wolf against him, Cassiel didn't care anymore. Those teeth could tear him to shreds, but he would give Dyna his blood.

But he arrived in camp to find they were no longer alone. A cluster of colorful butterflies fluttered around the tent. No. *Fairies*, he realized as he landed. Males and females, no bigger than his forefinger, in bronze armor. Each carried sharp glaives the size of needles. They now stood guard outside the tent, their translucent wings flapping in the breeze. Rawn faced off with them, attempting to placate the growling wolf at his side. No more sounds came from within the tent.

"What is the meaning of this?" Cassiel asked.

"As I said," Rawn murmured, "this is fae territory. A delegate of the court has come to investigate our matters here. She has already gone inside. Her guardsmen will allow no one near, and if we are wise," he added, glancing meaningfully to the wolf who looked ready to spring, "we must wait."

Cassiel groaned and rubbed his face. "We have no time. I could not find any fairyweed, so I must go to her. I care not what you say, Zev. I will—"

Zev ripped from Rawn's hold. He charged at the guards. A streak of gold dust burst from the tent and collided with his snout. The wolf went flying and crashed clear across the camp, hitting the ground hard. He snarled and rolled to his feet.

"Stand down," Rawn insisted. "You cannot fight these fairies. They are as strong as they are—"

But Zev ran right at that tiny bulb of light. It burst in a rain of gold dust, and in its place rose a human-sized girl with rich dark skin, her long black braids flaring behind her. She caught Zev's jaws and slammed him on the ground with a delightful giggle, as if he weighed nothing at all.

"—small." Rawn sighed. "This is Princess Keenali of the Morphos Court," he told Cassiel.

"Morphos?"

"It is a small but wealthy court in the northern, mid-west side of Urn."

"Call me Keena, Lord Norrlen, if you please." The fairy girl pinned Zev beneath her knee. No matter how much he struggled, he couldn't break free. He resorted to snarling and snapping his teeth. Her full lips broke in a smile, the firelight glinting on her translucent yellow wings. Her skin glittered and shone like she had been dusted with gold powder. The glossy red petals of her dress and the diadem on her brow made of black and gold beads glinted in the dawn.

"Now, now, wolf. I asked you to wait patiently," Keena said, speaking in tinkling bell tones. At the shake of her head, pointed ears poked out from her hair. "Will you please stop antagonizing my guardsmen so I may save your friend's life?"

"We do not need you," Cassiel said once Zev stopped struggling. "I can dissipate the infection myself."

Her golden brown eyes met his, widening slightly as a new smile crossed her face, and she clucked her tongue. "Perhaps if you had treated her from the onset, but this may now be beyond you, Celestial. The infection has taken over, and she is but hours from death."

His heart shuddered as more of the bond fractured. It punctured something inside of him, and the pain nearly knocked him to his knees.

At their horrified silence, the faerie's wings fluttered, and she released Zev. "I must take her with me to King Dagden's court. There, she will be healed. You have my word."

"No." Cassiel moved forward, but Rawn took his elbow.

"If the fae have come, we must obey while on their land. We are trespassers here."

He jerked his arm free. "I do not care. I will not simply—"

Lucenna came out of her tent, carrying Dyna in a purple mist. Her face was gaunt; matted red hair sticking to the sweat on her face and neck. Her complexion had lost all color, with dark shadows under her eyes. The sight of her cracked something else behind Cassiel's ribs.

"Thank you, princess," Lucenna said, bowing her head. "Please take care of her."

Keena accepted Dyna in her arms. Zev launched at her, but Lucenna threw out a glowing tether and it whipped around his neck, muzzling his jaws.

"Heel," Lucenna ordered. "We have to do this or she will die."

Zev yanked so hard Cassiel thought the tether might snap. It only thickened, glowing brighter as Lucenna fed it more power. She wrapped it around her fist and reeled it in, dragging him to her. She stomped on the magical leash, and it forced him to sprawl on the ground at her feet.

Lucenna petted his head. "There's a good wolf."

A deep, threatening growl rumbled in Zev's chest. But she must have had him completely subdued, because he no longer moved.

Princess Keena grinned and nodded her thanks. "Come through the Wild Wood due west to be introduced at King Dagden's court. We will be waiting for you."

She carried Dyna towards the dense trees, her butterfly wings leaving behind a trail of gold dust. The tiny guardsmen followed her into the forest. Cassiel shook his head sharply, snapping himself back to reason from whatever despair had stumped him. They couldn't simply give Dyna to the fae.

Cassiel ran for the forest. When he reached it, there was nothing but the first morning light streaming through the still trees. The fairies had vanished into the dawn, taking the other half of his soul with them.

CHAPTER 23

Von

The coming of night greeted Von as he, Len, and Bouvier finally reached camp after two days' ride. The rows of tents appeared as they passed through the boundary of the cloaking spell. They cantered for the large black tent in the center. A young Raider appeared as they dismounted, taking the horses away to be brushed and fed.

"Master, I have returned," Von announced as they slipped through the entrance.

The last of the Forewarning Crystal's light faded as he took in the occupants inside. Tarn sat at the head of his table while Novo and Elon stood before him, mid-report. They were filthy and haggard from the road. The Maiden was nowhere in sight, but Tarn looked pleased.

"It seems you also return with good tidings," he said, taking a drink from his goblet of wine. "Elon, repeat what you have told me."

"Commander." Elon nodded to Von in greeting. "The Guardians thwarted our second attempt to take the Maiden."

"I see that." Von took in their battered appearance and the bloodied bandages. "What happened?"

"The sorceress has joined their company."

Ah. Well, that explained it. Elon was a powerful opponent in his own right, and so was the sorceress.

"We knew she would," Von said. "The Seer had predicted it."

"Her spells, paired with Lord Norrlen's skill, kept us at bay."

"And the Lycan took a few bites out of me," the young spy retorted. "Tell him about after, Captain."

Von frowned. "What happened after?"

"We continued to track them," Elon said. "They also seek divination from the fae and considered the scales of grindylows would make sufficient payment."

Von stilled. "They didn't go *there*?"

"Aye, straight to the fjord," Novo confirmed, visible excitement drawing him to answer. "The stupidest thing, really. They were surrounded and surely would have been rendered fish food if not for the Maiden." Grinning, he held the pause long enough to make it suspenseful. "She has magic, Commander."

He knew as much already. Geon told him Dyna had healed him in Corron, which he deliberately kept from Tarn for her sake.

Careful to play the part of the unsuspecting party, Von wore an expression of shock, even as apprehension washed through him. "Magic? Are you sure?"

"She lit up like a green star. I have never seen anything like it. Then her power torched the entire fjord, killing the little sea beasts. We were on the cliffs, watching from a distance, and yet the blast threw us off our feet."

Von glanced at Elon and he nodded.

God of Urn. There would be no hiding Dyna's abilities now. Tarn liked magic and would collect her, as he had everyone else who was useful to him.

But it begged the question: what was she? Humans couldn't use magic, so how could she?

Tarn's eyes glinted in the candlelight and Von read the satisfaction there. "We are to make our way around the Zafiro Mountains for the Port of Azure."

"At once, Master. I will pass on the order."

"Dismissed." Tarn waved them away, barely sparing a glance at Len and Bouvier.

Von stepped forward. "I have more to report."

Tarn flipped through some scrolls on the table. "Go on."

"King Lenneus—" Von started, but Tarn's cold stare cut to him. "The Azure King," he amended, "has called on the Azure Knights."

"That is to be expected."

"And ... The Skulls."

Tarn straightened in his chair and uncrossed his leg from over the other. Without a sliver of dread, a slight smile hovered in the corners of his mouth—a vicious mirror of the one Von had seen from the mercenary in the capital. If Tarn ever laughed, perhaps he might have at that moment.

"The Skulls?" Novo repeated, his tone appropriately alarmed.

"We encountered two of the mercenaries at the prison," Von said.

"And you lived to tell the tale, mate?" Novo elbowed Bouvier, smirking.

Bouvier grinned. "By the grace of the fates."

"How did you break out of the prison?"

"Blew it up."

Novo groaned. "Blast. I wish I could have seen that."

Tarn sipped from his goblet, reading a map among the missives in front of him. "I presume these mercenaries swore to hunt me down."

"Yes, Master," Von replied.

"I welcome the attempt."

"But it's strange. They were men of Azure," Von said. "I believe they are from Old Tanzanite Keep."

Tarn's expression shifted. "Why is that strange? Old Tanzanite Keep was once the kingdom's capital. The population remains ample."

"It was the way he fought, Master. I know I have seen that dual blade technique before."

"Because it is the fighting style of the north. Don't waste my time with such pointless details."

Yes, but there was something about the way he moved that nagged at Von's mind. He couldn't quite place it.

Tarn's fingers drummed against his wine cup as he frowned at the warding spells dangling from the ceiling of his tent. "Bouvier, when were you captured?"

Bouvier stepped forward. "They captured me at the Warrant Authority office, Master."

"After placing the anonymous warrants on the Maiden and her company."

"Yes."

The drumming stopped. "Then Von was seen breaking you free from prison. The Azure Guard will soon make the connection behind the anonymous warrants to me."

Damn, he was right. That made Dyna a person of interest to the crown.

"They will search for her as well," Von concluded. The bounty was now working against their favor instead of for them.

Tarn stood, fixing them with his icy gaze. "Make way for the port immediately."

They bowed their heads and backed out of the tent. Outside, the spies turned to Von for his command.

"You heard the master. There is no time to rest. Prepare to move."

They nodded and split in different directions to pass on the order. Soon the camp was in an uproar as the men disassembled their tents.

The Raiders saluted to Von with a fist over their hearts as he made his way through the camp, barking orders. It used to be Lieutenant Abenon's task to handle these things before his untimely death. How many more men would he lose before this was over? None of that mattered to him right now.

Von kept going, with only one destination in mind. When he saw his tent, his steps quickened, desperate to reach it. He practically ran inside, and Yavi yelped at his sudden entrance. The smile crossing her face stole his breath.

Home.

It didn't matter where they went, what hovel they stayed in, or what curse broke the sky. She was his home.

He marched toward her.

Yavi stood from where she had been folding clothes into their trunk. "Von—"

He caught the lovely sound in a crash of lips. She gasped against his mouth, opening further, meeting the slide of his tongue. Her soft moan ignited him with liquid heat. She melted into his arms as he trailed kisses from the curve of her soft neck to the corner of her lips. He would never be tired of the sweetness of her skin. He pressed into her so she would feel exactly how much effect she had over him. Their mouths met in an urgent kiss, fierce and desperate to get lost in one another. The feeling of her soft lips consumed him whole.

"I missed you," he said against her mouth, his voice husky. "I need you."

Her nails dug into his arms as her breath quickened. A sly smile spread across those lips. "I know."

Von grabbed Yavi's hips and hoisted her up. She clamped her thighs around him, snaking her arms around his neck, fingers fisting in his hair. Their mouths locked as he carried her to their small dining table. Yavi ripped at his bandolier, nearly tearing the buckle before he got to it. She yanked off his coat, and he tugged at the bodice strands as they grasped and kissed, teeth nipping at lips and skin.

They came together in a crashing wave. Her head flew back with a delicious whimper, giving him access to her throat. Von groaned against her rapid pulse, holding her tight. So perfect. The feel of her tangled around him, with him, against him. All of it, absolutely perfect. She was all he would ever need, a need that never was sated.

Desperation took over, fast and hungry, not at all tender as she deserved. Yavi's nails dug into him with the same frantic need. She clung to him as if he was the only thing solid in the world. Yet he was as insubstantial as air, lost in never-ending chaos, and she was the anchor.

"I love you," he said, taking the back of her head to draw her into a kiss.

The phrase was too simple to describe what she meant to him. Yavi was branded on his skin, embedded in his heart. Without her, he couldn't breathe.

She smiled against his mouth and repeated the same line she always said to his confession, "How much?"

"This much."

Von carried her to the brink as they quickly rose together, and he silenced Yavi's cry with a kiss as they careered over the edge. He plummeted with her into a waiting cloud that carried him away. They held each other through the shudders as her pulse raced beneath his palms. She dropped her head against his chest, panting to catch her breath.

It was over too soon. Much too soon. Perhaps he was greedy, but he wanted more of her. *For her.* Not these short, stolen moments that came too far in between. It wasn't ever enough.

He gently pressed his lips against her temple. "Next time, it won't be like this."

Yavi smiled at him lazily through lidded eyes. She took it as wistful words said from the fog of satisfaction and not the promise he intended it to be. Other obligations would always intervene, but he truly meant it.

He would care for her better in every way.

Von ran his nose along her shoulder, planting a kiss on her soft skin. "Next time, I'll take my time worshiping every inch of you."

A breathless laugh escaped her lips. "Keep speaking like that, and we won't get on with our duties."

He cursed under his breath and groaned, making her laugh again. With much regret, he slipped free and went to the basin of water by the trunk. He took the cloth soaking inside and carefully cleaned her, then himself.

"You're drinking the tea?" he thought to ask as he buttoned his trousers.

Yavi slid off the table and straightened her dress, giving him a short nod.

"Good. A babe wouldn't do now, would it?" Von kissed her and started packing their belongings. He made quick work of it as he told her a short version of Bouvier's rescue and the encounter with the Guardians. When he stripped the last cot, he realized Yavi hadn't moved. She was staring at the ground. "What are you doing? We're in a rush, love."

A tear spilled from her lashes, trailing to her chin.

"Yavi." Von rushed back to her. "What is it? Was I too rough? Did I hurt you?" Guilt struck him. He'd been rabid as an animal and had been too lost to think—

"No." She wiped her cheek. "No, it's not that."

He brushed the dark tendrils of hair back from her cheeks, caressing his thumb over those satin pink lips he adored. "What is it?"

Yavi curled her hands over her heart. "Would it be so terrible if we had a child?"

A new sort of guilt hit him, along with an echo of pain. Once upon a time, before his life became what it was, he had imagined having a house of his own, set upon the land he would cultivate with his family. But that was an old dream from another lifetime he had forgotten. When Yavi came into his life, he dared to keep a small sliver of that dream of having someone to love, but he wasn't foolish enough to reach for more. As long as they remained chained, their secret marriage and stolen moments were all they could have.

Von closed his eyes, resting his forehead against hers. "You know we cannot. If Tarn learned of it ..."

Gods. He didn't want to think of what Tarn would do to her. To them.

It was against slave edict for life-servants to have any life-mates or children. Their sole priority was always to the master. Von had heard of several cases where other masters either disposed of the babe at birth or disposed of the mother while she was carrying, if not the father as well.

Tarn would probably do the same.

"If we were in a world where we were both free of chains," she said, "would you want a child?"

Where we were both free...

A dark, mocking thought reminded him that the Azure King had abolished slavery. He was an Azure citizen, and Yavi was his servant, so it applied to them both. But Von didn't speak the news aloud. He couldn't bring himself to tell her when he knew it couldn't be. The God of Urn's law superseded the law of men, didn't it?

Tarn would never allow it.

"In another world, we're happy and free." He cupped her face. "We have a home on a hill full of laughter and love and farmland to pass on to our five children."

"Five?" She laughed weakly, at last smiling even as her tears spilled over his fingers. "Mighty ambitious of you."

He nodded, completely serious. "Four boys with the countenance of their father and the intelligence of their mother. They will grow tall and strong, so they may watch over their little sister, who will come as a surprise we didn't expect, but a precious gift that made us complete."

Von could picture it. He could see his family, hear their laughter, and feel their joy. The possibility of that future felt so real—and out of his reach.

Yavi's face crumbled, and she hugged him tightly, shuddering with quiet sobs. "What a beautiful dream."

And that was all it would ever be.

A beautiful dream.

CHAPTER 24

Everything was bright. A stark contrast to the darkness that had haunted her, which faded quickly with the chill in her bones. The light was so strong it filtered through Dyna's eyelids. She groaned and tried to move her arm to cover her face, but she couldn't find the strength to lift it. Everything was heavy and tender, her bones feeling brittle. The thought summoned images of the bleached white mountain constructed of skulls with a black storm spiraling at the peak. Dyna had climbed and climbed, but no matter how many bones she scaled, she never reached the top.

"Ah, you're awake," someone said.

It was a voice she didn't recognize. One made by the sound of tinkling bells. Something as soft as silk fluttered against her cheek.

"What happened?" she rasped.

"You were at Death's Gate," the voice said. "I brought you here before you crossed the threshold."

Death's Gate. The land of nightmares had been cold and dark as she visited the dead. Had her soul been preparing to cross? Her body was warm and heavy now, but she didn't feel uncomfortable. There was a sense of safety in this place, but deep within her was a cloud of worry.

"Is this Heaven's Gate?"

The bells tinkled in a series of high tones, and she realized the voice was laughing. "No, silly girl. This is Faerie."

At the shocking answer, Dyna snapped her eyes open and immediately closed them at the sharp pins that struck her vision. She sucked in a sharp breath and slowly opened them again.

The first thing she saw was a ceiling, or what she thought was a ceiling. Vines of full green leaves hung like banners overhead. Their little white blooms glowed softly, providing light. The walls were round and made completely of wood. It was a small room with equally tiny windows looking out to greenery beyond. Little shrubs of fragrant flowers and bioluminescent blue mushrooms grew in the corners of the wall. Beyond the bed she lay in was a sitting area with couches upholstered with moss and seats carved of stone. The sheets wrapped around her were made of a white translucent material that glided over her skin like clouds. Gentle water trickled like soft music and the trilling of birds.

"I'm in Arthal?"

"No, you're in what we call the Phantasmic Moors," the voice said. "The Court of King Dagden, ruler of the Wild Fae."

Dyna glanced at the one beside her, and her mouth fell open. The faerie girl was beautiful. Young, perhaps younger than her, with skin of rich sepia. Her eyes were a golden brown woven through with olive green. Behind her beat translucent yellow wings that glimmered under the light. Every twitch released a sprinkle of gold dust into the air.

And the fairy was no bigger than about four inches.

She smiled warmly and tilted her head in greeting. "Hello, Dynalya. I am Princess Keenali of the Morphos Court. Please, call me Keena."

"I ... hello. Oh, forgive me—" She scrambled to stand on her feet to give the princess a proper bow, but the sheets tangled around her legs and she tripped.

The fairy burst into a shower of gold dust and caught her arm before she hit the ground. With surprising strength, Keena steadied her back on her feet. Dyna blinked repeatedly, stunned by her sudden change in size. The fairy now stood a little taller than her.

"Careful," Keena said. "You have been unconscious for three days. Give your body time to settle."

"How did you do that?" Dyna asked. "You were tiny before. Or am I still dreaming?"

The fairy giggled again. "I can temporarily change my size with pixie dust."

"Oh..." Well, that made sense, she supposed.

The sounds outside grew clearer. Once she got her bearings, Dyna made her way to the window. She was high above the ground, with a view of the vast forest below. Fairies of all kinds mingled about, hanging banners and adorning tables. Some flew through the air in glittering forms of all colors. From this high up, she realized she was in a tree. *Inside* of a tree.

"What is happening?"

"They are preparing for a royal wedding," Keena said, though that's not what Dyna meant, and came to stand beside her. "It will be tonight, so we must dress in our finest and pay our respects to the king. He graciously permitted me to bring you here to be healed."

"I was sick?"

Keena nodded, glancing at Dyna's knee where the skin had puckered with fresh scars. "Grindylows are filthy creatures. The wound had become infected. It was good I came to you when I did. Fae medicine works quickly." She frowned and crossed her arms. "Though, the Celestial could have healed you at any moment. Why did he leave you to perish?"

Dyna brushed her matted hair from her face. Cassiel must not want to give his blood anymore, not after it had bound them in a way neither of them wanted. No. The thought didn't fit. They may be at odds, but Cassiel wouldn't leave her to die. There must be a reason.

"Did he refuse to heal me?"

The fairy princess sheepishly shrugged. She played with the shawl necklace of interwoven brown and white glass beads that spanned her shoulders. "No."

"So why take me?"

"I wanted to meet you."

"What? But—" Dyna gasped when the reminder of Cassiel pulled her out of whatever dream-like trance she was in, and everything came rushing back. Her journey. The events of the fjord. Her friends.

"Where are Cassiel and the others?" she asked. Zev would never let her be taken.

"Worry not. They are on their way. My guardsmen reported they have entered the Wild Wood and will be here soon."

Dyna relaxed. Fairies couldn't lie, and Keena's soft eyes were clear and kind.

"Come, we have much to do." The princess sniffed and a little curl formed on her nose. "And we will start with a bath."

Dyna moved to follow her when something shifted inside of her muddy boot and pricked her calf. She peeled it off and a small item landed at her feet. The iridescent cerulean surface shone like a tiny pool of water under the light.

A grindylow scale.

CHAPTER 25

T he Wild Wood was eerily quiet. The sun had long since set,
    leaving shadows to grow among the barren trees. He kept his
    knife out at the ready as Rawn did his bow and Lucenna her
magic. Zev stalked beside him, his yellow eyes glowing in the night.
They were on high alert, not knowing what they would encounter,
even if Rawn said he had visited the Court of the Wild Fae many years
ago. The fae changed their moods as often as the weather.

"There," Rawn announced, pulling Fair's reins to a stop. He
motioned at a path of stone steps coated in moss, emerging from the
carpet of fallen leaves. It led up a steep hill into the dark forest
beyond. "The road into Faerie."

Cassiel gripped his knife, feeling a sense of dread that warned him
to turn back, but he wouldn't leave without Dyna. They followed
Rawn along the steps toward the shadowy trees. When they crossed
the last step at the top, the land changed. They had left Autumn
behind and stepped into Spring. Cool air wafted through the forest.
Flowers and toadstools speckled the soft, mossy ground, the green
canopy overhead lush and full, with tiny lights flickering among the
branches like fireflies. Cassiel's dread faded like an old memory.

The forest appeared to creak and move within the shadows—and
he realized it was. The trees walked on legs made of their roots, each

step slow and creaking with the groan of wood. They stopped and gawked at their gnarled frames and knotted faces layered with moss and lichen.

"Tree folk," Rawn said.

The mystical trees paid them no mind. They swayed with an unheard song until Cassiel heard it, the soft lilting of a flute, soon accompanied by a fiddle and drums. They followed the sound, their steps sinking into the plush soft ground as pink and purple flowers dangled from the branches overhead. The air smelled of a sweet garden and impossible dreams. Flower petals drifted in the air like snow. More fae appeared from the trees: ogres, pixies, fawns, selkies, and nymphs, among many others. All heading toward a soft light in the distance. It grew brighter as they neared. Lucenna waved a hand over her face, her image turning into that of the old crone.

Rawn shook his head. "King Dagden can see through such things, my lady. It is best to be truthful here. The fae cannot lie, and they certainly resent it in those who can. Be wary herein, but I suspect they know exactly who we are."

Lucenna let her glamor drop. The stone path brought them to a cluster of stands and tents where merchants sold a variety of wares. Cassiel glimpsed clothing made of vibrant fabrics, mirrors with moving pictures, decorated masks, glass flowers, and jewelry fashioned to look like dragons, spiders, or snakes. Rows upon rows of merchants selling hundreds of other items. He ignored their calls, having no interest in whatever they offered. The fae enchanted nearly everything they touched.

Further along the path, familiar fairies in brass armor greeted them. "Come," a female said. "She is waiting."

At the notion of finally seeing Dyna again, Cassiel and the others picked up the pace. The guardsmen brought them to a set of tents away from the others, where Princess Keena fluttered. She was dressed in a gown of deep blue flower petals with gold cuffs on her upper arms and neck. White paint adorned her face in dots and swirls.

Zev's fur gave away to flesh, and he stood, snarling at the tiny fairy. "Where is she?"

In a unified front, the guardsmen immediately shielded the princess and pointed their glaives at him. They were no bigger than his finger, but Cassiel had already seen how strong they were.

Keena looked Zev up and down as she giggled behind a hand. "Oh my."

Cassiel handed Zev a pair of trousers, which he quickly yanked on.

"Don't be troubled," she told them. "Dynalya awaits you at court."

"What is this?" Lucenna asked as a parade of fae danced by.

"This is merely the beginning of the festivities. The real revel is within the borough. There is to be a wedding."

"Yours?"

"Oh no, not mine." The fairy laughed like it was the most hilarious thing in the world. "This is not my court. I came to pay my respects to the bride and groom on behalf of my father. Princess Calixta, well, queen after tonight, is to marry King Dagden. Their union will combine the Court of the Moors and the Court of the Saxe Sea into one and bring peace to the east."

Her yellow wings glimmered as she flew around them. "King Dagden has extended you an invitation. But first, you must change and make yourselves presentable as my guests. You are not allowed in beforehand."

Cassiel exchanged a look with Zev. It was odd that a king they never met would invite them to a private event. But they were in dire need of washing. His clothes were beyond filthy. So were the others. They reeked of stagnant water and charred fish.

"Go on." Keena held out a hand at the two tents behind her. "Women on the left and men on the right. I'll wait to accompany you."

She flew away with her guardsmen and lingered nearby.

"This is good," Lucenna said. "They have invited us to court. This means we can meet the Druid."

"All you care about is the damn Druid," Cassiel said.

Zev frowned at her. "This is about reuniting with Dyna."

"Of course, it is, but my goals haven't changed."

Rawn said, "However, we arrived without payment, my lady."

"Then we'll win his favor another way. I'll not waste this opportunity." She turned away and slipped into the left tent.

Cassiel paused on the stone path. Dyna was close. He could feel her. The bond had grown stronger the day prior, and the ache in his knee had faded, letting him know she was healed. Why was he feeling her pain? Cassiel couldn't let himself think about it now. Princess Keena had kept her word, so he had to find the patience to believe they would see her soon.

"We find Dyna, and we leave," Cassiel said. "Tonight. Regardless if we meet the Druid or not."

The fae made him nervous. He didn't want to stay any longer than they needed to.

Zev and Rawn nodded. "Agreed."

Cassiel walked into the right tent after Rawn, and Zev followed. Three steaming baths made of brass waited inside. Each with a small bench of oils and soaps. Clothing neatly hung from the rafters. There were no privacy screens to be had. Well, then. Now certainly wasn't the time to be fastidious.

He stripped off his clothes, ignoring the others. As soon as Cassiel stepped into the hot water, he nearly groaned in content as it soothed his aching muscles. He heard a slosh as Zev and Rawn did the same. They scrubbed off the filth from the past three days. Steam filled the tent, mingling with the scent of fragrant soaps. If it had been any other day, Cassiel would have stayed in the bath until he became a prune. They quickly got out, dried off with the provided towels, and sorted through the clothing laid out for them. It was easy to tell which belonged to who.

The first set was a dark green brocade jacket and cream-colored trousers. On the right breast was the insignia of a Dynalya flower in open bloom. The sigil of Greenwood. Rawn frowned at it thoughtfully.

For Cassiel, they had laid out black pants, a loose black shirt, and a formal black jacket embroidered with silver threads. On the right breast was the insignia of Hilos: wings expanding from a crowned sword lit aflame. The clothing had a special fold on the back, as did the clothing of Celestials to accommodate wings. Some fae had wings, but for it to be embroidered with the sigil of his kingdom was unnerving.

Cassiel got dressed and slipped on his enchanted coat over his clothing.

For Zev, they'd chosen a deep blue tunic made of fine cotton and dark gray pants. No sigil, but a small embroidered crescent. Once they were finished, they made their way outside. Lucenna waited for them with the fairies in a gown of shimmering layers of deep purple wrapped around her lithe frame. It contrasted well with the lilac of her eyes. The outline of her diamond-studded medallion shone beneath the sheer layers.

"They won't allow us to bring our belongings," Lucenna informed them.

"For the safety of the king and his court, weapons and travel bags must remain here," Keena said, her slippered feet landing on Lucenna's shoulder. "We must take your horse to the guest stables as well. I give you my sworn word we will keep your belongings safe and waiting upon your return."

And because the fae swore nothing they couldn't keep, Rawn accepted on their behalf. Cassiel reluctantly handed over his pack. They each put their bags within Lucenna's enchanted satchel, which she spelled against anyone opening. Then one of the guards changed size in a sprinkling of gold, standing tall and imposing in his armor. Taking the reins from Rawn, he led Fair away with their belongings.

They followed the princess and her guardsmen into the borough. Drums beat in coordination with a flute and lute. Soon they came upon a row of immensely tall, pale white trees, forming a wide corridor made entirely by their trunks. Overhead, the canopy of branches wove together in a deliberate design. The music grew louder, combining with the hum of joyous voices.

"Hurry along now," Keena told them with a brilliant smile. "We're already late."

They followed her into the borough packed with fae. Most danced while others ate the delicacies piled on the tables decorated in moss, flowers, and dew. There were so many creatures. It was hard to differentiate them all. Some even looked human, or perhaps they were.

A woodland nymph spoke animatedly with a young woman in a white gossamer dress. Pin thin straps held it in place, leaving her shoulders bare. Sheer sleeves covered the bottom half of her arms, cinching at her wrists, and the flowing skirts ended above her knees. A crown of white flowers sat on her head. Brilliant red hair fell in soft waves around her shoulders.

Cassiel knew it was Dyna before she met his gaze. The floating lights overhead glinted in her emerald eyes. She was as beautiful as the rising dawn. Something swelled in his chest, lifting the heavy apprehension he'd been carrying. Her gaze crossed his face with a softness that eased the remaining weight off his chest. Trickling through the bond came Dyna's relief and a flash of what he thought might be happiness. His first instinct was to wrap his arms and wings around her, to physically feel that she was safe and whole.

Her health had tremendously improved since he'd last seen her. Nothing was out of place, but...

Cassiel glanced at the pale scars above her knee. The sight of it filled him with irritation and guilt. He should have gone to her, but his feet stayed rooted on the ground. That sliver of an opening closed, and Dyna's wall solidified in place, barricading her end again. He should never have told her how to block him. Weeks ago, he had wished to stop sensing her. Now that hardly anything came through the bond, he never knew what she was thinking.

Zev rushed past him and yanked her into an embrace. "Dyna, I was so worried about you."

"I'm perfectly well." She gave him a wavering smile. The one she offered Rawn and Lucenna was more genuine. Slipping away from Zev, she hugged them both.

"I'm glad you are back in good health, Lady Dyna."

"You look much better after nearly crossing Death's Gate," Lucenna said.

"Keena said I was sick."

"I had to send you with her. The fae have healing magic I don't possess. Zev and Cassiel hated it, naturally. They were beside themselves to get here."

Again, Dyna's gaze fleetingly met his, then Zev's. Her expression tightened. "The fjord ..."

Lucenna nodded, shooting a warning glance at Keena. "We will speak of it later. How are you feeling?"

"Better."

"I trust they treated you well, my lady," Rawn said.

Dyna smiled at the small fairy playing with the locks of her red hair. "Yes, Princess Keena has been most gracious."

"Of course, I have." She beamed. "Come, we must present ourselves."

Dyna grabbed Lucenna's arm and held her back, letting the fairies move ahead. She looked at the others, and they instinctively gathered around her.

"It wasn't all for nothing," Dyna whispered. Between them, she held open her palm where a single blue scale gleamed.

Lucenna's eyes widened. "You got one. How?"

"By some luck." Dyna frowned. "It's strange, really. I found the scale in my boot."

It was an odd coincidence, Cassiel agreed, but those creatures had swarmed them. They must have gotten close enough for a scale to catch on her somehow.

Dyna seemed to deliberate something, then said, "We should share it. A question for each of us."

"I only need to ask the Druid one thing," Lucenna said, nodding to them. "One of you should take the third question."

Rawn motioned at Cassiel and Zev. "I am of no concern. Choose among you two."

Cassiel worked his jaw, frowning at the scale. He had questions, but if Zev was going to ask on the matter he suspected, then that took precedence.

"There you are." Keena flew back to them, fluttering around Dyna. "Come along. The king is most excited to meet you."

Dyna passed Rawn the scale, and he slipped it within his pocket. They followed the fairy along a new path made of the softest grass spotted with white flowers. It brought them to a dais where well-armed sentries in iridescent black armor stood guard. The stairs of the dais were interwoven tree roots braided together, rising to a platform carved within an enormous tree. Upon twin thrones of bark and moss sat two of the most striking beings Cassiel had ever seen.

King Dagden, he assumed, looked at them with deep-set, garnet eyes. Not quite red, not quite amber, but with the warmth of autumn leaves. He had a long flowing mane of light gold locks touching on silver. On his head rested a crown of gilded antlers, flanked by a pair of pointed ears. Pale complexion, firm mouth set on a face that drew the awe of his court. A decorative plate of gold armor circled his shoulders and collar, leaving his muscular chest and torso bare. Gold bangles adorned his upper arms, offset by the scarlet robe circling his waist. His skin shimmered with a faint layer of gold dust under the fairy lights.

While he was a depiction of the earth, his bride could only be of water. Queen Calixta's hair was the aquamarine of the sea, flowing around her on invisible waves. Her eyes were the green of seaweed, with a dress in all the shades of the ocean. Her ears were long and webbed, same as her bare feet and delicate fingers. On her head sat a crown of coral and pearls. She had a dreadful beauty, cold like the ocean—deep and merciless.

The hobgoblin herald standing at the foot of the dais announced, "Presenting Princess Keenali Eveleigh of the Morphos Court and accompanying guests!"

Cassiel and the others took their bows with her.

"Royal Majesties of the Phantasmic Moors, it's an honor." Keena rose from her deep bow. "May the gods and the fates bless this union for as long as you reign. I hope the gifts I bring will please you."

Her tiny guards carried large crates and placed them at the foot of the stairs where other gifts had been piled. Mounds of gold, pearls the size of Cassiel's fists, gleaming jewels in every color, shimmering silks, and instruments gilded with gold.

"Oh, bring it here," Calixta said, wiggling her fingers in a come-hither motion. The guards opened the lid from a crate and brought her a small, frothy white vial with pink liquid inside. She popped off the glass cork and breathed in the contents with a satisfied smile. "The best perfume in all the land."

King Dagden tilted his head. "You honor us, Princess Keenali, to have come so far. Give your father my thanks for these gifts."

His garnet eyes moved to Dyna, then the others, with an impartial expression that wasn't the least excited. Swirling tattoos covered the left side of his neck along his shoulder to his chest. A geas, Cassiel realized. The fae like to seal their deals with such things. More swirly symbols marked King Dagden's fingers on his right hand. Queen Calixta bore the same on hers.

"Be this the company that sought refuge in my court?" he asked. "Introduce me to your rather curious companions."

"Ah, well, we recently met outside of the Wild Wood," Keena said. "I have not all of their names yet."

Rawn stepped forward. "Sire, if I may."

"Ah, now there is a face I recognize." King Dagden motioned him forward. "Rawn Norrlen of Greenwood, I have not seen you in—how long has it been? Ten years?"

"About so, sire. It pleases me to greet you once more. Allow me to introduce my companions: Lady Dynalya of North Star, Lady Lucenna of the Magos Empire, Zev of Lykos Peak, and Prince Cassiel of Hilos, third son of the High King."

Cassiel winced at his identity being revealed. Lucenna stared at him, and the courtiers quieted. As much as he hated the feeling of being exposed, there was no danger of them knowing who he was.

King Dagden's neutral expression shifted. "I sense the divinity flowing in your veins, Cassiel Soaraway. I know your father, though it has been some time since I saw Yoel last. This court adheres to the Accords. You need not be afeard, nor hide here, divine prince." He held out a hand, the indication clear of what he wanted.

Every instinct bracing, Cassiel inhaled a breath and slipped off his coat. The fae gasped at the sight of his black wings. The king and queen didn't seem shocked by his appearance, however. He had to assume they were really old for it not to startle them.

He bowed. "You are most gracious, sire."

"Do give my best to your father."

Cassiel's stomach clenched. He most likely wouldn't tell his father about this meeting. He had left Hilos under the guise that he would go to Hermon Ridge and stay with his uncle. If his father knew he was gallivanting about Urn, risking the exposure of Celestials, there would be repercussions.

"Forgive our intrusion. We were not aware we had arrived on such an auspicious day," Rawn continued. "We were traveling through your land when Lady Dyna became gravely ill. By some miracle, Princess Keena arrived precisely at the right moment. Thank you for allowing her to be brought here for healing. You have our utmost gratitude."

Pursing his mouth, King Dagden sat back on this throne. "Ah yes, *that one* said you lot would be coming. He was right, after all. I do hate it when he's right."

Rawn raised his eyebrows. "Pardon?"

"The Druid foresaw your arrival," Keena whispered to them.

Cassiel stiffened and exchanged looks with the others. Well, it certainly explained some things, like the fairy princess appearing at random and the prepared clothing.

"It so happens that we wish to meet the Druid, Your Majesty," Rawn said. "We seek his counsel."

Queen Calixta grinned, exposing a row of sharp teeth. "Interesting."

King Dagden crossed a leg over the other. "I trust you did not come to my wedding asking for favors without bearing gifts for my queen."

Cassiel expected nothing less. The fae always made deals. One could not receive without offering, ask without giving.

"My gift to Your Majesty would be a gown that changes color," Lucenna announced. "Whatever color you desire."

Calixta pursed her lips. "Impossible."

Lucenna waved a hand in a show of anticipation.

The sea fae twirled a lock of blue hair around her finger pensively. "Very well, let us see this miracle."

Lucenna snapped her fingers, and Calixta's gown changed to all shades of purple, then pink, and peach. She laughed gleefully as it shifted to yellow.

"Marvelous."

"A sorceress," King Dagden mused. "I have lived for many ages and seen more than you can imagine. But a sorceress, now there is a true rarity to behold, as is the laughter of my bride. To witness this is a gift enough." He glanced at the queen and his stern face softened ever so slightly. It faded when he looked at them again. "That dastardly Druid may be somewhere hereabouts. Search for him if you must, but I ask you to do so without disrupting the festivities or causing any harm to those in my court. This is my wedding after all."

"You're welcome to eat, drink, and gorge at your leisure," Calixta added, her sharp nails tapping on the arms of her throne. "Let it be known in kingdoms far and wide that King Dagden is a gracious host."

They bowed again and backed away from the dais for the herald to announce the next royal guests. A courtier greeted Keena, and she stayed behind, roped into conversation.

"How did you make her dress change colors?" Dyna asked Lucenna curiously.

Lucenna smirked. "A simple illusion. Nothing more."

Cassiel shook his head. Then it wasn't truly a dress that changed colors, only a spell that made it seem so. She sure enjoyed playing her tricks.

"It is perhaps best not to consume anything here," Rawn said under his breath to the girls. "Faerie food is as mischievous as the Folk, I have come to find. The wine especially. Drink it, and you may lose yourself."

That was the intention of wine. To lose all reason and care for nothing but keeping your cup filled. Celestials were not allowed to drink, but Cassiel had once, and he liked the fog. Until it led to waking half-naked with Dyna in his arms. As if she read his mind, her face flushed when they glanced at each other.

"Even with the king's welcome, be careful with your words in this place," Rawn added. "Take care not to offend or to enter any bargains. Leave no advantage against you."

Dyna and Lucenna nodded.

Cassiel stood near them as he watched the crowd. Glaring at the males who looked at them too closely. Why did the princess choose such revealing dresses? The thin layers hardly covered Dyna's skin. His eyes followed the trail of old jagged scars, starting from her right collarbone and descending to her chest. Lacy embellishments highlighted soft curves he had no business noticing. With each step she took, the gossamer skirts twirled around her thighs. A passing fawn with deer horns eyed her legs, and Cassiel stepped in his view, looming over him. The fawn scampered off.

"We should split up to look for the Druid," Lucenna said. "What does he look like, Rawn?"

"He..." Lord Norrlen blinked, frowning in confusion.

Zev crossed his arms. "Have you forgotten?"

"No. Pardon, it's been many years since we last spoke. Leoake is a stocky, hunched fellow with an ashy beard long enough to touch the ground, and he carries a gnarled staff."

"I'll accompany Dyna to look for him," Zev said.

"Accompany Lucenna," Dyna suggested instead, looking away.

"What—"

She shook her head, refusing to look at him, but Cassiel saw the tears gathering on her lashes.

"Dyna," Zev croaked, his voice ridden with guilt.

He reached for her, but she pulled her arm free and winced at the same time Cassiel did. He glanced at his unblemished wrist where he felt Zev's nails had scratched him. Nothing was there, but Dyna had a shallow cut on hers. A chill washed over him as he rubbed his fingers over the stinging spot on his wrist.

Devastation contorted Zev's features. "Dyna, I'm sorry. I—"

She pivoted on her heel and slipped into the crowd. He lowered his head.

"Watch her," Zev mumbled at Cassiel as he stalked in the opposite direction.

Lucenna smirked and crossed her arms. "Well, go on then, *Prince* Cassiel."

He glowered at her, annoyed that she knew who he truly was now.

Rawn sighed. "Very well, I will accompany Lady Lucenna if you will accompany—"

"Lord Norrlen," Cassiel cut him off. "In the future, if I wish to reveal who I am, that will be by my doing alone."

"Ah, forgive me. We cannot speak an untruth here, and the fae are bound by—"

"You will not speak for me again." Cassiel left them, not sure why a fog of anger followed him. He tugged on that invisible strand in his soul absentmindedly, letting it guide his steps to the beacon he didn't want to think about.

Yet he couldn't ignore the fact that he could feel Dyna's pain. His wrist faintly ached in the same spot she was cut. He didn't know what any of it meant, and he didn't want to. Cassiel glanced at a table with a fountain of gold wine spilling over the tiers.

He didn't want to think of anything at all.

CHAPTER 26

Fae danced to the hypnotic music in a wave of bodies as a tune played on lutes and drums. Dyna drank it all in, wanting to remember every detail. King Dagden's court was a blur of color. The air was heady with sweat, wine, a sweet woodland scent, and something ... carnal. Some had dressed in mere scraps of sheer fabric or nothing but gold and silver paint. Many had swirling symbols on some part of their body that looked much more permanent.

Every so often, pairs would break away from the dancing mass for a tryst among the shadowy trees. Dyna focused on the music. It drummed in her ears, beating against her heart, filling her head like a siren song. The atmosphere thrummed with a dark energy that moved around her.

Her jumbled thoughts of Zev and Cassiel loosened as the music lulled her into swaying with the rhythm, fading all her pressing worries. But a warning coursed through her mind, snapping her back to clarity. She shook her head, getting a hold of herself. There must be something in the air. A notion told her if she danced here, she wouldn't be able to stop.

Dyna stumbled away from the crowd to search for a face she knew and bumped into someone with a yelp. He grunted in surprise and turned, holding out his arms away from his beautiful jacket layered in silver leaves. Which was now drenched with golden faerie wine. It dripped from his hem and splattered his fine boots. An apology caught in her throat when she noticed his face.

He had the delicate beauty of the fae, like a gilded rose, too unnatural in a way that made her stare. Tan skin smoothed over high cheekbones, painted with silver swirls, ears rising to delicate points. His long hair was deep evergreen, like the color of summer trees. He kept it tied with a gold pin at the base of his neck, leaving the tail end to fall like a sleek stream over his shoulder.

"God of Urn, please forgive me." Dyna grabbed one end of her skirt and dabbed over the front of his jacket. Instead of the stiff, dry surface of leaves, his jacket was as soft as velvet beneath her palms—and thin enough to feel every ridge of his chest. She quickly stepped back.

The fae's glower switched to a sly smile. "No, please, *continue.*"

Taking her hand, he pressed it over the pulse of his heart and covered it with his palm. It was cool, the long slender fingers bedecked in rings. The twinkling lights overhead caught on his strange golden irises, ringed in black.

Dyna's cheeks flushed as hot as two coals in the night chill. "I'm terribly sorry for your jacket."

"And how will you repay me?"

Anything you wish had almost left her lips by some compulsive urge, but she quickly closed her mouth. Such words were a dangerous thing to offer here. The fae were tricksy folk. And she knew exactly what he intended with that question when his smile widened, as if he had been caught. *Careful with your words in this place.*

"I will wash your jacket and return it to you as clean as possible within my capability," she offered, slipping her hand free.

He clicked his tongue, giving her a playful pout. "Clever mortal. It's rarely one should wander into the Phantasmic Moors, even rarer that they should have a good head on their shoulders."

Dyna swallowed, a part of her doubting she would have been smart enough to be careful with her words if not for what happened in Landcaster. Von had used a truth spell on her to steal secrets from her mouth against her will, but the lesson remained.

"And who do I have the pleasure of acquainting with?"

She took the edges of her stained hem and dipped in a curtsey. "I am Dyna … of Azure," she added awkwardly.

A vague answer, but no less accurate.

"Charmed." He elegantly crossed an arm over his chest and bowed. "It's a pleasure beyond telling to meet you, Dynalya Astron."

Her reply stalled for a moment at the use of her full name. He must have been present at her introduction to the king and queen. If so, why ask? Unless it was to be polite. The fae were nothing if not proper.

"Azulo told me your name," he said before she could ask how he guessed.

Who?

Dyna yelped as something soft brushed against her ankles. A small blue fox with a diamond patch on its forehead looked up at her with vibrant, aqua blue eyes. It was the one she had met in the forest days ago. It twirled around her feet, then leaped into the fae's arms and nibbled on one of the acorn buttons of his jacket.

"Azulo told me the tale of a girl who freed him from a thorn bush," he said, scratching the fox's long ears.

Dyna smiled at the adorable creature. "Hello, sweet one."

The fox yipped.

"He is indebted to you."

"You understand him?"

"Of course. He's my familiar."

"Oh." She blinked, surprised to hear fae had familiars. "And may I know your name?"

He chuckled, turning to the table beside them. It was piled with custards and pies, with bowls full of colorful berries, and platters of slivered meat. After giving Azulo a piece of ham, the fox jumped down and darted under the table with its treat. Three fluffy tails poked out from beneath the tablecloth, wagging back and forth.

From one of the several decanters, the fae male poured more wine into his goblet. "I thought you were astute. You should know better than to ask a faerie his name."

"I didn't mean to ask for your true name," she said, fearing she had offended him again. That sort of information was more guarded than wealth.

"Surely." He took a drink, golden liquid glistening on his lips. "You may call me Aston. What has brought you to the Moors? Are you a guest of the bride?"

"I'm afraid not. My companions and I are searching for the Druid. I believe he is called Leoake?"

Aston's pointed nose curled ever so slightly. "Ah. *That one.*"

They didn't seem to like Leoake around here. Maybe he was an unpleasant fellow.

Regardless, she stepped closer to Aston, excited to at last have some lead. "Do you know where I may find him?"

Motioning for her to come closer, he leaned in conspiringly while looking out at the crowd. "The Druid is a wily one who enjoys hiding in plain sight," Aston whispered in her ear, his breath tickling her cheek. "Look close and keep your eyes peeled lest you miss him, clever mortal."

Pulling back, he popped a berry into his mouth and flashed his teeth in another grin at her frown. He was toying with her. She watched him take another drink of wine, and he offered her his cup.

Dyna shook her head. "I shouldn't."

"It won't harm you." Aston shrugged, wearing a mischievous smile. "It's no more than wine to the Folk, but for others, it makes them drunk with desires they wish to deny. You merely seek that which you secretly want, and wouldn't it be a wonderful thing to behold?"

His insistence only made her wary.

The golden liquid shimmered alluringly, but the thought of drinking the wine made her stomach pitch. She didn't want to acknowledge the nagging voice that had wormed its way in the center of her chest. The one suggesting that perhaps her feelings had been forged by the bond, and none of it was ever real. If she drank the wine, what would she go after?

Dyna lifted her chin. "Right now, I only desire to find Leoake."

"Suit yourself. Though, I wonder what a mortal could want from that old Druid."

"I must find him," Dyna grumbled. She searched the dark corners of the forest for any inconspicuous lurkers who may fit the look of an old man with a scraggly beard littered with moss and sticks, and perhaps a worn robe. But all the fae she'd seen were beautiful and extravagant. "I have questions I must ask him."

"A bit of advice—be careful what you wish for. The truth isn't always the answer you seek."

"Be that as it may, it's the truth I need."

Aston's smile widened, and he looked out to the crowd as the jaunty music ended. A fae woman made entirely of gold came through the throng carrying a golden harp. Ram horns protruded above her pointed ears, a long mane trailing on the ground behind her like a gleaming veil. Her sleek dress slipped around her dainty form like liquid gold. All eyes were on her, a hush falling over the revel.

She sat with the musicians and brought the harp on her lap. Her gilded eyes fell closed and her long fingers plucked the strings. A gentle melody wove through the trees. Her haunting voice harmonized in a spell-inducing lilt, filling Dyna's head.

Listen to me, my dearest
From the ashes came two seeds
The one of life and never endings
The other of death and foul deeds
Eat the right fruit and be made anew
Eat the rotten core for all to undo
Listen to me, my dearest
Snip the tie, and two will bleed
Seek truths within the carvings
For lies hide within those freed
Seek me in the land of glittering gold
Lose me in the shadows mighty hold
Listen to me, my dearest
Lend an ear ye fair maid
Fortune is lost to the shimmering sea
Let nothing else consume thee
Lest ye never return whole

Listen to me, my dearest
Lest ye never return whole

The haunting song ended, releasing Dyna from its trance. She shuddered at the odd crawl that skittered along her spine. The melody left something cold and clammy on her skin. Then the bard began another song about a king who begat a son born from cruelty and ice.

"Do you believe in fate?"

Dyna jumped, having forgotten the fae beside her. "I ... well, I'm not sure."

Aston laughed, and the twinkling lights reflected off his painted cheekbones as he leaned in close. "That is the question, isn't it? An interesting debate. The fates present us with a path of destiny, but do you reach it because of chance—" he cocked his head, grinning, "or choice?"

Was the future predetermined or brought about by action? If she believed in fate, was her father meant to die on that frozen hill? He chose to sacrifice his life for her, for North Star. She left her village to find the means to defeat the Shadow. She chose to come here.

"Perhaps the fates plan our destinies, but I believe we ultimately reach our futures by will," she said. "We have a say over our lives."

"If so, why seek the Druid to tell you of your fate?"

"Another seer has given a divination about my life," Dyna said. "I would like to ask if he could reveal its details so I may decide what to do next."

"I see." Aston stroked her crown of white flowers and loosely coiled a red lock of her hair around his finger. "Then shall we make a deal? I'll find the Druid for you in exchange for a favor of my choosing."

Dyna dug her nails into her palms at the tempting offer. She needed Leoake to discover who the rest of her Guardians were, but at what cost? Aston clearly was attempting to trap her in some agreement. His expression of mischief grew predatory at her wavering will when she didn't answer right away.

Leave no advantage against you.

"I—"

Awareness prickled down her spine, and she knew Cassiel was near before he yanked her from Aston. Her back collided against the hard wall of his chest as black wings enveloped her in a cocoon. Menace rolled off him in waves. His arm around her waist was like a brand, his palm hot against her ribs.

Protective.

Possessive.

Her face blazed with heat, and she attempted to pull away, but he held her firmly against him. Through the splayed feathers, she saw Aston's golden eyes widen. Not with fear, but with interest.

"Ah, the other end of the string." He gave a slight nod in greeting, wearing a conspiring smirk as he admired the sleek wings.

Cassiel's steely gaze pinned on the fae, threat oozing from his pores.

Aston grinned and took a step back. "Well, it seems I must be on my way. Before I do, I will leave this with you." He slipped off his jacket, exposing his bare skin to the night air.

Dyna's eyes snagged on the faintly glowing markings across his chest, shoulders, and arms in whirling vines and symbols. Geases. Markings of deals he had made with others and had yet to collect on. A quiver passed through her at the thought of almost becoming another mark on his body.

"I expect you to return it as good as new." Aston passed her the jacket, giving her a wink. "Protect your head, clever mortal. It's the only one you will get."

It sounded like advice—or maybe a threat.

Suppressing another shudder, she accepted his jacket and vowed to return it by tomorrow. Best not to get involved with the fae any more than necessary. Aston walked away, revealing the geas of a tree running from his neck to the end of his spine, the branches spanning the entire width of his back. As if he sensed Dyna's stare, he raised his hand in a lazy wave as he stepped into the throng and vanished from view.

Dyna didn't move, nor did Cassiel. His tension left her stiff, his warm breath raising the fine hairs on the back of her neck. But his touch, she missed. It was a secret craving uncovered by the grasp of his palm, and she didn't have it in her to move yet.

"I thought I warned you," he said, his tenor rough. "You must stay near, or you will be spirited away."

She shifted back, causing his hold to slip away. His wings flared behind him, the impressive wingspan twice as wide as he was tall, before tucking against his back. There was fire in the way he looked at her, the glow of heated metal in his stare. And gold stained his lips.

She noticed the empty goblet he held, and gasped. "You drank the wine?"

The beautiful angles of his face sharpened. "What of it?"

His irritation sat bitterly in her stomach, heating her skin. He was irate with her. With Aston and the dress, by the way he scowled at it. His attention snapped to a pair of male fae ogling her. One look at Cassiel made their complexions pale, and they took an unsteady step in retreat.

"Your pardon," one said, with a weak clearing of his throat, and they made a quick escape.

A rough sound rolled in Cassiel's throat, and his cool gaze fixed on her again.

"Why must you wear this wretched thing?" He brushed a finger over the thin dress strap, sending goosebumps down her arms. His jaw clenched as his gazed slowly roved over her exposed skin.

She'd never seen that look on his face before. Anger mixed with something else that burned in his eyes, wide pupils nearly swallowing the silver. He leaned in so dangerously close, his breath coated her lips. It smelled of sweet faerie wine and ... desire. Her throat bobbed, a rush swooping through her.

"Why," he asked in a low rumble, "must you tempt me?"

Her heart raced in her chest. "Prince Cassiel, you're not yourself."

It was the fairy wine, nothing more. But Aston's words taunted her. *It's no more than wine to the Folk, but for others, it makes them drunk with desires they wish to deny.*

His expression tightened. "That is my title, but when you say it with such formality, it sounds like a barb."

"It's not."

It was a separation to remind herself of who he was. They were two different people from different societies and ranks. She had become too comfortable with him beyond what was appropriate. She had her place, and he had his.

Dyna pushed past him, heading away from the revelry. Which direction had the others gone? Perhaps they had better luck. At least those were the thoughts she forced into her head.

"Please." The plea in his voice was so incredibly soft. Cassiel took her wrist and his thumb faintly caressed the scratch there, making it throb. "Do not run from me."

"I wasn't the one who ran first."

He had been the one to push her away. The one to construct his wall.

His gaze held her captive as he closed the distance between them. For every step he took, she retreated one. He kept coming until her back pressed against something firm and rough. Dyna's nails dug into the bark of a tree.

Cassiel's stare bore into her, and she did her best to look anywhere else but him. "I did not run."

As he stepped closer, his feathers lightly caressed her upper arms, firing tingles all over her body. His warm breath wafted over her skin, and her mind stalled, air locking in her lungs. Those silver eyes gleamed—dilated and pronounced in the faerie lights. Spelled by some magic.

"That's a lie," she whispered. He was so close. As close as he was that day on the cliff.

Cassiel observed her, considering. Deciding. He looked at her the same way he had when his lips grazed hers in a promised kiss that didn't come to pass. She should move, but she couldn't look away. His gaze dropped to her mouth, and the forest spun. A long moment passed where he didn't move, where she didn't breathe—then he leaned down. Dyna gasped, and he froze. For a second, his control slipped on his side of the bond, and she was hit with chaos and want and war.

"You call me a liar, but was it not you who lied?" Cassiel murmured. "I recall your promise not to turn your back on me."

Dyna tried to answer, but only a shallow breath left her mouth. She had meant the promise when she said it, and meant it even now. But she couldn't talk to him like this. Not when he looked at her as if he would kiss her at any moment, and when she thought she might want him to. Her body tensed with anticipation as his lashes lowered, heart trembling at the base of her throat.

Cassiel inched closer, bringing his body a hairsbreadth from hers, and her breath caught when his head dipped low. His soft lips brushed against her earlobe, sending a current of shivers across her flushed skin. "Do you hate me, Dyna? Or do you hate the bond that makes you mine?"

Her heart pounded so hard she could hardly breathe. He lifted her chin, and fire danced along her skin. His ambrosial musk fell over her and she leaned into his touch, a part of her not able to deny his pull. Dyna read the intent in his hooded eyes as he drew her mouth to his. A wild breath rushed through her chest—then panic. She tore her hand from his grasp and slapped him.

Shock flashed across his face.

The pink imprint of her hand marked his cheek and her own stung as if she'd struck herself. It lasted for a fleeting moment before fading with the mark. Gods, she hadn't meant to hit him. It was an instinctual reaction. She had imagined kissing him before, desired for it, but not like this. She didn't want a kiss tainted by the taste of fairy wine and anger.

"Good," Cassiel said, the one word sounding coarse and thick. All heat left his expression as it fell to resignation. "Hate me."

His answer was a surrender, the indifference in his tone the end of the war. Yet why did she feel like the one who lost? Tears burning in her eyes, she couldn't do anything but stand there, too jumbled to form a reply. Something was cracking inside of her. Dyna wrapped her arms around herself, afraid she would shatter.

Rawn approached warily, his gaze flickering between the two of them. "Is everything all right, my lady?"

Cassiel moved back, taking his warmth with him. "I leave her in your care, Lord Norrlen."

He walked away and leaped into the sky, his wings carrying him toward the glimmering stars. Dyna watched him go, her heart racing and face burning.

Stupid Celestial.

The thousands of things she should have said only occurred to her when he was already gone. There was nothing else to do but bottle each one and lock them away in her heart.

CHAPTER 27

Zev

The music filled Zev's head, and the drums beat in his ears. Voices all around swarmed together in a meaningless hum. There were too many sounds. Too many smells. The earthy scent of the forest mixed with the aroma of roasted meat, wine, and something heady filtrating through the court. It made his head spin and churned his stomach. But he couldn't get the sad look on Dyna's face out of his mind.

She knows of your cowardice, the Madness taunted, cackling in delight. *Of your weakness and plight.*

He growled.

Sad, sad, beastie. Not even death can you accomplish. Are you not tired? Rest.

He would rest when he was beneath the ground.

Something prickled against his senses, and Zev met the gaze of a dainty fae female. Long black hair decorated with beads and silver strands streamed around her pale face, her irises so red they looked like pools of blood beneath the faerie lights. Her full ruby red lips curved in a slow smile. He stiffened when her bare feet crossed the mossy carpet for him in a slow, sensual gait. Her dress was a sheer green thing with a long, thin train falling in the front and back, leaving every curve and swell exposed.

Zev swallowed. Hard. All mad thoughts fell silent. His veins rushed with a flash of heat, and every muscle in his body tightened as he forced himself to look away from her body and focus on her face. It was then that he finally noticed the carnal haze that permeated the air. The revel had turned a new tide. He thought of leaving to find the others, but the fae's scarlet gaze held him captivated. Her seductive smile grew wider when she came to a stop in front of him, revealing a tiny pair of fangs.

He cleared his throat. "Ah, good ... evening?"

She giggled, and the sound was the trilling of a creek. Her hand trailed along his arm, the fingers ending in sharp black talons. He followed their journey as she traced the groove of every muscle, the scrape of her nail leaving gooseflesh in its wake. She stepped closer and tilted her head in what could only be an invitation. He inhaled a breath, and more heat dipped to his center. She smelled like a flowering meadow and sweet arousal. But beneath it lurked the scent of something else he had been searching for.

She grabbed a goblet off the table at his back and brought it to his lips. She looked at him from beyond the rim with a smile that was a honeyed promise. Firelight gleamed on her soft cheeks, flushed with warmth, haloing around her head. A sudden urge to touch her burned through him, but he didn't dare. The females of Lykos Peak never approached him. He was accustomed to disgust, not desire. But he was a full-grown unmated male, and at the moment, she was exuding great interest.

His wolf bristled with wariness, but also with curiosity. The faerie was beautiful. Deadly. He had the sense she was flame incarnate, but he didn't mind getting a little burned. Zev's wolf released a low rumbling growl in agreement as he held her eyes and lifted the goblet.

The gold liquid inside sparkled, alluring him with a fruity fragrance.

Don't drink, the Madness hissed.

Zev smiled. He tipped back his head and drank the wine in one swallow. The warm liquid slid down his throat and pooled in his stomach, sending a hazy fog through his head. Magic floated through his veins with ecstasy, and the world swayed in soft waves. There was only one wish on his mind, and the one to provide it stood in front of him.

The faerie laid a delicate hand on his arm and drew him into a dance. Her soft form rocked to the hypnotic music, pressing into him in sinful ways he would never protest. He held her to him, leaving his hands to trail to the curve of her small waist. She smiled encouragingly and stood on her toes to wrap her arms around his shoulders. Her lips brushed over his collarbone, pressing her breast against his chest. A rumble of content vibrated in his throat, and he almost shredded her flimsy dress with his claws.

It startled him at first, at the animalistic need to take her then and there. He shook his head to clear it. The wine was making him devious. As if she sensed it, her mouth curved in a wicked smile. They danced and danced until his legs were limp and they glistened with sweat. Her small hand slid in his and she led him into the shadowy trees, away from the music and lights. He stumbled after her into a clearing of flowers and moss glittering in the moonlight.

His wolf snarled at him to turn back, but Zev shut him out. He grabbed the faerie by the waist and flipped her around. She giggled as he brought her to the moss bedding below. Wrapping her arms around his neck, she pressed her body against his. Her sharp nails raked across his back slowly, sending a pleasing punishment to his skin. He wanted to bask in the feel of her and what she did to his body. He needed it after feeling nothing but agony and rage for years.

Her neck arched back as he kissed the swell of her throat. He latched onto her beating pulse, tasting her soft skin. She grasped his shirt and pulled it off over his head. Her red eyes widened as they took in the ugly scars marring his body. A flash of pity crossed her face, but she captured his lips in a deep kiss that took all his focus. He held still, letting her guide him in a new dance of their mouths.

Could the faerie girl speak, or had she chosen not to? Did she know exactly what he had needed all along?

"I feel I should—" he said between their urgent kisses. "—ask for your name."

She pulled herself onto his lap and her light voice surprised him when she answered, "Richël."

Her legs wrapped around his waist. His breath came out in rapid, shallow pants as she rocked against him, sending fire through every nerve. Zev wove his fingers through her silken hair, holding the back of her head as he fitted her mouth in his. Her sharp teeth scraped against his bottom lip, eliciting a satisfying sting.

"I know what you want." He pressed the words against her cheek. "Take it."

Richël paused, a new, hungry gleam sharpening her features. "Do you know what you ask, wolf?"

"I give it freely." Zev drew her mouth to his in a deep, slow kiss. "Take it all."

Richël's eyes glowed softly in the night as she studied him. Perhaps searching for any hesitation, but he had none. He was ready.

With a strength he didn't expect, she rolled him onto his back and straddled him. The moonlight shone over her pale skin as she let the sleeves of her sheer dress fall. A heavy breath shuddered through him as he admired every soft curve of bare skin. Her slender fingers tugged at the ties of his trousers, but he caught her arm.

"No." His baser instincts ached to go further, but that's not what he came for.

Richël's head tilted questioningly, and nodded at whatever she saw on his face. Her hair curtained around him, briefly buffering the brisk air as she kissed his forehead gently, almost tenderly. Again, that recognizable metallic scent of sour blood reached him, hidden beneath the heady arousal. The smell of endings, decay, and the darkness beyond.

She smelled of death.

Richël took his face and pressed her mouth to his, soft and sweet, as if they were merely lovers in the woods. Her satin lips trailed over his jaw and neck as her hips continued rolling against him, enveloping him with her heat. Every taut inch of his body burned with need. Zev dug his fingers into her hip to resist the urge. Richël pried his hand free and cupped it on her breast. The other she lifted to her mouth. His next inhale of air stalled in his lungs.

Holding his gaze, she kissed his wrist, then gently drew her fingernail across it. Warm liquid spilled down his arm in dark red trails. She lapped it up with a swipe of her tongue, and her moan vibrated against his pulse, sending a heated flush through him.

The flash of Richël's fangs glinted in the moonlight as she latched onto his wrist. After the initial sting, it wasn't painful. Though he was sure she could have made it so. Her soft moans as she drank were a symphony, rippling a wave of pleasure that liquified his body, rendering all else meaningless. The faint howl of fury from his wolf and the Madness faded along with every fault weighing on his soul. He let it all go. Strength faded as his mind grew foggy, life leaving him with every tug against his vein. Zev slid his eyes closed, satisfied with this way of ending. With a passionate embrace and a scorching kiss.

There was no thought. No more pain. Nothing but her sweet lips.

"Get your nasty face off him, wretched slag," a voice hissed.

Light blazed behind his eyelids, and Richël let out a furious screech as something wrenched her off him. Zev blinked dazedly, a purple glow bleeding through his blackening vision. He tried to move, but his body was a sack of congealed matter. It took every ounce of strength to turn his head.

The faerie stood half-naked across the clearing; her face contorted with rage. She faced off with another fierce woman with a cascade of white hair.

Richël's fingers curled into claws, her lips glistening red. She bared her fangs in a feral snarl. "He's mine."

The glow in Lucenna's eyes flashed brighter as violet light ignited over her hands, spiraling up her arms. "Go find your meal somewhere else."

"Mine!" Richël launched at her with frightening speed.

Zev's useless body jerked, instinct flaring to protect Lucenna. But she hurled a purple sphere of fire at Richël, and Zev ducked from the explosion of light. Her scream echoed through the forest and faded into the night. He moaned, his aching head ringing.

Boots shifted over the ground until Lucenna appeared in his dizzying sight. Her cool eyes narrowed on him. "What were you doing?"

"I think you can imagine," Zev grunted, well aware of his bare chest and his trousers hanging half undone on his hips.

Lucenna's cheeks darkened, but she held her glare. "Do you have any idea what you were kissing? Why didn't you fight her off?"

"Why does it matter?" Zev gritted his teeth, his body throbbing painfully.

He groaned and lifted a limp hand to his face, finally feeling some strength return. Except for the two puncture wounds on his wrist, everything was intact.

"You had a nightwalker on your face, you fool. That thing was feeding on your blood."

"I know. I allowed it."

"By the gods, have you gone mad?"

Yes, yes, he had.

"You saved my life," he said instead. It belonged to her now, if she wanted it. Then he'd have some purpose. "Shall I call you master or mistress?"

Lucenna scowled, her lilac eyes flashing. "I will not take you as my slave, Zev."

Shame fell over him, and it had nothing to do with the state of his appearance. He knew better than to suggest that to her, not after what the women endured in Magos.

"Then don't interfere in my business." He used whatever might he could muster to stand, and his legs wobbled. Lucenna took his arm, steadying him. "What happened to Richël?"

"Who?"

"The nightwalker."

Lucenna rolled her eyes. "She's gone."

Zev froze as the remaining blood left in him ran cold. "You killed her?"

"She attacked, so did I."

Guilt sank in his stomach like a pile of stones as the Madness snickered. *Poor beastie. You led the little fae to her death, and you've doomed the sorceress, too. Everyone around you continues to perish, and you're left to watch.*

Pushing Lucenna behind him, Zev searched the trees as his heart raced. They had to leave. Now.

"What is it?"

"We're guests here," he growled. "Invited to a wedding where you have killed a member of the court."

Lucenna inhaled sharply and her heartbeat quickened. Zev backed towards the revel, keeping her shielded. A branch snapped, and the wind changed with the approach of fresh scents. It seemed he might get his desire after all.

CHAPTER 28

Something eerie and violent clung to the night air, thrumming in Lucenna's veins. Zev's reflective eyes gleamed in the dark as he studied the trees, a forceful reminder of what he truly was. His wolf rose beneath the surface at whatever threat he must have sensed in the wood. She filled her hands with magic, and he crouched in front of her protectively, releasing a snarl so vicious it promised death to whoever came forth.

There was movement in the shadows of the trees. The king's guard marched forward, their armor catching in the moonlight. They withdrew their swords as one. Ten against two, Lucenna liked those odds—until a cluster of arrows burst from the trees and pierced the ground at their feet.

Damn.

She eyed the branches, but the archers were cloaked in the darkness.

A goblin guard with a long, beak-like nose stepped forward. "You have violated the peace in the Moors. Now you must come with us."

"And if we don't?" the question rumbled in Zev's chest.

Even Lucenna knew that was a bad idea. She extinguished her magic. "It's all right. We will explain to King Dagden what occurred here."

They followed the guards through the woods and into the borough. The music stopped playing, and the court watched them pass, whispering and tittering among themselves. A procession of fae followed as the guards brought them before the dais once more. King Dagden lounged in his throne, one leg crossed over the other, as he balanced his crown of antlers on his foot. Queen Calixta sat beside him. Courtiers huddled around her throne, Princess Keena fluttering among them.

Rawn and Dyna were already there, looking as nervous as Lucenna felt. Zev moved to Dyna's side.

King Dagden eyed them as he took a drink from his goblet. "Well, well, it appears I have invited murderers into my court."

Lucenna opened her mouth to answer, but Rawn slightly shook his head.

"Who was killed?" Calixta asked nonchalantly as she played with a lock of ocean-blue hair. They didn't truly seem to care, so why the fuss?

"A nightwalker, Your Majesty," answered the goblin guard. "Demolished by her sorcery."

"Our sister. She killed Richël!"

A group of scantily clad fae with red eyes screeched and wailed. They sprang forward, but the king's guard held them at bay.

"Give her to us, my king," cried the one with short, dark purple hair. Her glistening red eyes fixed on Lucenna as they attempted to claw their way to her. "We demand retribution for our sister."

King Dagden raised a hand lazily, silencing them. "Bring forth the body, Gremly."

The goblin guard replied, "We didn't find a body, sire. Nothing left of her but bones and ash."

The nightwalkers shrieked so loudly Zev winced.

"Ash?" King Dagden's eyes widened as they fixed on Lucenna. He leaped to his feet and wildly searched the crowd, his forgotten crown tumbling down the steps. "Where is the Druid? Where is that conniving rat? Find him, Gremly. Drag him here by his ears if you have to."

Gremly bowed and marched off with a handful of guards. Lucenna met Dyna's startled gaze. What did the Druid have to do with this?

Calixta tittered behind a hand. "Oh, I doubt you will find that one now."

The king dropped onto his throne with a scowl. He glared at Lucenna and the others. "I should never have welcomed you here."

"And what will you do with them, my great wise king?" his queen asked with a pout. "A great transgression has been committed against your court."

"I'm sure there is an explanation, sire," Rawn said. "If you would allow Lady Lucenna a moment to explain."

"Speak, then."

She raised her chin. "It was self-defense. The nightwalker attacked Zev, and I stopped her."

Richël's sisters hissed, baring their fangs.

The one with purple hair gave Zev a sharp smile. "We don't feed without permission in the Moors. The male must have granted it."

"You mean your sister rendered him an idiot with her seductions," Lucenna snapped.

Zev frowned but didn't argue. Lucenna would slap him this instant if he so much as agreed with them. She saved him, and now they were in this mess.

The queen leaned forward, her long nails clicking against the arms of her throne. "What shall we do with them, then? The sorceress defended her companion, but one of ours is dead. Shall we let her go, or shall we make her pay?"

"Pay!" the fae hooted in unison.

Calixta's lips parted in a sharp smile, exposing her pointed teeth. "And will she pay with blood or boon?"

"Blood. Blood. Blood." The wild chant beat against Lucenna like a drum.

The fae pressed forward, hunger and eagerness shining on their wild faces. Gone was the mystic haze and whimsical music. The fairy lights vanished, and the flowers no longer bloomed. Heady bloodlust permeated the air.

Essence roiled in Lucenna's veins as her palms lit with power. Zev became a blur of fur, claws, and glistening teeth.

"Stay behind me," Rawn said, bracing himself.

Dyna cupped her hands, and the center glowed faint green.

"I'll make an opening, and you run," Lucenna told her. "Run and don't look back."

"No." Dyna shook her head. "I'm not leaving you."

A burst of wind and a flash of black whipped through the borough as something slammed into the ground, the vibration running up Lucenna's legs.

Cassiel.

His large wings twisted, throwing back those who had gotten too close. His coat flared open with a flare of blinding white, and a tremendous heat pressed against her. The fae cried out, leaping back from the sword of divine flame. It blazed in their startled faces smeared with paint.

"Take another step forward," Cassiel said, his voice laced with quiet wrath, "and I will cut you down."

King Dagden's face darkened. "You dare bring weapons here?"

"You truly believed I would allow you to disarm me? Evidently, my caution was warranted. You forget, in the agreement of the Accords, every mystical kingdom is to extend welcome to my kind and those in our party. Yet there is no welcome here."

"I forget nothing, Prince Cassiel. The sorceress slew a member of my court. Rectification is to be had by the family."

His eyes cut to her, wide and furious. "Then it shall be had."

The purple-haired nightwalker pointed a sharp fingernail at Lucenna. "I will take you as our boon, and we will seal it with a geas. To be released after one hundred years of service is complete or until you are no more."

"I refuse," she hissed.

"Then you will die," the queen said, straightening her skirts as they transformed into the green of seaweed. "Only boon or blood will pay for your crime."

Clenching her fists, Lucenna considered spelling her clothes to look like mud instead.

"My lady," Rawn called to the nightwalker. He stepped forward and took her hand, bowing. She simpered, giggling to her sisters. "Please, see reason. It is not feasible to ask her to serve for a century when her years are not as plenty as ours. Could she offer something else to ease the passing of Lady Richël? Her most prized possession, perhaps?"

No, not that. Lucenna would sooner burn down the borough than relinquish her medallion.

"Lord Norrlen," she warned.

"Yes." The nightwalker's sharp smile returned. "I'll take your prized treasure. Give it to me."

"Never."

Rawn looked at her somberly. "Forgive me."

Her hands crackled with electricity. If he thought she would—

Lord Norrlen reached into the folds of his clothes and held out his hand. The pearlescent blue scale gleamed on his palm. A choked gasp lodged in Lucenna's throat. The nightwalker snatched the scale in her claws and cackled gleefully. Something splintered inside of Lucenna's chest, some line of hope or sanity.

She dropped her hands, and her spells fizzled to nothing. She stared at the ground, seeing the faces of every sorceress suffering in the Magos Empire. So close. She had been so close to saving them. The scale she worked so hard to get, every drop of blood she had shed, every moment she had nearly died, the magic she lost—all of it rendered meaningless. Everything she had carefully planned vanished.

Lucenna's eyes welled as her mother's face surfaced in her mind.

The nightwalkers delighted in her misery, dancing around her as they laughed, mocking the tears threatening to fall. They didn't care about the scale, only that they took something she wanted.

"It is done," Cassiel said.

King Dagden nodded. "So it is. Now that all is well between us, you are welcome to stay the night if you so wish."

"Thank you, but I am disinclined to accept the invitation," Cassiel said coolly. He sheathed his sword and turned away. "We are leaving."

He motioned at Zev to lead the way. Someone took Lucenna's arm and gently pulled her along.

"Prince Cassiel," King Dagden called, his tone cautious. "No violation against the Accords has occurred."

But of course. Who would want Hilos and the Four Celestial Realms as an enemy?

"A truth to be said once my companions and I safely leave your court, Great King." Cassiel tilted his head in a curt bow. "I shall endeavor to pass on your greetings to my father. He will be interested to hear of tonight's events, I'm sure."

King Dagden stiffened at the underlying warning. So the Celestial knew how to act like a prince after all. If Lucenna hadn't been reeling, she might have laughed.

The King of the Wild Fae said no more, and the guards moved back at some signal. The grip on Lucenna gently tugged her again, leading her through the borough. No one attempted to stop them. They crossed the hall of trees where the lights once again glowed, and eventually, the path of moss and stone gave way to dirt as they entered the Wild Wood. The graying sky leaked on the horizon when they reached the end. All dreamlike signs of the Moors faded with the dawn. She stood at the tree line in a daze. What was she to do now?

"Forgive me, my lady," Rawn said, releasing his hold on her. "It was the only thing that occurred to me at that moment."

"Yes, what a grand plan it was." A bitter laugh slipped out of her. "Thank you, Lord Norrlen, for giving away the one thing you had no right to give. Now every sorceress in the Magos Empire is doomed."

CHAPTER 29

Lucenna

Lucenna wasn't one to be dramatic, but she had no other way of describing what would befall her people now. Gods, she needed to lie down. But her bag and all her belongings were in the possession of the fairies. She cursed and paced back and forth. Maybe it would be better to destroy something instead. The others watched her warily, following her clipped pace.

"You don't know what this means. I needed that scale." Lucenna thrust out her hand and released a burst of pent-up blast with a frustrated scream. Purple scorched through the air.

"You should have thought of that before killing someone," Cassiel said coolly. "You attack first and think second. This is the result."

"Rawn saved us, Lucenna," Dyna added. "They were ready to end us. It had to be done." She faced Zev. "What happened?"

He groaned and rubbed his face. "Ill-conceived notions led by a cup of fairy wine."

Lucenna smirked. "If that's what you want to call it, wolf. Truth be told, this is all your doing."

He growled. "You shouldn't have interfered."

"Then you would be dead right now."

"I do not follow," Cassiel interjected. "What led to this?"

"Zev thought kissing a nightwalker would be a splendid way to pass the evening." Lucenna crossed her arms, glaring at him. "She nearly killed him too, if I hadn't arrived. Shall I tell them what you told me?"

Fur rippled across his arms as his eyes flashed yellow. "That is none of your business, Lucenna."

He was mad. Good. She wanted to make him mad. Wanted an excuse to unleash the power boiling inside her.

"A nightwalker?" Dyna's expression tightened as she searched his face. "Zev."

He turned away, and his clothes fell as he shifted. The large wolf stalked away into the clearing, heading for the nearby stream. *Coward.*

Lucenna dropped to the ground and buried her face in her hands. Maybe if she went back to the fjord, she could get another scale. The risk may be less now with more than half of those creatures gone.

She must have been speaking aloud because Dyna said, "Even if we get another scale, we need the Druid. I had no luck finding him. Did any of you?"

Lucenna already knew the answer. Before she had seen Zev being led away by the half-naked faerie, she had spent the night searching for the old Druid or anyone that matched his description. Apparently, he liked to stay out of view.

"Why do you need the scale?" Cassiel asked.

Lucenna glared at him. "I have stayed out of your matters, prince. Stay out of mine."

"I should like to know what you risked our lives for."

"As if you have not risked mine."

"You toss out spells carelessly," he pressed on. "You strike and kill and destroy without thought."

"My magic saved us. It saved you and Dyna and Zev." She got to her feet. "It's my power to wield, and I'll not apologize for it. Not when there are thousands of sorceresses like me who cannot."

Electricity crackled over her arms. She had no control over it, and she didn't care. She held Cassiel's hard gaze because she wanted him to understand. To see.

"I fight with my power because it's my right. A right the women of the Magos Empire are denied every day."

The scowl faded from his face. He glanced at Dyna, and she nodded.

"You are forbidden to use magic?" Rawn asked.

"By your manner, you've lived at least two centuries. In all these years, have you ever met a sorceress?" Lucenna watched his pensive eyes widen at the realization that he hadn't. "Women are never allowed to leave the Magos Empire, and outsiders are never allowed in. It's closed off from the rest of Urn to maintain the patriarchy that it's established on. The Mage Code of Law."

Why was she telling them this? She was spilling mage secrets, but she wanted them to know. The world knew nothing about what went on behind the walls of her home, and it infuriated her.

Rawn's eyebrows knitted together. "I am unfamiliar with this law."

"As am I," Cassiel said.

A vivid purple mist danced on Lucenna's palm. "The Mage Code is a regulation that oppresses sorceresses. It binds us, imprisons us. Our lives and our power belong to our fathers from the moment we're born. We have no rights, and we have no freedom. All of our moves are monitored and all of our decisions are made. We must never learn spells or try to leave the empire. The Archmage will execute any who dare."

There was no comment. Their breathing sounded loud in the shocked silence.

"It's done by siphoning," Lucenna continued. "Our Essence is as vital to us as air. Without it, we die. It's the source of magic and the one thing every mage wants. They take it from their wives and daughters, merging it with their own to gain more power. Girls that have little power are sold in marriage before their first courses. Most of them die—from rape or in childbirth."

Her throat caught with the tightness that gripped her chest. She had seen it happen many times in the empire, and she had been powerless to stop it.

The silence was so heavy Lucenna made herself look up. There was no mistaking the sincere dismay Rawn expressed. Cassiel's expression hardened with sullen anger. Zev watched her from a distance, his ferocious yellow eyes luminous in the night.

Rawn pressed his fingers against his eyelids. "The mages I met in Greenwood had been kind. I am ashamed to have admired them. Their atrocities are unbeknownst to the rest of Urn."

"Why would they speak of it?" Cassiel said. "They know the rest of the world would condemn them for it."

"It's awful," Dyna said softly.

"Are any so fortunate to escape?" the elf asked quietly.

Lucenna sighed. "Of course, but the Enforcers capture most. Their sole purpose is to seize refugee sorceresses and return them to Magos, where they are publicly executed in the capital to discourage others from doing so. It offends mages that we would dare to aspire for independence. We are nothing more than property to them."

"But not all mages can possibly believe that," Dyna said. "Azeran didn't believe that."

Lucenna nodded, feeling a mixture of admiration and sadness. "No, he did not."

"Azeran did form a rebellion against the Archmage that led to civil war," Dyna told Cassiel and Rawn. "That much is true. But the War of the Guilds wasn't for his gain of power. It was for freedom."

"When he ascended as head of the Lunar Guild, he fell in love with a Sun Guild sorceress and she with him," Lucenna said. "But it is against the Mage Code to marry outside of our guilds. They eloped, and the Archmage had them hunted down. He forced Azeran to watch his wife be siphoned."

Cassiel looked away, and Lord Norrlen lowered his head.

"And that led to war," Cassiel said.

Lucenna nodded. "Azeran found he wasn't the only one who wished to dismantle the Mage Code. Reyes Fuego, Head of the Sun Guild, joined his rebellion. Along with the thousands of mages in their guilds who wanted to fight for their families."

"The Earth Guild remained in league with the Archmage," Dyna said, standing beside her. "The war tore through the empire. Many died. With the Sun and the Moon against the Earth, Azeran had the advantage. They were winning, but..."

Lucenna clenched her fists. "But Andrez betrayed him."

Dyna sighed, glancing at her sympathetically. "He was Azeran's brother."

Electrical currents seeped through Lucenna's taut fingers. The Magos Empire hailed him as a hero. They built monuments in his memory and consecrated his name.

"The War of the Guilds was lost, but the Lūna Medallion saved them," Dyna continued, motioning at where it hung from Lucenna's neck. "The Moonstone it once contained had the power to open portals. With it, Azeran and Reyes escaped the empire with as many mages and sorceresses as they could take. Each went their separate ways to establish the sanctuaries: The North Star Village in the southeast of Azure and the Sōl Aubade Village in the north-west of the United Crown."

The news sent a soft shiver through Lucenna. Most considered the existence of the sanctuaries as a legend. No one knew where they had settled and she never would have guessed they remained in Urn.

The early dawn grew cold with the passing wind. Invoking a bouquet of purple flames, Lucenna placed it between them on the ground. The enchanted campfire exuded soothing warmth, casting a hue on the grim faces of her audience. Zev didn't join them, but he lay at a distance and she knew he was listening.

"The Archmage did not pursue them?" Lord Norrlen asked.

Dyna shook her head. "Azeran warded the sanctuaries from outsiders. They were free."

The back of Lucenna's eyes stung from the bitter envy but also joy that they succeeded in at least that. "Freedom is but a dream in Magos. The Archmage ruling now is more ruthless than his predecessors."

"The Enforcers that came for you," Lord Norrlen started. "They said any who should interfere in your capture risked war. Why would the Archmage go to such lengths to obtain you?"

Lucenna gritted her teeth, and purple electricity coiled around her body. "Because my Essence is rare, and the most sought after in Magos."

Dyna smiled. "You're a Transcendent."

Lucenna stared at her, surprised that she knew about that as well. How much had she learned from Azeran's journals? "Yes, I am..."

"I realized it the first time I saw you fight against the Enforcers."

Cassiel's brow furrowed. "What is a Transcendent?"

"It's those born with the Essence to transcend the elements of all three guilds," Lucenna said. "That ability is extremely rare and highly valued, for it can be siphoned or passed on by birth. Transcendent newborn girls are sent to live in Castle Ophyr. They are to one day marry into the royal family and provide the next generation of rulers with the ability to transcend."

Rawn's eyebrows rose high. "That is why the Archmage wants you."

"That part I understand," Cassiel said, his jaw clenching. "The makings of thrones and power is a game rulers play to make sure they keep it. Who are you to marry?"

Lucenna twisted the pink gemstone around her finger. The ring was a tiny shackle that she couldn't bring herself to part with. It was the embodiment of the future decided for her at birth, but it also held a pledge that had embedded in her heart. A face rose from her memories with a smile that reflected the warmth of his amber eyes. An old longing stirred inside of her.

"I'm promised to Prince Everest of House Terra," she said, dropping her hand. "Heir apparent to the throne of the Magos Empire. He is to be the next Archmage ... and I'm to be his queen."

Lucenna smirked at their stunned reactions. It sounded strange saying that aloud. Her, the future Queen Consort of Magos—and the one who hoped to dismantle it all.

"My twin brother Lucien and I were born with the ability to transcend," she told them. "Our birth marked history, for it was completely uncommon for not only two to be born in the same year, but for a male to be born Transcendent without a Transcendent mother. The Archmage took us from our family, and our House gained more wealth, land, and my father ascended to Head of the Lunar Guild."

The icy wind tugged at her hair as a breeze passed over them, and she rubbed her arms. "We were raised lavishly in Castle Ophyr, but we didn't understand that we were prisoners in those walls. We were blind to what was happening outside in the rest of the kingdom, and I dutifully obeyed the Mage Code. Until one day, Lucien and I witnessed the execution of a Sun Guild sorceress. Her crime was practicing magic. Before they could siphon her, she shouted she was free and invoked a wave of fire upon herself, taking her own life."

Closing her eyes, Lucenna could clearly remember the shout of liberty as a magnificent tsunami of fire consumed the sorceress in a protest that was both beautiful and heart-wrenching.

"That had been the first time I had seen a sorceress use magic. I questioned why she had to die because of it. Our Essence is ours. What right did men have to take it from us?"

"Thus, you began to use it," Rawn said.

She nodded. In secret, Lucien taught her spells. The more executions she witnessed, the more spells she learned to honor them.

"It came easy to me." Lucenna invoked a blaze of fire in one hand and shards of ice in the other. "But I only feared it because I knew once I gave birth to heirs with my ability, they would take it from me. That was my future."

Everest wasn't like the other mages. He was kind, gentle, and irrevocably had won her heart, but their union came at the cost of her power. She would have given him anything except that.

"But you're here now," Dyna said. "You escaped."

"Yes, with some help. The rebellion is alive in the empire. They call themselves the Liberation." She clenched her fist, extinguishing the spells. "For years, they have been helping sorceresses escape. They are planning another uprising to overthrow the Archmage and dismantle the Mage Code. My brother and I joined the cause."

Lucenna brushed her fingers over the crevices of the carved runes on the pendant around her neck, its weight reassuring. "Azeran created The Lūna Medallion to hone his power. It would aid the Liberation against the Archmage, but the Moonstone is missing. From the history records, Andrez claimed Captain Ida took the stone during the confusion of the war. So, my mother and I accepted the mission to find Mount Ida."

A slow smile spread on Dyna's face. She glanced at her companions, and they gave her varied expressions of astonishment and wariness.

"The Liberation staged our escape to fall on the eve of my wedding."

Memories of that night surfaced in Lucenna's mind. Everest had caught her trying to scale out of her bedroom window. She had been afraid of him at that moment, afraid that his true character might appear at her disloyalty.

Everest didn't question her or call the guards. Instead, the prince kissed her and let her go with a promise. *"When it's finished, I will find you."*

Somehow, he must have known she'd joined the rebellion and didn't accept the Mage Code. What did he think of her now?

"Your brother didn't escape with you?" Cassiel asked.

Lucenna shook her head. "Lucien stayed behind to maintain appearances. The Liberation needs a spy in the Archmage's regime."

"How long has it been since you left?" Dyna asked next.

"Four years. My father has been searching for us ever since, but my brother would always call to warn us whenever he got too close."

"Through the orb," Rawn said.

"I spelled it so no other can intercept our calls." Lucenna itched to return to the Wild Court to get her belongings. She wanted her orb back. "Because of him, my mother and I evaded capture. We spent most of that time searching for Mount Ida, but we failed to locate it. The Liberation then requested that we search for black clovers instead."

Alarm crossed Rawn and Dyna's faces.

"What are black clovers?" the prince asked them.

Rawn frowned. "It is a hybrid herbaceous plant derived from dark magic."

Cassiel curled his lip, his eyes narrowing again. "Now, I know that pertains to witches."

Dyna removed a small notebook from her satchel and flipped it open to a page for him to see. It was a sketch of a clover with three heart-shaped leaves filled in with black graphite. "Black clovers aren't natural. Witches created them to steal power from each other. If used on a mage, it could siphon them to the point of death."

Rawn frowned. "My lady, black clovers are treacherous. It wouldn't do well to be involved with anything of the sort."

She shook her head, frustrated that he didn't understand. "Black clovers are the only absolute defense that exists against mages. It would give the Liberation the upper hand."

"Even at the cost that comes with black magic?" Dyna asked her gently.

Lucenna turned away at the sudden weight compressing her heart. "I already paid the cost. Witches are difficult to find, nor are they willing to share such a powerful weapon. After years of searching, I was tired of knowing other women were dying because we couldn't find them."

Her hands trembled, and she gripped the medallion so tightly the diamonds cut into her fingers. "I used a potent earth spell to make black clovers, but all it did was attract my father's attention. He found us ... and my mother sacrificed herself so I could get away."

Lucenna fought the stinging in her eyes. Lucien never blamed her, but she wished he would. She was the reason their mother was dead.

"I am sorry for your loss," Rawn said, his tone a soft whisper.

The dried leaves on the ground shifted as someone sat beside her. Dyna's hand laid over hers. There was no judgment or rebuke on her face, only understanding. Lucenna's vision blurred.

Dyna brushed the wet strands of hair from Lucenna's face. "You have a mission, and I want to help you complete it. Black clovers are black magic, but where there is darkness, there is also light. Four-leaf clovers grown on the earth are a natural protection against spells. Azeran wrote of it."

"What?" Lucenna gasped. "Four-leaf clovers?"

Dyna smiled. "It's autumn now, but in the spring, we can search for them. As for the Moonstone, I may be able to help you with that as well."

She looked at her companions, and alarm crossed their faces. Their gazes flickered between Lucenna and Dyna, and she realized something was being decided in the silence. The wolf approached to stand between the prince and the elf. Cassiel's mouth formed a tight line.

Dyna sighed. "Cassiel—"

"No."

She scowled. "It's not your choice to make."

"We can vote on it if you prefer." He crossed his arms. "However, I'm sure the others would agree."

They were having a conversation Lucenna didn't understand, but she had a feeling it involved her somehow. Before she could ask, a cluster of fairies appeared from the trees.

Princess Keena and her guardsmen flew to them in a cloud of gold dust. "There you are. I was hoping I'd catch you. You forgot your things."

Her guardsmen brought forward Fair by his reins and Lucenna's bag. She snatched it from them with a sigh of relief.

"Thank you, Your Highness," Rawn said, stroking Fair's muzzle.

"I'm sorry for what occurred," she said.

"It was not your doing."

"And yet I feel responsible." Keena linked her hands, lowering her head. "I shouldn't have believed him."

"Who?" Dyna asked.

"Leoake."

Lucenna whipped around. "You know the Druid?"

The fairy princess nodded, her nose curling in annoyance. "Yes, he's somewhat of a friend. He said you would come and that I should bring you to the court. He ..." Her gaze flickered to Dyna, then away. "Leoake is tricksy as most seers tend to be."

"You knew we were searching for him," Dyna said. "Why didn't you tell us?"

Keena flew to her. "He said your paths may cross."

"They didn't."

The fairy glowered at the woods, though the edges of her mouth softened with fondness. "That dastardly Druid. He is long gone now. Seers are mighty convenient to have in one's court. King Dagden bound him in a geas, but Leoake set the terms. 'Serve you I will until the day comes the moon renders death to ash.' Such strange terms, and yet no one questioned it since it seemed so silly and impossible. Us, who are so careful with words." Keena met Lucenna's gaze and smiled. "His geas was broken after twenty years when a Lunar sorceress vanquished a Dark Fae of demise."

No wonder the king had been angry. He'd lost a valued member of his court.

"That is why you expected us," Cassiel said.

"Leoake advised King Dagden travelers would come and that allowing you into the court would endow the Phantasmic Moors with great amusement on his wedding day."

That they certainly did.

"Do you know where he may have gone?" Dyna asked.

"Most likely as far away from King Dagden as possible. He wasn't treated poorly, but Leoake hated being trapped here." Keena fluttered around Dyna and landed on her shoulder. "He may very well be headed for Arthal."

"That is across the ocean," Lucenna said in alarm. "We need to find him as soon as possible. We have questions to ask of him. Where can we find him?"

The fairy shrugged as she knotted a lock of Dyna's hair in a braid. "I suppose he may pass through the Port of Azure."

"Good," Cassiel said. "We are headed there as well."

"How much time do we have to find him?" Dyna asked.

Keena bit her lip. "The next ship to Arthal leaves in one week."

Rawn bowed his head. "Thank you, Princess."

The little fairy curtsied back. "If you need anything, I will be in the Moors."

"Ah, yes, I must return this jacket." Dyna motioned at the folded silver fabric in her arms. "But it's too late to go back now."

"Then I'll return to escort you in the morning." Keena waved farewell, and they flew away in a mist of gold dust.

"I need to sleep," Lucenna grumbled. She wouldn't be able to function without at least a few hours. "Do whatever you want. I'm making camp."

With a wave of her hand, she tossed out everyone's belongings from her satchel. Her tent floated out and expanded as it reached the ground. She went in, ignoring the hum of the voices outside. She peeled off her flimsy dress and put on a black chemise before flopping on her bed.

But sleep proved difficult when her mind wouldn't quiet. She would have to contact Lucien tomorrow and admit her setback.

The scale had fallen into their hands and slipped out of their fingers all in the same night. The medallion glinted on the pillow beside her. She needed the Moonstone, but if she had only one question to ask the Druid, it wouldn't have been about that.

Dyna poked her head inside the tent, and she smiled tentatively. "May I come in?"

Lucenna nodded.

"I'm sorry to disturb you. I know you need your rest, but I fear I'll not be able to sleep at all if I don't understand what happened at the fjord."

Lucenna gave her a languid smile. "What is there to understand?"

Dyna came to sit beside her. "What was that?"

"*That* was the most powerful Essence Blast I have ever witnessed. A concentrated explosion of pure energy that burns hotter than any fire."

Her eyes widened. "Is that why it hurt?"

"There was too much coming out at once," Lucenna said. "Your magic was contained for so long, it has accumulated. When it released, it came too forcefully through your Essence Channels that are not used to such power."

"Contained?" Dyna shook her head. "That wasn't my Essence. If not for Cassiel's feathers, I wouldn't have been able to cast such a powerful spell."

The destruction in the fjord had been alarming and awe-inspiring. Lucenna hadn't sensed the depth of Dyna's power because it had been hidden. Until it surged, unlike anything she'd ever seen.

"Where do you think the magic came from?"

Dyna frowned. "You said feathers are like crystals."

"They are the same in the sense that both heighten power." Lucenna sat up and propped against her headboard. "Mages use crystals to enhance the strength of their Essence, but they are merely enhancers. Celestial feathers are conduits. They draw the entirety of your Essence to the forefront at once. Neither one can produce spells beyond your capabilities."

Dyna's eyes widened. "Do you mean..."

Lucenna smiled and nodded. "Yes, that was your true power."

A shaky breath left Dyna's lips. She curled her fingers into loose fists, staring at them as if they weren't her hands. "To have wielded so much. To feel it burning me from the inside. It was frightening, but I had never felt more myself than in that moment. It's as if my Essence was kept behind a dam. The little I have been using all these years was merely what leaked through the cracks. But at the fjord, the dam dropped, and I was flooded with so much power I didn't know what else to do but let it go. Why couldn't I use it before?"

"After what I witnessed, I see now there *is* a barrier that is containing your power," Lucenna said. "But I don't understand why."

Dyna sighed. "It must be my heritage. My human blood is too strong."

Could that really be it? The Magos Empire forbade mages to take human wives or to marry outside of their guilds because they said it dampened the power in their descendants. But Dyna's power wasn't dampened.

It was locked away.

"I'm going to mention this to Lucien. He may know something," Lucenna said as she studied her with a frown. "But other than this barrier, your mind also holds you back, Dyna."

Magic fed off emotion, and Dyna's fear wouldn't allow her to wield it. That sort of thing could kill her in a dire moment.

She hunched. "I panicked."

"I know, but you cannot allow that to happen again," Lucenna said sternly. "Losing yourself to fear could be the difference between life and death."

It was a lesson Lucenna learned the hard way, and she would make sure Dyna wouldn't repeat that mistake.

CHAPTER 30

Zev

Zev heard the crunch of dried leaves as footsteps approached. He growled in warning, but didn't move from the spot where he lay with his head resting on his paws. He kept his eyes closed, wanting to sleep and forget the night in the Moors.

"Get up," Cassiel said.

Zev ignored him. He had left the camp because he wanted to be alone.

"I know you hear me, Zev. Answer me, or I will step on your tail."

He bared his teeth.

"I will not leave here until I get an answer," Cassiel snapped. "You better shift back or—"

Zev launched to his feet in a blur of receding fur, towering before him in a blink of an eye. "Or you'll what, Your Highness?"

"That's better." Cassiel crossed his arms. "What is wrong with you? After the ludicrous mess you caused, the fae wanted blood, and we lost the scale. Explain."

Zev scoffed. "I don't owe you an explanation."

"You wanted to sacrifice yourself to that nightwalker," Cassiel pressed. "As you did at the fjord. Do not deny it."

"I don't." He marched away, heading deeper into the woods.

Cassiel's quiet voice reached him. "Ending your life would not cease the pain. It merely burdens someone else."

Zev faltered in his steps. He didn't need to say it. Zev knew Cassiel meant Dyna. If he left her behind, it would break her heart.

She was his other half. The person he could always count on to be there. But Dyna saw more than he wanted her to. She knew what he had tried to do, so he'd hidden. Which was what he'd been doing until an irksome prince came to pester him.

"I'm not the only one with problems," Zev said, narrowing his eyes. "What have you done to Dyna?"

A flush rose to his face. "If you are referring to last night—"

"What? No. What happened last night?"

"Nothing." The hitch in Cassiel's voice proved otherwise.

Zev stepped into his space. "You both are at odds, but neither one of you will explain why. Answer me this, why does she *glow*?"

He moved back. "Glow?"

"When I'm a wolf, I see things that humans don't see," Zev rumbled through his teeth, tone growly and deep with his wolf surfacing. "Celestials glow as bright as stars in the night, and now, so does Dyna."

Cassiel tried and failed to hold his gaze. The rhythm of his heartbeat increased. "I do not know."

"Liar," Zev growled.

Cassiel took a step back, probably now wishing he'd left him alone. His throat bobbed. "Perhaps it is a remnant of my blood."

Zev studied him, following every twitch and flicker of his face. "Oh, I know your blood changed her. It changed her scent too, and now she radiates light."

"Is that why you refused to let me heal her?" Cassiel demanded, his eyes sharpening. "She nearly died, Zev."

"I won't allow you to use your blood on her again until I know what you've done." His nostrils flared as his head heated, every muscle tensing. He knew Cassiel was hiding something. "How did you find her in Corron when I couldn't?"

Cassiel didn't answer. He stared back at him as if he feared Zev would rip out his throat.

Zev clenched his teeth. "Tell me."

Cassiel lifted his chin, the haughty air of royalty returning to his demeanor. "Why does it matter? I found her, and she is safe. Who are you to question me?"

Zev scoffed. "Aye, and I can ask you the same. Don't pester me with your questions when you refuse to answer mine."

"Is this your poor attempt to change the subject at hand?"

Zev turned away.

"I'm not finished," Cassiel said.

"I am."

"Get back here."

Zev growled. "I'll take no orders from you, Your Highness."

He kept going, needing to escape the rage and turmoil bubbling inside of him. The Madness cackled. Claws caressed his mind, digging into his being. It would never stop unless he made it stop.

"Are you so determined to die?" Cassiel shouted.

"Yes!" Zev roared.

And there it was. The ugly confession of it all. He stared at nothing as the world distorted around him. He had sought death. Reached for its veil but was refused. His life had become a constant well of emptiness, for the loss of his father became the loss of him.

"Yes." His vision blurred.

He was a monster. He had to die. There was no other way.

"Zev, I misspoke—"

He shook his head. "The Madness seeks to take me, Cassiel. I fear I'll not be able to resist much longer. If I succumb, I ask you to end my life."

"What?" he breathed.

Zev faced him. "When I look into my future, I find only darkness. Once I lose all sense of myself, I will become the feral beast you thought me to be. I cannot be allowed to live should that happen."

Cassiel grew serious at the realization it was a genuine request. "Do not ask this of me."

Zev grabbed Cassiel and shook him. "For once in your life, do something selfless. If not for me, then for Dyna's sake. I'll stop seeking to end my life and go as far as I can on this journey if you swear to put a knife through my heart when the time comes. Do it before I hurt her or someone else. Swear you will protect Dyna. From me and the world when I'm gone." He choked on a sob as he laid his forehead on Cassiel's shoulder. "Please."

The broken plea settled between them, laden with the grave wish. There was no one else he could trust with this.

"I will," came Cassiel's soft promise as he rested a hand on his back. "You have my word."

When Zev returned to camp, everyone was asleep except Rawn. He rode Fair in a distant field, steering the Elvish stallion through an imaginary obstacle course as they leaped and bounded. They moved with a swift elegance that only came with a horse and rider that truly knew each other. Zev strolled over, following the light of the moon.

Rawn circled the field and drew Fair to a stop when he noticed him. He wiped the sweat from his forehead. "Oh, pardon, did I disturb you?"

Zev blinked, taken back by the question until he understood Rawn meant the sound of the cantering, as they both had sensitive hearing. "Oh, no. I was awake. And you? Couldn't sleep?"

"Occasionally, I like to ride under the night sky. It helps to settle my spirit." Rawn patted the horse's neck. "His too."

Fair nickered, ears folding back as he eyed Zev.

"I don't think he likes me."

Rawn chuckled. "He senses your wolf and is not sure what to make of it yet."

Odd. Zev never thought he would have something in common with a horse.

Rawn dismounted and released the reins, allowing Fair to trot away.

"Does he understand when you speak to him?" Zev asked.

"Elvish horses choose only one master in their lives. It forms a bond that binds us in a way where I simply comprehend him and he comprehends me." Rawn gathered his long blond hair and tied it back with a thin strip of leather, pulling it away from his pointed ears. "But I take it you wished to discuss something else. It is unusual that you should seek me out."

Zev hid a grimace. He really hadn't been kind to Rawn.

"I ... I owe you an apology, Lord Norrlen." He dropped his gaze to the long grass, watching it undulate in the wind. "I have been short with you, and it was undeserved. I selfishly resisted handing you the position of Guidelander when God of Urn knows we would have avoided several troubles if I had only listened to you." Exhaling heavily, he admitted, "It was nothing you did. I merely wanted to be the one Dyna turned to for guidance. Until now, it had always been us, and I didn't know how to make room for others."

"I understand," Rawn said, nodding to his horse. "For the last twenty years, I had no one in my company but Fair. It has certainly been an interesting change to go from a group of two to six."

Zev smirked at that. "I think you mean tiresome."

Rawn smiled. "Perhaps."

"Well, I'm sorry for my part in it. I should not have taken this long to say so, not when my stubbornness nearly killed you."

There was no judgment on Rawn's face, no resentment, no anger. The elf only looked at him with an open kindness Zev didn't deserve.

"I'll no longer impede your decisions. She didn't say it, but Dyna chose you as our leader. It's time I respect that."

"Then the fault of what occurred at the fjord lies with me as well," Rawn said. "Every choice a leader makes is to the benefit or the detriment of those in the group. I failed to conduct proper guidance, and it led to nearly losing my life. However, you dove into those infested waters at your own risk and made sure I survived. For that, I am grateful."

"I have enough blood on my hands. I couldn't have yours too. Is that strange, hearing it from a predator whose first instinct is to kill?"

"No." Rawn rested a hand on the hilt of his sword. "Even soldiers tire of taking lives."

Zev curled his clawed fingers, the points as sharp as any blade. "Death is constantly lurking, snuffing the lives of anyone it wishes except those who deserve it."

Each of the Seven Gates had a god, and he was the most familiar with the God of Death. It mocked him, lurking within the shadows, waiting to strike everyone but him. That was his comeuppance.

He dreaded the end of the day, for those thoughts kept sleep at bay. Beneath the moon, all that was good faded, leaving the past where it was moored inside of him.

"There are things in life in which we have no say," Rawn said, searching the starry sky. "The coming of death is one of them. We may never know why it happens for some and not for others. All we can do is strive to live each day we are given to the fullest and leave the world a better place once we are gone."

Was that possible for someone like him with a rabid beast inside? He couldn't control the Other, let alone the Madness. If there was a way, maybe the Druid would know.

"Thank you for the wisdom, Lord Norrlen," Zev said. "But I don't think it's possible to truly live when I spend my days fighting myself."

Rawn fixed his turquoise gaze on him in a way that seemed to see beyond the scarred layers. "If I may share one more piece of wisdom? Cease to fight yourself, Zev. There are many battles we must face in our lifetime, but fighting against one's nature is a battle already lost."

CHAPTER 31

Dyna inhaled the crisp air to steady the nerves fluttering in
her chest. A swath of pink and orange sky met a sea of blue
with the dawn. She forced her expression to remain blank
and kept each step even as she walked through the dewy grass.

Cassiel waited in a field coated in frost some distance away from
the camp. Six feet of lean muscle, profile strong and steady. His wings
swayed gently in the mild wind where he stood in the gray shadow of
the forest, out of the sun's reach. He'd rolled the sleeves of his white
shirt to his elbows, exposing the planes of his forearms that had caged
her. The ring on the chain around his neck caught the light. A lush
blue stone nestled in a simple but intricate weaving of silver.

His stare slowly roved over the leather armor she wore. It clung
to her body like a second skin. Rawn had given her the armor last
night after he'd made a trade for it in the fae market while searching
for the Druid. The armorer had enchanted it to give the wearer
quicker reflexes. Good, she would need that.

Cassiel's gaze dragged down her body to her feet, then back to her
face. He cleared his throat. "Dyna, about the other night—"

She attacked. He lurched backward, scarcely evading her knife.

Cassiel armed himself. "What are you—"

She pivoted and came for him again. Their knives crashed.

"Dyna, I should never have—" He dodged her blade before it took his nose. His eyes widened. "—touched you that way."

Sunlight glinted off the edge of her knife as she slashed for his gut, missing by a fraction.

She bared her teeth, her pulse thrumming. "Stop. Talking."

He parried her next swing. "I understand why you are angry—"

Dyna arced the blade, slipping past his defenses, and brought her knife to his neck. He froze, his throat bobbing.

She wasn't angry. She was furious. "If you speak another word, I'll stick this knife in some part of your body."

Cassiel's eyes widened further, but his mouth sealed shut. Dyna unleashed every convoluted emotion as she attacked again and again. At first, he held back, defending instead of attacking, and it only made her livid. She swiped at him wildly, nearly cutting him several times. There was no more speaking as he met her, swing for swing. Every contact of skin burst like fire and electricity, igniting the depths of her being.

The armor didn't make her better, it only made her faster, but he attuned to her newly heightened reflexes and pushed her until they were both panting and drenched in sweat. His shirt stuck to his body, outlining every dip of muscle.

How was he going to approach her the way he did, and look at her in a way that confused every part of her, then leave her to deal with it on her own? He always retreated, and she was tired of it. As frustrated as he made her, she wasn't ready to surrender to the war in her heart.

"You do things to provoke me," Dyna said through a heaving breath. "To make me despise you. Well, it won't work. I'm not turning my back on you."

She came for him again, but Cassiel caught her wrist and spun her around. Her back slammed into his chest. The irony wasn't lost on her. His arms clamped around her, binding her arms to her sides so she couldn't move. But Dyna didn't struggle. The fight melted out of her. She was finished.

"So, please don't push me away," she murmured, blinking away tears as she watched the sunshine bathe the field. "I don't want that."

Cassiel remained quiet for a long moment, his heavy breaths tickling the back of her neck. His feelings catapulted through her. His dejection. Regret. The hollow pang of misery inside him. He held her pressed against him so firmly she felt his rapid pulse on her spine. Her arms tingled where his fingers found her skin.

"Dyna—"

She flipped the knife in her hand and jammed it into his thigh. He released her with a curse. The apology rushing to her tongue cut off at the sharp pain shooting through her. Cassiel stumbled away, and her stomach churned at the sight of the knife handle sticking out of him. Not because of the blood leaking down his leg, or even the fact that she'd done it. Dyna pressed on her thigh and bit back a whimper. It throbbed in the exact spot where the blade pierced him.

His silver eyes flashed, but his mouth curved with ... *pride*. "That hurt."

She winced. "I warned you."

Cassiel stared at her strangely, as if he couldn't believe she said that. "It seems you have a hidden violent side."

He gripped the handle, and a flinch went through her at the sudden jolt of pain.

"Wait."

"It's fine. I will heal."

"No, wait. Don't—"

Cassiel yanked it out, and she dropped to her knees with a cry. He was at her side in an instant. "What happened?"

Dyna gripped her thigh, pressing on the invisible wound. But there was no blood. No knife.

"I felt it," she whispered, gawking at him. "When the blade went in and when it came out."

He stared at her thigh, something like horror crossing his face.

"Cassiel?"

He shook his head as he moved away, his expression frozen.

She grabbed his arm before he could stand. "No more of this. Tell me what this means."

His uncertainty flickered through her, mixed with alarm. "I ... I'm not sure."

"You lie." She let him go, slumping back. "You lied about the bond and you lied to me again. I think ... that is why I'm angry. You didn't trust me to understand, as you don't trust me now."

He lowered his gaze to the ground, his jaw working. The gentle breeze flowed across his shirt, fluttering the ends of his inky hair.

"Can you feel my pain too?" At his silence, Dyna glared. "Shall I stab you again?" He nodded, and she let out a groan. "We cannot continue like this, Cassiel. We are bonded. I don't fully understand what it means, but I know it means something, and we have to address it."

"I was not meant to be bonded, Dyna." He sighed heavily and dropped his forehead against his hand. "There was no plan for it, so I did not bother to learn what it entailed. I do not know what to do about it or any of this." He motioned to the world around them. "And now ... I'm afraid I have made a rather big mess of everything. The entire ordeal has become so tangled, I'm at a loss of how to unravel it."

Dyna heaved a deep breath. "You don't have to do anything. What's done is done. I say we shouldn't try to unravel it and simply start from the beginning." She held out her hand. "Let's start over, agreed? Hello, my name is Dynalya, but friends call me Dyna. Occasionally, one of them likes to call me stupid human."

One end of Cassiel's mouth lifted in a faint smirk. He took her hand, and it sent an electric flutter to her stomach. "Hello, stupid human. You may call me—"

"Stupid Celestial?" She grinned. "It's only fair."

His expression twitched. "Should you get bored with that one, I answer to Cassiel as well."

"Hmm, and what is it you do, Cassiel? I studied to be a healer, and now I hold the trade of a Herb Master."

He leaned back on his hands in the grass, giving her an appropriate expression of surprise, pretending this was the first time she'd told him. "Impressive. Did you always want to be a healer?"

Dyna tucked her hair behind an ear and bit her lip. "No ... I wanted to sing."

His eyebrows shot up. "Oh?"

"When I was a little girl, I heard the most talented singers in all of Azure perform in the Blue Capital before the Azure King. I thought perhaps that would be me someday." She blushed under his stare and fidgeted with her scabbard. "I could sing, once upon a time. Don't ask me to now. It wouldn't be pleasant to your ears. I ... the day after my family died, I became ill. My throat caught an infection, and well, that was the end of that."

God of Urn. Why did these conversations always have to become so depressing?

"I am certain you had a beautiful voice."

"How would you know? You haven't heard it."

He shrugged. "Something tells me it was."

She smiled. "And you?"

"There is nothing remotely interesting about me. I'm a prince. It was decided at my birth, and I had little choice in the matter." He picked at the frayed edges of the new hole in his black pants. A darkened spot encircled it, but the wound had long since healed. "I have little choice in anything."

"I very well doubt that. Your flute, for instance. That was something you learned on your own, was it not? The music you play, there is a fondness in it." Well, there had been. "I don't hear you play anymore."

"There has been little time for it these days." Or rather, he had lost his joy for it. She saw it in his frown.

"It's important to you. Was it a gift?"

Cassiel frowned. "It is hardly worth a conversation."

"So, it was a gift, then. By your father?"

"No. My father bestowed upon me a crown and a sword, and both came with responsibilities I did not ask for." His wings spread wide, the splayed feathers fluttering in the mild wind. "No matter how far I fly from Hilos, I do not have the power to refuse their burden."

A trickle of his anger carrying a tone of anxiety settled in her chest. Cassiel had left home for a reason connected to Mount Ida, but it was also more than that.

"Is that why you've come?" she asked softly. "To escape your father?"

Contempt twisted his lips. "Him. That place. The throne."

Dyna balked. *The throne?*

"He means to make you High King?"

Cassiel braced his elbows on his knees and kneaded his forehead. "Ridiculous, is it not? Malakel should be the High King. He is the firstborn and a pureblood. It is his birthright. Should the queen learn my father plans to put me in his place..." He shook his head, closing his eyes. "That is not something she would accept, let alone the Realms."

He didn't want it, Dyna realized. Many people lusted for power, position, and wealth. But here was a prince who wanted none of it. That was why King Yoel chose Cassiel to succeed him. Other than his son being the bridge between Celestials and humans, he didn't covet the throne. And those who didn't want power were the ones best chosen to have it.

"No reign is ever perfect, but I think you would be a great king," she said.

He scoffed dryly.

"It wouldn't be so bad, would it? You could finally order your family not to be such—" she hesitated, "...turds."

Cassiel stared at her in bewilderment, then threw back his head and laughed. "Not even by the power of *Elyōn* do I think that would be possible. They would have a fit if they heard you referred to them as turds."

He laughed again, so freely Dyna laughed with him. It was a rare thing, and she treasured every moment of it.

"It may not come to pass," Cassiel said once he'd calmed himself, his smile fading. "I assume my father will no longer find me worthy once he learns I have killed humans."

"You think he would change his mind?"

He plucked a blade of grass and wound it around his finger. "I'm not one to guess the workings of his mind. Suppose it does come to pass, do you think you would make a great queen?"

"Me?"

His eyes gleamed in the sun as a smirk once again settled on his mouth. "Through whatever means, we are wed. By law, you are now Princess Consort of Hilos. If I were to become the High King, well, that would make you the High Queen."

Cassiel was teasing, but the air trapped between her lips. God of Urn, she hadn't thought of that. She was a princess now.

The edges of his subtle smile grew. He stood and helped her to her feet, a soft tingle passing through their joined hands. "Do not be frightened. I would never subject you to such a terrible fate."

Dyna fell into step with him as they walked back to camp. "Oh, I don't know. I may like to stride the grand halls with a pretty crown."

"If it is a crown you want, that is nothing. I will give you as many as you desire."

She widened her eyes, covering her mouth with false surprise. "Would you? Crowns made of gold with glittering jewels?"

"I will bedeck them in so many jewels you will hardly be able to lift your head. Only the best for the High Queen."

"Well, that doesn't sound awful at all." She giggled and adjusted her leather greaves. "Though, I'm jesting about the crown. I'm more comfortable in armor."

It made her feel sure of herself. An added layer.

"Like the Valkyrie," Cassiel said.

"The what?"

"I have mentioned them to you before. Those who protect Hermon Ridge are a legion of all-female warriors we call the Valkyrie. The Watchers of Hilos pale in comparison. If you ever fear our kind, fear them, for you will have marched through the Seven Gates before feeling the divine fire of their blades."

Dyna smiled at the admiration shining on his face. She tried to imagine a fierce female Celestial and felt proud as well.

"They certainly would not hesitate to stick their knife in someone either," he added.

"I won't apologize," she said, though a part of her almost had. She still wanted to say it.

"You should not." He sighed, coming to a stop. "I should, however. My behavior was wholly beyond the bounds of propriety. You have my word I shall never touch you in that manner again." Cassiel's stare roved over her armor, and something crossed his face that made her pulse speed.

Without your permission, she thought, he said, but he hadn't spoken. The way he was looking at her, however, said enough.

Dyna arched an eyebrow. "We're learning many new things about each other today. I'm violent, and you're forward."

"I beg your pardon," he said with mock offense.

"Well, when you drink." She laughed, continuing onward. "It's all right. Let's blame the fairy wine."

"I will not." Cassiel's stride ate the distance between them until he stood over her. His hair shone midnight blue under the sun, a lock falling over his forehead. His gaze flickered to her shoulders, and she shivered at the phantom touch of his fingers where they had caressed her.

"My actions were my own, and I take responsibility for them," he said.

She held his gaze, lost for a moment in the silver. They shone like pools of starlight, as if the God of Urn had gathered his two brightest stars and placed them there.

"I ... I don't hate you," Dyna whispered, at last saying what she meant to say last night. "I'll never hate you, Cassiel."

He only observed her silently. She didn't hate the bond either, but it frightened her. It tied them in a way she didn't understand, and it was growing—binding them further.

"Whatever comes about because of the bond, we'll figure it out together," she said. "All I ask is that you no longer lie to me."

He rubbed the back of his neck.

She glowered. "If you do..."

"It will result with another knife in my body," he concluded.

"Good. We understand each other." Dyna glanced at the forest as Princess Keena appeared in a cloud of gold dust. She flew toward Rawn Norrlen, where he was brushing Fair's coat. "I have to go. I need to return Aston's jacket."

"I will accompany you." Cassiel crossed his arms at her frown. "If you thought I or any of the others would have allowed you to go without an escort, you are gravely mistaken. Regardless if you can somewhat defend yourself, the fae are not to be trusted."

Somewhat?

She scoffed. "You truly don't trust anyone, do you? Not Rawn or Zev, not Lucenna—"

"Especially not her. There is only one person you can trust in this world, and that is yourself."

Her heart sank at the implication in his words. "Well, I trust her. You could at least trust me."

Cassiel's eyes narrowed. "I hope you are not insinuating what I think you are, Dyna. You cannot tell her about ..."

He trailed off, but the notion was clear.

Dyna clenched her fists. The map was hers, and she could share it with whoever she pleased. "She needs our help."

"The whole world needs help. You cannot save everyone."

She glanced at Zev, where he sat on a short hill in the distance. The wind rippled through his clothing as he stared blankly at nothing. The detachment on his face, the emptiness, made her stomach twist. She had yet to speak to him about what happened in the fjord.

"I can damn well try." Dyna snapped her gaze back to Cassiel. "I know what she wants, and it's *there*."

"I do not care. You will not tell her."

They glared at each other in a silent standoff. In the bright, early morning sun, his features were colder, harsher, and yet beautiful.

Right as she thought they were beginning to understand each other, the delicate bridge they'd built unraveled and carried them apart. Cassiel was only a jump away. So close she could almost reach him.

If only he would take her hand.

The fae market buzzed with a medley of voices. Many wandered about, but the paths were not as full as last night. Due to what happened at court, Zev and Lucenna had to stay behind, so Dyna found herself accompanied by the fairy princess, Cassiel, and Rawn.

"I don't believe I have met Aston," Keena said thoughtfully. "I know quite a few courtiers, but hundreds of fae came to the wedding. What does he look like?"

"He has long green hair, and he's a few inches shorter than Cassiel. He had a blue fox with him."

"Did he wear livery? Symbols of any kind?"

Dyna shook her head. Aston didn't display any crests that she could remember. He only wore the jacket of silver leaves now tucked into her satchel. When she had washed it in the stream that morning, the wine stains washed away without trouble. She hardly needed to scrub.

"Hmm, perhaps he is a forest nymph," Rawn suggested.

It was all they had to go on. He and Keena split off from them as they searched the market for someone matching his description. Dyna and Cassiel did the same. They were moving on for the Port of Azure after today, so she had to find him. But as the day wore on, they had no luck. No one knew Aston.

Dyna paused by an armory, eyeing the bows.

"These are the perfect size for you, milady." The fae at the counter motioned to a set of smaller bows.

Cassiel picked one with polished gray wood embellished with silver. "What do you think of this one?"

It was a pretty bow, but when he passed it to her, it invited something clammy over her skin.

"I wouldn't," Keena said as she and Rawn joined them. "That bow is enchanted to shoot true, but it will shorten your life by one year for each life that you take."

Dyna quickly put it back. Rawn and Cassiel glowered at the merchant, who wore a dark smile.

"Did you have any luck?" Cassiel asked them as they moved on.

Rawn shook his head, and Dyna groaned. Did they come here for nothing?

"Let's keep looking. If you need a bow, I'll find you a better one," Keena offered.

Not wanting to give up yet, Dyna followed the fairy and they continued searching for that sly male. Keena flew among the armory stands, studying each weapon on display carefully.

"Can you see enchantments?" Dyna asked.

"All royal fae have the ability." Keena fluttered around her and patted her leather chest plate. "This is good armor. Decent enchantment. It will make your natural reflexes twice as fast as they normally are."

Cassiel arched an eyebrow at Dyna. She gave him a small smirk back.

"And it comes with no nasty repercussions, as some fae like to add to their wares," the fairy added.

"Do the fae enchant everything?"

"Nearly so."

Dyna removed the jacket from her satchel. "How about this?"

Keena's golden brown eyes widened. She burst into a cloud of gold dust, appearing in front of her in full size.

"Oh yes, this especially." Keena lifted the sleeve, making the polished acorn buttons glitter in the light. She traced the distinct lobes of the silver leaves. "Someone enchanted it to turn away any spell or weapon, even the elements."

"Like armor?"

"More of an impenetrable shield. Quite rare. I imagine your acquaintance will certainly want it back."

They continued until the fairy stopped before another bowyer stand belonging to a blue-skinned male with black hair and short antlers. "Ah, the one I was looking for. Weyden is a little kinder in his creations."

He grunted to her in greeting and allowed her to study the small display of weaponry.

Dyna pointed at a bow made of dark wood. "This one?"

Keena shook her head. "That one will never miss, but only if you use ash arrows. Run out, and you'll find yourself in a predicament." She flew to another bow, completely plain. "Perfect. Take this one."

"Are the enchantments safe?"

"The bow isn't enchanted. The bowstring is." Keena plucked it and lifted the bow by the thin strand. "Spelled to never snap."

"That will certainly be of use," Rawn said.

Cassiel agreed and handed the bowyer a few gold coins before Dyna could ask for the price.

"Do you perhaps know someone by the name of Aston?" she thought to ask Weyden.

He scratched his beard. "No."

They collectively sighed.

"But I have heard the name. My neighbor was wailing it last night."

Dyna blushed at the insinuation. "Oh, where can we find him?"

"Hem lives in the Gathering Tree."

Keena flashed him a smile. "Thank you, Weyden."

The bowyer nodded, and they went on their way. The Gathering Tree turned out to be the tree where Dyna had first woken. It was a gargantuan sequoia with a rope bridge spiraling around the massive red trunk. Each landing had several doors and windows of different shapes and sizes. Asking for Hem easily led them to a round yellow door about halfway up the tree. Below sprawled the entire court of the Moors. She knocked, and a young fae in rumpled clothing answered. His curly blond hair fell over his brown eyes, swollen red from crying.

"What?" he snapped.

She winced. "Sorry to bother you. I'm searching for Aston."

A bitter smile crossed his face. "You're too late, mortal. That conniving pile of muck already left for his court with the others."

"Oh, uh, but I have his jacket. I've come to return it to him."

Hem glanced at the silvery leaves in her arms, and his mouth quivered. "He loved that gaudy thing, probably more than me. Yet he didn't care to leave it behind, either. Burn the jacket or toss it in the Lost Well for all I care. If you ever find him, toss him in there too."

Then the door slammed in her face.

CHAPTER 32

Dynalya

When Dyna entered Lucenna's tent later that evening, she found the sorceress laying in her bed, staring at the ceiling with defeat. Losing the scale had really brought her down. Dyna sat beside her. "Are you all right?"

Lucenna sighed and finally glanced at her. She arched an eyebrow at the sight of the silver jacket she wore. "I will be. I take it you had no luck finding the fae?"

"No. Aston returned home. With how valuable his jacket is, you would think he would have sought me out before leaving. It's enchanted to protect the wearer."

Lucenna sat, life sparking back to her face. "Is it? Enchanted clothing is quite rare. Well, if he cares nothing for it, perhaps we can use it to trade with the Druid."

Dyna played with the soft leaves. "Well, you may not need the Druid. I think I have the answer you're searching for." She reached in the jacket and pulled out the journal. "Can you cast another containment dome?"

Lucenna didn't hesitate. She waved her hands in a circle, and a dome of gold light appeared around them.

"A long time ago, I ran away instead of fighting," Dyna said, watching the softly glowing round walls. "I couldn't protect my family then, but I swore to myself I wouldn't let that happen again. That's why we're here. I'm on a mission to find the one thing that will protect those I love." Her gaze flickered to the medallion. "I suspect it's being held in the same place you also search for."

Lucenna stilled.

Dyna traced the embossed shape of a crescent moon entwined with vines on the cover. Azeran had dedicated his life to helping those in need, and the journal was part of that legacy. In her heart, Dyna sensed it was right to share its secrets with Lucenna when she was fighting to continue what Azeran started.

Hovering her glowing green palm above the journal, the clasp came undone. The old yellow pages crinkled as she gently turned them to a blank section. She brought it close and whispered, *"Tellūs, lūnam, sōlis..."*

Gold dust swirled on the page, mixing with a flare of purple magic tinted green with her own. Majestic black ink swirled across the surface, quickly forming the country of Urn. The last to take shape was the glowing beacon of the hidden island within the Leviathan Ocean.

Dyna smiled at Lucenna's shocked face. "We're also going to Mount Ida. Join us."

She expected Lucenna to leap for joy, or cry again, or simply say yes to her offer. The sorceress didn't do any of those things. Lucenna stayed unmoving as her gaze fell out of focus. Perhaps the revelation had been too much.

"In Corron, when you said you knew where the stone was, you meant you knew how to get there," she finally said.

Dyna nodded. "The map is our secret. I couldn't tell you before."

"Why are you telling me now?"

"I know what's at risk and who you fight for."

Lucenna curled her fingers around the medallion. "Now I understand why your companions are so defensive. I take it you asked me to make a dome because they don't know you're sharing this with me."

"They wouldn't want me to."

"Perhaps you shouldn't have."

Dyna frowned. "You don't wish to join us?"

"I don't think I can. It would be too dangerous for you to stay near me."

In reality, that fact was the other way around. It was more dangerous to be in their company because of Tarn. She opened her mouth to say so, but then closed it. Revealing that would discourage the sorceresses from uniting with them. Dyna didn't want to scare Lucenna away. She enjoyed having her around.

"How did Azeran get a map to Mount Ida to begin with?" Lucenna asked.

"He went there himself. He recorded his vast knowledge of advanced spells and runes in a grimoire. During one of his travels, Captain Ida stole it. Azeran followed him, but after reaching the island, he let the grimoire be."

"You're risking your life for a spellbook?"

"No. I'm searching for the Sōl Medallion. It's the counterpart to yours."

Lucenna's white brows rose high on her forehead. "Reyes Fuego created it. The embedded sunstone contains dreadful power. Why do you want such a thing?"

Dyna looked at the dangling charms on the ceiling, listening to the moan of the wind. She thought of the forest surrounding her home and how the wind howled that winter night. "I need to annihilate a shadow demon."

Lucenna stiffened, her throat bobbing. "Shadow demon?"

"It killed my family and many others. Soon it will return to kill again. It hunts in my village every ten years. The Sunstone is the only weapon that can defeat it."

"Few would dare to face such a thing."

But she had no choice. "I must save my sister."

Lucenna's expression softened. "I didn't know you had a sister. How old is she?"

"Lyra is nine years old, smart and sweet." Dyna's eyes misted. She missed her so much.

Lucenna smiled at that. "I hadn't thought to ask if you had more family."

"I have my Grandmother Leyla and Zev, of course."

"Zev?" Lucenna's eyes widened. "He's family?"

"Yes, he's also an Astron." Dyna laughed, remembering how Cassiel reacted when they told him. "He's my cousin on my father's side, but I consider him a brother."

The sorceress glanced past her and winced. "Well, I believe your *brother* is angry with you at the moment."

She turned to find the men standing at the tent entrance. Rawn rubbed his forehead. Zev's wide yellow eyes stared at her. Cassiel's expression was as hard as stone, his anger swarming through her head. He motioned for her to get out of the dome. Lucenna waved a hand and dropped the spell.

"We agreed not to share this with anyone," Cassiel snapped.

"I didn't agree to anything," Dyna said. "You *ordered* me not to."

"For your safety. How can I protect you if you keep making thoughtless decisions?"

"Lucenna needed to know."

"No, she did not."

"This was something you should have discussed with us first," Zev said.

Dyna crossed her arms. "Oh, don't get me started on things that we should discuss, Zev." He looked away. "Lucenna's mission is as important as ours."

"Did you even stop to think of what could have happened? You are so reckless it is no wonder you need Guardians." Cassiel stormed out of the tent.

Dyna went after him, refusing to let him have the last word.

"Because you question my ability to make decisions?" she said at his retreating back.

"No, because I question how naïve you are." He whirled around, his wings arching. "You are too trusting, Dyna. We hardly know her enough to say you can trust her."

"Curious. I could say the same about you," she threw back. "We had only met when I allowed you to join us on our journey. According to you, I should only trust myself. Then that means I shouldn't trust you either."

At his cold gaze, she scowled back. Cassiel wouldn't order her around anymore, even if he thought it was for her wellbeing. She made her own choices perfectly well before he came along. Even if they weren't the right ones, they were hers to make.

Lucenna interrupted the dragging silence by clearing her throat. "So, what is your reason to go to Mount Ida, Lord Norrlen?"

"I am searching for a weapon on behalf of my kingdom, my lady."

"I'm here to protect Dyna," Zev answered next.

Cassiel scowled when they looked at him expectantly. "My business is my own."

Zev winked at Lucenna. "He has yet to tell us."

She wiggled her fingers. "Well, I could get it out of him with a simple truth spell."

Cassiel walked away and leaped into the sky. Dyna watched as he flew over the treetops and wondered what his reason to go to Mount Ida could be that he wouldn't tell them. She had asked him once before, but he refused to answer.

"He escaped," Zev said.

Lucenna snickered. "I wouldn't have done it, but I enjoyed his reaction."

Dyna sighed and rejoined them. Cassiel could be angry with her all he wished. The truth was out now.

She took Lucenna's hands. "So, you will come with us?"

The sorceress's smile wavered as she thoughtfully searched her face. "I'll consider it."

Dyna woke with a startled gasp, slow to distinguish the canopy draped over the large bed she lay in. Her clothing stuck to her damp skin, her heart racing from the remnants of a bad dream. She covered her face, holding a cry so she wouldn't wake the others.

By the soft candlelight, she noticed Lucenna observing her from where she sat at the desk, hunched over a thick tome. "Nightmare?"

Dyna sighed. "I have them on occasion."

"Yes, I can imagine why." Lucenna flipped a page of her book and reached for the small iron kettle beside her. Steam billowed from the spout as a dark liquid poured into a ceramic cup.

The scent of cinnamon wafted in Dyna's nose. "What time is it?"

"Late. I've been reading." Lucenna held up the book to an opened page with an illustration of red eyes staring out from a cloud of darkness, the same red eyes from Dyna's memories.

A chill skittered across her skin.

"It's a history book on demons. After what you told me about the Shadow, I couldn't sleep. My nursemaid used to tell me that if I didn't behave, the Shadow demon would come to my bed and swallow me in one bite."

What a horrid thing to say to a child.

Dyna forced herself to look away from the pages. "I researched it as well. The Shadow is intangible, born from hellfire smoke. It's impossible to capture and beyond a mortal's ability to kill."

Lucenna turned to another page. "It says here demons once roamed the Mortal Realm during the First Age. It was a time of ash and blood. Humans were nearly extinct until the Seraphim appeared. They led a thousand-year campaign against the demons, dedicating themselves to hunting them until the last demon was vanquished. The Seraphim then locked the Netherworld Gate so no more demons could enter this realm. How did a Shadow demon arrive in your village?"

Dyna rolled onto her back and rested her arm over her clammy forehead. "Before Essence waned in North Star, many were eager to learn magic. A young man inherited a grimoire on portals. On the first day of winter, he attempted to form one with black magic and inadvertently opened the Netherworld Gate. The Shadow came through and possessed him. It consumed so many children before my grandfather could cast it back to the Netherworld. But he didn't have enough power to seal the Gate. Now every ten years, it reopens and the Shadow returns."

Lucenna was quiet for a moment. "Why do you think it only eats children?"

"Because innocence is delicious," Dyna quoted, her stomach churning. She read that excerpt in a demon glossary.

The sorceress shuddered again. "God of Urn."

"The only thing to extinguish the dark is light. The Sōl Medallion contains the power of the sun. With it, I can destroy the Shadow and close the Netherworld Gate permanently."

Lucenna searched her face over the rim of her cup. "You're quite brave to take this on yourself."

"No, I'm simply doing what I must to save my sister and the other children of my village."

The sorceress gave her a calculative look. "Is that truly the only reason?"

A coldness came over her when she remembered the dream on the snowy hill. "What other reason would I have?"

Lucenna continued to study her with a cold sort of sternness Dyna didn't expect. "What was your dream about?"

It was always more of the same. Dreams of terror and shadows lurking within the confines of her mind.

"The darkness and all it contains," she said.

Lucenna closed the book. "Nightmares are often a reflection of what is burdening us. But like all burdens, it serves no purpose other than to hold us back. You must face it for what it is."

Dyna shook her head. The past had ingrained itself in her. It was part of every step and thought. The Shadow left a mark on her life, and it wasn't something she could take away.

"I think this is something I'll always carry with me, Lucenna."

A faint glow sparked in Lucenna's eyes as they narrowed. "That type of mentality will only hinder you."

Dyna sighed as she looked at the beautiful sorceress, seeing the fierceness in her, and the strength. Lucenna's power was a soft hum in the air, palpable and always ready to answer her call. It didn't matter how much Dyna trained. They weren't the same, even if she wished to be.

"Have you thought about joining us?" she asked, changing the subject.

Lucenna sat back in the chair, watching her oddly. "The others are right, you know. You have taken a significant risk in telling me about this. What led you to trust me?"

"Should I not trust you?"

"I survive by being cautious. Azeran trusted his brother and we know where that brought him."

Dyna laughed sleepily and closed her heavy eyes. "Our situation is hardly the same. It's not people I fear."

Maybe it was because they were distantly related, but she was at peace around the sorceress. Lucenna was a good person, fighting for what she believed in. That was enough.

Lucenna's whisper drifted through the fog of sleep that drew her in. "What do you fear more than the darkness?"

"Failure."

CHAPTER 33

Lucenna

The sky was dark as Lucenna packed her things and slipped out of the camp with the journal. After cloaking herself, she left the others asleep by the dying fire. The stolen item was a block of lead beneath her arm as she headed north without stopping. The autumn chill brushed against her cheeks as she hiked. A hint of sunlight rose on the horizon, and in the distance, she heard a faint scream.

Lucenna halted in place, her heart beating in her throat. It really would be so easy to keep walking and completely disappear in the mountains. They would never find her. There was so much at risk. Too many delicate plans in place. It all rode on the Moonstone, but if she couldn't find it, then there would be no saving the women of the Magos Empire. She had to do everything in her power to get it, or they would never be free.

Dyna's cries carried on the wind.

Lucenna conjured a sphere of magic in her hand and the purple light glinted off the crescent sigil of House Aston on the journal. There was so much history behind it. So many wishes and dreams. It was once a symbol of hope. She accepted Azeran's mantle on his behalf and for the women of her country. For the sorceresses she swore to protect.

Sorceresses like Dyna.

Desperation and greed whispered that she had every right to take the map. It was the property of the Astron family, and she needed it.

Lucenna spoke the passphrase. The journal clasps unlocked, recognizing her as kin, but her finger froze on the first page. She hadn't earned the right to open it.

"Lucenna!" Dyna came tearing out of the bushes with the others behind her. "No, no, I sensed her power here. She was here!"

"She's gone," Cassiel grated. "I told you not to trust her."

Dyna spun as she wildly searched the glade. "She wouldn't do this to me. She wouldn't."

"What do we do?" Zev asked Rawn. "I lost her scent."

Lord Norrlen rubbed his face with a heavy sigh. "I may be able to track her on foot."

Zev shook his head. "Dyna, why did you tell her about the map?"

"Lucenna was searching for Mount Ida too, Zev. But she wouldn't do this. I told her what I need to do. She knows what's at stake. She wouldn't steal from me. I know she wouldn't. Lucenna!" Her broken cry ripped through the forest, startling birds out of the trees.

It squeezed something in Lucenna's chest, but she didn't drop the invisibility spell. Not yet. Dyna may hate her at the end, but she needed to learn this lesson. Have it pierced right through her so she wouldn't ever forget.

Green light sputtered in Dyna's hands. It was there, waiting to be unleashed, but she curled into herself and dropped to her knees. Lucenna shook her head. The girl was too soft.

"Dyna." Cassiel approached her.

She flinched away. "Please don't say it. I know I'm stupid. I'm so stupid."

But she wasn't stupid, only full of so much doubt. Lucenna was sick of it holding her back. She increased the gathering of Essence in her hand. Dyna gasped, and her head snapping to the spot where she stood.

"Show yourself." She got to her feet. "I know you're there!"

Dropping the invisibility spell, Lucenna threw a wave of purple at the men. Cassiel dodged, but it wrapped around Zev and Rawn in a misty cloud. She flicked her finger, lifting them in the air. Zev snarled, while Rawn merely looked at her with disappointment. No matter how much they struggled, they couldn't break free.

Cassiel withdrew his sword, and white flames spiraled around the blade. "Come on then, witch."

Lucenna gave him a cruel smile. "Gladly."

With a wave of her hand, she sent a blast of fire at him. The flames caught on his coat and he yanked it off. It was all she needed to distract him. She snatched him in a purple shroud and placed him with the others in the air.

Dyna stared at her with wide eyes. "Why?"

"Why?" Lucenna retorted. "Because you made it too easy to take from you, Dyna. If you want the journal back, then come get it."

Twirling her hand, a translucent containment dome encircled them in a wide berth. It hummed with gold light as static prickled gently against her skin. No magic would be sensed outside of it. Dyna slid into a defensive stance and her hands flickered green, but she hesitated.

Lucenna clenched her teeth. "I *stole* from you, and yet you don't fight? Pathetic."

She thrust out a spell and struck Dyna, sending her crashing across the forest. Cassiel bellowed in rage.

"Lucenna," Zev roared, his yellow eyes blazing. "Stop!"

With a snap of Lucenna's fingers, the purple mist wrapped around their mouths. Dyna rose to her knees, wincing in pain as she clutched her bleeding arm. She needed to stand when things were hard. To fight and not back down. Lucenna waited for her to counterattack, to do something. *Fight me!*

But she only wobbled to her feet and did nothing else.

Lucenna shook her head in disgust. "You're right, Dyna. You're a soft and scared little girl. A sorceress cannot afford to hesitate. She cannot afford to be careless or to trust anyone, or she would die."

She attacked with a purple blast, and Dyna hit the ground with a cry. Gods, she didn't block or even dodge. The spelled bindings muffled the men's furious responses, but Lucenna read the hate in their eyes, the need to rip her apart. They didn't understand why she was doing this. None of them did. They didn't know the injustice in the Magos Empire or how easily the powerless were crushed.

She was done being helpless and done seeing it in others.

"You have always had someone there to protect you, didn't you, Dyna? A big strong man to take the blows for you. To fight for you. Kill for you. Well, I have taken them away. Now what will you do?"

Tears glistened in Dyna's eyes. "Why are you doing this?"

"The time for crying is over. Get off the ground."

"Tell me why."

"Get. Up. Stand on your feet, or I will break your legs and leave you here."

Dyna pushed off the ground and faced her, clenching her fists. Finally, some sign of anger.

"I taught you how to use magic," Lucenna said. "I gave you the lessons. I showed you how to reach it so you may protect yourself and those you care for, yet it sits uselessly in your hands. You don't deserve to have the journal."

She cast out another Essence Blast.

Dyna rolled out of the way, barely evading the attack. "Is that it, then?" she demanded. "Now you have it, and all we went through means nothing to you?"

It meant a lot more than Lucenna had let herself see, but it was there, raw and new. A kinship grown over shared days of training and a mutual understanding of loss. But she refused to let that show on her face. Dyna didn't understand what this was about. Lucenna would have to rip it out of her. It was the only way she would make it in this world.

"I told you from the beginning, *no one* will stand in my way," Lucenna said, laying a hand over the Lūna Medallion. "I know what I'm fighting for. Do you?"

Dyna scowled. "I fight for my village."

She chuckled dryly. "No. You wish and pray you can save them while hoping for luck to help you. When things get hard, you drown in your panic and wait for the others to rescue you."

Her face flushed red. "That's not true."

"Say it again and mean it. Why are you here?"

Dyna blinked, taken back by the question. "The Shadow—"

"Why are you here?" she repeated, circling her.

Dyna's boots scuffed in the dirt as she turned with her, keeping her in view. "I told you. To save my sister from the Shadow."

"Stop lying to me." She threw another spell.

But Dyna thrust out her power, and the spells clashed in an explosion of light, knocking Lucenna back a few paces. "I'm telling the truth!"

She laughed, surprised by the counter and the claim. "You have lied to yourself so much you believe it."

"You don't know what it's like to be me!" Dyna shouted. "To be so weak and helpless and to be hunted, fearing one day to be captured because you couldn't defend yourself."

Fury flamed through Lucenna and light spiraled along her arms. "Don't I?"

From the moment she was born, someone had sought to control her, to steal that which wasn't theirs to take. The Archmage, her father, the Enforcers—there was no one there to hold them at bay, no protectors to keep her safe. She had no one to rely on but herself.

In this world, she couldn't afford to let anything impede her, or it would be a death sentence. She'd seen what was holding Dyna back, and there was no way to get rid of it other than to face it. Otherwise, the girl would never survive.

Dyna's throat bobbed. "I didn't mean—"

Lucenna lifted the journal in a cloud of purple flames and fueled it with enough power to singe the edges.

"No!" Dyna held out her hands pleadingly.

Lucenna snatched her in a blanket of purple mist and drew her forward. "Answer the question," she said stiffly, her patience wearing thin.

Betrayal and hurt swam in her wild eyes. "I told you why!"

She shook her head and hissed a sharp breath. "There is only one way this ends, Dyna. Only one of us will leave with the journal today."

"Family means nothing to you," Dyna said, tears running down her face. "As it meant nothing to Andrez."

The accusation impaled Lucenna's ribs like a knife. She tossed her to the ground.

"Lie to me one more time, and I will destroy the journal," Lucenna hissed. *"Why are you here?"*

CHAPTER 34

D yna's heart rammed in her chest as the journal hovered in the air. Lucenna stood confidently, her hands and forearms alight with crackling streams of light. The answer to her question would never be the right one, because she couldn't win this battle, not against her.

Clenching her fists, Dyna summoned her Essence. It hummed faintly beneath her skin. "I don't have the power to fight you."

Lucenna's eyes flashed a vivid purple, and she threw out a streak of lightning. Dyna pivoted, but not fast enough to avoid it fully. The blazing spell caught the edge of her arm, and she cried out at the searing of her skin.

"What was that power on the fjord?" Lucenna shouted. "A fluke? The power idling in your veins is wasted on someone who refuses to use it."

Dyna shook her head. "That hadn't been by my means. I can't access it on my own!"

The sorceress released a fierce growl through her teeth. "Stop making excuses. That is your magic, Dyna. Use it!"

Her magic? Dyna balled her fists. How could she have that inside of her? Her whole life, her Essence had never been enough. Maybe the one who wasn't enough was her. Whatever was keeping her power locked away, there was only one thing that set it free.

Cassiel couldn't speak or so much as move his head, but she saw the answer burning in his eyes.

Do it! She could almost hear him say.

Dyna ran to his extended wing and plucked a feather. It immediately flared gold, and power rushed through her veins, so hot it burned her body from within. The barrier swung open, and Essence rushed through her pores, bathing her in green light. It convulsed inside of her, effortlessly rising to her call with a vengeance. The sting of betrayal fed the incineration of her anger. Green flames climbed up Dyna's arms as she faced her opponent.

The disadvantage vanished, and so did her hesitation.

Dyna hurled a firestorm at Lucenna, commanding blast after blast. Lucenna effortlessly deflected each attack. Purple met green, each explosion ripping through the forest within the dome. With a frustrated grit of her teeth, Dyna waved her hand, and a boulder came flying from the right. Lucenna's eyes widened. She leaped away, only for another to come flying from the left. It knocked her off her feet, and she slammed on the ground.

Wincing, Dyna instinctively jerking toward her. "I-I'm sorry, I—"

Lucenna laughed. She brushed dirt from her cheek and stood, a harsh smile tugging at her lips. "Good." Her eyes glowed as light swarmed over her body. "Now the real battle begins."

Chest heaving, Dyna moved in formation. Lucenna came at her at full force. Spears of water, cyclones of wind, fissures in the earth. Magic, Dyna hadn't learned.

"I have the advantage here," Lucenna goaded. "Show me what you'll do."

Dyna could only run and dodge as she flung Essence Blasts to meet each attack. Their spells clashed, making the ground tremble at her feet.

"You have more power," she panted, wiping the sweat from her forehead.

"There will always be someone more powerful than you," Lucenna said. "No matter how much you train, there will be someone faster and stronger. Do you remember what I once told you? What is the alternative to strength?"

Dyna couldn't recall what Lucenna was referring to. Streaks of purple lightning came for her. She thrust out her arms in the formation of a shield spell she hadn't properly mastered. The spell hit, and she dropped with a pained gasp. She'd seen Lucenna kill with lightning. This attack was mild, but the pain stole her breath as her body spasmed. She clutched at her throbbing chest, smoke wafting from her singed clothes.

"If you don't know the answer, then I don't know if there is any hope for you."

Dyna spat out a wad of blood and rolled over. "I don't understand."

"Yes, you truly don't," Lucenna said somberly as she approached.

"What is the point of all this? Making me fight you in a battle I clearly can't win for a lesson to teach me what? That I can't trust you?"

"This was never about me." Lucenna stopped in front of her. "It's about you, Dyna. You're not here for your sister. You're not here for North Star. You're not even here for revenge. Admit it."

Fury ravaged through Dyna's body. Green spilled from her in droves, flooding the ground in a misty fog. "You know nothing."

"It's you who knows nothing because you refuse to acknowledge it." Lucenna's white hair fluttered with the wind churning around her. "Tell me the truth, Dyna. Why are you here?"

She squeezed her eyes shut. The answer hovered on the tip of her tongue. A truth she didn't want to admit. It was a black abyss that waited to embrace her each night. At that moment, she despised Lucenna for making her see it.

"Stop this," Dyna said, past anger and hate. She shoved Lucenna back with a discharge of power. "I'm finished."

Magic flashed in Lucenna's eyes, teeth bearing around her hissed words. "We are not finished until you answer me."

The sky darkened, and storm clouds closed in. Thunder cracked in the distance. Lucenna's power pressed against Dyna, demanding and merciless. It tore at the edges of her stability, breaking down the stronghold she'd hidden in. Essence slipped through her fingers as the barrier fell back into place.

"Why are you going to Mount Ida?"

Legs trembling, Dyna staggered back. "I left to destroy the Shadow. It killed my family and it will come for my sister next if I don't stop it."

"All I hear are excuses. Pretty lies. We would like to think we're noble and selfless. The truth is, we're all selfish. We all want things." Lucenna motioned at the men who fought against their magical restraints. "Even those three, who would do anything to protect you. They also have selfish reasons for being on this journey."

Dyna's gaze flickered to them. Even with his arms clasped at his sides, Rawn somehow moved his hand enough to work on freeing his enchanted sword from its scabbard. His fingers bleed as he nudged the blade out inch by inch. He was going to cut through the spell soon.

Lucenna didn't notice as she continued circling. "While you may appear to be perfect, you're not. So, why are you here, Dyna? Perhaps you left it all behind and abandoned the village to die."

"No!"

"Then why?"

Her chest heaved with shuddering breaths. "I—I—"

The Shadow flashed through her memories. Thane's empty face. Her father's screams echoed in her ears as she ran and ran from it all.

Dyna stumbled away, but purple light snatched her off the ground and whipped her around. She had nowhere to look but into those two glowing points. Her body seized with panic and the desperate need to escape, but there was no place to hide. Her shell had cracked and peeled away.

"Why?" Lucenna shouted in her face. "Tell me why!"

"I'M AFRAID!" Dyna's scream rang in the forest. The purple bindings vanished. She collapsed on her hands and knees, shuddering as she faced the truth.

When she had taken the first step outside of her village to find an impossible place, she knew it would be dangerous and difficult. She had told herself it was to save her sister from the fate of her brother and parents.

But she left to save herself.

To search for the one thing that would destroy the shadow demon and the fear buried inside of her. It had latched onto her bones, buried deep within the marrow. Her desperate attempt to stop her father from opening the Seven Gates had caused his death. It was her fault the Shadow would return.

Hot tears rolled down her cheeks. "I left so I wouldn't be afraid anymore."

"I know." Lucenna kneeled and embraced her tightly as she sobbed. She rocked her, holding her tenderly like a child. "I know," she whispered. "I know."

But Dyna couldn't save her family during the Shadow Winter. Why did she think she could now?

"How will I save them when I cannot save myself?"

"Knowledge conquers fear. Knowing how to defend yourself, how to outwit your enemies, those are things you own. They belong to you and only you."

It finally came to her then, what Lucenna had told her before. *Whatever challenge you may face, the advantage of your opponent doesn't matter. Be smarter than them, and you will win.*

"I want you to have the security of knowing how to fight within your heart, so you don't have to rely on anyone to save you from it." Lucenna cupped her cheek. "One day, you won't be afraid anymore, Dyna. I promise you that."

The Shadow's red eyes stared back at her within her memories. A part of her never left that snowy hill. The fear was always there, but maybe … maybe one day it wouldn't be.

Exhaustion dropped over Dyna like a heavy blanket. Her Essence had drained to the dregs. Several footsteps rapidly approached. A clawed hand wrapped around Lucenna's throat and yanked her away. Dyna tried to protest, but her body keeled over. Strong arms caught her and cradled her against the steady warmth of a firm chest. Soft feathers brushed her cheek.

"Give me one reason why I shouldn't kill you." Zev's furious voice rumbled in the fog as the world faded.

"No…" Dyna croaked—or tried to. Her tongue had become sand in her dry mouth. *Don't hurt her.* She reached out for the fading light as she sank again into the land of dreams.

Golden rays bathed the dewy meadow, birds chirping a morning song in the trees. Dyna studied Lucenna, where she sat on a fallen log some distance away, watching the sunrise. Rawn, Cassiel, and Zev stood silently behind her. To Dyna's relief, Zev hadn't killed Lucenna. They'd left the decision of what to do with the sorceress to her.

She took the kettle hanging over the fire and poured tea into two cups. Her boots glided through the wet grass as she walked over to join her. Lucenna accepted the offering, and they quietly observed each other as the heat from the cup seeped into her palm.

"I think it's your turn to tell me the truth," Dyna said.

Lucenna dropped her gaze, gripping the Lūna Medallion. The sun glittered over the diamond on her finger as she stroked the empty groove.

Dyna sighed. "Are you searching for the Moonstone?"

"Yes."

"Is that why you wanted to find the Druid?"

Lucenna's white eyebrows furrowed. "That was my original intention, but if I could ask him only one question, I wouldn't have wasted it on asking him how to find Mount Ida. I told you we're all selfish, Dyna. Me most of all. I would have asked him how to use the Time Gate to reverse time and prevent my mother's death."

Dyna recalled their first meeting when Lucenna had made the world pause. *Time is a peculiar thing. Try as I may, I cannot manage it to go forward or backward. But I've learned how to make it stop.*

Lucenna frowned at her cup. "Perhaps it would have been a waste to ask it. My wish is impossible. Time cannot be changed."

Stopping time was one thing, but to go back in time to change events was a power that belonged only to the gods. If Dyna had the chance to change the past and prevent her family's death, she would have opened all Seven Gates, if needed. No matter the cost.

"Did you plan to steal my map?" she asked.

"I was tempted to take it from you, so very tempted." The light caught on Lucenna's white lashes as she looked at the field. "But I'm not Andrez. I lived my life with the promise that I would undo his deeds, and that includes protecting every sorceress I can. In a way, I hope it will one day right the wrongs against Azeran."

An old sadness crossed Lucenna's face. "I see myself in you, Dyna. I know what it is to fear not being enough for those you love the most and carrying the deaths of those you couldn't save."

She set down her cup and released a heavy sigh. "I lied yesterday. Being afraid doesn't make you weak. Your strength is your loyalty to your friends, your bravery, kindness, and mercy for your enemies." Her lilac eyes rose to hers. "Those qualities are far more valuable than physical prowess. They are not easy to find this world."

Such simple words, but the ones Dyna needed to hear. Since they had crossed paths, Lucenna helped her, even when she didn't want it. Resulting in inner growth, as well as a magical one.

The fates had given her Guardians, and while they protected her every step of the way, that didn't mean she was helpless. Instead of running away with the map, Lucenna stayed and made her face the darkness she hid behind. It was brutal and painful, and her soul had needed it.

Fear was a shroud she would peel away, one piece at a time.

"Thank you." Dyna inhaled the crisp morning air and released the last of her anger with the next exhale. She glanced at Zev and the others, who watched them warily. "You had to know they would have tried to kill you."

Lucenna closed her eyes. "If it's not worth dying for, then it's not worth fighting for."

It was the same thing Azeran once said when he risked it all for what was right.

With a soft smile, Dyna sat on the log and rested her head against Lucenna's shoulder. "You will be the redemption of House Astron, Lucenna. I'm looking forward to seeing it."

They said no more as they watched the sunrise on the horizon, and Dyna pretended she didn't hear Lucenna cry.

CHAPTER 35

Zev

Z ev's paws stopped at the edge of a rocky precipice as he sniffed
the chilly air, the wind pulling at his thick fur. Evening's amber
light bathed the small fishing town of Argos Valley in the
gorge below. For three days, they had traveled across the Moors.
After nothing but endless trees and stone, he was glad to see some
sign of civilization.

A thin strip of washed-out blue painted the distant horizon.

"The Saxe Sea," Dyna said beside him. "We're close."

It seemed a lifetime ago since they left their little corner of Azure.
The world was much bigger than he could have imagined. Instead of
wonder, it only made him feel small and insignificant.

"Zev." Dyna rested a hand on his head, massaging his ears. "What
are you thinking?"

He drew away, and she dropped her hand with a sigh. He had
spent the journey as a wolf to avoid Dyna, lacking the bravery to
speak to her. In this form, he didn't have to talk with anyone. Most of
his thoughts were scents and sounds, dulling even the Madness.

Dyna wrapped her arms around his neck. "I'm sorry for being so
cross with you. Whatever happened at the fjord, you don't need to
explain it to me, but please come back, Zev." She buried her face in

his fur, trying to hide the sadness in her voice. "Please talk to me. I miss you."

But Zev didn't shift. He wasn't ready to face her or the mad thoughts. If only he could stifle the whispers that condemned him for every horrifying sin he'd committed.

At his silence, Dyna let him go.

"It's all right. I'll be waiting when you're ready." She lifted his face so he'd met her gaze. "Don't surrender."

The plea made it hard to breathe in that moment, reminding him of his father's last words.

Don't surrender, Zev.

She joined Cassiel and Rawn, where they were studying the map in the journal. Lucenna held on to Fair's reins, watching him silently. Zev drew his lips over his teeth. Dyna may have forgiven her, but he hadn't. His heart wasn't as good as hers.

"There is a path through the gorge that leads to Argos Valley," Rawn said as he closed the journal. "We can replenish our wares there and lease a carriage to take us to the Port of Azure. It will be a two days' ride."

Zev met Rawn's gaze and nodded. He trusted him to guide them where they needed to go. Dyna mounted Fair's saddle and followed Lucenna and Rawn down the ridge through the trees. He continued watching the horizon for a moment longer.

Cassiel ambled to his side as he took in the view with him. "I take it you remain angry with Lucenna."

He answered with a low growl.

"Well, I'm impressed by your restraint. I expected you might attempt to take a bite out of her at any moment."

Even if he'd wanted to, Lucenna was family, however distant. He scented it during his first breath inside of her tent. She was another Astron descendant. While Zev didn't like Lucenna at the moment, he had no urge to harm her. At least not now.

When she had attacked Dyna, his wolf wanted to rip out her throat. He had seen Dyna grow, lived with her, loved her like a sister. Their familial ties were stronger. It didn't matter that Lucenna was trying to help in her own way. All he'd understood was the attack and his need to defend.

Then for Dyna to break under the weight of her fear, he hadn't been able to bear it. She was petrified of the dark, and to see the extent of how deep her trauma had gone saddened him.

"What happened the night the Shadow came, Zev?"

He only knew what he'd been told. He hadn't been there to witness it. By the time he arrived, North Star had become a graveyard of mutilated bodies, and Dyna had disappeared. When he finally found her on the frozen mountain, she was curled within the burrow of the *Hyalus* tree. Her skin was blue from the cold, terrified eyes staring at nothing as she repeated only one thing.

"The Shadow is coming."

Cassiel rubbed his chin. "Whatever happened, I assumed it was revenge that drove her on this journey and the determination to save her village, when it was fear. A fear so suffocating and heavy, she would do anything to remove it." He shook his head and wrapped his fingers around the sapphire ring hanging from his neck. "Lucenna's right. We all have selfish reasons for going to Mount Ida. What is yours?"

To protect Dyna.

Cassiel eyed him, guessing his response. "I think a part of you believes that, but I do not. Neither does your wolf."

We know the true reason, don't we, beastie? The Madness whispered.

Zev dug his claws in the dirt. He'd left Lykos not because they despised him, but because he feared what would happen if he succumbed to the Madness. It was growing stronger, determined to take over, and one day it would. He was an imminent danger to everyone, so it was best to leave and put an end to his misery.

But then the quest gave him a way out.

From the moment of her birth, Zev had cared for Dyna and her happiness. He would always to protect her, but he hadn't deliberated about joining her on this dangerous journey because he knew in one shape or form, they would reach a pivotal point where her survival may require the loss of his. It was the perfect opportunity to die— and for it to mean something.

He'd been a mad fool at the fjord, then a drunk one at the Moors, searching for an easy escape while forgetting the real reason he'd come. There was only one person he would give up his life for. Dyna needed him, and he would go as far as he could to keep her safe.

Zev's stiff body sagged as the Madness retracted its claws and withdrew into the depths of his being. Not gone, but lurking, waiting, now that all sides of him understood his intention. Letting go of his wolf, Zev shifted. He stood on two legs and inhaled a steady breath, filling his lungs with the frosted air.

He would no longer chase death.

When it was time, it would come to him.

"We all have our reasons, Your Highness. I, at last, understand mine."

Cassiel opened his mouth to answer but glanced down, then rapidly away. "Dress yourself at once, you unrefined lout. I cannot have a serious conversation with you when you are naked as the dawn."

Zev chuckled and mussed his hair. "Why? Yours is the same as mine."

Cassiel flicked his hand away. "No. No, it is not."

Once Zev dressed, they caught up with the others on the path to the fishing town. He waved and called Dyna's name. When she saw him, Dyna broke into a relieved smile and brought Fair to a stop. She slid off the saddle and ran for him. Zev caught her in his arms.

"I'm right here," he said. "As long as you need me, I'll be right here."

Dyna squeezed him tight. "I will always need you, Zev."

Perhaps not always, but until then, he would stay.

CHAPTER 36

Von

Silent like a cat, Von stalked behind Dalton and Geon, where they crouched by a wagon. The boys snickered quietly as they peered at four Raiders sitting by a campfire, enjoying their evening meal. Dalton flicked his finger, and a pebble went flying. A Raider jumped up and cursed, rubbing the back of his head. The boys ducked, smothering their chortles.

Geon elbowed him. "Do Gord next."

Dalton grinned and wiggled his fingers. A bald, stout Raider roared when his mug burst and soaked him in ale. The boys fell back on the ground, rolling with laughter. It soon died when they noticed Von standing over them. They leaped to their feet, shrinking under his glare.

He crossed his arms. "I believe we can find a more productive use of your abilities, Dalton. Set to work on creating more Witch's Brew for the Master."

"Yes, Commander." Dalton scurried away.

Von fixed his gaze on Geon, and the boy winced sheepishly. "Return to your duties, lad. The camp will move again soon."

"Aye, sir." He saluted and dashed for the cook's tent.

Von chuckled and shook his head. His role as commander aside, he secretly liked that they found time to be boys.

With the receding daylight at his back, Von slipped into the woods on the outskirts of the camp and followed the sound of water trickling to a creek. A basket rested by the bank, full of freshly washed uniforms.

"Yavi?" he whispered.

A hand slipped in his as she appeared at his side, giving him a sly smile. "Did anyone see you come?"

He wound his hand around her hip and drew her close as he brushed his lips over her cheek to her lips. "No."

Her mouth opened against his, and he drew her into a kiss. Since he promised to do better by her, he attempted to make these moments more frequent. No matter how tired he was, Von stole away with her into the wilderness to be together. To be present, to converse and love her, to be the man she needed. It was the only time when nothing else mattered, and he saw the difference it made. Yavi looked happier. She smiled and laughed more.

But in the back of his mind, he knew this was merely a sliver of what she deserved.

Yavi tugged him along, and he followed her deeper into the trees. She led him to a ridge where a blanket was stretched out on the grass with another folded on top. It overlooked what he thought was the sea until he realized it was a valley of crushed sapphires. They were near the mines. With the rays of the sunset, the blue valley created an illusion of a vast, glittering ocean.

They sat, and Yavi nestled in between his legs, leaning against his chest as they watched the sun slowly descend into the horizon. It bathed her in soft, warm hues, illuminating her hazel eyes and freckles. He couldn't remember the last time he had a perfect moment like this.

"When I lived in the United Crown, we'd only heard stories of the sapphire sea in the Azure Kingdom," Yavi said. "I thought it would be bigger."

He brushed a lock of hair behind her ear. "I'll write a letter to the Azure King recounting that you were greatly disappointed by one of the kingdom's wonders."

She snorted. "The Hashell Ruins of Harromog Modos, now those are a wonder. The structures rise like jagged dragons of stone, and when the wind passes through, it creates a haunting song that touches your very soul. It's guarded by the Desert Fae so no one can get close, but they say that at the center of the ruins lies the Lost Well. It's a well that carries no water, only the wishes it was given."

"Why is it called the Lost Well?"

"You lose that which you love the most to gain your wish."

He laughed. "What an awful trade. Who would do that for a wish?"

"The desperate?" Yavi shrugged. "Those who have nothing else to lose. Otherwise, why guard it?"

He had to agree she had a point.

Twilight fell as the last of the rays faded, painting the sky in rich blues and pinks. Yavi reached for a lantern he hadn't noticed by the folded blanket and lit a match to light the wick. She yelped, dropping the match, and clutched her fingers. Von pried her hand open, and an echo of dread passed through him at the pink blister.

With each passing day, his worry grew, but he couldn't bring himself to tell Yavi about the Seer's divination. He hadn't told her about the ending of slavery in Azure, either. Yavi wouldn't understand his reason to remain a life-servant, nor would she understand the wrath of the fates.

Once before, he had dared to turn his back on a holy vow, and it had resulted in a tragedy that changed everything. The fates had punished him severely, and he bore the weight of it on his shoulders. The thought of disobeying again sent a wave of dread through him.

He knew what the punishment would be.

Yavi.

The blister, every flicker of flame, was a warning. A reminder of how easily she could be taken from him if he defied the God of Urn again. With her death, it wouldn't matter if the fates damned him. Without Yavi, he would be.

Von pressed his trembling lips to her fingers. "If one day it was all devoured in flames, I would give up everything to wish for you back."

She cocked her heat at the dejection he couldn't mask in his voice. "What are you saying?"

"Only that I love you with all that I am." He cupped her face, stroking his thumbs over her cheeks. Yavi's satin lips curved and he and pressed a kiss to her temple. "You're never more beautiful than when you smile."

A pink flush colored her cheeks. "Stop it. I'm already yours. No need to whisper sweet nothings in my ear."

Von grazed his mouth along her neck, smiling against her fluttering pulse. "Then do you prefer wicked nothings?"

Her fingers coiled through his hair as she exposed more of her throat to him. "Perhaps."

"Hmm."

Von skimmed his fingers down her arms, and she shivered, her breath catching. He kissed along her shoulders, his fingers continuing to circle patterns on her flushed skin, roving over her collarbone and arms. He teased and stroked, whispering every wicked thing he planned to do to her.

He'd intended to play with her a little longer, but one heated plea from Yavi was all it took to roll her onto the blanket and strip her bare. They became lost in each other, letting go of all else but the embers created between them. Diving deep with a frenzied need to become one as they moved together, rippling waves of pleasure searing into his heart. It was always within her arms where the world, at last, felt right. There was nothing but the fire created between them.

If he could, he would choose to burn with her forever.

When the last tremors faded, he eased Yavi onto his chest. He stroked her back, her arms, her hair, memorized every part of her, desiring for a different life where his dream could be a reality. Where they were free of chains.

If only, if only.

The vast shimmering night sky was his only well. A never-ending deep blue that gazed upon the world. Wishing on stars was for the desperate or the wistful. For those who had nothing else but fragile hope.

For those like him.

Closing his eyes, Von held his love close and made a wish.

The next day, Von stood before Tarn in his tent, giving his daily report on their progress to the Port of Azure and about a message that arrived from Bouvier. He'd sent the spy to Beryl Coast to find intel on the whereabouts of another Sacred Scroll. But Tarn didn't seem to be listening. His pale gaze fixed dazedly on the blood-red Crystal Core hanging from the tent ceiling, among the other wards and charms. Sweat beaded his forehead. It seeped through the creases of his clothes, even though it was bitterly cold outside.

"Master?" Von called for the third time. He reached out. "Master—"

Tarn caught his wrist with lightning speed, and his pale eyes sharped. "Do not *touch* me."

"Pardon." Von stepped back. "You were gone for a moment."

Tarn leaned forward in his chair. His white-blond hair curtained around the sharp angles of his face as he rubbed his forehead. "I was not. I'm fine."

"Master, the Witch's Brew wasn't meant to be taken this long. You haven't slept for years and it's beginning to take its toll." Von swallowed when those icy blue eyes narrowed on him. "Your body needs rest. I will post men outside of the tent and guard you myself day and night, so you may sleep. I fear if you take the potion any longer, it may have repercussions."

Tarn went to a trunk set at the base of his unused bed and pulled out a dark gray tunic. He removed his sodden shirt, exposing the jagged scars all over his body.

"Neither gods nor men would ever persuade me to leave myself that vulnerable," Tarn said as he slid on the clean tunic. "Suggest it again, and I will kill you right here in this dismal place."

Von bowed his head, holding in a sigh. "Yes, Master."

"I will rest once I have the Unending." Tarn went to the table and poured himself a glass of wine. He pulled out the vial of potion from his pocket only to find it empty. He exhaled a sharp breath and pressed on his eyes. "Bring me more."

"Right away. I believe they should be finished by now."

The Forewarning Crystal announced Len's arrival before she slipped inside. On a silver tray, she carried a new vial full of shimmering black liquid laying on a velvet cloth. Bringing it before Tarn, she bowed with a small smile hovering at the corners of her mouth. But he took the vial without so much as looking at her, and it faded. Len was a simple girl. All she wanted from him was an acknowledgment, but Von had long learned not to expect anything from their master.

Tarn poured a few drops of Witch's Brew into his cup and swallowed it to the dregs.

"Leave me," he ordered. They bowed and turned to go, but his sharp gaze locked on Len, and he snatched the white item sticking out of her pocket. "What is this?"

The blood left her face. She backed away as Tarn unfolded the crumpled piece of paper. Every angle of his face hardened.

Von glanced at the contents on the page, and a coldness fell over him. It was the king's notice declaring slavery abolished in Azure. The one he had crumpled and thrown behind him in the Blue Capital—leaving for Len to pick up.

"You wish to forsake me, Len?" Tarn asked, his voice too calm. He stalked after her, and pure fear washed through her features as she stumbled backward through the entrance. "Have I not been good to you?"

Len dropped to her knees before him, bowing until her head touched his boots.

"I fed you, clothed you, and trained you. Yet you conspire against me."

Len's tears pebbled in the dirt, stunning Von. No matter how wounded she'd been, he'd never seen her cry. The Raiders gathered, watching within the recesses between the tents. Novo jerked forward, but Elon held him back.

Len clung to Tarn's legs, shaking her head. For the first time since Tarn bought her, Von heard her speak.

"Nan," she said in the language of Versai. The sound of her voice rang clear in the shocked silence. *"Samajuni arajuk, Fasa."*

"Fasa?" Tarn repeated the word as if it were an insult. "I'm not your father, Len. Who do you serve?"

She lowered her head. *"Masada."*

Von found Yavi's face in the crowd, and she held his gaze solemnly as she mouthed the translation. Master.

"Until when?"

"*Alhaya.*"

Eternally.

Tarn looked down his nose at Len, unmoved by the tears staining her face. "You serve at my leisure. Never forget it." His cold eyes fixed on the gathering. "Who do you serve?"

"You, Master," Von recited in unison with the others.

"Until when?"

"Until you deem my service complete, or death releases me through the end of my life or thy own."

Most of the men were not slaves, but they bowed nonetheless. Tarn stalked back inside his tent. Von glimpsed him tossing the page into the fire as the tent flaps settled back in place. Novo picked Len up and led her away, hiding her beneath his cloak. At Von's command, the others dispersed. He went in one direction, Yavi in the other, and they met in their tent minutes later.

"Not even parental love will he risk." She shook her head, mouth pursing tightly. "Len thinks of him as a father. He knows this and offers her only humiliation and malice. Why was he angry?"

Von rubbed his face, sighing heavily. "Len ... was caught with a notice from the Azure King."

"Well? What did it say?"

Hesitating, Von braced himself. "He has abolished slavery in Azure."

Yavi dropped into the chair at their table. She covered her mouth, too stunned to say anything. But the joy entering her face filled him with dismay.

"You're free." She said, her eyes misting. Yavi jumped to her feet, looking around the tent like she didn't know what to do first. She laid a hand on her stomach, inhaling a gasping breath. "God of Urn. Von, we're free!"

"Yavi."

"What should we pack first?" She turned away with a laugh and began rummaging in their trunk. "Should we bother with the cots?"

Von heaved a breath. "Yavi."

"No, I don't want any of it. Let's only take the clothes on our backs, Coal, and enough food to get us to the nearest port."

"Yavi!"

She froze. At the grim expression on his face, her smile faded.

He exhaled heavily. "We can't go."

"What do you mean? You're free. *We* are free." She stood and stared at him incredulously. "This is what we have been waiting for, Von. We returned to Azure in time for you to regain your freedom."

How convenient. It was almost as if King Lenneus had decided it when he learned of Tarn's return. Would he enact a law that would change thousands of lives to impede Tarn? For what was at stake, Von had a feeling he would.

"The king has cut your bonds. He has cut mine, too." Yavi took his arms. "We don't have to serve that monster anymore."

Von shook his head. She didn't understand. "Who are men to defy the will of the God of Urn?"

"Who are men to *decide* the will of a god?" she shot back.

Von groaned and rubbed his face. "Tarn would never allow any of us to walk out of here and live. I knew that when I found the page. Azure laws mean nothing to him."

"Found the page?" She dropped his hands and backed away. "When did you find it?"

He immediately regretted the slip of his tongue. "That's not important."

"When did you find it!"

He winced at her scream. "In the Blue Capital."

Her mouth fell open as pure betrayal and hurt contorted her features. "Why didn't you tell me?"

He tried to answer, but no words would come out.

A gasping breath left her. She stumbled backward and crashed into the table, nearly knocking over the oil lamp.

He rushed to her. "Yavi."

"Get away." She shoved him. "Don't touch me. Don't touch me!"

"Yavi, calm down."

"No, you don't get to tell me that. You have known this whole time we were free, and you kept it from me." Tears pooled in her eyes. "Is this why you have been more attentive? To keep me complacent in this life? Bed me daily, and I'll forget about everything else, is that it?"

"No, love." He reached out to her again, but she jerked away. "I'll find a way to help you escape."

"Me." Yavi's face crumbled as she sobbed. "You always say you will set me free, but not *us*. You will never turn your back on him, will you? There is no hope for us. No hope for our future when you have already chosen this one. Why can you not understand that this is wrong? Why do you refuse to see?"

How could it be wrong? Von had been raised strictly by the laws of the God of Urn. He knew each one by heart, where they had been hammered like nails. Obey the God of Urn. Seek the God of Urn. Revere the God of Urn. Lest you be damned.

Von clenched his roughened hands, riddled with scars he'd earned serving his master. He was bound to this life. "This is the holy law. I made a vow."

"What of the holy law regarding marriage?" she demanded. "You also made vows to me."

He had no answer to that, too dumbfounded to reply. Which vow superseded the other?

Yavi shook her head, staring at him as if she didn't know him. "You want to be his slave. That is who you are now. I'm nothing to you."

"You're my wife."

"No," she hissed. "I'm the mistress who warms your bed in secret whenever you wish. Tarn is the one who ruts you."

He inhaled a stunned breath, his fists clenching. "I understand your anger, but you will not speak to me that way, Yavi."

"Or you'll have me whipped, master?" She faced the table again as more tears fell.

"I promise you will not always be a life-servant."

While Tarn claimed Yavi as his slave, she truly belonged to Von by holy law. The right to free her was his. They only had to wait for the opportune moment she could escape.

Yavi scoffed. "You cannot keep your promises to me, Von. All of your pretty words are empty. All of your assurances are lies. He will always come first. No matter what I want or what you say, whatever

Tarn commands you obey. He could order you right now to ride across the world on any errand he demands and you would do so without question."

"Not without question," he said, and his tongue soured.

That was the thing about lies. Sometimes they tasted like truths until one swallowed enough to tell the difference.

Yavi laughed, but there was no humor in it. The light of joy had left her eyes, and the warmth had left her face. She looked at him, and her distant gaze broke him in two.

"*Alhaya,*" she murmured. "You're shackled to him, Von. Forever. Even with the key in your hand."

CHAPTER 37

C assiel listened to the gallop of horses as the dark carriage
rocked and rattled over the bumpy road. Silvery moonlight
trickled in through the small, round windows. Night had
arrived and the late autumn chill fogged the glass. Lucenna kept
Rawn company in the coachman's seat as he steered the carriage at a
steady pace. Zev ran alongside them somewhere in the wilderness.
He'd opted for the outdoors rather than the cramped quarters.

A lantern hung on a rusted hook from the ceiling, creaking as it
swayed back and forth. It was for Dyna's sake, but he couldn't sleep
with it on. She lay curled against the carriage wall with her head
pillowed against her forearm. As soon as the sun sank on the horizon,
she had fallen asleep. Cassiel guessed they would arrive in the Port of
Azure by morning. They'd ridden non-stop since leaving Argos
Valley yesterday.

They were fortunate to have a moment of rest. It wouldn't last.
Too much had happened since their journey began. And Tarn wasn't
the only hindrance in their way.

"Cassiel," Dyna mumbled and blinked drowsily at him. "I sensed
your worry in my dreams. Are you having trouble sleeping?"

He rubbed the back of his neck. Gods. It shouldn't surprise him that she could feel him in her sleep when he could feel her fear during nightmares, too.

"A lot burdens my mind."

Dyna stretched her lithe arms above her. "Tell me."

"The odds are against us. Each of us has a threat hanging over our heads. Tarn is after you, Red Highland hunts Rawn, Zev is in the depths of despair, and Lucenna is on the run from the Magos Empire." He nodded at the alarm appearing on her face. "A lot impedes us from reaching Mount Ida. I don't know how long we can avoid—"

"What do you know about Zev? Did he say something?"

A part of Cassiel wanted to tell her what Zev had asked of him, but it didn't feel right to share it. He knew Dyna had noticed the signs of Madness—the moments when Zev was more animal than man.

More dangerous.

Dyna read his grim expression, and her face fell. "At the fjord, he chose to stay, hadn't he?"

It wasn't really a question.

"The anniversary of his father's death is in a few days."

Well, now it made sense why Zev was more erratic. He seemed better recently, but it would be foolish to trust it. Zev stood on the edge and anything could push him over.

"I thought … if I promised to chain him for the rest of his life, he would live," Dyna said.

"The guilt is too much."

It was hard to live when you couldn't breathe, and guilt was suffocating.

Something Cassiel knew all too well when the deaths of the Raiders had weighed on him like an immense boulder he carried everywhere he went. But Rawn was right. He'd done what he had to do. This journey would likely put him in more situations where he would have to protect Dyna at the expense of others. She was his bonded. He would keep her safe, and no one would impede that.

"But how do I take it away?" she asked. "I've told him several times it wasn't his fault."

"It is something he has to forgive himself for."

It had been years since Zev had accidentally killed his father. He had held onto the blame for so long, maybe he couldn't forgive himself now—and it may be the death of him. Cassiel wasn't cruel enough to tell Dyna that, but he didn't need to. She already knew. The moonlight shone on her misting eyes.

Cassiel shifted in his seat, not knowing what words of comfort to say to her or how to find them. He leaned his head back to watch the sway of the lantern. They sat in silence as the carriage rocked them along the road. She attempted to muffle her sniffing as she wiped her face with the sleeve of her dress.

By the gods, he should at least offer her a handkerchief. But his fingers brushed along the trimming in his coat pocket, remembering he didn't carry one.

"What is the threat hanging over your head?" she asked after a moment.

Cassiel frowned. "Well, I should think it is quite obvious. Should poachers capture me, not only would I lose my life, the discovery would lead to Celestials being hunted again."

"I'll ask Lucenna if she can spare some stardust for your clothing," Dyna said. "Its magic is rather versatile. Lucien says it can do more than create space. They also use it to light their homes in Magos."

Cassiel rolled his eyes as she rambled on about how great the mage was. Since their meeting, Lucien always called through the orb to speak to her in the morning and evenings. She appeared to enjoy his attention, always giggling as they conversed for hours. Having a *grand* time.

"You are quite taken with him," he said aloud, much to his horror.

She tilted her head, her confusion fluttering through him. "Taken with him?"

"If you are not speaking to him, you are speaking *of* him."

Dyna bit the corner of her lip, frowning at the tone that he couldn't seem to soften. "Oh, I didn't notice. It's been pleasant getting to know Lucien. Shall I introduce you? He's kind and charming."

"Is he now? He will make a perfect love-mate for you, then." Cassiel clenched his teeth, wishing he could have swallowed his retort as soon as it left his mouth. The mage's character was everything he wasn't.

The carriage creaked in the void of silence between them, making the air thicken.

"I think you have misunderstood," she said. "There is nothing of that sort between us. He is only interested in Azeran."

A mixture of relief and confusion clouded his mind. "But Lucenna said..."

Dyna's brow furrowed for a moment, then she chuckled. "Oh, you mean her note? There was no truth to that. I thought you knew she was jesting."

Cassiel's jaw worked as he glared at the carriage ceiling. Lucenna had caused him unnecessary aggravation, and he suspected it was intentional.

"You assumed Lucien was courting me?" Dyna muffled a giggle behind her hand.

He looked away to the window, ignoring the heat washing through his face. "What else could I assume with your nose pressed against the orb every day?"

A twinge trickled through the bond.

Why must he be such a lout? Dyna didn't deserve his callow behavior. An apology lingered on his tongue, but he couldn't bring himself to say it aloud. He couldn't trust himself to say the right words.

As she observed him now, her eyes said too much for his comfort. "I'm sorry."

He cringed. "No, you have no reason to be. Speak to the mage all you wish."

An awkward silence filled the carriage. He knew she was studying him, trying to make sense of his annoyance. It made no sense to him.

A lock of hair fell in Dyna's face, and he fought the urge to tuck it back. It was unnerving how much she affected him, but he missed her occasional touch that would give him a view of her soul.

It must be the bond. Nothing about it was normal or logical.

"When are you going to tell Lucenna about Tarn?" Cassiel asked to distract her, or perhaps himself.

"I will after we leave the Port of Azure."

"I didn't take you to be so deceitful."

She balked at the accusation. "I'm not."

"You are keeping information from her. That is deceit."

Dyna's mouth pinched. "Are we to compare our manner of dishonesty? If we are, then may I point out your long list of deceptions?"

"List?"

"You know well and true what I speak of," she said pointedly.

Cassiel shifted in his seat with the subject switched back on him. When the bond first established, he'd kept it a secret for reasons she didn't need to know. But the changes it was going through now ... How could he reveal that when he didn't yet understand what it meant?

Dyna crossed her arms. "Bearing in mind the obvious, you also refuse to tell us why you seek Mount Ida."

What was their obsession with his reason to go? It was none of their business.

"I do not wish to speak of it," he finally said.

"You have avoided the conversation long enough, don't you think?"

Cassiel crossed his arms and leaned back in his seat, closing his eyes. "That is not your concern."

"We have all shared our reason to go to Mount Ida except you."

"I'm going to sleep now."

"I'll keep pestering you all night," she vowed.

Cassiel groaned and sat straight. "I will share my reason if you tell me what happened the night the Shadow came."

"Done."

He thought there would be more resistance to revealing that. He frowned as he observed Dyna's open expression. She probably had nothing to hide.

"I'm searching for someone," he said.

"Who?"

"That is all I will say."

"You're coming with us to Mount Ida because you're searching for someone? But I thought the island was impossible to find."

An icy wave sunk in his chest.

"Cassiel?"

He wrestled to contain a spiteful retort. Why was it difficult to tell her the truth? It wasn't a real secret. He simply found it wearisome to speak of.

Dyna sighed and took out a book from her satchel. She opened it to a page in the middle and read by the low light. No matter how rude he was to her, she never changed. It was chiseling at his defenses. He wanted to trust the kindness she offered. Never had he received it from others before, and he didn't want to lose it now.

"I'm searching for my mother," he admitted in a whisper.

His confession weighed in the silence.

He had been only a child, but that night was clear in his memories. The moonlight had illuminated the determination on his mother's face when she said goodbye. Her long black hair brushed his cheek as she lowered to kiss his forehead and place her ring in his small hand with a promise to return. Then she slipped out of the kingdom's gates, her retreating back fading into the night.

"She was ... human." It cost him to say those words.

There was no judgment in the bond, no disgust or surprise. Dyna already knew what he was. Regardless, he couldn't bring himself to see what her expression would tell him.

"Because of it, the Celestial society censured and despised her, no matter that she was my father's consort. The queen would often confine us to our room when he was away tending to the Realms." He traced his fingers over the foggy window, drawing shapes. "My mother would turn those days into a game. She said we must hide in the castle to see how long it would take for anyone to find us or how sneakily we could reach the kitchens for something to eat. It wasn't until I was older that I realized she did this to protect me from the queen's scorn and to make sure I was fed."

Dyna didn't move or speak. He continued drawing.

"When possible, we would go to my father's study. No one would venture there. We were free to simply be, and read from his private library most of the day about the adventures of other worlds. Then my mother found tales about Mount Ida and the pirate who hid magical relics there—one had the power to grant humans the gift of flight and long life."

The stars in the night sky took the shape of his past, painting those days. His mother's voice drifted through his memories with the stories she read to him. As a child, he'd thought that island was a wondrous place full of dreams and happiness. He knew better now.

His finger moved over the pane, the image slowly taking form. "A disillusion grew in her mind that if she had wings, the Realms would accept her, that long life would grant her more time with my father. It became an obsession. The more the queen ground my mother under her heel, the more my mother sought a new reality. All of her time was spent studying every book on Mount Ida in the library until one day she discovered its location. Then she left to search for it … and never returned."

Cassiel dropped his hand. The drawing of his mother's face on the glass lasted a fleeting moment until it faded beneath the fog once more.

"I read every one of those books a thousand times over. Whatever led her to that cursed island didn't reveal itself to me. I could only wait for her return. After so many years, I gave up hope. Then you appeared with your map." He met Dyna's sad gaze. "At first, I was angry that another human was committing my mother's same mistake, but then I realized you were the means to find her. That is why I followed you, Dyna. I need to know if…"

However many times he had avoided letting himself think of it, he knew there was little chance she lived.

Cassiel glanced at the flute peeking out from the top of his pack. "Her music was the most beautiful sound to ever be heard. A melody so enchanting, any thereafter could never compare. But she is gone, and she left nothing behind."

Dyna moved to sit beside him. "She left you behind, though."

The matter of his existence was the only proof his mother was ever real. And yet, sometimes, she didn't seem to be. He knew nothing of her family, of her past, or where she came from. As if she was the fairy tale from a book and had slipped into the pages of a world he couldn't reach. He had nothing left of her but fragmented memories, a sapphire ring, and a broken promise.

"Yes," he agreed. "She left me behind."

She abandoned him for an impossible dream that had surely cost her life. He was left to continue hiding from the derision of the queen, to endure the cruelty of his brothers, and to scavenge for scraps when the servants conveniently forgot to bring his meals.

"But your father..."

Cassiel scoffed. "I was a walking reminder of what he lost. He couldn't stand the sight of me, so I was sent to live in Hermon Ridge."

If it wasn't for his uncle, he may not have survived much longer on his own.

Dyna laid a hand on his arm and Cassiel stiffened, instinctively wanting to pull away from any form of affection or comfort, but receiving it from her left him weightless. The bond hummed, carrying away his strain like a stream. If she wasn't touching him, he thought he would drift too far away from his reality—one he couldn't ever let himself forget.

"Perhaps I fooled myself," he said, shifting slightly away. "My mother may have left under the guise of travel to spare me. Her life was a miserable one. She must have wanted to forget the revile of Hilos, and the creature she'd given birth to."

"That's Prince Malakel speaking on your tongue."

The sternness in her glare and the statement stunned him for a moment. "That does not diminish the truth. I'm a half-breed, Dyna."

Queen Mirah never let him forget it. *The crown on your head is a pretense. You will never compare to my children. They are purebloods. Heirs to the Realms. You are nothing."*

So simple a thing to exist and yet not. To breathe, and walk, and see, and feel, with no purpose, no path or place. Aimlessly wandering and fitting nowhere, for he was an abomination against *Elyōn's* natural creation. To be a Nephilim meant to be a mistake. A nothing.

"That's not true." Dyna shook her head, and he realized he must have said that aloud. "For you to be, you had to come from something."

"And what would that be, as you see it?"

"The union of your mother and father."

He smirked. "Well, clearly."

Dyna smiled and swatted his arm. "I'm not referring to that, though it's certainly part of it. For you to be, your father and mother had to exist. There's a story in their meeting, and they created your story from a single page of theirs. You came from their love, and it's written right here, waiting to be read." She placed a hand over his heart, where his pulse spiked under her fingertips.

He lowered her hand, holding on a second longer before letting go. "Are you not listening? Nephilim are an error of nature. Creatures incapable of normal sentiments like compassion and empathy."

"You protected me several times. What was that if not compassion and empathy?"

Did she always have an answer to his every verity? Whether Dyna was wrong or right, in time, he would be gone and forgotten. No mention of him would ever be written in Celestial history. At the end of it all, it didn't matter. Though he couldn't help but wish for her to be the one witness of his existence.

Her expression tightened, as if speaking about the state of his being hurt her. "Sometimes the world is cruel," she said. "It can be lonely, and dark, and convince you that you're worthless. The reality is, it takes courage to find worth within yourself. Each life is valuable, each given a purpose, regardless of whether you believe it or not. I know your worth, Cassiel. So should you."

He sighed, giving up on arguing over the matter.

"It is enough if you believe that for the both of us," he murmured. "It is enough."

Dyna laid her head on his shoulder, and a single, beautiful tear trailed down her cheek in a stream of starlight.

"Why do you cry?" he asked, genuinely surprised.

Her sadness flooded through him. "You must have felt so alone."

More tears fell like glass pearls, little treasures of lament on his behalf. Tears that could no longer be extracted from his own well that had long gone dry. He hadn't wept since he was a child, and he would never do so again.

"Do not cry, stupid human. Not for me." Cassiel gently wiped beneath her lashes, gathering each droplet on his fingers, wishing to preserve them somehow. Like rare relics, he could bring out later to remind himself that someone had cared enough to shed them for him. "I have long become used to having nothing."

Dyna took his hand. "You have me."

Something shifted inside of him. A fracture in the rock he carried within his hollow chest, another minuscule rotten piece chipped away.

A soft current ran along his skin where they touched. He looked into her glistening eyes as the Blood Bond coiled through them, reminding him of his transgression against her. He should pull away, but he couldn't bring himself to when a part of him had been missing her touch. Letting their fingers link together, Cassiel found her hand fit perfectly in his. He drew in a breath and opened himself to her soul, sighing as the electrifying colors of green and gold filled his vision.

He needed this, a connection with another person. The future was uncertain, life a precarious thing, but he was secure with her beside him, with her hand in his own. So, for now, at this moment, he dismissed all worries and doubts.

He allowed himself to be.

Cassiel rested his head over Dyna's, inhaling the sweet honeysuckle scent of her hair. "Thank you," he whispered.

The bond flared and slowly danced between them to an unheard song that faded all manner of thought. For one night, he would think of nothing and care for nothing else but this.

CHAPTER 38

Dynalya

D yna stepped out of the carriage into the bustling city at the center of the Port of Azure. The midday sun shone in the clear blue sky, but a chill clung to the air. She shivered and slipped on her velvet capelet, and Lucenna buttoned up her redingote. Cassiel and Zev gathered their bags as Rawn untied Fair's reins from the carriage. Someone from the stable they had stopped in front of came out to take the leased carriage and payment from Cassiel.

Dyna bounced on her feet excitedly as she viewed their surroundings. The air carried the salt from the ocean, and seagulls cried above them as they flew through the towering stone structures. Effigies of dragons and gargoyles adorned the colossal stone buildings. A group of Azure Guards marched by, appearing regal and polished in their uniforms and swords sheathed at their hips. The busy streets bustled with people and creatures from all over Urn.

A great black Minotaur passed by, the ground trembling with its massive steps. Dyna stared at the centaurs cantering along the road, with the carriages and wagons taking goods towards the market. A nymph and a satyr passed by in a cart, laughing over some private joke. A procession of tiny pixies with glittering wings zipped overhead. They were no bigger than her forefinger, but they carried large bags of luggage with a link of rope.

"Are all fairies strong?" Dyna asked, thinking about Keena. The fairy princess must have already returned to her court by now.

"Not all, my lady," Rawn said. "Those who are, have the strength that can equal about ten times the strength of humans."

Once done speaking with Cassiel, the coachmen climbed into the driver's box and snapped the reins. The carriage horses neighed and pulled away.

"The coachman suggested the Cobalt Tavern. It has a stable for horses, and it's near the pier."

"Thank you for paying for our ride," Dyna said, her breath clouding in the air. The icy wind bit at her cheeks and nose.

"Yes, thank you," Rawn said.

Zev and Lucenna nodded.

Cassiel slid on a pair of leather gloves. "Do not expect to continue relying on my finances. My pockets are not limitless."

"I will pay for lodging tonight," Rawn said. "It is fair to share the costs of our travel."

Lucenna frowned at Cassiel's enchanted dark gray coat. The tattered ends were seared black. "Perhaps now would be a good time to accept my offer," she said. "You need to dispose of that."

He glowered at her. "No."

If his wings were exposed, Dyna imagined he would tuck them protectively against his back. He wasn't so willing to trade his feathers with the sorceress now.

Lucenna rolled her eyes. "Does your pride mean that much to you?"

"It is not a matter of pride," Rawn said as he tied his pack onto Fair's saddle. "Prince Cassiel cannot permit the trade."

"It's not allowed," Zev added. "It's illegal for his kind to trade or sell."

Lucenna crossed her arms. "Then your second option is to present me with a formal apology for calling me a witch, Prince Cassiel. Then I'll be gracious enough to give you stardust."

Dyna bit her lip. Cassiel was a stubborn one and most likely would refuse, but for once, she hoped he wouldn't. His safety was more important than saving face.

Cassiel's expression dulled as he said in a deadpan tone, "I beg your pardon for calling you a witch because I witnessed you use magic, and you attempted to harm me with it. On several occasions."

Lucenna scoffed. "Is that your manner of an apology?"

It wasn't much of one, but Dyna could count on one hand how many times Cassiel had apologized for anything.

She fixed the sorceress with a pleading pout. "Please? You did ruin his coat."

Lucenna rolled her eyes and handed her the velvet pouch. "Fine. Take it. Use a pinch of stardust, then return it to me."

"I will, thank you."

"You're welcome," Lucenna cut in pointedly, giving them both a look that sent a flush of heat to Dyna's cheeks. "Well, let's get on, then. We must stop by Cobalt Tavern to secure our rooms." Twirling her fingers over her face, Lucenna's features changed to that of a wizened hag with straw-like hair. Her iris color remained the same. It was the only thing the glamor spell couldn't change. She tied a sash around her eyes. "I have to be careful. There are mages in this city."

"Yes, I must be discreet as well." Rawn raised his hood over his head to hide his face in shadow. It reminded Dyna of the bounty Red Highland placed on him. He secured his bow and quiver on his shoulder and hid his sword beneath his cloak.

"Should we split up to search for Leoake?" Zev asked. "We will cover more ground that way."

Even without the scale, they'd decided to continue searching for the Druid until they had to leave Azure. Dyna wanted to find her Guardians, and the others had questions, too. If they found him, perhaps he might take something else as payment.

"It's too risky for me to wander the city," Lucenna said. "I will have to leave the search to the rest of you."

Dyna nodded. "It's best if you stay out of sight."

"You must be careful, too. Even if your Essence isn't potent, any mage can sense you."

Cassiel crossed his arms. "Only if one comes near her. We will keep her safe."

Zev agreed in a rumbling growl.

"Very well," Rawn said. "I shall accompany Lady Lucenna to pay for our lodging and leave your arrangements under my alias, Nelrron. Rest tonight. Tomorrow morning, we shall board a ship to Dwarf Shoe, regardless if we find the Druid."

Dyna smiled when everyone nodded without protest. They finally accepted him as their Guidelander.

Rawn offered an arm to Lucenna, and they walked ahead together, appearing like a guide for the poor blind woman. Dyna waved to them as they departed down the street.

Zev pulled off his shirt. "I'll shift and search the west end of the city."

"Then I'll search the east." Cassiel glanced at her. "You may come if you wish."

He headed for the street without waiting for a reply. Dyna hesitated to follow, torn between who to choose.

"You want to go with him?" her cousin asked.

She shrugged. "Yes, if you don't mind. He's headed for the market, and I'd like to explore."

It was a poor excuse, but Zev smiled and patted her head. "Make sure not to leave his side. I'll accompany you first."

They headed into the street. The crowd gave her a wide berth, wary of the large black wolf at her side. But as she passed the current of people, she didn't spot Cassiel anywhere in sight. Somehow, she sensed his presence near, so she kept walking, letting this new instinct guide her.

Dyna reached a market street when a sudden tingle of roiling energy pressed against her back. She spun around and spotted Cassiel across the street. His gaze stayed on her as he moved through to the crowd in her direction.

"There he is. Well, I'll meet you at the tavern," Dyna told Zev. His cold nose nuzzled her palm, and he went on his way. She waited for a cart to pass, then darted across the street to Cassiel.

"I found you," he said.

"No, I found you."

Had an odd sense of direction led him to her, too?

Cassiel ran a hand through his inky hair. "I ... thought you would not wish to come."

"Why?"

He looked away and cleared his throat. "Never mind. Come on then, stop dawdling."

People packed the streets, and Azure Guards patrolled every block. They spent hours searching for any clue on the Druid's whereabouts, asking any fae they met if they knew where to find him. No one did. And no one fit the description of Leoake.

They searched nearly every corner of the market, visiting countless vendors with unique offerings for sale. The merchants sold everything from rice to unusual fruits, vegetables, and cured meat. The colorful spices and herbs filled the air with potent scents. The following streets each contained various wares, from furniture, scribes, furriers, goods from overseas to clothing. There must be hundreds of other streets than they could explore in one day. And she had a feeling the Druid would be in none of them.

Even though their search was fruitless, Dyna secretly enjoyed spending the day wandering aimlessly with Cassiel. He was quiet, but he never left her side as she continued inquiring about the old fae. She often caught him watching her with a soft smile that made her stomach flutter.

They briefly stopped by one of the surrounding clothing shops to pick out a new jacket for Cassiel. Music filled the city square as a procession of dancers in shimmering red and orange garments pranced by, waiving decorative ribbons to celebrate fall's harvest. Strolling past a large fountain, Dyna noticed a crowd had gathered to listen to a little hob with a red cap dance and play his lute, singing a jaunty tune.

> *The wealthy king gave his queen three castles and a throne.*
> *Sadly, from her barren womb, no male heirs were born.*
> *Thus, the king begat a son on a naughty night.*
> *Now the prince seeks to put his head on a spike.*

Laughter responded to the scandalous song. A pair of Azure Guards pushed through the gathered crowd, and the hob scampered away, slipping out of view. The people tittered amongst themselves, gossiping about who the song referred to.

"As if these kings have nothing better to do than to father bastards," Cassiel said. "Then they want nothing to do with the result."

His bitter anger fell over Dyna as he stalked away. She watched his retreating form pass through the crowd. Cassiel's family broke his ability to trust when they cast him aside. Beneath the crown and arrogant facade was someone who hid behind a wall of stone, so no one would have the chance of hurting him again. He had already turned his back on the world, and she worried one day he would do the same to her.

Cassiel stopped when he noticed she had stayed behind and hurried back to her. "What are you doing?"

Dyna shrugged, rocking on her heels. "Dawdling."

Grousing under his breath, Cassiel's frown softened as he took her wrist. "Keep close, stupid human."

They continued searching, and by the time evening arrived, her stomach rumbled in protest. Cassiel chuckled and steered her towards the stands selling cooked food. They chose one where a woman was selling a variety of broth and stews. The smell of fresh bread came from a bakery next door.

"I'll buy some rolls. You stay in line."

Cassiel's brow tightened, and his apprehension brushed against her. This reminded him of Corron. He didn't want her to go alone, but she didn't want to live her life afraid of her own shadow anymore.

"It's all right." Dyna gave him a reassuring smile. "You'll be steps away and I'll stay by the windows where you can see me."

To her surprise, Cassiel didn't argue.

"Be careful," was all he said, and his gaze followed her to the bakery.

The little bell above the front door jingled as she went inside. Large baskets on tables along the walls were full to the brim with a variety of bread.

"Hello," a plump woman said as she came out of the rear door.

Dyna glimpsed the baker putting fresh mounds of dough in the stone oven before the door closed behind the woman. She had a soft face, with a few gray strands peeking out from beneath her bonnet.

The woman wiped her flour-coated hands on her apron as she approached. "What can I get for you, dear?"

"I'll take two rolls, please."

She went to a table and lifted the lid off a basket. She placed two on a piece of parchment paper before handing it to Dyna. "That will be four russets."

The price was unexpectedly high. A bag of a dozen rolls in Corron had only cost her one russet. Flustered under the woman's waiting gaze, Dyna rummaged in her satchel for the money she knew she didn't have.

A hand reached past her to give the woman a silver coin. "I'll pay for whatever the lady wants and half a dozen of your rye loaves."

The woman blushed, patting down her disheveled hair. "Of course, milord."

She took his money and hurried off to package the order.

Dyna glanced at the man standing beside her. At first, she thought she recognized him, but he wasn't anyone she'd met before. A long, dark blue frock coat fit his tall frame, laden with leather armor and weapons. Embellishing his baldric was the metal emblem of a bird's skull. Tousled blond hair fell in soft waves around his jaw covered in a short layer of stubble. He had a rugged attractiveness with a jagged edge—one that surely broke a few hearts.

"Your pardon, lass. I hope I have not offended you," the man said. His northern Azure accent was thick, the brogue timbre more apparent. But he spoke formally and gave her a polite tilt of his head.

"Not at all, sir, thank you," Dyna replied.

"If it pleases you, allow me to introduce myself." He bowed, holding out his hand in the manner of nobility. "I am Klyde of Old Tanzanite Keep."

Dyna paused, surprised to hear the name of that city.

The bell to the bakery jingled loudly when another man wearing the same coat and emblem came through the door. Dark brown curls framed his face. He wore an eye patch, the surrounding skin scarred.

His one good eye landed on Dyna, then flitted to Klyde. "Captain, I found the location."

Captain? Klyde bore no sign of his rank and his coat was a darker shade of blue than the Azure Guard uniform. Perhaps he was of a different division.

"Good," Klyde replied. "I'll join you momentarily, Lieutenant." But the man hesitated to leave.

"Eagon, it's fine." The captain frowned. "Wait for me outside." Eagon nodded and strode away to where two horses idled outside the windows.

The woman soon returned. "Here's your order, milord."

"Thank you, madam." Klyde accepted the burlap sack she offered and opened the door for Dyna. "Shall I escort you somewhere, lass?"

She hurried outside, bashful by his charm. "There is no need for it, sir. You have done enough for me today. I can find my way."

"May I have the pleasure of knowing the name of such a lovely lady?" he asked, taking her hand. His blue eyes shone as his amiable smile widened, revealing two dimples on each cheek.

"My name is Dynalya," she said, dipping in a curtsy.

"Ah, and a well-suited one it is." The captain lifted her hand gently and kissed the back of it.

She was jerked free from Klyde's fingers. Her skin vibrated under the steel hold, and she found Cassiel at her heels.

"I ask you kindly to mind yourself," Cassiel said, not at all kindly.

Klyde chuckled and lifted his hands. He backed up a step towards the lieutenant, who watched indifferently from his horse. "Begging your pardon. I was merely introducing myself."

"If your business is finished here, good day to you, then."

"Aye, good day," Klyde smirked, dropping his formal tone. He headed for his companion. The two short swords strapped to his back partially covered the garish embroidered symbol of a bird's skull. He took the reins of an onyx thoroughbred with a glossy coat and mounted the saddle. "The city is no place for the lass to wander unescorted, mate," he said. "Keep her close."

There was a true warning in there, as much as his stern expression conveyed. Cassiel's fingers tightened around her wrist, his unease winding around her. Klyde clicked his tongue, and the hooves of their horses beat on the cobblestone as they rode away.

"Who was he? What did he say?" Cassiel asked her.

"This is the first we've met. He only told me his name and nothing else of consequence."

"That man was a Skull..."

"A what?"

"Nothing." Cassiel exhaled a forceful breath and rubbed his forehead. "Dyna, I understand you do not want to be afraid, but I am. Please be careful. If you were taken again, I ... I may lose my mind."

She couldn't find the means to reply. From his eyes came a gentleness she hadn't seen before.

"I will."

They walked in silence through the active streets. The chilling breeze bit at Dyna's cheeks. Her numb hands had grown stiff and ruddy with cold. She blew into her palms and rubbed them together.

"Here." Cassiel peeled off his leather gloves.

"But then you'll be cold."

"That is the least of my worries."

Did he worry about her?

Dyna deliberated for a second before saying, "I have a better idea."

She took one of his gloves, slipped it on, then took his bare, warm hand in hers. A soft electrical current passed through them, seeping more warmth through her as it reached her cheeks. Cassiel froze in place for a moment, staring at their entwined hands as if he didn't know what to make of her boldness.

"Sorry." She started to pull away, but he tightened his grasp and slid their fingers together.

With a clearing of his throat, Cassiel continued down the street, holding her hand as if it was the most delicate thing in the world.

CHAPTER 39

Lucenna

Lucenna hated to admit it, but being out in the open among so many people made her nervous, especially with mages about. The presence of their power drifted in the air like the humidity of summer. Not potent enough to belong to an Enforcer, but any mage could attempt to capture and return her to the Magos Empire.

Keeping a clipped pace through the city, she wanted to reach the tavern as soon as possible. But Rawn slowed, bringing Fair to a stop on a street corner. She followed his line of sight to a courier office on a busy road and read the debate on his face.

"You need to send a letter?" she asked, smiling tightly.

Rawn nodded, though he looked hesitant at her obvious unease. "Letters to my wife. I do well to send her one every month, but I have been delayed for unexpected reasons. I have two letters to send now. She must be worried."

"You send them by courier portal," Lucenna concluded.

Portals were difficult to make and required a lot of power. The mages who could manage a small one offered their services in courier offices, and that office most certainly had a mage. She could feel it.

"Go. I'll wait here." She sighed.

"I will not be long." Rawn handed her Fair's reins and crossed the road.

"Come along, Fair." Lucenna led him to a shadowy street around the corner from the courier office.

It held a few merchant stalls and even fewer people. Perfect. It may serve to pass the time while she waited. Fair's hooves clopped loudly in the quiet as they strolled through. The offered wares were merely threadbare clothes, overripe food, and rusted tools. Grim people eyed her with mean gazes from their stalls.

"Witch," they hissed.

"Hide before she speaks to us," a merchant whispered to another, thinking she couldn't see them.

The glamor of an old hag and sash over Lucenna's eyes did well to disguise her as a blind witch. The merchants dropped the canopies over their stalls, closing their shops. People on the street took one look at her and walked in the opposite direction. Lucenna flashed a harsh grin, releasing a cackle. May as well play the part.

She stopped before a shoemaker's shop at random, and the man waved her away. "Begone. We don't serve your kind here. Go to the Briar Witch for your business."

Briar Witch?

He motioned to a dark alleyway with a faint red light glowing beyond. There was a witch here. Her heart jolted as goosebumps rushed across her arms. Finally, she'd found a lead to what she'd been searching for. But when she took a step, Fair neighed, pulling on the reins.

"Stop that." Lucenna frowned. He pulled again, shaking his head. "Don't tell me you're scared. Elvish horses are to be brave, and you serve the Norrlen House. You have a reputation to uphold." At that, Fair settled with a nervous twitch of his ears, and he flicked her with his tail. She patted his neck. "Come now, Rawn left me in your care. Will you accompany me, please?"

Fair nuzzled her cheek with a wet snort.

"Thank you."

Lucenna held on a little too tightly to the reins as they approached the eerie alley. Black mold covered the damp stone walls. Water dripped, pattering in an unsteady rhythm. Rats scurried by her boots and hid beneath the broken crates left to rot in the corners. Red highlighted everything in a sinister hue. The strange light came from a rusted lantern hanging above a round, black door at the end of the alleyway. No windows or signs, save for a knotted symbol painted in the center of the door with red paint.

She wasn't the only one who came to meet the witch. A man with an eyepatch stood silently in the shadows, holding on to the reins of two horses, one black and the other brown. He was dressed in dark blue and layered with leather armor and metal plating. The man watched her approach without a word. Fair tugged against the reins again, his breaths coming in heavy. If the horse was frightened, perhaps she should be.

"All right, all right," she whispered. "Wait for me here."

Lucenna tied the reins to a rusted iron wheel resting against the wall and approached the door. The witch's symbol faintly glowed. Shivers traveled up her spine like crawling ants.

She glanced at the one-eyed man again, and he stared silently back.

Is it safe to go in? She wanted to ask, but it was ridiculous. Why should she be scared? Her magic protected her.

Lucenna swallowed and reached for the knob, only to realize it was made of bone. Animal or human? *Don't think about it.* Grabbing it, a shudder passed through her at its porous texture, and she quickly opened the door. Before she could change her mind, Lucenna slipped inside.

It was dark and cold. Then the smell hit her. The rank stench of spoiled meat, foul herbs, and sour urine choked her senses, making her eyes water. Smoke wafted in the air. A thick canopy of interwoven thorns hung from the rafters. The room was full of random furniture, barrels, and cages with chickens and pigs, squealing and clucking in their filth.

Voices drifted from deeper within.

"You're a pretty thing," came a raspy, female voice. "It's not every day one with a face like yours comes to see old Briar. What brings you here? A charm? A potion? Poison, perhaps."

Lucenna crept closer.

"None of the mentioned, madam," a man answered, in a deep, brogue accent. "I've come to inquire about Witch's Brew."

The Briar Witch cackled, and another shudder passed through Lucenna. It was nothing like the performance she'd given on the street. It was a dry, wicked sound that reminded her of wind rattling through brittle branches.

"Does the pretty one have trouble sleeping?" the witch mocked. "The darkness finds its way into all of our dreams. Well, I have none on hand at the moment. I can have it for you at dawn within two days' time."

Lucenna peered out from behind a pillar. By the hearth crackling in the corner was a tall, broad-shouldered man in a long dark coat and leather armor, similar to the man waiting outside. He faced the fire, and the flames highlighted the gold of his hair and the bristles on his jaw. His back bore the white sigil of a bird's skull.

An old woman in a dark red robe stood before him, the hood covering most of her face. The folds of her cheeks lifted as her dry lips cracked in a smile. Her gnarled fingernails walked a path up the man's chest. "What shall we trade for it? The color of your eyes or a kiss from those sensual lips?"

He shifted back. "You misunderstand, madam. I want to know how it's made. What are its full effects?"

The Briar Witch cackled again and turned to stir a pot simmering over the fire. "If you think I'll tell you trade secrets, then you're not very smart, my pretty."

"I have no interest in making a profit from the wares of a witch. I seek only to know its purpose." He dropped a heavy sack on a cluttered table. It rattled loudly as gold coins spilled on the tabletop, glittering in the firelight.

The witch ran her fingers through them. "You have spilled much blood for your wealth."

"And more is yet to be spilled."

Her dry mouth split in a grin, revealing yellowed teeth. "I knew I liked you. Well, come closer. I'll not share secrets where *others* can hear."

Lucenna's heart dropped in her stomach, feeling she'd been caught. The Briar Witch stood on her toes to whisper in his ear, her dry lips caressing him like a lover. He jerked back when she finished.

The witch cocked her head, wearing a simpering smile. "Not what you expected to hear?"

"You have been ... helpful, madam. Thank you. Good day." He nodded and swiftly headed for the exit.

Lucenna ducked behind the pillar. When he passed, his gaze flickered to where she hid for the briefest of seconds, then he slipped through the door. He'd moved too fast for her to get a good look at him.

"Come out, come out, wherever you are," the Briar Witch sang. "I sensed you as soon as you crossed the threshold, sweet meat."

Lucenna bit back a curse. Goosebumps pricked her skin as every instinct told her to leave. Immediately.

Taking a breath, she rose and faced the witch with a blank expression. "Pardon, madam. I didn't wish to interrupt," she said in a practiced, croaking voice. "I, too, have come to inquire for some knowledge. Might you have black clovers for sale or know where I may acquire them?"

The witch threw back her head and laughed, giving Lucenna a view inside of her slimy mouth full of sores. "You're no witch, or you would know the proper etiquette by which we hold. A witch does not ask another for the power to kill her."

She snapped her bony fingers, and a cold smoke snatched Lucenna in the air. It pulled her close enough to smell the witch's revolting breath. Lucenna bucked wildly, but the invisible hold kept her in a vice grip. Panic flooded through her veins. The Briar Witch lowered her hood, revealing milky gray eyes and a sunken face. Thorns outlined her eyebrows and the back of her knuckles.

"Such power you have. Such delicious power gifted by the moon. You hide behind enchantments, but I can see your beauty and youth. If you seek what is mine, then I'll trade for what is yours. Black clovers for all ..." She ran a nail down Lucenna's cheek, pulling down the sash. "That you have."

Lucenna's glamor spell fell off the way a snake shed its skin. It dried and peeled, withering away. Her white hair whipped forward as she kicked and thrashed.

"Release me!" She called on her Essence, but it sparked uselessly in her hands.

"You have no power here." The Briar Witch flashed her a feral smile and nodded to the blood-red symbols painted on the dark ceiling. "My wards keep out all magic but my own."

Lucenna stifled a whimper, refusing to show fear. Inside, her mind screamed. Never had she been so stupid. Her heart thrashed behind her ribs, breath coming in heavily as her mind grasped for a clue on how to escape. It reminded her of the men when she'd kept them trapped in her spells. Was this the helpless desperation they experienced?

The Briar Witch went to a table and rummaged in the mess. "Did you know, we witches are polite folk? We don't go sneaking into another's dwelling without permission. If we did, well, it never ends favorably for the intruder."

She turned, and Lucenna inhaled a sharp breath at the sight of the dagger in her hands. Firelight shone through its translucent edge. The blade was made of pure white crystal.

"What are you doing?" Lucenna demanded. "Stay back."

"I'll not kill you, sweet meat. But merely take what we bargained for. I promise it will only hurt a little."

"We didn't bargain for anything. I no longer want the clovers. Let me go!"

"And relinquish the chance to be beautiful? I think not."

When she neared, Lucenna threw back her head and smashed into the witch's face, knocking her back into the table. The witch whirled around with a red welt on her forehead. She hissed, curling her fingers into claws. Cold smoke ensnared Lucenna's neck and head, locking her in place.

"Hold still. I don't want to scar that pretty face. It'll soon be mine." The witch snatched a handful of Lucenna's hair in her fist and lifted the crystal dagger to her hairline.

The scream she'd been holding back tore from her throat.

Heavy footsteps thudded behind her, and something white hit the witch. Then she was the one screaming. The Briar Witch tripped backward, howling and clawing at her face as her skin sizzled and blistered. The hold on Lucenna vanished, and she hit the floor.

"On your feet, lass." A hand hauled her up.

It was the man who'd been there moments before. She fell against his firm chest as his arm wrapped around her waist so tightly, she could feel every muscle. His mouth curled in a smirk, and he heaved her to the door with him, tossing handfuls of sand across the ground as they retreated.

No, not sand.

Salt.

He yanked Lucenna out into the alley. His companion with the eyepatch slammed the door shut behind them, dumping more salt along the threshold.

"Get to your horse." The man shoved her toward Fair, and they ran for theirs.

She didn't need to be told twice. Yanking the reins free, Lucenna swung onto Fair's saddle, and they raced out of the alley. She dared to glance behind her in time to see the entrance seal shut with a brick wall. Lucenna didn't stop until they entered the busy road bathed in sunlight. With a heaving breath, she leaned on Fair, hugging his neck as she waited for her heart to stop racing.

"Are you all right, lass?" The man chuckled behind her. "You're nearly as white as your hair. That was foolish. She had you in her snares. If I hadn't been there—"

"Yes, thank you," Lucenna said testily, annoyed that a *man* had saved her.

"Hmm. She doesn't sound particularly grateful," he said. "Does she sound grateful, Eagon?"

"I wouldn't say so, Captain."

"I'd be more grateful if you hadn't waited until the last moment," Lucenna growled. "She nearly carved off my face."

She whipped around to yell at the man, only for her glare to melt away.

Gods.

She took in the angles of his face, the cheekbones, and ... sensual mouth. Eyes the color of the clearest sky looked at her from behind thick lashes, woven through with the deepest blue of the sea. Dark blond hair curled at the nape of his neck. It fell forward around his chiseled jaw, layered in stubble, brushing over his dark brows. Her stare dropped to the black trousers that clung to his thighs wrapped around his steed, moving to the many weapons and dark blue coat he wore. It fit him indecently like a second skin, straining against his broad chest and arms, showing every groove and ridge. Her stomach dipped, remembering how they had enveloped her.

"That would have been a pity," the captain said in that interesting accent. It was thicker than the one she was used to hearing in Azure, a lilt pleasing to the ear. He smiled, and two dimples appeared as his gaze roved over her face. "The witches have a set of rules by which they live. In regards to their homes, you must knock to request entrance, or you forgo any truce. Perhaps next time you'll think twice before wandering into a witch's den without permission, aye, lass?"

"Don't call me that," Lucenna snapped.

He chuckled and with a click of his tongue; the captain drew his onyx horse astride to hers. "Then do tell me your name, so I may thank the Heavens for bestowing me with the chance of meeting such a rare beauty."

She rolled her eyes. His allure was fading fast. "Do such charms always work on women?"

Eagon snorted. "You'd be surprised."

With a face like that, she wasn't.

"Well, if you'll not give me yours, then allow me to give you mine. Please call me Klyde." He took her hand and brushed his soft lips over her knuckles. His breath tickled her skin, eliciting tingles along her arm. "If I'm so blessed, may you whisper it to the stars when you think of me."

A rush of heat rose to Lucenna's cheeks, and she snatched her hand away. "If I may say so, *Captain*," she said, her tone scalding. "Should I ever recall your name, it would be to remember the man who found enjoyment in exaggerated flattery and forward behavior."

Eagon folded his lips inward, muffling a snort.

Another grin broke on Klyde's face, this one more genuine. He opened his mouth, but the gallop of incoming horses interrupted whatever he planned to say. Three armed men in the same blue coats rode toward them.

One with a mop of ginger hair nodded as he approached. "Captain, we have a lead."

Klyde's face completely changed. Gone was the playful man, and in his place appeared a sharpened soldier. She realized that's what he was when she inspected his uniform, the metal-plated leather armor, and the weapons peeking out of his coat. Past his shoulders, she glimpsed the skull-shaped pommels of his short swords.

Klyde's gaze lost all warmth as the churning blue frosted over. He nodded and tugged on the reins, leading his horse away. But he paused and glanced back at her, the edges of his mouth softening for the barest of moments. "It was a pleasure, lass. If the fates are so kind, may we meet again."

Then he signaled his men, and they galloped away. She watched him go, their coats flaring with the garish sigil on their backs. Klyde turned on a street corner and disappeared from her life as quickly as he entered it.

"Lady Lucenna?"

She jumped.

Rawn frowned at her, his sudden presence snapping her back to reality. "Your disguise."

"Oh!" She waved her hand, slipping the glamor back into place. "Did you send your letters?"

He sighed. "Unfortunately, mail to Greenwood will be sent tomorrow. I must return in the morning."

She mumbled some empathetic reply, her mind too scattered to offer anything else.

"Did Fair behave?"

Lucenna petted his head. "Oh yes, he was a good boy."

The willful stallion gave a short neigh that sounded like a complaint.

Rawn raised his brows. "And did Lady Lucenna behave?"

Fair snorted and stomped his hooves. He was definitely complaining.

She chuckled nervously and gave Lord Norrlen a sheepish grin. "I may have asked him to escort me on a stroll. Nothing more."

Fair jerked on the reins, shaking his head.

"Hmm."

"He's so silly." Lucenna hugged the horse's neck and discreetly whispered in his ear, "Hush or I'll braid your mane with frilly bows."

Fair settled with the tiny threat, and they continued on their way to the Cobalt Tavern. Due to embarrassment, she rather to tell Rawn about her foolish detour—or about the rugged captain who had eyes the color of the sky.

CHAPTER 40

Dyna fell into comfortable silence with Cassiel by her side as they made their way through the seaport city. They reached the pier, where several large ships came into the wharf to moor and unload their cargo. Their search proved futile when the harbormaster said there was no one of the name Leoake or the Druid listed to board the ship to Arthal.

"I think we may have missed him," Dyna said once they had left the harbormaster's office.

Cassiel frowned. "No, the ship is here. Leoake wants to avoid being found. Either he is using another name, or he didn't come to the city at all."

Dyna sighed heavily. The Druid was on the run from King Dagden, so it made sense he would stay out of sight. "You may be right. Let's hope the others had better luck."

Cassiel led her to a cluster of wooden tables set outside a line of shops selling fried fish on the pier and motioned for her to sit. "Let us tarry here for a moment. I'm sure you are hungry."

He removed a new wineskin strapped to his rucksack and took out two wooden cups as she sat next to him. He popped off the lid and poured the steaming broth into a cup for her. It smelled of rich herbs and vegetables. She handed him a roll, and they ate while they watched the ships sail on the horizon. The sunset radiated like gold silk over the surface of the ocean. Seagulls squawked and flew through the large mounds of clouds moving across the sky.

"The tavern should be down this street." Cassiel nodded to the right of them as he ate.

"Have you been hereabouts before?" Dyna asked him.

"Yes, but I have not been this deep in the city. I lodged at a small inn on the outskirts to avoid any attention. Poachers centralize here."

She stiffened at the mention of poachers, but he remained relaxed. His new jacket hid his wings well. They'd already enchanted it in an alley so he could change into it. The fine, deep navy fabric was adorned with silver trim on his collar, lapels, and shoulders. He wore a matching shirt underneath, fastened with silver buttons.

The wind tousled Cassiel's soft locks over his forehead, his distant gaze fixed on the horizon. Not wanting to disturb him, Dyna reached in her satchel and thought of Jökull. The familiar heavy shape of a book landed in her hand, and she pulled it out. The silver lettering on the cover shone under the low rays of the sun. *Lord of the Everfrost.* She traced her fingers over the beveled words and the sigil of the phoenix crest beneath it. The pages fluttered against the wind as she opened it to an illustration of a great, pale blue bird on a backdrop of snow and a woman in white furs riding its back.

"What are you reading?"

Dyna looked up to find Cassiel watching her inquisitively.

A blush crept up her cheeks. "Only a book of fairytales … and romantic tragedies."

The corners of his mouth quirked. "Any specific one in particular?"

She showed him the front cover. "It's about the tale of the Ice Phoenix. Have you heard of it?"

He shrugged nonchalantly. "Tell me about it."

"At the beginning of the First Age, before the time of demons and Celestials, snow covered the land of Azure. It was called the Everfrost, and ruled by Jökull, the Ice Phoenix king." Dyna flipped the page to the illustration of a striking man sitting on a throne made of ice. His long blond hair was so pale it was nearly white, with eyes the blue of frost. The page after it bore an illustration of Jökull shifting into an immense bird with light blue feathers.

"He was harsh and cruel and cared for nothing but his power. All manner of creatures bowed before him, for he had unparalleled and destructive magic—Jökull was master over life and death. Not only did his power make him invincible, he was immortal. He ruled for a thousand years and may have ruled forever if he hadn't met Sunnëva Morkhàn."

Dyna turned the book to show him the image of a woman dressed in gray furs holding a spear. Her blond hair flared around her face, fixed in a feral glare as she faced off with the Ice Phoenix.

"She was a warrior and daughter of the head of the Morkhàn clan that lived in the east. But her people were starving from the lack of food. Everfrost was a tundra of Jökull's making, and the conditions made it nearly impossible to survive. Sunnëva came to challenge him for their sake, even at the cost of her life. Taken with her ferocity and devotion, Jökull agreed to withdraw his power from the eastern edge of the Everfrost if she would remain with him in his castle until the end of her days. The head of the Morkhàn clan readily agreed and sold his daughter to the Ice Phoenix."

"I take it this did not sit well with her," Cassiel said.

"Oh no, she was furious. Sunnëva thought of Jökull as arrogant and unpleasant. She did all she could to escape with little success. His spell had bound her to the castle. The only way to free herself was to kill the Ice Phoenix. So she pretended to befriend him, hoping to discover his weakness."

"And low and behold, that is when she fell in love with him."

"I thought you never heard of this story," she said, glowering playfully.

He hid a smirk and motioned for her to continue.

"Yes, Sunnëva fell in love with Jökull, as he did with her. He made her queen of the Everfrost. She softened his frozen heart and his ways, but she worried about her people. He wished to make her happy, so he gave up his form of the phoenix and bestowed her with the magic of life and the ability to fly."

Dyna flipped the page to another illustration of Jökull and Sunnëva, wrapped in a kiss, with crowns of ice on their heads. The frosted outline of wings rose from her back.

"By giving away his wings and half of his magic, the land thawed. Green grew nearly everywhere but in the north where their castle stood, which is now known as Old Tanzanite Keep. Jökull then only had the power of death, for he gave his immortality to Sunnëva. He was a mystical being and could have lived forever, regardless. They had many years together, and she bore him three children. They were happy ... until the clans of the east rose against them."

The wind tugged at the pages, turning several until she brought her hand down over another drawing of Jökull in Sunnëva's arms, bleeding out on the frozen steps of his castle.

"They killed him in his home, and his power passed on to Sunnëva. Enraged by the loss, she used her new magic to take away life instead of giving it, wiping out the eastern clans. Many came from far and wide to witness Jökull's funeral. She built a great pyre for her husband. Then before the eyes of thousands, she cast aside her immortality and walked into the flames, ending her life." Dyna blinked back the sting in her eyes. "For she chose to be with him in death rather than not at all."

She sighed and closed the book.

Cassiel tilted his head. "It is only a story."

"I know, but it's sad and romantic."

He snorted. "Romantic? The fool relinquished his wings. I would never do that."

Dyna rolled her eyes. "I suppose it's not a tale you'd appreciate."

"I did not say that. Besides, you missed the best part."

She smiled. "I knew you'd heard of it."

His mouth hitched in a smirk. "Of course. Everyone in Azure knows the story. Some even consider it history. But I read more books on the tale when I came across it during my research on Mount Ida. They are connected."

"What?" She flipped through the pages. "I don't think I've read that part yet."

"The story continues that the pyre burned all night," Cassiel said. "And when the fires died at dawn, from the ashes, they found two seeds. But their children didn't plant the seeds. They feared the fruit it would bear."

"Were the seeds ever planted?"

"Yes. A thousand years later, by Jökull's descendant. They were right to fear it, for the seeds grew into two majestic trees which bore fruit that could grant anyone with his frightful power. The trees were taken and hidden on an island, lost to the ages until—" Cassiel paused as he leaned in close, "—Captain Ida discovered a Sacred Scroll that revealed its location."

A soft gasp left her lips.

"He ate the fruit and became so invincible he could have wrought destruction on the world if he so wished. But because magic had inadvertently given the island life, it somehow trapped him there, or so the legend goes."

Dyna sat back in her seat and stared at him. She hadn't known that part of Mount Ida's legend. There were so many versions of the story, she assumed most of them were merely tall tales.

"God of Urn, do you think it's true?"

"That is the thing about stories. They change over the years with each retelling, and by the end, no one can truly know which part was true."

"I mean the part of immortality."

He shook his head. "Immortality is for the gods. No being within our world is immortal."

"Not even the fae?"

"It could be possible for them to live nearly forever, but they cannot fully escape death. It can find them through iron, curse, or wound."

But what if the story of Jökull and his power was real? Her only concern had been reaching the island, not what or who may be on it.

"Cassiel, what if Captain Ida is alive?"

"He will defend his treasures." Cassiel nodded at her horror. "Do not dwell on it. We will concern ourselves with the possibility when we get there."

She grinned.

"What?"

"You said *when*, not *if*. Does that mean you're confident I'll survive the journey there?"

Cassiel rested his elbow on the table, propping his chin on a fist as he gave her a faint smile. "You have surprised me at every turn, Dynalya. I expect you will continue to do so."

The sound of her name on his lips elicited a flutter in her stomach. He rarely said it, rendering each moment he did memorable. The way he looked at her now, the softness of his voice, reminded her of what he'd said at the fjord. He believed in her even when she didn't.

"What did you say to me at the fjord?" she asked. "What does it mean?"

Ett haor sheli. The words slid across her mind like a veil gliding across her skin.

Cassiel shrugged. "Nothing."

"Tell me."

"I have truly forgotten."

She glowered, not believing him in the least. "Have you taken to calling me stupid human in your language now?"

He smirked. "If I were, I would call you *haddam lonavon*. Unwise human."

She couldn't help but laugh. "And how do you say Celestial?"

"There was no word for Celestial when the Seraphim fell. If there is one now, we do not know it."

Cassiel crossed his arms, and her eyes fell over the sharp, elegant lines of his new form-fitting jacket. Without his wings, he passed as human, if one wasn't looking too closely at his unearthly beauty and luminance. Enchanted clothing was a manner of safety, but he had refused to trade for it.

"What would happen if they caught you trading your feathers?" she asked quietly, making sure no one was around to listen. The tables had momentarily cleared.

"The same that would occur if my father learned I have given you my blood," he said, matching her volume. "It would mean my exile, without question."

She clenched her hands on her lap. "How is a Celestial exiled?"

"The wings are shorn. Then the High King compels them to forget. He erases the memories of their past and replaces them with new ones as a precaution, as not to lead humans to the Realms."

That stunned Dyna into momentary silence. She'd known the removal of the wings was part of it, but the revelation that his father could alter their memories left her a little startled.

She recalled King Yoel's threat to Prince Malakel in the dining hall. *I will have you exiled with the removal of your wings. Then you will resemble the very humans you loathe so much.*

He would do that to his sons?

"I didn't know your father had that ability," she said, shifting nervously in her seat. If he so wished, King Yoel could have made her forget ever meeting Cassiel. Fortunately, he'd allowed her immunity.

"Compelling minds is one of a few powers he has," Cassiel said. "The abilities of the High King are passed on to the heir once they ascend to the throne."

Her eyes widened. Cassiel may have that power one day.

"Exile is a severe sentence in the Four Realms," he said, looking at the evening sky. "Not only would an exiled Celestial never fly again, the source of their power is lost. Without our wings, our blood loses its ability to heal, and we become mortals."

"Why did you risk that for me?"

"You were bleeding to death. I couldn't leave you to die." He sighed, seeing the conflict on her face. "The only way I could save you was with my blood. But I had never used it to heal someone before. Without thinking, I cut my palms and placed them on your wounds, inadvertently..."

Warmth flushed through her cheeks. "Creating the bond."

Cassiel nodded, fidgeting with a cuff on his sleeve. "When my kind began the trades with humans before The Decimation, they only sold their blood in vials. Never directly through contact. Giving blood is one thing, and something else entirely to exchange it with another. It is a sacred act reserved only for when a Celestial has found a mate."

The nervous flutter in her stomach moved to her chest.

"One must choose carefully, for it is permanent and can never be undone." Cassiel traced the grooves on the wooden table, and she wondered if he was thinking of the Druid. He'd said he wanted to ask if there was a way to break the bond.

"Has anyone regretted bonding with another before?"

"It has happened more times than you would imagine." He traced the silver embellishments of his sleeve. "The bond merely binds your souls, not your heart. If it could forge love, I imagine many like my father would be much happier."

Tingles rushed down Dyna's arms. The bond didn't influence how she felt. That one fact had her shoulders sagging with relief. Her feelings were never false.

"I hope one day you could forgive my mistake," Cassiel said, the lump in his throat bobbing. "You are not obliged to me in any way. The bonding happened without your consent, and you are human. Our ways do not apply to you." His silver gaze flickered to her, then fell away. "You are free to marry whom you wish when the time comes."

Marry whom you wish.

He was freeing her. Giving her the choice to live how she wanted, and yet ...

Dyna looked out at the sea and listened to the water lap as an ache filled her chest.

"Do you despise me for what I have done?" he asked softly.

She shook her head. "Your selfless act saved me. I don't hold it against you."

His cool fingers turned her face so she would look at him. It sent a tingle across her cheek. "Then why do I sense you are troubled?"

"What does the bond mean to you?" Dyna asked, unable to mask the break in her voice. "Does it mean nothing?"

Cassiel simply stared at her, and his hand slipped away. She resumed watching the sea, suddenly self-conscious for being so candid. She hardly understood the aspects of a Blood Bond, but she knew in her heart it was important. He said himself it meant marriage. That made him her husband and she his wife. She couldn't simply ignore that and marry another. Dyna glanced down at Cassiel's loose fist resting on the table. Those hands had bonded them, but it had nothing to do with her heart.

"Well, the deed is done," she said faintly. "You have my word that I shall not reveal it to another Celestial on my part. I don't wish for you to be exiled at the expense of saving my life. It was a mistake after all."

"Saving you was not a mistake," he replied, his tone careful. "That I do not regret. There is a chance my father may pardon me for giving you divine blood as it resulted in a bond. If so, your immunity now extends to all Four Celestial Realms." His expression shifted. "And well, now he cannot foist me into marriage."

Because he had been forced into one with her. Dyna couldn't help the slight sting the thought invited. Cassiel was studying her, and she made sure her walls were in place.

"Wait, what do you mean he cannot?" she asked.

"A bonded life-mate truly is for life. I can never exchange blood with another because it would taint the bond we have. I hear doing so is not only akin to adultery, it is a disgrace and physically agonizing. That applies to you as well. You cannot mix your blood with another unless you wish to do me harm."

Dyna scoffed. "I'm sure there is no risk of another Celestial willing to impose their divine blood upon me."

The corner of his mouth quirked. "You are probably right."

Even if they kept it a secret, King Yoel would eventually find out when he attempted to arrange a life-mate for his son.

"Will your father be angry?"

"Oh, I certainly expect to sustain his displeasure." Cassiel sighed. "For other than this reason, I did not go to Hermon Ridge as he believed. Lord Jophiel must have notified him by now that I failed to arrive within the allotted week after leaving Hilos."

She gasped. "Cassiel, your father will assume the worst has happened to you."

He frowned and rubbed his forehead. "I had not considered that. I could not tell him I would go to the place that took my mother from him. He would not allow me to go."

The night she showed King Yoel her map to Mount Ida, he'd been shocked. She must have reminded him of his lost love. He accepted the loss, but Cassiel still clung to the hope his mother was alive. Dyna heard it in his voice last night and could see it now.

"Will he send the Watchers after you?" she asked.

He shook his head. "No, that would put the Realms at risk."

"But you're his son."

"One life weighed against the security of the Four Celestial Realms holds no contest."

Dyna couldn't believe that King Yoel would abandon his son, no matter what was at risk. A parent was meant to protect their child.

"We're near Hermon Ridge," she said. "Perhaps he would send the Valkyrie to your aid."

Cassiel's eyes widened as his complexion paled. "I certainly hope not. Yelrakel frightens me."

"Who?"

"Yelrakel is the Captain of the Valkyrie. Sowmya is her second. Both wield blue fire."

"Wait, what?" Dyna straightened in her seat, remembering what he had told her about it once before. "I thought those swords were kept locked away."

"The original Seraph swords created in the Heavens are. In some rare instances, *Elyōn* may bless a Celestial with blue fire. They are among the few chosen. All the females within the legion are gifted warriors, but those two..." He shuddered. "They are something else."

Dyna hid a smile. If they frightened him, they must certainly be something.

Once they finished their light meal, they gathered up their belongings and made their way through the pier. Idle ships dotted in the Saxe Sea. A group of Azure Guards marched past in perfect unison, their coattails flaring behind them. The leader glanced at them as they passed. He had a stern face; dark brown hair kept neat and short, like his beard. He commanded presence and authority in his regimental blue coat. Dyna held her breaths under his peering gaze, but the guard moved on.

"There are many guards around."

"The kingdom receives cargo from all over the world, so guards make sure the ports run smoothly," Cassiel said.

The Azure Guards stopped at a docked merchant ship further down and the leader spoke to the ship's captain. The annoyed man begrudgingly handed over his ledger as the guards began breaking open barrels and crates.

"What are they doing?" she asked.

"They are inspecting cargo to make sure no one is smuggling goods that carry high taxes. The city profits off of it, so they cannot allow the loss."

The lead Azure Guard signed off the captain's paperwork and moved on with his men to the next ship.

"Occasionally, they catch those attempting to smuggle opiates into the city or slave traders attempting to smuggle orphaned children out."

Her stomach rolled. "Children?"

"The slave traders will take the destitute without families to Versai, a small country in the east that actively buys and sells slaves. They are rarely successful," he added, seeing her dismay. "The Azure Guards do well to keep the city safe."

Von and his life-debt to Tarn came to mind. Azure didn't permit slave trades, but it had permitted the life-debt, and it was essentially the same. But the life-debt was abolished now. Von was free now. Had he left Tarn's side? With what she knew of that man, most likely not.

She really had been so naïve of the outside world, sheltered in her village, believing people were kind and good. It saddened her to realize it wasn't always true.

A large ship sailed into the harbor and docked in front of them, flying the symbol of an ax. The white sails deflated as the ship's anchor dropped with a loud splash. Sailors called to each other while they pulled on the ropes and worked on lowering the sails. They dropped a gangplank on the deck and unloaded large cages with wild animals inside. The sound of their cries and growls filled the pier.

A muscle in Cassiel's jaw flexed. "Regrettably, poaching remains legal in Azure. Come, we should make our way to the tavern."

But he wandered to the cages, and Dyna followed. Restless large cats paced in their cages, and the reptiles snapped their teeth as they passed. There were a variety of brightly colored birds. Parrots with vivid green, yellow, and red feathers and short curved beaks squawked at her.

"Oh, look at this one." She pointed at a massive cage behind the others.

It held a noble bird a head taller than her, with feathers a deep red blending into a fiery orange and yellow at the tips. Blue feathers lined its black eyes. One eye fixed on them and its long, sharp talons scraped against the bottom of the cage as it rotated its large body to face them.

Cassiel froze, his mouth parting. "It's a fire phoenix."

The bird let out an angry screech and reared, opening its lethal pointed beak. Within its mouth, an orange glow grew. Cassiel tackled her to the ground before a gust of flame blew over them. He protected her head with his own until the heat passed. Dyna peeked through her squinted eyes at him, highly aware of his body pinning her down.

Getting to his feet, Cassiel helped her stand and backed her away from the cage. The phoenix squawked at them, attempting to flap its wings in the narrow cage. It was a massive bird, but only an eighth of the size of the Ice Phoenix in the book.

Cassiel smiled and shook his head. "I have never seen one in person before. They are highly rare and so incredibly hard to catch."

"Aye, but no' for me master," said a haughty voice. A scruffy dwarf hobbled out from behind the cages. He gave them a toothy grin. "Master Draven has caught and sold every creature imaginable, including this beauty." He jabbed a thumb in the bird's direction. "Are ya interested in the phoenix? I could sell it to you for fifty thousand gold pieces. That is the best deal you'll ever find, considering—"

"They are almost extinct." Cassiel grabbed the dwarf's shirt and lifted him into the air. "Release it at once."

The dwarf rolled his eyes and bellowed at the ship. "Master Draven, we have another zealot here!"

The door to the captain's quarters busted open and a burly man stepped out. Leaping over the railing of the boat with a length of rope, he landed near them on the dock and approached in long, confident strides. A fur shawl rested over his bulky shoulders, the rest of him wrapped in leather armor.

Cassiel dropped the dwarf and took Dyna's arm, pulling her back as the man approached.

Draven clutched a long battle-ax, the wooden handle adorned with braided leather and embellished steel. He pointed the two-headed edge at Cassiel. "Don't touch my dwarves," he said in a coarse voice. The sea breeze whipped at his dark brown hair streaked with gray. A thick beard framed his squared face, tanned and weathered from life at sea. "If you're not here for business, then off with you, mate."

Neither of them replied because dangling from the neck of Draven's ax was a tassel of charms, three of which were grindylow scales.

"Cassiel," Dyna called under her breath. His hand slid down her arm to take hold of hers and squeezed gently, signaling he noticed them too.

"You cannot cage a phoenix," he said. "They are nearly extinct because of people like you."

Draven sneered. Scars marked his thick, muscular arms, left behind by teeth and claws from his catches. Four long, jagged scars ran down half his face through one eye, leaving it milky white. "Then it shouldn't surprise you that I have one, aye? There is no law against it."

"Well, there should be," Dyna huffed.

"You'll keep that woman quiet lest I tan her hide."

"I beg your pardon?" she snapped before Cassiel could reply.

The poacher's glare fixed on her, but it faded as a slow smile spread across his dry lips.

"Fine little minnow you've got here," he said. The abhorrent way he looked at her left a clammy sensation on Dyna's skin.

Cassiel's back tensed and he shifted his stance to block the man's view.

Draven merely moved to keep leering at her. "Well, are you here to trade, mate?"

"The scales," Cassiel said through his teeth, and Dyna sensed how much he hated saying it. "I will purchase them from you."

Laughing, Draven crudely tickled the cluster of charms. "You want these wee things? Nearly lost me other eye to get them. I have another offer for you, honest business." He nodded at Dyna. "I'll give you a scale for her. I'm in need of a bonnie lass to clean my cabin and to keep me warm at night."

What the poacher implied struck her as if he'd slapped her. Cassiel's entire demeanor changed. Something dark and cold filled her mind as the planes of his face hardened into stone.

"What did you say?" he asked, his quiet voice coated in icy wrath.

The poacher grinned, exposing all his teeth. "I want to mount your woman until she knows nothing but my name."

Cassiel's eyes burned like silver flames. He drew his knife, his jaw tight with tension. "Dyna. Go."

She stiffened as his intent washed through the bond. Any reservations he had against bloodshed were gone. He would kill this man.

A group of dwarves and men clambered down the gangplank to join the poacher's side. A lanky young man with fewer scars, Draven's same features and contemptible sneer followed behind them.

"Come on then, boy. I could do with a fight." The poacher widened his stance and readied his battle-ax. His assemblage snickered, taking out serrated daggers.

Dyna clutched Cassiel's sleeve and tugged him back. "Let's go. The others are waiting for us."

But he wouldn't budge.

"Is there a problem here?" a voice asked.

The unit of Azure Guards who had been inspecting cargo stood behind Dyna and Cassiel with their swords drawn out. The leader regarded all of them with calm brown eyes. He stood tall in his fine regimental coat; dark brown hair perfectly swept back from his handsome face. A brass badge shone on his left lapel with the Azure sigil of an interwoven seven-pointed star.

The dwarves cursed under their breaths. She heard them whisper the name Veron and read the nervousness on their faces.

Draven straightened from his stance. "You needn't trouble yourself, Commissioner. We were merely exchanging pleasantries, is all."

"I see nothing pleasant about it."

The poacher shrugged innocently, leaning on his ax. "Well, there may have been a dispute over the trade of a slave and our nightly endeavors."

Cassiel gripped his knife, a vein pulsing in his taut neck. "Speak another ill word."

"Stay your weapon," the commissioner ordered. "Now."

"Cassiel." Dyna took his arm. The muscle was as hard as marble beneath her hand. The Azure Guards were ready to cut him down if he disobeyed. "Please."

His jaw flexed, a moment dragging before he conceded and sheathed the knife.

The commissioner motioned at the guards to lower their swords.

"This is not the conduct I will have in my city," Veron told them, his Azure accent smooth and casual. "I take it you're not from here, so I'll disregard this with a warning. Any fighting on the streets will be met severe consequences." His gaze pinned to the poacher next. "It would be wise to cease harassing the travelers, Draven. Your lawlessness won't be tolerated, no matter the provocation. There are quite enough complaints against you already. One more violation and I will revoke your trade license indefinitely. Am I understood?"

"Of course, sir."

"Good. As you were. I will return shortly to check your logs." The commissioner glanced at Dyna and Cassiel again. "Come."

The guards surrounded them and forced them to walk behind the commissioner. Cassiel's hand found hers as the guards led them away from the ship. She glanced back at Draven and his dwarves, and they grinned at her. She exhaled a low breath. Cassiel would have fought them if the guards hadn't arrived.

The setting sun layered an amber glow over his wary expression trained on the Azure Guards. His worry swam through her.

"Who are you?" Cassiel asked the leader. "Where are you taking us?"

"I am Veron Moreland, Commissioner of the Azure Guard in this city. And to answer your question: nowhere on my account. I simply meant to escort you safely away. Draven Skinner has always been a disagreeable man, and you'll do well to stay away from him. May I ask where you're lodging?"

Cassiel hesitated before answering. "We are staying at the Cobalt Tavern."

"That is nearby." Veron stopped and motioned at a guard to come forward. "It's run by the family of Corporal Willam."

The corporal had a kind face, short reddish-brown curls, and a thin nose. His soft brown eyes nearly disappeared behind his spectacles when he smiled at them. The man reminded Dyna of her little brother. Her heart clenched when she imagined he was who Thane might have grown up to be.

"Corporal, please escort them to the tavern. Make sure of their lodging, then return. We will continue inspecting cargo here."

"Aye, sir." He saluted, then motioned for Dyna and Cassiel to follow him along the pier. "My name is Kye Willam, and yours?"

"I'm Dyna, and this is Cassiel," she said as they walked alongside him. "It's a pleasure to meet you."

"Likewise. How long are you staying in the Port of Azure?"

"Merely passing through," Cassiel replied.

"We're planning to board a ship to Dwarf Shoe," Dyna added.

Kye chuckled. "Fine that. We receive quite a bit of transit business since the bridge was closed off to travelers fifteen years ago."

"The bridge?"

"Aye, it's a narrow isthmus bridging Azure to the rest of Urn. It lies north from here, west of the Hermon Mountains."

"He is referring to the Troll Bridge," Cassiel said, and she recalled he had pointed it out to her on the map before.

"You know of it then," Kye said. "The isthmus was well-traveled before. There was a small town there once, by the name of Azurite, in honor of our kingdom. Sadly, cave trolls overran the isthmus, and they ravaged the town. No one survived."

Dyna sighed. "That's awful."

Kye tilted his head in condolence. "That it is. Crossing Dwarf Shoe by ship was once costly, forcing the impoverished to risk crossing Troll Bridge only to meet their demise. The ship captains decreased their fares to make it more affordable for everyone to sail."

He shook his head with a heavy sigh. "Only the brave and desperate go there now. Every winter, King Lenneus offers prisoners in his kingdom the chance to regain their freedom should they be able to eradicate the trolls. None have returned."

Dyna covered her mouth at the news.

"You mean the Azure King sends people to their deaths for the slight chance that he may recuperate that land," Cassiel said, a bite lacing his tone.

"Aye, and I don't agree with it either," Kye said with a weak clearing of his throat. "But I don't have any say in the matter."

"Oh, don't mind him," Dyna said, giving Cassiel a frown. When the corporal walked ahead, she whispered, "You ought to be kind to humans, Cassiel."

"What would that serve? Protecting you is my only priority." His fingertips brushed her temple as he swept a lock of hair from her eyes.

The touch sent a course of warmth through her, heating her cheeks where his fingers touched. But Cassiel froze, and he dropped his hand. With a deliberate step, he backed away, taking her brief happiness with him.

CHAPTER 41

Cassiel winced at the look on Dyna's face. He backed away, and she glanced away to the ground, rubbing her arms. The feel of her skin hummed on his fingers. The touch was intimate, unsuitable, and beyond the boundaries of their association. He couldn't seem to maintain his wits about him when it came to her.

When Dyna had asked him if he thought their bond meant nothing, he couldn't reply. He had been fighting the answer to that question since the moment they exchanged blood. Thinking about it meant he would have to think about other things. He didn't want that vulnerability, but she continued to chip away at his walls.

It was ludicrous. He was a Nephilim, and she was a human.

Their bond couldn't amount to anything.

Corporal Kye Willam cleared his throat. "In any case, you will enjoy my family's tavern, I assure you. Come along. It's around the bend here."

They continued their walk in silence. Cassiel peeked at Dyna from the corner of his sight, remaining close by her side. She kept her gaze downcast, watching her boots move over the worn cobblestones of the street. Evening was descending and the temperature with it. Their breaths clouded in the air.

"How long has your family owned the Cobalt Tavern?" Dyna asked the corporal.

"It has been in my family for three generations," Kye said. "My grandfather worked in the mines, mining sapphires, and other precious stones until he had enough to have the tavern built. It's been passed down in my family since."

Dyna smiled. "That's lovely."

"Aye, my mother is the owner now. Her name is Annora. I'll have her give you two a cut-rate." He winked at her.

"Oh, that's very kind. Thank you."

"It's my pleasure, lass." Kye chuckled, but it faded when he noticed Cassiel's glower. He cleared his throat again. "Right, well, here we are."

They came before a towering stone structure with three chimneys on the roof. Hundreds of windows decorated the elevation, all of them made with stained blue glass. The two wide doors at the entrance were painted rich cobalt. The bustle of voices and music leaked from inside. A couple of men on horses pulled astride the tavern. Stable hands came out to take the reins, leading the horses to the stables beside the tavern.

They followed Kye through the front doors. A colorful throng of bodies packed the lobby, the voices merging into a boisterous roar. The hot and stuffy air carried the scent of sweat, stale mead, and roasted meat. The Corporal motioned them to follow. Cassiel took Dyna's elbow and kept her close as they made their way through the mass, but he soon lost sight of Kye. There were too many people. Elves jostled past them. He scarcely dodged the hooves of a centaur and swatted at the fairies flitting past his ears. A drunken man stumbled against Dyna and leaned in close, chortling in her face.

"Watch it, sodden fool." Cassiel shoved him back into the crowd.

"This way!" Kye waved at them over the crop of heads.

Cassiel guided Dyna in front of him, shielding her from the multitude of people. She made it to the bar and pulled him through the last wall of bodies to Kye's side. The Corporal leaned over the bar counter and waved at the young barmaids who shared his features, but they were too busy attending the demanding crowd. He gave up calling them and yelled through his cupped hands at a pudgy woman rushing to pour ale from a wall of stacked barrels into mugs. She wore a dark navy dress under her dirty apron, brown curls tied in a messy braid. Sweat gleamed on her forehead and flushed cheeks.

"Mother!" Kye put force into his shout, rising above the noise. "Mother!"

She beamed at the sight of her son and hurried over. "Oh, thank the heavens you're here, Kye. The gods know I could use the help."

"Sorry, I have to return to cargo duty. I brought you a couple more patrons." Kye clapped Cassiel's arm. "They require lodging for the night. Dyna, Cassiel, this is my mother, Annora."

She cocked an eyebrow at them. "You promised them a cut-rate, didn't you?"

Kye patted her chubby hands. "Be a dear. You can't turn away this young man and his bonnie wife."

Cassiel coughed at the sudden lump in his throat. He wanted to protest the assumption, even though it wasn't incorrect. He thought Dyna would clarify the mistake, but she blushed and fidgeted with her dress sleeve.

"You embarrassed them, Kye." Annora laughed and smacked his shoulder with a wet rag.

The corporal winked at them. "Don't you worry none. My mother will see to you. Enjoy your stay." Then he slipped into the crowd and disappeared from view.

Annora sighed and shook her head. "My son loves to bring me customers, but he forgets how quickly the rooms fill. I only have one room left, and I know it's taken." She motioned at the back wall, where a large placard held rows of hooks set above black numbers. One brass key hung on a hook in the third row.

"That one is certainly mine," Cassiel said.

Annora chuckled. "You're not the first to say so, sir."

"A friend of ours should have arrived earlier to reserve our lodging, mistress. His name is Nelrron," Dyna said, mentioning Rawn's alias.

"I hear too many names in a day to remember them all, lamb."

Cassiel exhaled sharply. "He's an elf. Tall, blond, with the speech of another age. Dresses like a vagrant."

Annora's face lit up, and a giddy smile broke through. "Oh, yes, now I remember! He came through early this noon. Handsome gent if I ever met one, and *courteous*," she added, giving Cassiel a disapproving frown. Annora brought out a thick, heavy book from under the counter and opened it to a section bookmarked with a blue ribbon. She ran a finger down the list of guest names. "Nelrron, Nelrron ... aye, here it is. Nelrron reserved three rooms. He noted here the last key is for a young man, but no name, only another alias. How do I know it's you?"

Cassiel groaned. "He chose an alias for me?"

"Aye, in good faith, I'll allow you a guess."

He raked a hand through his hair, trying to remain calm. Rawn didn't mention he would use an alias for the rest of them. He didn't know what it could be. The elf referred to him by royal address. So did Zev.

"Could it be ... Your Highness?"

She grinned. "I can see why he chose that."

Cassiel glowered at Dyna playfully when he caught her hiding a smile.

Annora snatched the key off the wall and handed it to him with a flourish. "Welcome. Your room is on the third floor, *Your Highness*."

"Thank you," he sighed in relief, ignoring the tease. For a moment, he'd worried there would be no lodging for the night.

Annora winked at them in the same manner her son had. "It gets quite busy this time of year. Thank sir Nelrron for reserving the last room for you and your wife."

The lump returned to Cassiel's throat, leading to a coughing fit. Dyna patted his back.

"Oh dear, he must be knackered," Annora told her. "Better get him to bed, then. I'll send meals to your room. Your friend noted you abstain from meat. I'll have the cook make something special." With that, she tucked away the reservation book and rushed off.

"Wait," Cassiel called, but the innkeeper disappeared into the kitchens. He gripped the key in his hand.

"Rawn forgot to mention the room is only for you," Dyna said. "I was to board with Lucenna."

"Well, how are we to know in which room you need to stay? We cannot stay together."

Cassiel cut back into the crowd to search for the others. There were too many people, too many faces to make sense of any individual one. He circled the floor, but there was no way to find them among the throng. They were unlikely to be in it. Rawn and Lucenna needed to remain out of sight.

"They will not be here," Cassiel said to Dyna, but at her silence, he turned around to find her gone. He was an idiot. Her petite frame must not have been able to follow him through the crowd.

He took a breath to regain the calm he didn't feel and closed his eyes. Searching for her through the bond, Dyna's presence hovering around his senses pulled him back to the bar like a glowing torch in his mind. Cassiel elbowed a path through the wall of bodies to get to her, ignoring the shouts of protest and outrage.

"An apology is a common courtesy," a deep voice growled.

"You would not need one if you had not been in my way," Cassiel said. He didn't have time for this.

"Come again?"

Gritting his teeth, Cassiel spun around, only to meet the hairy chest of an orc. The creature's colossal body towered a few feet over him, his complexion green as moss with angry cat eyes. Sharp canines jutted out of his swollen lips, and long, pointed ears stood out amongst the orc's dark green hair tied in a tail. Leather boots fitted his massive feet, leather gauntlets, and armor protecting his body as thick as a tree and fists the size of Cassiel's head. In one mammoth hand, he carried a huge cudgel hammer. With the other, he grabbed the collar of Cassiel's coat and yanked him into the air.

The orc shook him back and forth until his vision spun. "Apologize."

"All right! My apologies, Master Orc."

It took a few seconds for his sight to focus. At this new height, he locked on the familiar red of Dyna's hair at the other end of the tavern. His relief was short-lived. A group of dwarves surrounded her, jeering and pulling on her dress. Cassiel shouted her name, but the chorus of voices and music swallowed his call.

"Is that your woman?" the orc asked, following his gaze.

Cassiel flushed at the question and tried to pry the creature's thick fingers from his coat. "You have no right to my business. Release me at once."

"You left her alone in this swarm? That was unchivalrous of you."

"I will take no lectures from an orc. Now unhand me."

The orc shook him again, and Cassiel nearly fell out of his coat. He desperately clung to the lapels, fearing to be ousted in front of hundreds of people. The buttons strained as the fabric slipped through his sweaty hands. One popped off, and he dropped half a foot down.

"By all the gods." The orc gaped at the sight of a few revealed feathers past Cassiel's shoulder. He quickly fixed the coat properly to hide his wings again. "You're foolish to come here, divine one, even with your enchantments," he said in a harsh whisper. "Too many poachers hereabouts. Are you fixing to get yourself killed? You must be on your way before you're discovered."

It was then Cassiel remembered Rael's Accords also bound the orcs. A colony of them lived near Hermon Ridge and were on good terms with his uncle.

Cassiel's heart slowly calmed from his panic. "I was doing so until you stopped me, Master Orc."

"Aye, call me Elric."

"A pleasure. If you will excuse me, I have a dire matter to see to." Cassiel squirmed in his grasp, trying to break free.

He cursed as the dwarves yanked on Dyna's arms, dragging her towards the entrance. The drunken crowd gathered to watch the struggle in amusement.

Elric growled. "Them lot are poachers. Is she another like you?"

"No."

"Who is she to you, then?"

Only the truth would convince the orc to let him go. Heat rushed to Cassiel's face as he spoke the words aloud. "She is my wife. Now, will you please release me?"

"I'll do you one better." Lifting his hammer, the orc roared at the crowd.

They scrambled out of the way, and a path formed for them. Elric's heavy footsteps thudded on the floor as he carried Cassiel to Dyna. Her voice filtered towards them as they approached.

"Unhand me." She kicked a dwarf in the groin and punched another in the face. She quickly took out the knife strapped to her calf, holding it so well it made him proud. "Touch me again, and I-I'll put another hole in your face."

Elric chuckled, and Cassiel grinned. She fixed the dwarves with a fierce glare. But to him, the dainty human with the pointy knife looked rather adorable.

"Come with us," another jeered. "Master will pay your sire finely for the service of your comfort ..."

The dwarf trailed off when Elric stomped over to them, releasing Cassiel. He landed on his feet beside Dyna. Their beady eyes flickered from him to the gargantuan orc repeatedly. They were Draven's dwarves.

Elric roared, sending them scrambling under the tables. He cackled. "I quite enjoy doing that."

The crowd laughed with him. Most were drunk and swaying on their feet, their jolly complexions colored crimson.

"Are you hurt?" Cassiel asked Dyna.

"I'm fine," she said a tad sharply, sheathing her knife.

"What is it?" He lifted her chin.

Dyna's wet eyes shone under the chandeliers above them. She jerked her chin away, hiding beneath her hair. "I thought you'd left me behind."

He frowned.

Elric nudged him with his hammer. "Apologize to the lass."

"Forgive me," Cassiel mumbled and cringed at how difficult it was to say. Apologizing wasn't something he did often, but in this case, she made him want to change that.

"Louder, so we can all hear you!" someone in the crowd hollered. Several agreed in loud cackles.

He might have spat a curse if he hadn't noted a smile pulling on the corners of Dyna's lips. Well, if it would make her happy, he'd gladly comply.

"I'm sorry," he announced. A collective cheer and laughter went through the crowd, and they clapped in approval. She allowed him to adjust the sleeves of her dress and right her tousled hair behind her ears. "I left in a hurry to find the others, but I assumed you followed. I did not intend to leave you. That is one thing I would never do."

Dyna's eyes lifted to him and held.

"Now kiss her!" another hooted.

The people whistled and jeered with mocking laughter. Cassiel rolled his eyes. They were out of their bloody minds.

The orc chuckled. "You said she's yours. What man doesn't give his mate a kiss?"

Dyna's eyes widened. Well, it wasn't as though he spoke a lie. She was his, in a manner of speaking. In an unauthentic, insignificant, meaningless manner of speaking.

"Husband," Dyna said, her voice sending a tingle down his spine. A small smirk played on her mouth. She startled him when she rose on her toes and lightly pressed her soft lips to his cheek. "Come, I'm tired and would like to retreat for the evening," she said aloud for others to hear, and linked her arm through his.

Their audience erupted in protests.

"Enough!" Elric parted the throng of drunks aside with a threatening wave of his hammer. Cassiel led Dyna after his rumbling steps until they reached the stairwell at the other end of the tavern.

"Thank you, Elric."

The orc grunted. "Think nothing of it. Have this teach you it won't do to leave a lady unescorted in this city or any other."

It was the second warning given to him that day. Cassiel instinctively tugged Dyna closer.

"You'll do well to keep yourself out of sight as well, divine one."

"Unfortunately, he knows my secret," Cassiel told Dyna at the jolt of her alarm. "He nearly tore off my jacket."

Elric winked at her. "Aye, we were in a bit of a scuffle. Not that he didn't deserve it, mind you. If he was any other bloke, I would have felled him."

Dyna smiled. "Thank you for your help."

"It was my pleasure, lass. You tell me if he makes you cry again. I would be more than pleased to teach him to mind his manners." Elric gave Cassiel a warning glare before heading back into the crowd.

Once the orc left, they idled in the stairwell, with the tumult of the busy tavern between them. His cheek still tingled where her lips had touched him.

"Did you find the others?" Dyna asked.

Cassiel scratched at his neck, feeling her stare. "No. They must have retired. We don't know what rooms they are in, and there is no way to contact them. I suppose this means ..." He swallowed; his throat suddenly dry. "We will share a room tonight."

"Oh ..."

"There is no other option." He climbed the stairs, struggling with a sudden bout of nerves. There wasn't anything else he could do about the situation.

What would the others think of this? The question sprouted a layer of sweat along his back. What choice did he have? If Rawn and the others had been in the lobby, they would have found them. No one could have missed the spectacle they made.

All he could hope for was that Zev wouldn't kill him.

CHAPTER 42

When they reached the third floor, Cassiel paused at the tug of Dyna's fingers on the edge of his sleeve. Flickering sconces dimly lit the long hallway. The window at the end was black with the night. Her wide eyes fixed on the dark corners of the hall, and a trickle of her fear came through the bond.

He took her hand. "Come along. It is all right."

Together, they checked the brass room numbers on each blue door until they reached 311. By the door was a wooden tray with two covered plates. He inserted the key through the lock and pushed open the door. The room was pitch black inside. She hesitated at the doorway, staring into the darkness. He frowned and went in first, dumping his pack on the bed. There was an oil lamp on the bedside table. With the matches he found in the drawer, he lit the wick and illuminated the room.

A single bed rested against the wall, a fact Cassiel ignored. At the end of the room was a screen to hide the bathtub and chamber pot from view. A set of doors led to a small balcony, but not much else was in the room besides a small dining table with a single chair and a wardrobe. Dyna lifted the tray of food and hesitantly came in, her eyes flitting to the shapes crawling on the walls.

"Are you really so afraid of the dark?" Cassiel asked.

She placed the tray on the table, not turning to look at him. "I know such a thing is unbecoming."

He looked around the room, fidgeting with the loose button of his coat. "How have you endured it at home?"

"I share a room with my sister, and I keep the lamp on all night."

Cassiel sighed. He may as well accept he wouldn't rest fully tonight. "Then we will keep it on all night."

"Thank you," she said, her soft voice lifting the sharp edge of his irritation.

They stood still and quiet in the room, too aware of each other. Well, if he was alone, he knew what he would have preferred to do.

Cassiel cleared his throat, fighting the heat surfacing on his face again. "I will give you leave to bathe and prepare for bed."

Before Dyna could reply, he took a plate for himself and stepped out onto the balcony, closing the door behind him. The platform was a small wooden ledge enclosed in an iron railing. He sat down and uncovered his meal, revealing a roasted acorn squash stuffed with chickpeas, grains, and herbs. The twinkling lights of the city served as a view while he ate. Once his belly was full, he stood and leaned against the railing.

The bustle didn't end with the night. Lampposts illuminated the streets as several people milled about, and Azure Guards patrolled the area in pairs. He smelled the brine in the air as a breeze blew past, rippling through his hair. The nearly full moon shone in the sky, its silvery light reflecting over the surface of the sea. The sight of it drew his thoughts to Zev. His next change was coming in a few days. They needed to make sure Rawn and Lucenna were prepared for it.

His gaze lifted at the movement of birds soaring past the moon, their wings rapidly slipping into the wispy clouds. For a moment, their large, elongated shapes almost resembled Celestials.

He must be really exhausted to be imagining things.

Cassiel stayed out on the balcony until he couldn't withstand shivering from the cold. He dared to peek inside the room, and found Dyna already asleep. She lay curled under the white bedsheets, damp hair splayed on her pillow.

He slipped inside and headed for the screen divider to wash up. She had already used the bathwater, but he couldn't call down for more without waking her. The water wasn't murky. Besides, he hadn't washed in too many days to be fastidious.

Cassiel stripped off his clothes and sunk into the tepid water. He used the salts and oils on a tiny bench next to the bath to clean himself and rapidly scrubbed his body. The privacy screen hid him well, but he hurried lest she woke. It was the quickest bath he had ever taken.

He got out, patted himself dry, and dressed in clean black trousers and a dark green tunic. His bare feet slinked across the cold wooden floorboards to the wardrobe. Within its shelves were folded piles of blankets. He pulled out several along with a pillow and made himself a spot on the floor next to the bed.

Cassiel tried to get comfortable, but his body was restless and stiff. The light from the lamp filtered through his eyelids, keeping sleep at bay. Tossing and turning didn't help to ignore it. Dyna was already asleep. She didn't need it anymore. He reached out for the lamp's dial and doused the lamp. Pitch black filled his surroundings, as he liked it.

Resting on his stomach, he stretched his wings as far as they could go, then brought them down and covered himself with their warmth. Laying this way on the floor near Dyna reminded him of their night in Corron. In his drunken logic, he had wanted to comfort her, so he brought her under his wing. How had he done it so blatantly? Perhaps it was because of saving her life so many times, or the bond had something to do with it.

Dyna was too trusting of the world. Cassiel had to shield her from it. But when did his self-preservation take second place to hers? The questions he struggled to understand spun in his head, fueling his restlessness. Cassiel groaned, burrowing into the pillow. He wanted to sleep and forget everything else.

Something shifted inside of him as he was struck with horrid panic. The sudden onslaught gripped his bones, and his heart hammered behind his ribs. It was coming through the bond. A sharp scream shattered the darkness. Dyna thrashed and kicked wildly on the bed.

Cassiel scrambled to light a match, her deafening screams piercing his ears. After the third match, he lit the wick of the lamp, and the room filled with soft light. Dyna writhed and shrieked against an invisible foe. Her wild eyes bulged with horror at something unseen, her face wet with tears, and the sheets tangled around her limbs. She hyperventilated, her chest rising rapidly.

Cassiel held her down. "Dyna, calm yourself. Breathe." She gulped in air, and her crazed eyes focused on him. "It is me."

Her small body shook beneath his hands. He carefully freed her from the tangled sheets, and she latched herself onto him. He let her embrace him, too stunned to care. Her arms trembled around his neck as sobs wracked her body.

Cassiel shifted his position to sit on the bed, hesitating before pulling Dyna onto his lap. He sat there rigidly, not sure what to do. Her tears soaked through his tunic, and he worried she would cry all night. She trembled against him, whether from fear or cold, he didn't know.

He wrapped her in his wings and hoped it would help. Opening himself to the bond, he sent a sense of calm through until soothing energy coursed between them. He gently ran his fingers through her hair, his fingertips tingling with each stroke that brushed her skin. Her cries slowly quieted. After a few more minutes of sniffling and hiccups, she fell silent.

Cassiel waited another minute, then asked, "Are you feeling better?"

She nodded against his chest.

"Do you care to tell me what that was about?"

Dyna shook her head. Embracing him tighter, she tucked her face against his throat.

Her nightmare had already terrified her, then she woke to find the room ... dark. Zev had always gathered extra firewood to keep the campfire going until sunrise. Now he finally understood why.

It's not the dark I fear, but the things that may lurk within it.

"You fear the Shadow that only appears at night," Cassiel said. She stiffened, and he briefly closed his eyes, annoyed with his stupidity. He should have known. "I have done nothing but fail you today. Forgive me for dousing the lamp. I swear I will never leave you in the dark again."

Dyna's hands trembled on his back, and she released a shaky breath at his promise. It was the first pact between them. Cassiel shuddered as it settled over their bond, branding his words. He stilled.

The bond continued to do things he knew nothing about. It made him question everything he learned and didn't yet know. Why'd he been so foolish to ignore his studies? He had preferred to stare out the windows, watching birds soar through the sky, envious of their freedom.

"When I was a child, my brothers found it amusing to lock me in a birdcage," Cassiel told her after some silence. "Malakel said if I made a sound, the poachers would find me and sell parts of me for gold. They left me in the castle garden alone. I hardly fit in the cage, and I could not move. Too afraid to call for help, I was trapped there for a day."

Dyna didn't comment, but a flash of her irritation swept through him.

"The gardener eventually freed me, but it left me with a fear of cages. It mattered not how small it was. The sight of one terrified me. You can imagine how my brothers found enjoyment in this." He worked his jaw as the sound of Malakel and Tzuriel's mocking laughter echoed in his mind.

"My uncle set to plucking that fear out of me immediately. He forced me into a cage and left me there for an hour each day until I learned how to break it open." Cassiel smirked and shook his head. "It was an eccentric way of doing things, but it worked. He taught me I had the means to free and defend myself. I despise poachers, though. It angers me to see animals in cages. They cannot free themselves or call for help as I can. I have half a mind to return to that poacher's ship and release them all."

His teeth clenched at the thought of Draven. The man had the audacity to send his dwarves after Dyna. That was something he wouldn't let pass. He'd inform Zev about it first thing tomorrow, and they would take care of it.

Cassiel looked down at her face, marred with tears. "By this, I merely wanted to explain that our fears are sometimes unfounded. You said yourself the Shadow arrives each decade. You are safe."

Dyna slipped out of his arms and moved away to curl under the sheets with her back to him. "I saw it," she whispered. "I saw the Shadow the night it took my brother."

She looked so small and frail. His chest hurt, and he pressed a hand over it, knowing the pain came from her. He couldn't say anything, so he only listened.

"The Shadow came to our house first," she said, her voice straining to speak. "It was a black shapeless cloud with eyes like fire that held more evil than all the wickedness in the world. My father had made Waning Amulets that harnessed the moon's power into a cloaking spell to protect us, but we had failed to give it to my little brother in time. The Shadow snatched Thane through the window and devoured him before my eyes..."

Cassiel watched her shoulders silently shake, aghast at what she had seen. He couldn't imagine it. Her sadness and helplessness flooded their bond, drowning him. He wanted to erase her pain, but he didn't know how.

"My father opened the Netherworld Gate to cast the demon back, not caring that it would claim his life. I tried to stop him, but I lost my amulet. The Shadow came after me, and my father sacrificed himself to save me."

Dyna shook her head, coughing on another heartbreaking sob. "He told me to run. So I did. I ran through the woods, blinded by the snowstorm. I made my way up the mountain. I tripped down a ravine and sprained my ankle. I couldn't stand on my feet, but I dragged myself through the snow until I found the glass tree outside of North Star."

He hadn't known there was a *Hyalus* tree in her village.

"When the Shadow found me, I thought I was going to die. But white light attacked the Shadow when it tried to come near. The glass tree protected me."

Cassiel frowned at that. *Hyalus* leaves gave off a pure white light at night, but there was nothing known about it being sentient. Then again, it was a sacred tree.

"So, the Shadow retreated into the darkness and waited. I hid in the hollow under the tree and stayed there all night, watching those flaming eyes. Every faint growl, every snap of a branch or gust of wind struck me with terror. Knowing at dawn, when the Glass Trees' magic faded, it would come for me."

He held his breath.

"But then ... my father came."

Wasn't he already dead?

"Somehow, he made it to me," she said, staring at the wall, lost in her memories. "He could barely stand, leaving a trail of blood from the gash in his stomach. With his last breath, my father told me I would be safe. He opened the Netherworld Gate and shoved the demon through—going with it."

Shudders crawled along Cassiel's spine. *May Elyōn have allowed him a swift death.*

Dyna laid an arm over her eyes, tears trickling down her face.

"How long were you out there?" Cassiel whispered after a long pause.

She sucked in a shaky breath. "Zev... found me later that morning. I was nearly frozen to death. He took me to Grandmother, and she gave me tea that put me to sleep for days. Months passed until I was sane of mind and able to accept my family's death. I had to find a reason to go on. I focused on becoming a Herb Master and searched for a way to end the Shadow. After a while, it wasn't so difficult to smile again, but the darkness always brought me terror. Those red eyes follow me in the shadows of night and my dreams."

Their bond hummed as another decision entered him. "You have my word that I will help you find the Sōl Medallion, and we will destroy the shadow demon. Together."

Dyna was silent for a moment, staring at the ceiling. "You will?"

"I promise."

His words seared over them, again branding the pact within their bond. She buried her face in her pillow so he couldn't hear her cry, but her shoulders still shook. Cassiel searched the flickering shadows in the room for the answers that would comfort her. They offered no wisdom. There was nothing else to do but sleep. Cassiel moved to get off the bed, but Dyna reached behind her and grabbed the hem of his tunic.

"Will you stay with me?" she asked.

Stay with me.

The back of his neck became hot. "What? On the bed?"

"I don't want to be alone."

Cassiel waited for her to say something else, but there was only silence, and her trembling hold on his tunic. He took a deep breath, hoping it would calm the nervous tension stiffening his body.

It didn't.

"Very well..." Cassiel sat there, though, finding it hard to make himself move.

It took great effort not to think about the thin fabric of her white chemise or glance at the soft swells not fully covered by the low, lacy neckline. Gods, he shouldn't be on this bed. He shouldn't even be in this room. But she asked him to stay. Swallowing once, then twice, he gingerly laid down on the edge, staying on his side so his wings wouldn't be in the way.

Dyna held out a hand to him. He hesitated before he took it. Her slim fingers wove through his, and the energy of her touch fell over him. She was trembling.

"Come here," he said, his voice sounding too thick.

She hesitated only a second before moving closer to him, seeking his warmth. He pulled the blanket over her, his fingers inadvertently brushing her bare arms, covered in gooseflesh. It took a few more breaths before he brought his arm carefully around her, then his wing.

"You have nothing to fear so long as I'm with you." It was the same vow he gave her at the inn.

If Dyna remembered it, she didn't say. Her fear had flayed the armor she had been building around herself, leaving her as small and vulnerable as the day he met her in the woods. And like that day, he wanted to keep away anything that could ever cause her harm.

Dyna rolled on her side, causing her neckline to dip further. He shot his gaze to the ceiling. Damn that chemise.

She curled their entwined hands close to her mouth, her lips inches away from his knuckles. "Thank you," she whispered.

Cassiel pulled the sheets to her chin and tucked them around her. "Get some rest. We set sail tomorrow."

Dyna closed her swollen eyes, unshed tears rolling down her temples. After a few minutes, her breathing deepened with sleep and peace came over her face. Her long, wet lashes were like threads of silk. They made little shadows over her flushed complexion. An endearing shower of freckles sprinkled across her nose, though her full mouth was his favorite feature.

Long had he noticed her beauty, but he'd held the thought at bay, not wanting to acknowledge it because Dyna already put him on edge. Having her inches away from him made his pulse thud in his ears, drawing the feel of her lips on his skin like a brand.

Wife.

Husband.

It was a formality, nothing more.

Dyna whimpered, her features tensing with another nightmare. Cassiel shifted closer and stroked her hair, murmuring that he was there. Energy pulsed where the tips of his fingers brushed her cheek. It immediately cast away her fear, and soon she settled. Her arm wrapped around his torso, and he stiffened as she nestled into his chest. After a moment, he relaxed.

Being here with her, in this room, in this bed, didn't feel immoral to him, although it should. There was a rightness to it. She fit perfectly by his side, in more ways than one. But he shouldn't want this. Wanting, desiring something more than he'd ever had before, was terrifying. Foolish. It had to be wrong. He knew it deep in his bones.

His second sight surfaced, and he Soul Searched. It came easy to him now. The colors of Dyna's soul illuminated inside of her as she slept. He listened to her gentle breathing, and studied the soft curves of her face. Everything about her was a force that pulled him in, drawing him helplessly like a weed starved for sunlight.

Every rational thought told him he should go back to the floor. He shouldn't get close to her. He couldn't afford to. Each second he lay beside her was torture. Every minute he didn't move away was another step he took toward crossing lines he shouldn't cross. Allowing whatever this was wouldn't end well for either of them. Even as he told himself this, Cassiel settled his head on the pillows.

He had to stay. It wasn't easy protecting someone. Though, it's easy to say you would. It was harder to do it. If protecting her meant she was free from fear, free to smile and laugh and hope for the future, then he didn't care how black his soul became. He would stay by her side until whatever end.

Such a thoughtless declaration.

"What are you doing to me?" Cassiel whispered.

He forgot what he was and who he was meant to be when in her presence. His eyes fell on Dyna's lips, and he had the insane need to know how they would feel against his own. Such a thing could only bring him to ruin. As Cassiel looked at her and wondered why she affected him so, he had no other answer but one.

"You are made of magic."

Sleep came to him soon after, taking him into a dream where he had the courage to dare.

CHAPTER 43

Lucenna

Lucenna yawned, squinting against the rays of the morning sun streaming in through the glass-stained windows. It filtered blue light across the wooden floor of her room. Sitting at the small bureau across the bed to brush her hair, her temple pulsed with Lucien's call. She pulled out her illuminated orb from her satchel, and the white fog within cleared.

"Good morrow, dear brother of mine." Lucenna set down the orb in front of her and ran a brush through her silvery locks. She smiled, remembering how Lucien had broken another orb at the revelation of Azeran's map. He was ecstatic, to say the least. "Dyna isn't with me at the moment. Therefore, you're graced with my presence instead."

"Unfortunately, I'm calling on a serious matter," Lucien said. At his tone, she focused on his tense expression. He sat at his desk with the morning light shining on his face.

"Forgive me for not contacting you sooner," she said. "We made it to the city. All is well."

"No, I'm afraid it isn't."

Lucenna put down the brush. "What do you mean? What happened?"

Lucien leaned in to whisper, "Early this morn, father received a letter by a courier portal, and he immediately called to have an audience with the Archmage and Prince Everest."

At the mention of her betrothed, she fidgeted with her engagement ring. "Why?"

"I know not, but I don't think it's good. The Archmage is old and losing patience with father for not locating you. Prince Everest is of age to rule. However, he needs to wed before he can ascend to the throne to fortify his reign. There is no other Transcendent to replace you. The Archmage is considering passing the throne to Ender."

"Ender? But he's second born."

"And he's wed to a Transcendent," Lucien said. "If she conceives, Everest may lose his position as heir apparent."

The reminder of princess Ava made Lucenna scowl. She'd rather not think of her old friend and the pain she caused her brother. But Lucien continued without a shift in his expression.

"Father is desperate, Lu. If you're no longer the future queen, he will lose his position at court and his position as Head of the Lunar Guild. He is using every spell imaginable to find you. When he received that notice this morning, he was thrilled. Whatever it was, I have an unsettling feeling about it."

Lucenna frowned. "But I have been careful. I've made sure of it."

"Where are you now?"

"I'm at the tavern with the others. We will board the next ship to Dwarf Shoe today."

"Good. Don't linger, please. Depart from that city without delay."

"I will."

Lucien glanced at something behind him. "I have to go. Stay safe."

His image disappeared, and the crystal orb cleared. Lucenna stared at her engagement ring, absorbing what she heard. If the Archmage forced Everest to abdicate the throne, that meant her father would no longer hunt her. She could at last be with Everest without any political conflict. This must be what he meant.

When it's finished, I will find you.

She only had to evade her father a little longer.

Lucenna cast her glamor and strolled out the door with a smile. She reached the stairwell at the end of the hall, and her boots clacked on the wooden steps as she made her way down quickly, excited to start the day. She reached the first-floor landing, only to ram into a boy running up the stairs. He fell with an *oomph*. A cluster of rolled parchments flew out of his satchel, scattering at their feet.

"Pardon me, madam," he said, hurriedly gathering them up. "I forgot to mind meself."

"It's fine." She helped him up as he adjusted the cap over his ginger hair. "Where are you off in such a hurry?"

"Work, madam. Time is money." He grinned and eagerly offered her one of the rolled-up parchments. "Daily news? Only five russets."

"No, thank you."

"Are you sure? It's full of juicy gossip, and it lists the highest bounties the city has ever seen."

She smiled at his efforts. He couldn't have been older than twelve years old. "I'll do without, but here is a russet for your trouble."

He accepted the copper coin gratefully. "Thank you! You be careful now, madam. Lots of dangerous folk about."

With that, he scampered up the stairs, most likely to sell the rest of his parchments to other patrons.

Continuing on her way, Lucenna strolled into the empty and quiet lounge. It carried the scent of fresh bread and cinnamon. Sunlight streamed in buttery shafts through the tall windows. Several round tables were set around the vast room, with a bar along the back wall. There were a few patrons seated as they ate their morning meals. Barmaids carried trays of food and steaming pots of tea. She found Zev and Rawn sitting at a table in the center.

"Good morrow," Lucenna said as she slid into the seat across from them.

Zev mumbled a greeting before shoveling a pile of fried eggs and sausage into his mouth.

Rawn set down his spoon in a bowl of porridge and smiled in welcome. "Good morrow, Lady Lucenna. Did you rest well?"

"I'm afraid not. My room was on the second floor. The noise kept me awake until late."

"Mine was on the fourth," Zev said between bites. "I slept great."

"How wonderful," Lucenna retorted playfully. She couldn't help the smile that wouldn't leave her.

Rawn chuckled. "Deprivation of sleep did not hinder your pleasant mood."

"I received excellent news today," she said as a barmaid came by to pour her a cup of tea. Lucenna asked for an order of cinnamon bread and fruit to accompany it.

"What news?" Zev asked her after the barmaid left.

Lucenna continued to smile while she sipped her tea. She wanted to enjoy the news for a while before she told them.

"Did you hear? Rubin swears he saw a Celestial flying over the city last night," a voice said.

Rawn and Zev stiffened, alarm crossing their faces. Lucenna carefully peeked at the bearded man sitting at a table beside them, talking to his scraggly companion dressed in fine furs.

"Swears by it," he said.

"What bollocks. Was he drunk again?" the scraggly one asked.

"Aye, damned sozzled. He couldn't stand straight without falling into his shite."

"There hasn't been a Celestial seen in these blasted parts for five hundred years. They've all returned to Heaven's Gate."

The bearded man grunted. "Right, but Rubin kept wailing that if he had a pint of divine blood, he could have saved his children from the pox. Sad loss it was."

"Blast, if I had some divine blood, I could sell it for a chest of gold instead of meandering across the kingdom hawking furs. Imagine if Celestials existed and established trade again. We'd all be better off for it."

"Poor old bastard. He must have seen a griffin or a great bird."

"That must be it, eh? A poacher was selling a phoenix in the market yesterday."

"You don't say? Not every day you see one of those," the bearded man said as they gathered their belongings and started for the entrance. "But that's not as impressive as a Celestial, is it?"

"The poacher had no luck selling the phoenix. Who wants an enormous bird that spits fire? You can buy enchanted fire from any mage merchant these days. It's a lot less expensive, and there's no upkeep."

"I wish I could say the same about my wife."

They made their way out of the tavern, their laughter fading behind them.

Lucenna exchanged startled looks with the others.

"Cassiel isn't foolish enough to fly over the city, is he?" she whispered.

Zev shook his head. "He knows better. You heard them. The old man was drunk."

"Well, best we leave this city right away."

"Yes, agreed," Rawn said. "Cassiel has yet to wake, I believe. Will Lady Dyna be joining us soon?"

Zev glanced at Lucenna expectantly.

She frowned at them. "What do you mean? Dyna didn't stay with me."

Zev's eyebrows rose high on his forehead. "What?"

Rawn straightened in his seat. "Come again?"

"Dyna never arrived night," Lucenna said. "I waited for her, but after a few hours, I assumed she stayed with Zev."

"She didn't." He dropped his cutlery, and they clattered loudly on his plate. The sound drew the stares of patrons at nearby tables.

Lucenna hadn't thought to seek Dyna out last night. After Rawn had secured their rooms yesterday afternoon, he gave her a key, saying she was to share a room with Dyna. Then they went their separate ways.

"How did this happen? Did you not inform the tavern keeper of our arrangements?" she asked Rawn.

"I requested her to hold a key for Cassiel." His brow furrowed as he glanced at the bar, and his posture stiffened. "I failed to mention Dyna."

"What happened yesterday?" she asked Zev. "Was she not with you?"

"She was with Cassiel." Zev slammed his hands on the table, rattling the dishes as he stood. "He will know where she is."

Lucenna then relaxed. If they were together, the prince would keep Dyna safe. "But where is Cassiel?"

"I'll ask the tavern keeper," Zev said, and charged to the bar.

Rawn sighed. "I pray they have not found themselves in a predicament."

The barmaid returning with Lucenna's cinnamon bread had caught the last part of the conversation. "Predicament, milord? Are you unhappy with your stay?"

"Oh no, I haven't any complaints," Rawn told her. "We are attempting to locate two of our companions. A young woman, petite with red hair, and a man with dark hair and a permanent scowl on his semblance."

The barmaid laughed. "Oh! Yes, I know who you speak of. The life-mates made quite the spectacle last night."

Arching an eyebrow at Rawn, Lucenna chewed her bread.

He frowned. "Life-mates? You must be mistaken. Did she have green eyes and his gray?"

The barmaid nodded with a big smile as she refilled his teacup. "Yes, milord, those are the ones. My mistress gave them a key to their room last night."

Lucenna choked. She guzzled her tea to swallow down the dry lump of bread stuck in her throat, only to scald her tongue. She winced and coughed, rubbing her stinging lips.

The barmaid chuckled. "She attracted some trouble with a handful of redcaps who wanted to feast on her flesh, but then her husband gallantly arrived on a unicorn to her aid."

Lucenna shook her head. No way was any of it true.

"It's true. I heard it from the other barmaids." She clasped her hands together, swooning. "Well, you know how stories alter as they're passed around, but doesn't it sound lovely?" With that, she floated away happily.

Lucenna smirked. "You don't believe her story, do you? It sounds ridiculous."

"The tale was rather outlandish," Rawn agreed. "However, she described Lady Dyna and Prince Cassiel."

"But to confuse them as husband and wife is..." Lucenna wanted to say it was also ridiculous, but when she had first met them, she too thought they might have been a pair. Prince Cassiel was protective of her and Dyna was always watching him as if she couldn't help it. Both would often fall into unspoken conversations with each other, seeming to communicate with nothing but a look. "Do you think there is something more between them?"

Rawn busied himself by brushing a speck of nonexistent dust off his cloak. "I suppose anyone could misconstrue Cassiel's willful protectiveness for that of a mate."

Lucenna eyed him, reading the evasiveness on his face. "That isn't an answer, Lord Norrlen. I imagine with your keen hearing you know more than you pretend."

He sighed and said in a quiet tone, "It is not my place to say, my lady. I ask that you please keep any suspicions to yourself. Zev would not receive the notion well, nor would Prince Cassiel for that matter."

Gods, it had merely been a guess, but Lord Norrlen had all but confirmed there *was* something between them.

Before Lucenna could reply, Zev returned to the table, glaring at him. "Why did I waste my time with the tavern keeper when you know which room Cassiel was to stay in?"

"Oh, right, of course." Rawn cleared his throat. "I reserved him on the third floor in room 311."

Zev barreled for the stairs. Lucenna and Rawn's chairs scraped against the floor as they quickly rose to follow. The pounding of their boots echoed in the stairwell as they hurried up the stairs. They reached the third floor and rushed together down the hallway until they arrived at Cassiel's door. Rawn took a deep breath and lifted his hand to knock, but a male moan from inside halted him in place.

"Oh, Cassiel. You look exhausted."

Lucenna gaped at the grains of the wooden door, not sure if she truly heard Dyna's voice. Zev stiffened in place.

Rawn shook his head. "No, Prince Cassiel would never—"

"Of course, I am," Cassiel grumbled. "I have been exerted to the point of exhaustion. Not to mention last night was somewhat eventful, mind you. I half expected to receive complaints."

Rawn covered his face. "God of Urn."

Lucenna stifled a snort. She hadn't thought Cassiel or Dyna were the type to indulge in the throes of passion so willingly, as both were prim and proper. It proved one couldn't judge character by appearances. Lucenna placed her ear against the door to listen better.

"My lady," Rawn chastised her quietly.

She grinned and motioned for him to listen.

"I'm sorry to have burdened you," Dyna said.

Cassiel was quiet for a pause, then said in a gentler tone, "It could not be helped. You were quite distracted at the moment, and I had some fault in it as well."

Lucenna's muffled laughter ended abruptly when Zev's shocked face turned red. His whole body shook as fur sprouted up his arms to his bulging neck. His eyes flashed yellow and his claws extended.

"I'm going to tear out his throat," Zev growled.

"We mustn't misconstrue," Rawn said in a low whisper. "Prince Cassiel would never partake in such debauchery."

"Thank you for allowing me to stay the night with you," Dyna continued.

"Think nothing of it. What kind of man would I be to turn you away? Now let us hurry and meet the others before they find us in such a disreputable state. Do you have your belongings?"

The door swung open, and Cassiel's impatient expression switched to shock to find them there. There was no time for Lucenna to shout a warning. Zev's fist smashed into the prince's face, launching him across the room.

Cassiel collided against the wall with an awful *crack* and crumbled to the floor.

CHAPTER 44

The world had gone black. Cassiel's skull throbbed like someone had cracked it open. A piercing ring filled his ears, muffling all sounds. The floor vibrated with heavy thuds. Dyna's alarm and pain blared through the bond. Who was shouting? The entire left side of his face and jaw throbbed as something wet leaked from the back of his head.

"Prince Cassiel, can you hear me?"

He groaned, his limbs twitching as feeling returned to his body. With Rawn's help, he sat and his vision swam.

"How dare you steal her virtue!"

Cassiel recoiled from the roar and met Zev's feral yellow eyes. "What?"

"I trusted you, and you took advantage of her innocence."

Cassiel stared at him, dumbfounded. What was he talking about? Slowly, his thoughts cleared. He and Dyna had spent the night together. This looked bad. Dyna laid on the floor by the bed where Lucenna was helping her up. She winced, holding her cheek. Gods, she must have felt the blow.

"I did nothing to her," Cassiel grated, lest Zev thought to hit him again. The skin on the left side of his face tingled as it went through the stages of healing.

Rawn tried to hold Zev back. "Cease this at once."

Zev snarled, ready to tear through him. "Step aside. I'm going to kill him."

"You will not," Rawn ordered. "Cassiel has denied these allegations, and I have a mind to believe him."

Dyna cut in front of Zev, trying and failing to shove him back. "You best calm yourself, Zev Astron. Nothing untoward has happened here, and I assure you, I'm quite capable of deciding the bounds of my own propriety. Now take a breath."

She was so small compared to her cousin. If Zev wanted to get to him, he surely could. The others must have thought the same, because Rawn shifted closer and Lucenna formed a glowing leash between her hands.

But Zev forced himself to inhale a deep breath. He blinked in surprise, and his nostrils flared as he sniffed the air again.

Dyna crossed her arms. "Do I smell mated?"

Zev grimaced sheepishly, and his yellow eyes bled back to green. "No ... But I should like to know what's going on."

"I should like to know the same," Cassiel said, rising to his feet. The last of the ache faded from his cheek.

"Why were you in the same room together?"

"You accuse me of something I will not dignify with words."

A menacing growl rumbled in Zev's throat. "I demand an explanation."

"The tavern keeper mistook us as married, and there wasn't a moment to explain," Dyna said. "Cassiel tried searching for you, but it was impossible in the crowd, and we didn't know which rooms you lodged in for the night. Would you have preferred for him to abandon me to sleep in the lounge alone in the dark?"

At that, his hardened expression faltered.

"I believe he's innocent, Zev, but if you would like, I could place him under a truth spell to quell any further doubt," Lucenna offered, letting her glamor spell fall away.

Speaking through his teeth, Cassiel said, "*Elyōn* as my witness, her honor is undefiled. What reason could you have to condemn me to such shame and reproach? Do you truly esteem me so little?"

Zev released a heavy exhale and rubbed his face. "Forgive me, Cassiel. It was a mistake."

"Mistake? If I had been human, that blow would have killed me."

"What else was I to think with your constant coquetry?"

Cassiel reeled back in disbelief. "What *coquetry?*"

"I'm not a fool!" Zev shouted, his eyes flaring yellow again. "Do you think I haven't noticed the way you look at each other? Are you courting her in secret?"

Cassiel's head heated, and he balled his fists. *"No."*

"Zev," Dyna gasped, her face reddening. "You've gone too far."

He heaved, his wolf surfacing. "I swear to the God of Urn, Dyna. If he—"

"There is nothing between us!" she shrieked.

A heavy silence fell in the room. Her words echoed in Cassiel's head as they lacerated him to the bone.

Nothing.

Well, at least he knew where they stood.

Dyna inhaled sharply, turning to him. "Cassiel—"

"There, you see," he said. "You heard the truth from her lips."

She shook her head. "That's not what I—"

"No, it is best we clear this now. The only thing between us is a stain on my integrity."

Dyna reached for him. "Wait."

"Stay away from me," he seethed, pushing all of his anger through the bond, flooding it with his contempt. "I find myself encompassed on a journey with a reckless human who fears everything and stands for nothing. Who needs Guardians to protect her from her naivety, to solve every hindrance." The bond flinched with each insult, but he continued, the spiteful words spilling from his tongue. "There is always a plight when it concerns you, Dyna. I have had enough of it, and I have had enough of you."

Hurt welled in her eyes. Cassiel held his glower, even as something tore into his lungs, drowning him.

A tear escaped, and it sliced through him as it slid to her chin. She turned away for the door. "I will wait outside. I need some air."

"I'll come with you." Zev took her arm, but she tugged it free.

"No," her voice broke. "I need a moment, please."

Rawn shook his head. "Wait, Lady Dyna—"

She rushed out the door, and the sound of her hurried footsteps faded down the stairs.

Zev growled at Cassiel. "You have now earned that blow."

He earned that and more. Her dejection came to him in droves, and he let himself feel it all. It was worse than anything Zev could do to him.

"I comprehend your ire, Your Highness," Rawn said coolly. "Yet at the moment, your conduct has fallen woefully short."

"She wasn't to blame for this," Lucenna added.

No, that only fell on him.

Slamming the patio door open, Cassiel stepped out onto the balcony. His breath shot out in white puffs as he released a string of curses. He was an idiot for letting himself get close to her. But guilt choked him as he thought of the tears in her eyes. He'd been the one to put them there with his instant retaliation to cut as deep as her words had. The rational part of him knew that wasn't her intention, but being told they were nothing, sat bitterly in his stomach all the same. He gripped the iron railing, fighting the urge to go after her. She wouldn't want him near right now.

Zev's heavy steps receded for the door. "I'll go find Dyna. Gods forbid anything else happen today."

Cassiel retorted to the sky. "Yes, nearly killing me first thing in the morning was more than enough."

"Can you blame me?"

"Yes, I can." He glared at him. "I thought you knew me well enough not to assume the worst of me. You were ready to end my life."

Zev dragged a hand down his face. "I'm sorry for my outburst. When I overheard your conversation, I assumed you'd lain with her."

Cassiel's face heated. "I-I did not."

"Aye, I know that now," he said, the lightness returning to his tone. "You're sputtering at the thought of it. Have you never—?"

"Do *not* finish that question," Cassiel growled, prompting Zev to laugh.

Lucenna rolled her eyes. "Men."

"Well, now that we have cleared that blunder, we should make our way to the pier and purchase our boarding passes," Rawn said. "If we have time, I may stop by the courier's office—"

A knock came at the door.

Cassiel groaned and entered the room. "What is it?"

"Daily news, sir!" a voice called. "Only five russets."

Sighing, he yanked the door open. A boy in a cap stood in the hallway, hugging a cluster of rolled-up parchments in his arms. He held one out, but when he saw Cassiel and the others in the room, he froze.

Cassiel took the parchment and reached in his pocket for a coin. "Thank—"

The boy ran away.

"Wait, you forgot your money."

The boy nearly tripped as he dashed down the stairs. Why did he look so frightened?

Frowning, Cassiel unrolled the pages and read the harsh black letters. The room skewed, distorting his surroundings as all air left his lungs. He stared at the words, an icy rush sinking through his body. The pages slipped from his fingers and he bolted out the door. His feet pounded on the floor, his heartbeat thudding in his ears. Dyna didn't want him to go after her, but he didn't care. He needed her safe. Needed her with him. He needed—

Her.

CHAPTER 45

Lucenna

The pages fluttered to the ground at Lucenna's feet. She stared in horror at the wanted posters with all of their faces and the large, bold lettering beneath them. She was hardly aware of the alarmed voices in the room. Lucenna couldn't tear her eyes away from the page with a rough illustration of her face.

MAGE WANTED
REWARD OF 5,000 GOLD PIECES
EXTREMELY DANGEROUS
CAPTURE ALIVE

They were searching for a mage. They were searching for *her*. Lucenna's fear nearly drowned out the cynical part of herself that wanted to correct the notice. The rest of Urn wasn't familiar with the term sorceress.

What did it matter? These notices must be all over the kingdom. Mages within Azure would be on alert, and more Enforcers would come.

She clutched the sheet, crumbling it slowly in her shaking grip. The freedom she had been aspiring for was slipping away.

Her father must be behind this, or so she thought, until she glanced down at the other wanted notice on the floor. It bore Cassiel's face and his first name, wanted for fifty thousand. Then she looked at the page in Zev's hand, and her breath caught.

WANTED

DYNALYA ASTRON

REWARD OF 100,000 GOLD PIECES

CAPTURE ALIVE

At Zev's violent curse, she flinched away from him.

"I'm going with him to find Dyna." He snatched his pack off the floor and scrambled around the room to gather Dyna's scattered belongings. "Go to the port. We might have time to board a ship."

"We must not separate." Rawn shoved Cassiel's pack and sword inside of his enchanted pack, and they vanished within. The movement was quick, but to Lucenna it was slow, time cruelly dragging as her mind spun. "We stay together and depart the city forthwith."

"This is Tarn's doing, isn't it?" Zev growled.

Rawn nodded. "Now that he knows who we are and the extent of our abilities, he is attempting to impede us."

The mention of this man briefly cleared Lucenna's fog of panic. It wasn't her father's doing?

"Who is Tarn?" she asked, her shocked voice barely a whisper.

"That means bounty hunters will be coming for us." Zev shouldered his pack, apparently not hearing her. "The city is rife with them. Is it too late to board a ship to Dwarf Shoe?"

"Most likely, but there is bound to be a merchant ship in the harbor that we can bribe for safe passage to a western port, but we must leave immediately."

They had formed a plan without consulting her. She didn't factor into their problems, let alone acknowledge her. They hadn't even informed her about this adversary.

"No one is going anywhere until I know who this man is," she hissed. "Who is Tarn?"

Zev and Rawn glanced at each other, then at the page in her clenched fist. Lucenna's Essence convulsed with her fear and anger. Her fingers sparked, and the sheet caught fire.

Rawn watched the ashes float to the floor by her boots. "Tarn is Von's master, the man you defeated in Corron. He is pursuing Lady Dyna for her map."

"You mean he sent those men to kidnap her?" Lucenna forced herself to take a deep breath. Otherwise, she feared she might destroy the room with the raging magic on the edge of manifesting. She had given little thought to why Von had gone after Dyna. "Why was this not mentioned before?"

Zev rubbed the back of his neck. "Dyna didn't want to say anything that would discourage you from joining us."

Lucenna shook her head, backing away from them. "Do you not know what this means? My father will see the bounty and know where I am. He will come for me."

Rawn took her trembling hands. "We will leave the city as soon as we locate Lady Dyna."

"No, I need to leave now." Lucenna blasted him with a minor gust, knocking him into Zev.

She placed an invisibility spell on herself and ran out of the room. They shouted for her to wait. She sprinted down three flights of stairs, but Rawn and Zev were right behind her. Their keen hearing easily followed the sound of her footsteps. She reached the lobby, and it was now swarming with people. She weaved through the mass of bodies, making way for the entrance.

"Wait!" Zev called behind her.

She didn't. This was the warning Lucien had tried to give her, the news her father received by courier.

She couldn't search for the Druid now. Grief and anger swelled in her. No matter what she did, something always impeded her mission. Her mother's face crossed her mind, and her vision blurred.

Lucenna busted out of the tavern's double doors into the sunny street. The city was now teeming with morning activity as people went about their day. She skidded to a halt at the sight of a huge green orc jostling Cassiel in the air.

"I warned you if you made the lass cry again," the orc growled.

"Please, Elric, I need to find her," Cassiel said. "She cannot be alone in the city!"

At his alarmed tone, the orc let out a low growl and carefully set him down. "I told you to keep her close, divine one. Well, go on, then. Your wife headed towards the pier."

Wife?

"Thank you." Cassiel sprinted away.

Elric grunted and bounded away, muttering to himself. "Those two and their silly tiffs."

Zev crashed into her back. Lucenna shrieked as she went sprawling. He caught her arm before she hit the ground face first and steadied her on her feet.

"I got her," he said, keeping a hold of her wrist.

"Good," Rawn said, his gaze following Cassiel's receding form until he disappeared around the corner of the street. "We must join him and board a ship immediately."

"Unhand me, Zev," Lucenna snapped, dropping the invisibility spell. Electricity surged over her arm and he yelped, releasing her. "I cannot wait. I must leave before my father finds me."

"Lady Lucenna, I understand your concern, but you must not flee on your own." Rawn rested a hand on her shoulder. "We must stay together. We are *stronger* together. Whatever may come to pass, we are here by your side."

Zev nodded in agreement. He must not hate her anymore. Surprised that they so willingly wanted to protect her made Lucenna's chest knot with emotion. No other man besides her brother had done so.

Rawn glanced past her and he tensed. "Steady."

A group of Azure Guards marched toward the tavern. They stopped before them, and the leader stepped forward. A gold badge with the sigil of Azure shone on the lapels of his regimental blue coat.

"I am Commissioner Veron Moreland of the Azure Guards," he said with a nod in greeting. "Lord Rawn Norrlen of Greenwood, I have heard much about you. It's an honor to meet your acquaintance."

Rawn warily nodded. "To what do I owe the pleasure?"

"It's unfortunate that we should meet in such a manner." The commissioner reached into his coat and pulled out a rolled document. "By order of the Magistrate, I have a warrant for your arrest and those in your company."

Shock sunk through Lucenna's body like heavy mortar, rooting her in place.

"On what charges, if I may ask?" Rawn said stiffly.

"Your crimes are conspiring with a man who has committed crimes against the Crown of Azure."

"What man?" Zev demanded.

"Tarn Morken." The reply hung in the air with the dead silence.

Rawn shook his head. "You are mistaken, Commissioner. We have done no such thing."

"I have never met Tarn, and I'll not be arrested under false charges," Lucenna said. "Now, make way lest I melt the flesh from your bones."

She conjured comatose spells in her hands, blue churning spheres crackling with power. While intimidating, the spells would only render them unconscious. But the Azure Guards didn't react to her threat.

Veron observed her inquisitively, a slight smile tugging at the corner of his mouth. "While I'm impressed by such bravery. I'm disinclined to heed your demand, Lady Lucenna of the Lunar Guild. Comatose spells are not fatal."

She flinched at her name. That information hadn't been on the wanted poster. To know who she was, proved the commissioner not only knew of the Magos Empire's secrets, he was in league with her father.

Lucenna's hands crackled with electricity as dark clouds shrouded the sky, and a threatening boom of thunder rolled overhead. "Well, if you wished for death, you need only say so."

"Wait!" Rawn shouted.

She refused to be taken. The women of Magos and the Liberation awaited her return. Being caught meant her mother died for nothing.

Veron swiped his hand sharply through the air. A force cleaved the Essence out of Lucenna's very veins and she screamed in agony. Purple light hurtled towards his open palm, where he absorbed it within seconds. She fell back with a weak gasp. Rawn steadied her against him. The clouds parted and sunlight spilled back into the street.

What happened? He took her magic. The commissioner raised his hand, and his coat sleeve lowered to reveal the glowing bracelet made of amber beads on his wrist. Within each bead was a black clover.

A whimper escaped Lucenna's lips, her shuddering body falling numb. She spent years searching for black clovers. Yet this man had a bracelet of them. No wonder they didn't fear her.

"My lady, shall you invoke another spell, I'll be forced to oppose you," Veron said casually, his demeanor unruffled. "Therefore, I ask that you please surrender at once."

Lucenna winced when her temple pulsed rapidly with Lucien's call, and the orb throbbed in her satchel in tandem. She should have heeded his warning and left the city when she had the chance.

Rawn stepped in front of her, shielding her with his body. "Stand back, Commissioner. Those black clovers could kill her."

Veron clasped his hands behind his back. "My intention isn't to harm you. The clovers are merely for our protection, and clearly, it's well within reason. Now, please don't cause us to use force. Come with us."

"And if we don't?" she asked, filling her hands with electricity.

The Azure Guards unsheathed their swords. Rawn swiftly loaded his bow, aiming it at the commissioner. Zev's claws grew, and he crouched to spring. Both flanked Lucenna on each side like sentinels of steel and strength, their hard faces highlighted by the glow of her Essence.

They would fight their way out with her.

"Our swords are tipped in silver," Veron informed them. "We will attack, should you be difficult. Not to mention the clovers would render all your magic useless. We are well prepared for any possible confrontation against all the beings of Urn, I assure you. Hence, I suggest you stand down. I would rather this go peacefully."

Lucenna tensed at the mention of silver, but Zev continued growling, his eyes reflecting a menacing yellow. His wolf hovered on the surface, inches from attacking.

"Calm down," she hissed at him under her breath. "You'll be killed if you're cut."

"We will yield peacefully," Rawn said, motioning for them to comply. "Zev."

Taking a breath, Zev loosened his rigid stance, but his throbbing body heat hovered against her. His hands curled loosely at his sides.

The commissioner nodded. "Your weapons, please."

Rawn set his bow, quiver, and sword on the ground.

"And where are your remaining companions?"

None of them replied. Lucenna peeked at the pier, hoping Cassiel and Dyna wouldn't come back this way.

"Corporal Willam, search the pier," Veron said, having noticed where she looked. A guard with curls and spectacles saluted and led a group of ten guards away.

Zev growled a curse, and she groaned.

"Come along." Veron turned away.

The guards kept their swords pointed at them until they reluctantly came forward and followed the commissioner away from the tavern. The guards marched behind them.

Lucenna walked between Rawn and Zev silently. She focused on filling her lungs with air and blinked away the bitter tears that wanted to spill. She had done her best to avoid any attention, always remaining alone and out of large cities, but all her efforts had been undone. The bounty would lead her father to her. She knew it in her bones.

Lucenna's temple continued to pulse with her brother's call. By now, Lucien must know their father was notified about her location. *He's coming for me.*

Rawn placed a hand on her shaking arm, but Lucenna jerked away from him. "I should never have joined you."

"We didn't know this would happen," Zev whispered.

"I will not allow any harm to befall you," Rawn said. "Trust me."

Lucenna glared at the ground. She didn't know how she could trust them after their lie led to her capture.

They walked in silence through the busy streets with the guards. People stopped to stare and titter. Lucenna shivered from the chill that wouldn't leave her. The further away they moved from the pier, the further away they were from their escape. Her mind raced with ideas to get away and find a place to hide. She couldn't let this render her mother's sacrifice meaningless and take away her chance of reuniting with Everest again.

They reached the city center and stopped in front of a five-story building. A wide set of steps led to a pair of archway doors. The morning sun shone on the many glass windows. Guards in blue coats went in and out of the building, some dragging chained prisoners through the doors.

"Headquarters of the Azure Guard," Rawn informed them quietly.

The guards forced them up the steps. Veron opened the door and motioned for them to go in. Only five guards followed them inside.

"Constable, I leave you to continue the search for the princess," he quietly said to a guard that remained outside. "We must find her, or this matter will have to be brought to the king."

A dark-haired guard saluted and led the remaining group of guards down the steps. Lucenna watched them go, hoping Veron would send the others away too. They were not the only people the Azure Guards were pursuing.

He led them inside to a spacious foyer with polished travertine floors. Ahead of them stood two guards at the attendant's desk. They saluted as their commissioner walked past.

To the left of the foyer, other guards were forcing people into rooms with barred doors. They headed to the right end of the building to another set of stairs. They walked several flights until they reached the fifth floor. Tapestries of Azure's sigil hung on the stone walls. Veron came to another door, and a guard held it open for them to go in.

A large window took over the southern wall. It had a vast view of the city and the ocean in the distance. The tips of the boat sails at the pier peeked out above the rooftops. At one end of the office was Moreland's large wooden desk. Behind it were bookshelves full of rolled scrolls and books. On the opposite wall was a large map displaying the city roads, ordinance laws, and a full display of wanted posters with their faces among them.

Veron lowered into the wingback chair at his desk and slipped off his white gloves as he began gathering the loose paperwork on his desk into a neat pile. "Sit."

The guards shoved Rawn and Zev forward. Well, they tried, but Zev's large frame didn't budge from their efforts. Lucenna didn't want to go in. If she did, it would leave her trapped. Rawn gently took her arm and gave Zev a reassuring nod. They came forward and sat on the bench placed in front of the desk.

The commissioner looked at them, and his gaze narrowed. "Now, do you wish to tell me why the most wanted man in the Kingdom of Azure has placed a bounty on your heads?"

CHAPTER 46

Dynalya

yna listened to the waves crash on the shore, letting the salted wind dry her eyes. Cassiel had been cold with her before. This time, it was different. His words, the look on his face when he threw them at her, crushed something in her chest. That pain mirrored his when she claimed there was nothing between them. His family told him he was nothing, and to hear it from her had penetrated so deeply it struck the bond.

Sighing, she pulled her hood over her head against the chilly breeze. Dyna looked out at the pier, where she sat at the tables outside of the fish shops. How could she tell Cassiel that it wasn't true at all?

"How much do you think the Morphos Court would pay for their princess?" someone asked behind her as they walked by.

The sinister question caught Dyna's attention.

Another answered with a gleeful snicker. "Enough to bloody retire. She's the only heir."

Morphos... Her mind raced to recall where she had heard that before. The thought drew the memory of a beautiful, dark-skinned fairy with yellow wings.

Hello, Dynalya. I am Princess Keenali of the Morphos Court. Please, call me Keena.

A cold wash of dread fell over her.

When the voices grew distant, Dyna glanced over her shoulder and recognized two of Draven's dwarves as they climbed the gangplank to their ship. After they had attempted to take her last night, she wouldn't put it past them to abduct someone else. If they had Keena, then she wouldn't sit idly by.

Dyna watched the ship, debating how she could board undetected. The answer came when Draven appeared. He clambered down the gangplank with his crew. They meandered away, laughing and cheering, perhaps celebrating a new fortune.

As soon as they were out of view, Dyna crept up the gangplank to the ship and peeked over the banister at the deck. It was empty. Nothing but her and the cages of animals. Her heartbeat quickened. No sane person would be here. It was stupid and dangerous, but no matter how scared she was, Cassiel was right about one thing.

She was reckless.

Dyna crept behind barrels and crates on the deck, listening for any sounds beyond the cries and mewling of the animals.

"Princess Keena?" she whispered. "Are you here?"

The boat creaked in the silence, swaying with the soft rock of the waves. Wind fluttered the sails, and seagulls cried overhead. She crept further on the ship.

"Keena?" Dyna called louder this time. She held her breath, waiting, hoping, praying. Maybe she was too late.

"Help me," came a weak whimper.

Relief and dismay churned through her at the sound of the familiar voice. "God of Urn, you are here."

"Please ... Please help me."

"I can't see you," Dyna called, spinning in place. "Where are you?"

"Up here."

A little cage about the size of a tankard hung from a hook on the mast, out of reach. A tiny hand reached out through the bars. Dyna cast out her power and unhooked the cage, levitating it to her hands. Inside was the fairy princess. Her once beautiful butterfly wings had withered into dull shades of yellow. Keena curled into herself on the floor of the cage, lost in a puddle of brittle pink petals that made up her gown. Her dark skin had taken on a horrible gray hue. Angry burns mottled her hands and arms.

"Please set me free," the little fairy pleaded. She looked at her with fatigued eyes, and they widened. "Dyna? Oh, thank the gods." She reached out pleadingly, her wrist brushing a bar. She cried out as her skin sizzled with more red welts. "The iron. It burns."

"Those fiends," Dyna hissed. She inspected the cage for the door and found the opening, but it was locked. "I need a key. Where's the key?"

Keena moaned and dropped her head, too weak to hold it up. "The poacher..."

Of course. Draven would have it, but Dyna couldn't wait for him to return.

"Don't worry. I'll get you out." Dyna tucked the cage in her satchel, leaving the flap open.

"What do you think you're doing?"

Dyna jumped at the snarl and spun around to find a man standing on the threshold of the captains' quarters. He resembled Draven, but he was younger and lankier.

His angry gaze dropped to the cage. "Wretched whore. Put that back."

"No." Dyna hurtled a surge of green flames.

He threw himself out of the way. The blast hit the wall, singing the wood. The poacher scrambled to his feet with a curse. She cast flare after flare to keep him at bay as she made her way back to the gangplank. He dodged them all. Her power quickly drained until the last spell abruptly stalled behind the barrier. Essence sparked uselessly in her hands.

The poacher grinned as he armed himself with a dagger. "Did the little witch run out of magic?"

Dyna took a step back, panic stiffening her limbs. She'd left her opal knife behind at the tavern, sitting beside Cassiel's sword. She was halfway across the deck. Escape was a mere handful of steps away.

The poacher saw where she was looking, and he blocked the way. "You're not going anywhere."

The sky darkened with a sudden call of storm clouds, blotting the sun. But the storm disappeared as quickly as it arrived. Something was wrong with Lucenna. She had to get back to her friends.

Dyna shifted, and her foot hit something, causing a heavy thud. A hatchet. She snatched it off the ground and braced her stance. Whatever happened, she would get off this boat.

The poacher licked his lips and swung his dagger around. "Good. I like it when they fight back."

She bared her teeth. "Come any closer, and I'll cut off some part of your body."

He laughed. "Not before I cut up that pretty face."

Forcing a steadying breath, she gripped the handle tightly and kept retreating until her back hit something hard. A loud caw made her flinch, and she found herself face to face with the phoenix. The massive red bird watched her through the cage bars, smoke billowing out of the sides of its large beak. Heat came off it in waves.

There was no time to debate. Dyna swung the hatchet down on the padlock. The bird squawked loudly, startled at the loud bang. She kept hitting the padlock repeatedly, casting sparks on the deck, but it wouldn't break.

"Stop!" the poacher charged at her.

The phoenix shrieked, scaring her into stepping back. It reared its head and blew a gust of flame at the poacher. He ran out of range, tripping over crates. The phoenix then aimed its fire at the metal lock until it blazed molten orange, softening under the heat. Dyna grinned and raised the hatchet, bringing it down with all her might. The lock cracked in half and hit the deck with a dull thud, sizzling as it charred the wood planks with its shape.

Using her satchel's flap to grab the cage bars, Dyna quickly yanked open the door. The talons of the phoenix scraped against the bottom of the metal cage as it stepped out. The bird reared on its legs with an angry caw and spat a stream of fire at the young poacher. He jumped backward out of the way, his foot caught on a mound of rope by the banister, and he fell over the side of the ship. His cry ended with a splash into the sea.

Dyna laughed and waved her arms. "Go."

With a flap of the phoenix's large red wings, a powerful gust blew through the ship. It gave her one last squawk before soaring into the sky. She watched it go until it was a speck of red. Freedom wasn't something that could be bought, sold, or given. No one belonged in captivity. She hacked away at the other cages, liberating most of the animals till they swarmed the deck. The parrots flew out to their freedom, streaks of color against the clear blue sky.

A hand snatched her hair, making her shriek.

"You're going to pay for that," the young poacher snarled in her ear. He yanked her against him so hard tears of pain sprang in her vision, and her scalp burned. His wet body soaked through the back of her dress.

Rapid footsteps pounded up the gangplank, and Draven stormed onto the deck with his dwarves. "Galen, why is my phoenix flying over the damn city!"

He roared in rage at the sight of the empty broken cages. Animals scurried between his legs and down the ramp.

Galen threw Dyna down before him. "It was her doing."

Fury boiled in Draven's discolored eyes, but they cut to Galen. "It's your job to mind the ship!" His fist pummeled into Galen's jaw, knocking him down next to her. "Useless bastard."

Galen cowed. "I'm sorry, brother."

"Where were you?" Draven growled. "You left again, didn't you? No doubt for a dalliance at the brothel."

"No, I may have been taking a nap, but I was here. I tried to stop her."

Draven grabbed Galen's throat and squeezed until his face turned purple. "I swear if we didn't have the same mother, I'd break your neck and toss your body into the sea." He shoved him aside and faced Dyna. "I hunted for months in the Misty Isles to capture that bird, you meddlesome little wench."

She glared at him. "It should never have been in captivity."

"You will pay dearly for what you have cost me." He raised his fist. She covered her face and braced for the blow, but he kicked a barrel instead. His chest heaved as he breathed deeply to rein in his rage. He huffed and righted his fur cape. "As luck would have it, you're worth more alive than dead. Tie her up."

The dwarves grabbed Dyna before she could run away. They tore off her satchel and tossed it down. Keena's cage peeked out from under the flap. Draven hadn't noticed her yet. The fairy reached out a trembling hand, her little frightened eyes watching helplessly.

Dyna kicked one dwarf in the groin and punched another. A satisfying crunch sounded beneath her fist. The dwarf released her, howling in pain as he held his bleeding nose. Galen surged forward and his fist rammed into her stomach. The air shot out of her. She dropped to the deck with a wheezing gasp. Stars danced in her sight and she nearly vomited.

The bond pulsed with Cassiel's presence and she heard him shout her name. He ran up the gangplank but stopped short at the chaos on the ship. They locked eyes through the wall of dwarves standing between them.

"Did you send her to release my bird?" Draven growled.

Cassiel glanced at the large empty cage that once held the phoenix. Dyna took advantage of the distraction and tried to run to him.

"You're not going anywhere." Galen grabbed her and roughly bent her arms behind her until a searing pain shot up her back, and she screamed.

"Unhand her." Cassiel reached for his waist, but *Esh Zayin* wasn't there.

Draven laughed. His dwarves took out their daggers and surrounded him. "She's mine now. The lass cost me substantial loss and I don't take too kindly to that."

"Name your price. I will pay you whatever you want, and we will be on our way."

A sneer twisted on the poacher's face. "Oh, you're not going anywhere either, mate. The bounty for the both of you is more than enough to mitigate my losses."

Cassiel went rigid.

Dyna glanced between them. "What bounty?"

Draven took two notices out of his coat and waved them at her. "Someone is willing to pay a hundred thousand gold pieces for you, bonnie lass, and eighty thousand for your master. I wonder why that is?"

She gaped at the pages, then at Cassiel. He mouthed Tarn's name.

Draven shrugged and neatly folded the pages before tucking them in his coat. "I don't care as long as I'm paid my dues. Tie them both and stick them in the phoenix cage."

Dyna hardly noticed the rope binding her wrists as the weight of dread suffocated her. Draven would soon find out he had captured a Celestial, and the result would be catastrophic for the Realms.

Cassiel paled as he stared at the cage.

"Run!" She bucked wildly as Galen began dragging her towards it. "Go. Leave me!"

His hair fell over his forehead as he lowered his head.

"Are you mad? Get out of here!"

"Please," he said softly. "Let her go."

Draven released a booming laugh, and his dwarves snickered. "Did you hear that? He said *please*. Well, now I may do so since he asked so politely."

Cassiel looked up, his face now devoid of emotion. "I have something far more valuable than the phoenix. It is more valuable than both of our bounties combined."

This caught Draven's attention, his greed conveying him to listen. "Oh?"

An icy wave fell over Dyna. "No. Don't do it!"

She called on her Essence. Begged for anything to surface, but it merely sparked weakly in her fingers. Damn whatever barrier that kept it locked away. She fought against Galen, and he backhanded her. The blow snapped her head back, leaving her ears ringing.

The angles of Cassiel's face hardened. "Hit her again, and you will get nothing."

"It really must be good if you're confident enough to make threats," Draven said. "Don't forget I have the advantage here."

Galen brought his dagger to her neck, and she inhaled sharply at the sting.

Cassiel gritted his teeth, fury darkening his features. "Believe me, it is well worth it. Have him remove the dagger."

"No, I think I won't. Not until I know what it is you're offering."

Dyna's vision blurred. This wasn't supposed to happen. "Don't." She pleaded. "Not for me."

Cassiel ignored her. He kept his gaze fixed on the poacher.

Draven glanced back and forth between her and Cassiel's resigned expression. "Well?"

"Have you seen a Celestial before?"

"Don't mock me, boy. They died out five hundred years ago."

"I am the last of my kind."

The poacher arched a bushy eyebrow. "Your kind?"

"I'm assuming you know how much we are worth." Cassiel slowly undid the buttons on his coat. "To have your own Celestial, well, that would make you as wealthy as a king."

"No," Dyna cried. "Cassiel, please don't do this. Please."

He took a deep breath and slid off the enchanted coat. His glossy black wings arched above him and gleamed in the morning sunlight.

The poachers gawked at him in wonder.

"By the gods..." Galen gasped and loosened his hold on Dyna. She didn't have the strength to stand anymore and her knees cracked against the deck.

Suspicion lined Draven's glare. "Celestials have white wings."

"Not all of us do." He held out a hand to him. "I will prove it to you."

The poacher took out a dagger from under his coat and pricked the tip of Cassiel's finger. They watched in awe as the cut healed in seconds. A greedy sneer took over Draven's face. "You're going to make me a lot of coin, mate. But what is to stop me from keeping the lass as well?"

Cassiel's eyes sharpened. "She is to go freely. My life for hers is more than fair. If you do not accept my terms, then you will lose in this deal. I have the ability to stop my heart. With my death, my blood and feathers become useless."

Draven's sneer faltered at the threat. "You lie."

She knew he was, but Cassiel's cold composure remained.

"Do I?" he asked the poacher. "Are you willing to risk it? I'm worth a hundred times more than the amount on that piece of paper."

Draven glared at him as he contemplated the risk. "Aye, you'll be more than enough. Let her go, Galen."

"What?" Galen said in disbelief. "Why? We have them both."

Draven cuffed him upside the head. "Do as I say."

His brother undid Dyna's bindings as the dwarves put shackles around Cassiel's ankles. His expression remained indifferent and withdrawn. He had yet to look at her. The dwarves shoved him into the phoenix cage. He flinched when the heavy metal door slammed shut behind him, and they quickly latched it with a new padlock. Only then did Cassiel's poise unravel. He hunched forward, his wings trembling on his quivering back. He feared cages, and her actions put him in one.

She fell before it, hitting the bars. "Why did you do that? Why?"

Cassiel shifted to kneel in front of her. Instead of anger, he tried to give her a brave smile. But he couldn't hide the panic in his silver eyes. He wrapped his hand around hers over the bar she clenched. "I'm sorry for what I said. It was not your doing."

"But this is my doing."

He sighed and wiped her eyes. "I told you not to cry for me."

But Dyna couldn't stop the tears from falling. "Why did you do it?"

"Since the moment I saved your life, you were mine to protect."

His words in the woods outside of Hilos came to her. *I will be damned if I am the one responsible for poachers returning to hunt my kind because I saved a stupid human.*

She had damned him.

Her head dropped against the bars. "You should never have come. How did you know I was here?"

"You are my bonded, Dyna. Wherever you are, I will always be able to find you."

She didn't fully understand, but a part of her did. They were connected.

"You must go. Your journey does not end here." Cassiel removed the chain around his neck and put it over her head, the sapphire ring now resting on her chest. "It belonged to my mother. Will you please find her for me?"

"No, you have to be the one to find her. You made promises to me." She pressed a fist over her chest. The weight of the oaths he made last night weighed on their bond. He placed a hand on his chest, too. "I can't leave you."

"You can and you will."

Sobs heaved out of her. "I want to stay. No matter the consequences, I want to stay with you."

She couldn't bear to lose him.

A broken look entered his eyes. He reached through the bars and pulled her close. With a soft sigh, he gently brushed his lips against hers. It was hardly a kiss, a light flutter, but it sent a bloom of heat through her veins and hummed on the surface of her skin. A caress of farewell.

No, she wouldn't let him go.

Through the wide bars, Dyna weaved her arms around Cassiel's neck and kissed him. He stiffened for a moment before his arms wound around her, one hand slipping into her hair and the other around her waist. Cassiel's mouth took hers, slow and tender, caressing every curve of her lips. He kissed her like he needed her to breathe.

Every part of her electrified with a fiery energy, leaving her breathless. It was like falling off a cliff again, floating through the air, trusting his wings to catch her. He wove his fingers in her hair, his lips soft against hers. She wanted this moment to last forever, but it was over too soon. His shaking hands released her, and his arms slipped away.

"Go," Cassiel whispered. He moved to the center of the cage and curled over his knees as he enveloped himself in wings.

His wings! Dyna threw her arm in to grab a feather, but Draven jerked her away from the cage, pulling her against him. His fur cloak stank of rank meat and his breath of sour rum.

"Oh, how sweet," he jeered. "I allowed you to say your goodbyes. Now, off with you. Unless you need a man to care for you, my offer stands."

She recoiled, but then spotted a small key peeking out from the leather straps of his fur cape. The key was the perfect size for Keena's cage.

"You can't take him!" Dyna pummeled Draven with her fists, snatching the key unnoticed. The poacher shoved her, making her trip on the deck. She crawled backward, keeping him and his dwarves in her sights. Her hands landed on Cassiel's enchanted coat and her satchel. She gathered them in her arms.

"The deal is finished." Draven's menacing shadow fell over her and he brandished his ax in her face. The grindylow scales glittered among the tassel of charms. "Get out of here. Be quick about it before I change my mind."

She ripped off the tassel and sprinted off the ship. Draven cursed, but he didn't chase after her. People stopped to stare at her as she ran through the pier. She had to find her friends.

Cassiel had given up his life—and the secrecy of Celestials. For her. How could that be right? It wasn't. Her life wasn't worth that sacrifice.

"Dyna," Keena whimpered from her satchel.

The iron was killing the princess. Dyna searched her pockets for the key she had stolen from Draven. Blinded by her tears, she rammed into a person in front of her. A man grunted, and firm hands steadied her.

"Your pardon," she said, wiping her eyes.

"It's all right, Dyna."

She jolted at the sound of that voice.

Looking up, she met a pair of sea-green eyes. Chestnut brown hair brushed back from his rugged face, curling at the base of his neck. He was dressed in all black with crossed bandoliers on his chest strapped with his many knives.

Von.

"Hello, lass."

They stood still in the crowded pier, oblivious bystanders continuing about their day, merchants hawking wares, peddlers pulling along carts, seagulls crying overhead. No one noticed them, and no one could help. Instinct told her to run, but she had no control over her rigid limbs anymore. But she wasn't alone. She was in the middle of the busy pier—surrounded by witnesses.

Dyna inhaled a deep breath and screamed.

CHAPTER 47

Everyone within the vicinity turned, startled by Dyna's screams. Von let her go, and she sprinted away. People quickly parted to let her pass. Once she got far enough in the crowd, she ducked into a dark alley set between two fish shops. Her running steps echoed in the cold, narrow passageway, but it ended in a brick wall. Dyna spun around, and her heart sank at the sight of Von's silhouette at the entrance of the alley.

She was trapped.

Dyna walked backwards until she hit a stack of broken crates. There had to be something she could use to fight back.

"Dyna," Keena rasped. "I can't stay here much longer."

Dyna quickly removed the cage from her satchel. Her shaking fingers fumbled with the small key as she jammed it into the keyhole. The lock gave a soft click, and she yanked the door open. Keena stumbled out, falling in a heap on Dyna's lap. Her tiny chest heaved with shallow breaths. She carefully gathered the fairy in her hands, trying not to touch the burns on her arms. She was cold and frail, her wings drooping like limp leaves.

"Please don't make this difficult," Von said as he approached. "I don't wish to harm you, lass."

A fractured piece of wood had split from an old crate beside her. Dyna broke it off and braced her stance, holding the long piece of wood like a knife. It wasn't a real weapon, but it was sharp. She would make sure to stab some part of his body this time. Her grip tightened around the rough edge as she cupped Keena close to her chest.

"Come any closer, and I will harm *you*."

The edges of Von's mouth slightly curved. "You think you can stop me with that?"

The confident way in which he stood put her on edge. This man was someone who could switch between the actions of a gentle smile to slitting a throat.

"Probably not," she said. "Regardless, I plan to be very difficult."

"We both know what resulted when you didn't comply last time." He glanced at her ankle casually, reminding her of her embarrassing tumble. "How is your ankle?"

Dyna narrowed her eyes, ignoring her flush. "I'm not the same girl from Corron, Von."

And she wasn't. Inside she was shaking, her heart racing, but on the outside, she'd fortified her will with determination to save her bonded.

Fear could wait.

Von's slight smile faded at whatever he read on her face. "Fight if you wish, but in the end, you're coming with me."

A deep male voice chuckled above them. "She's not going anywhere with you, mate."

They looked up at a man standing on the roof of the alley building. A black mask covered the bottom half of his face. The sun shone over his blond hair rippling in the wind. With a line of rope, he rappelled down the wall, and his blue coat flared with the sigil of a bird's skull on his back. He landed between her and Von as two long knives slipped to his hands from the concealed sheaths up his sleeves. His familiar blue eyes flickered to her, and she recognized the captain from Old Tanzanite Keep.

"Klyde," she breathed.

A look crossed Von's expression that told her he knew the man, too. There was no hesitation. He armed himself with two knives, hilts spinning in his palms, and attacked. They moved in wild but graceful aggression. Blades whistled as they slashed the air inches from each other in a whirl of clashing metal. They blocked each other's blows and kicks, equally matched.

Dyna could hardly follow their deft movements. Even if she had her dagger, she wouldn't have been a match for Von. He slashed for Klyde's throat, and the captain parried with a swipe of his blade. Their arms locked together, bringing them face to face with their knives, a mere hairsbreadth from their necks. Keena flinched in her hand, watching the fight with wide eyes.

"Do you remember all the people you've slain for him?" Klyde grated, his eyes like stone.

Von clenched his teeth. "I remember them all."

The captain rammed his knee in Von's gut and threw him over his shoulder. Von collided with the brick wall behind her.

"Go, lass," Klyde told Dyna. He withdrew one of the short swords strapped to his back as Von stood. The small polished skull of the pommel grinned back at her. "I'll take care of this."

Dyna nodded. "Thank you."

She sprinted past him to the street and kept running, not daring to stop.

"Where did that fine knight in no armor come from," Keena asked wearily. "Do you know him?"

"No." All she knew was his name.

"He seemed to know you."

She shook her head. "I briefly met him yesterday. I thought he was part of the Azure Guard."

Keena managed a weak laugh. "Oh no. That one is a Skelling Mercenary. Most simply call them The Skulls. You didn't recognize the emblem?"

The Skulls ... Cassiel had called him that before, but she had paid little attention at the time.

"They are notorious swords for hire. For whatever reason, he helped you. Why was that other man after you?"

"It's a long story." Dyna couldn't afford the time to think about Klyde or Von. She had to find the others.

"If it wasn't for the iron, I could have helped," Keena said as Dyna ran through the streets. "Iron is toxic for the Folk, and it's costing me to recover. Thank you for freeing me. I am within your debt."

"But I ..." A rush of emotions flooded in Dyna's chest, and her eyes welled. "It's my fault Cassiel was captured."

"He could have flown away to save himself. Instead, he traded his life for yours. But I won't let it come to that." Keena's tiny hand brushed her thumb. "You have my word that I will do all in my power to help you."

A small spark of hope filled Dyna's heart. "Thank you, Your Highness."

The fairy princess beamed. "None of that. We need to find a patrol of Azure Guards. My guardsmen must have notified them of my disappearance, and they will be searching for me."

"Wait, how were you captured?"

Keena fidgeted with a tear in her dress, looking sheepish. "I ... I followed you."

Dyna stopped to stare at her. "Why?"

"Leoake said if I did, I would find what I'm searching for. I was there in the crowd last night when the dwarves were trying to steal you away. I sent my guardsmen to your aid, but Cassiel arrived with the orc, so I stayed back."

Dyna had to fight the tightening in her throat at the memory.

Keena found the strength to fly, wings struggling until she landed on Dyna's shoulder and held on to a lock of her hair. "I wasn't paying attention to my surroundings and a dwarf trapped me in a cage. Draven wanted to sell me for ransom. The Morphos Court is known for its wealth. Our fortune lies in the highly sought perfume we create from the Aurora Blooms. It was so foolish of me. I nearly died because I listened to that dastardly Druid."

She hurriedly continued down the street. "What is it you need?"

Keena opened her mouth to answer, but then she glanced at the crowd and broke into a relieved smile. "Kye!"

Dyna searched for the familiar regimental uniform of the Azure Guards and soon found a unit of them standing on the corner of the street. Relief flooded her when she noticed the familiar corporal among them giving orders.

She called to Kye, running his way. He and the guards rushed to meet her.

"Dyna, what happened?" the corporal asked, but then did a double-take at the sight of the fairy and exhaled in relief. "Princess Keena, Commissioner Moreland has the entire squadron searching the city for you since your disappearance last night."

"A poacher held me captive," Keena said as she landed in his open palm. By their familiarity, Dyna took it they knew each other.

He scowled. "What poacher?"

"It was Draven," Dyna said, "and now he has Cassiel. You must help me free him."

Kye glanced across the busy pier toward Draven's ship, but he put an arm around Dyna and forced her to hurry away with him in the opposite direction. "It's best that you both accompany me. I shall get you to safety. Princess, you need nectar."

Dyna didn't understand his strange words. *Nectar?* "No, we need to go back. Cassiel is in trouble."

"I will report this to the commissioner, but first, I have to bring you to headquarters." His reply was careful, but she heard the nuance behind it.

"Why? What happened?"

He sighed. "A warrant has been issued for you and your companions."

Dyna jerked to a stop. "What? Why? We've done nothing wrong."

"Tarn placed the bounties on your heads."

"And that is a warrant for arrest?" She tried to run, but he caught her wrist. "Let me go!"

The sun reflected on Kye's glasses as he shook his head. "I'm sorry about this, but I have to do as ordered."

"It's all right, Dyna," Keena told her. "Commissioner Veron Moreland is a good friend of mine and my father's. I'll have a word with him about this."

Dyna was hesitant to go with the guards, knowing every minute counted against Cassiel's favor. She needed to find the others and save him as soon as possible.

Then Kye said the one thing that made her stop resisting. "We have already detained your companions."

The guards led Dyna to the fifth floor of the Azure Guard Headquarters. Zev's furious voice filtered in the hallway. She ran towards the sound, Kye following close behind with Keena in his hands. They reached a set of double doors manned by more guards. They opened the doors at the corporal's nod and let them into the large office.

Commissioner Moreland sat behind his desk, calmly listening to Zev shout that he needed to find his cousin. Rawn stood by Lucenna, where she sat on a wooden bench, her arms crossed tightly across her chest. Electricity flickered along her body and through her hair in purple flashes.

"Zev." At the sight of him, all the angst and fear she held at bay came rushing out.

He whipped around at the sound of her voice. "Dyna!"

She ran and threw herself at him. He pulled her into the fold of his arms, cradling her against him. The steady beat of his heart was all that held her together as she shook with silent sobs.

"What happened?" he murmured. "Where is Cassiel?"

She couldn't answer yet. All she could do was soak Zev's shirt with her tears.

"Something must have occurred," Rawn said.

Zev leaned in to whisper in her ear, "The commissioner believes Tarn is in the city. He wants to use us to draw him out."

"Perhaps he is," Dyna replied shakily under her breath, knowing Rawn and Zev could hear. She inhaled a deep breath and wiped her face. "I saw Von."

Zev held her back, searching her eyes in alarm. There was a question on their faces as to why she was unharmed if she'd encountered Von. Her thoughts were in too much of a disarray to explain Klyde's appearance. She didn't know who the captain was or why he had helped her.

"I found her and Princess Keena at the pier," the corporal announced as he closed the door behind him.

"Princess." The commissioner stood, visibly relieved to see the fairy. She flew to him and landed on the open palm he held out to her. "You look awful."

"Is that any way to speak to a lady, Veron?" Keena quipped, giving him a tired smile. "Might you have any nectar?"

"Yes, of course. Your guardsmen provided it in case we found you first." He reached into a small wooden box on his desk and pulled out a tiny barrel. He set it down on a tome and Keena popped open the lid, scooping out a golden dewdrop. She slurped it hungrily, reaching for more. The burns on her limbs were glaring under the sunlight streaming in through the window.

"Draven held her captive," Kye reported. "In an iron cage."

Veron's mouth forged into a thin, hard line. "Have him and his company detained immediately."

"Yes, sir. I have already sent word to her guardsmen. They should be here shortly."

"Thank you, Corporal."

Kye saluted, then exited the room.

The silence left behind drew Dyna to meet the stares of her friends. Lowering her head, she confessed what she'd done on Draven's ship and that Cassiel traded himself as payment. She didn't mention that he revealed his secret to the poacher, but she could tell by their startled expressions they knew what this meant.

"Your little righteous foray was rather foolish," the commissioner said as he took a seat in his chair again.

"No, it was brave," Keena countered. Gone was the gray hue to her complexion. She shimmered with a golden light exuding from her wings, strength returning to her features. The burns were almost healed now. The nectar must have been what she needed to recover. The scent of a wildflower meadow wafted through the office as the fairy flew to them. "Dyna saved me. I might have died on that ship if it wasn't for her."

Rawn bowed his head. "It is a pleasure to meet again, Princess Keena. I am sorry to hear what befell you."

"And you, Lord Norrlen. Thank you, but I'm afraid we must skip the pleasantries in favor of other dire matters," she said, giving him a meaningful look.

"Yes." Rawn moved to stand before the Commissioner. "Release us at once. Our companion is in danger."

Veron frowned. "Hardly. He will be fine. Once the guards have detained Draven, Corporal Willam will escort your companion here." He linked his hands on his desk, waiting until their responding protests quieted. "It seems I may have failed to convey the situation in which you find yourselves, so let me tell you. Lord Norrlen, you and your company have been *arrested*."

"On false charges," Lucenna snapped.

Zev growled in agreement. "We have no part in Tarn's illicit activities."

The commissioner's dull expression didn't change. "Withholding the truth is considered perjury."

Rawn exhaled a sharp breath. "We speak the truth, sir. The charges are a *farce*. He is no acquaintance of ours."

"Be that as it may, I must hold you. Tarn Morken has placed a bounty on each of your heads."

"And for that, we're considered his accomplices?" Dyna asked.

"Unfortunately, your association marks you as leads to his whereabouts," Veron said. "He has avoided execution for the last fifteen years, so forgive me, but we're going to implement this opportunity to capture him."

"You said he committed crimes against the crown," Rawn said, a question in his tone.

"Tarn murdered Rubin Afton, the Duke of Zircon—cousin to King Lenneus. He entered the duke's castle in the late hour, killed him in his bed, and emptied the coffers. By some mercy, Tarn didn't harm the servants. He told them his name and showed them his face."

"Thievery was not the primary intention," Rawn said, studying the commissioner's face. "He wanted it to be known he was responsible for Lord Afton's death. I assume you know the motive."

The commissioner leaned back in his chair, and Dyna followed his line of sight to the wall covered in wanted posters. Separated from the others was one for Tarn. She recognized the striking face, with a long scar running from his left brow, over his nose to the right side of his chin. His cold, piercing eyes stared back at her.

"Tarn's mother was quite beautiful, I hear," Veron said. "With hair like a river of gold silk, and eyes the pale blue before dawn. Her countenance was revered in all of Azure, but none coveted her more than Lord Afton. He claimed to have bedded her the night before she wed Thorne Morken, the Earl of Old Tanzanite Keep."

Tarn was from Old Tanzanite Keep? Dyna went rigid at the puzzle forming in her head. Goosebumps crawled over her skin when Klyde's face swam in her thoughts. The captain was also from the north. He was connected to all of this—connected to Tarn.

"Tarn was born shortly thereafter, and Lord Morken questioned if he was indeed his progeny. Most suspected him to truly be the Duke's son. His mother negated all allegations against her, but it caused many years of strife between Lord Morken and Lord Afton, regardless. The tension worsened, and their noble Houses brewed towards civil war. To appease Lord Morken, the king gave him peerage over the Azurite Isthmus. Better known as Troll Bridge."

Shocked silence filled the room. A shudder crawled down Dyna's spine, recalling what had happened to the settlement there.

Rawn glowered. "One could almost be forgiven to think that King Lenneus conspired to be rid of Lord Morken and his family in favor of Lord Afton. The Azurite settlement didn't last more than five years. Hundreds perished."

"Except for Tarn," Lucenna scoffed. "Well, then I think the Duke deserved what came to him."

But it didn't fully make sense. If the Duke was Tarn's real father, why would he allow him to be raised by the Morken family? Dyna sensed they were missing part of the puzzle. It involved the Azure King somehow.

"Naturally, the king favored his cousin," she said.

Rawn frowned. "It would seem so, yet Lord Morken was also a distant cousin to King Lenneus."

"Regardless of the reason, Tarn murdered a member of the royal family and countless others." The commissioner's jaw tensed slightly, the only shift in his stoic exterior. "For that alone, he must meet the executioner. Tarn will pay for his crimes with nothing more than his head."

He couldn't quite keep the tightening out of his voice at the end, and Dyna suspected Veron had history with Tarn as well.

"Then why hasn't he?" Zev asked.

"It's not for our lack of trying. With a considerable bounty of ten thousand gold pieces on his head, Tarn has been careful not to show his face in Azure. Yet after all these years, something brought him here, or someone." Veron's dark eyes narrowed on Dyna. "His bounty is considered a king's ransom, yet the one Tarn placed on your head is ten times the amount of his. It's rather curious that he would pay so much for you."

A deep, menacing growl rumbled Zev's throat. He, Lucenna, and Rawn immediately closed in on her protectively.

"You plan to fill your pockets with the reward, is that it?" Lucenna demanded.

"No." The commissioner's gaze flicked to her. "It's a third of the sum Lord Galveston offered for your extradition."

The color drained from her face. "You have been in contact with my father?"

"He sent a message by courier portal this morning to have you detained while he makes his way here."

Lucenna took a step toward him. Her shaking hands filled with flashes of purple electricity, and the room hummed with the pressure of her power. "You may have those black clovers to protect you, but I'll burn down this building with everyone in it before I let my father take me."

The guards moved forward at the threat. Dyna quickly yanked the sorceress to her side. Lucenna's Essence clashed with her own, the charge running currents against her skin. Zev snarled at the guards and shielded them both with his large body.

Dyna wasn't sure if she had heard Lucenna correctly. Had she said black clovers?

She peeked past the crook of Zev's arm at Commissioner Mooreland. He raised a hand to wave off the guards, revealing a glimpse of the bracelet on his wrist. It was constructed of amber beads dotted black in the center. She wasn't close enough to get a good look, but she could feel them tugging on the edges of her Essence, ready to siphon it should she use any.

"You have misunderstood me, Lady Lucenna," Veron said. "Not only did your father fail to provide legal documentation for the extradition, we never accept bribery, not while I'm in command. I'll not let you fall into his hands."

At his words, Lucenna's churning magic dissipated.

"I'm well aware of the deplorable customs in the Magos Empire. I wish I had the power to stop it. For those few refugees that escape here, we offer to ferry them discreetly across the Saxe Sea to Darrsho."

The capital of Dwarf Shoe, Dyna recalled from studying her map.

"The free state of the dwarves forbids extradition and the collection of bounties," Veron informed them.

"Would you be so kind as to ferry us there as well," Lucenna said, hope hitching in her voice.

"That isn't possible while you're in our custody."

A bleak tension fell over them.

Dyna glanced at the Azure Guards guarding the door, contemplating if they somehow could fight their way out. Time dragged by, and they were no closer to finding Cassiel.

She closed her eyes, wishing she could appear where he was. The bond stirred in her chest, tendrils of warmth moving through her senses. It filled her with his presence, drawing her towards the city. Instinctively, she knew if she followed the feeling, it would lead her to him.

You are my bonded, Dyna. Wherever you are, I will always be able to find you.

"I understand your position in this state of affairs, but I can assure you we are no acquaintances of Tarn," Rawn said. "We simply aim to board a ship and put a thousand leagues between him and us, for we do indeed have something he seeks." He looked at Dyna. "We must guard her at all costs, as you guard this city. Detaining us places her, and now our companion, in peril."

The head of the Azure Guard drummed his fingers on the desk as he observed them each individually, speculating on what it all meant. His calculating gaze fell on Dyna, and her friends shifted closer to her.

"Commissioner." Keena landed on his desk. She lifted the folds of her torn gown as her tiny feet walked past piles of documents and stacked scrolls. "I'm willing to vouch on behalf of Dyna and these fine people."

He shook his head. "Princess, I cannot involve you in this matter."

"I was involved the moment a citizen of your city held me captive for ransom," Keena said as she sat on a book resting by his hand. "All of this happened within miles of your headquarters, under the noses of your guards. What would my father think to hear that the fae are no longer safe in the Port of Azure, least of all his daughter?"

A flush rose to Veron's face. "I am deeply sorry for what befell you. If I had known you were here—"

Keena raised a hand, cutting him off. "I cannot imagine what would have occurred if Dyna hadn't rescued me. Instead of rewarding her, you have her arrested. My father would not be pleased, possibly offended even. Perhaps enough to end our trade deals with the Azure Kingdom, deals that would greatly displease the queen if they were lost. The Azure King wouldn't want to upset his queen, now would he?"

Commissioner Moreland stared at the fairy for a long minute, then motioned at his guards to leave the room. Once the door closed behind them, he faced away from them and pressed a curled hand to his mouth. At first, Dyna thought he was angry, but then he shook with muffled laughter.

"Keenali Eveleigh, when did you learn to speak that way?"

The fairy giggled and shrugged. "Well, attend enough noble gatherings, and you begin to speak the pompous language. Was I threatening?"

"Yes, extremely. I'm sure it would also displease my wife if the trade deals between the Morphos Court and the Azure Kingdom were to end."

At the mention of her, Keena's brow creased with worry. "How is Marla feeling these days?"

The commissioner's smile faded. A brief sadness reflecting in his eyes before it was gone. "She is doing well, thank you." He cleared his throat, regaining his composure. "Returning to the matter at hand, the Magistrate has ordered their arrests. My hands are tied."

Keena flew up to his face and poked his nose. "Veron, there is far more at stake here than capturing a wanted man. Their friend, the one I need to remind you a poacher holds captive, is a *Celestial*."

Dyna's heart lurched at the sudden revelation of Cassiel's identity to another human.

The commissioner's mouth opened and closed before it could form words. "A Celestial?"

"I bore witness to his self-healing myself," Keena confirmed. They stared at each other, seeming to silently share something.

Zev squeezed Dyna's hand as worry creased his face. Rawn and Lucenna braced themselves. She nodded to let them know it was all right. She trusted Keena, and if the fairy trusted this man, then so could they.

Veron snatched a quill from the inkwell on his desk and rapidly wrote on a page. "Celestials have not been seen in these parts for over five hundred years."

Zev glared at him. "And with good reason, if you know their history with humans."

"Yes, I'm fully aware," the commissioner replied, rather flustered. "What is his full name? The bounty only provided the first."

No one answered. They couldn't.

Dyna didn't know all the rules of her immunity, but the main clause was to never reveal the existence of Celestials. It barred her from ever speaking about them. But what if it could save Cassiel's life?

Veron looked up at their silence in exasperation. "Government officials of the Azure Kingdom are required to sign the Accords. I only know this because of my position. It's confidential information, and I could lose my head if I spoke of it publicly. I can assure you the secret is safe with me."

"Soaraway," she answered in breathless relief.

The quill snapped in Veron's fingers, ink splattering across the page. His eyes bulged wide. "Come again?"

By his reaction, he recognized the royal family name and the severity behind it.

Dyna squared her shoulders. "He is Prince Cassiel Soaraway, son of Yoel Soaraway, the High King of Hilos and the Four Celestial Realms."

"By the gods." He grabbed another quill, and the tip scratched quickly across a fresh page. "I'll deliver this news to the Magistrate myself. Corporal Willam will have organized a unit of Azure Guards by now to go after Draven. We will free the prince within the hour."

Zev growled. "We don't have an hour."

"By the time you run through all the legal channels, it may be too late for him and the secrecy of Celestials," Lucenna added.

Von's hand stalled over the page, sweat sprouting on his forehead. "But I cannot simply release—"

Keena laid her hand on his thumb. "Veron, you know no poacher would wait to sell divine blood. The prince may already be headed for the market as we speak."

Dyna came to stand in front of his desk, forcing him to look at her. "King Yoel bore witness to The Decimation of his people. He lost so many to the greed of humans, including his mother. He will *never* forgive another loss, especially that of his son. Cassiel is to be the future High King of Hilos."

Veron stiffened in his chair.

Zev shot her a startled look. She hadn't had the time to share that with him, not that it was her news to share.

"Do you understand what is at stake?" Rawn said before he could reply. "If we do not stop this, the Azure Kingdom will have violated the Accords. Allow the death of their heir, and that egregious move will not go unanswered. The High King would annihilate the port and the entire kingdom into obscurity."

The color drained from the commissioner's face, and he swallowed. "The grounds for your arrest are speculation, at best. Most likely, they will drop the charges. If you run, you'll become fugitives of Azure."

Dyna braced her hands on his desk, holding his gaze. "With all due respect, sir, I don't bloody care."

She waited for his answer, their hope riding on his decision to break the law for them.

Veron dragged a hand down the length of his face. "The gods forbid I am responsible for a war that could have been prevented."

A collective sigh of relief sounded in the room.

"Go. You have until noon before I raise the alarm of your escape. That is the only help I can give you."

Keena flew to join them. "I'll help."

"No. After this, they will be wanted by the crown. You cannot publicly involve yourself with them any further." Veron looked at Dyna and her companions. "The Azure Guard will search for you, beginning with the pier and at every port along our coasts. Get the Celestial prince out of my city and don't return." He stood and nodded to Zev, straightening his uniform. "Going out the front door isn't an option, nor can it appear that I aided your escape."

A wry smile crossed Zev's face. He clenched his fists, making the knuckles crack. "I apologize in advance."

He swung, and the punch sent the commissioner crashing across the room. He slumped against the wall, falling unconscious.

Keena winced. "That's going to leave a mark."

Lucenna cast a containment spell at the office door, coating the surface in a rippling purple magic. Guards banged on it from the other side, shouting in alarm.

"Time to go." Zev grabbed the bench and flung it through the window.

The loud shatter of glass rained down below. Rawn knocked away the remaining jagged pieces on the edges. He grabbed a rope out of his pack and secured it to an exposed rafter on the ceiling before tossing it outside. He motioned for Lucenna to come first. She grabbed the rope and climbed out the window as the Azure Guards started breaking down the door. Then Zev followed at Rawn's instruction and he held out his hand for Dyna to come next.

The fairy smiled at her. "Come visit the Morphos Court once this mess is sorted. My father would gladly receive you. We're within your debt."

"There is no debt to speak of."

"Wait," Keena called when Dyna moved to take Rawn's hand. Uncertainty crossed her expression, and she sighed. "If he hasn't reached it yet, you will find Leoake in Willows Grove, a day outside of the city. There is a hidden portal in the largest willow tree. A fae secret. It's how we travel between the courts."

By this, it was clear the fairy had known more than she let on. Their meeting couldn't have been a coincidence, but there wasn't time to question it.

She bowed her head. "Thank you. To the both of you."

Keena nodded. "Good luck to you."

"And to you." Then Dyna leaped out of the window.

CHAPTER 48

The cage was dark and cold. Uncontrollable trembling settled over Cassiel, and he wasn't sure if it came from the icy metal base or fear. It was a large cage, wide enough to stretch his arms on all four sides and stand without hunching. Almost as if it was made for him. As soon as Dyna left, Draven ordered the dwarves to cover it with a tarp. It failed to muffle their voices as they made their plans.

"Move out," Draven ordered, and the bustle on the ship grew louder.

"Brother, I think it's best we set sail for another harbor," Galen said. "We shouldn't sell him here. There are too many guards around."

"This is Azure. The Celestial hunts began in this kingdom. Everyone knows the damn value of divine blood. We will make a fortune here."

"But the girl—"

"Has a bounty on her head. If she's smart, she will have already left the city. Enough blathering. Let's go earn some coin."

The cage lurched, and the gears squealed as they pushed it across the deck. Cassiel slid on the metal base from one end to the other when they rolled it down the gangplank. They hit a snag, and Galen spat curses at the dwarves to be careful. The cage leveled once they had it safely on the ground.

The wheels rattled loudly as they rolled him through the cobblestone streets. With the breeze coming off the sea, the ends of the tarp fluttered at the bottom of the cage, letting in soft light. They pushed his cage for miles through the city. The dwarves called to people passing by to come see what Draven had captured. The sound of footsteps following them grew as more joined the procession, and their excited voices filtered around him.

"Sacred one."

"Celestial."

"Divine blood."

Cassiel's shaking hands gripped the bars as the cage shrunk in on him. He dragged in a breath and forced himself to calm down. A memory of his uncle's voice came to him, as it always did when he needed guidance. *"It is not the cage you fear. You fear what it means, but you are not trapped, and you are not helpless. This cage has a door. Find it."*

He reached for his right boot and pressed on the metal embellishments on the counter heel. A gold pin came free and fell in his palm. Cassiel exhaled heavily. He nearly forgotten he had pins made and embedded in all his shoes for this exact purpose. His old phobia of cages hadn't fully left him. Perhaps it was fate preparing him for this.

Grasping the pin in his sweaty fingers, he grabbed the padlock swinging from the chains on the door. He pushed all else from his mind, focusing on the gears in the lock. His shackled hands made it difficult to maneuver the pin, but he had practiced this enough that he should be able to—

The cage hit a pothole, and the pin slipped from his fingers, falling onto the street as they wheeled past.

Cassiel stared blankly at the padlock. This was how his story would end, as a pivotal moment when the world once again changed. He had exposed his people, and now the hunts would begin. But not before the poachers drained him of his blood. His uncle wouldn't know what happened to him. He hadn't arrived in Hermon Ridge as he should have. No one knew where he was. By the time his father learned of his death, the word that Celestials still roamed the earth would have spread throughout the kingdom.

Tucking his knees to his chest, Cassiel wrapped his arms around his legs and enveloped himself with his large wings. It didn't ward off the fear bubbling inside of him like a foul disease. He must be nothing. Feel nothing. He wouldn't die with terror as his last thought.

Cassiel shut his eyes and let his mind go. It brought him to the forest of Hilos. Birds chirped and sang among the indigo branches, thin rays of sun filtering through the massive canopy. The *Hyalus* tree stood like a silent giant among the trees. Its transparent glass leaves fluttered in the breeze, shimmering with an iridescent sheen.

It reminded him of the day Dyna stumbled into his life. Since then, things have changed. Bit by bit, day by day. He knew what would happen if he didn't stop it, if he didn't form a clear line between them.

But he couldn't.

It wasn't simply about the journey anymore. She'd taken root inside of him. He knew it was a mistake, but he found himself wanting what he shouldn't.

The cage came to an abrupt stop and his eyes opened to his reality when. He stiffened at the roar of so many voices swelling together. The cage moved again, and he held onto the bars as it lifted at a slant. The dwarves grunted while they pushed it up what he guessed was another ramp.

"Secure the wheels," Galen barked once the cage leveled.

There was a shuffle of small feet, then a screech of metal, followed by a heavy thud that jerked the cage firmly in place.

"Did you get it?" Draven asked.

"Yes, Master," a dwarf replied. "A crate of a hundred glass vials. Each holds an ounce. We loaded them onto the wagon."

A shudder crept down Cassiel's back.

Vials. For his blood.

"Good. Haul it here," Draven ordered.

"A hundred vials? That's excessive," Galen said. "He will die if you extract too much."

"He won't die. Celestials self-heal, idiot. He will replenish the blood as quickly as we take it."

Cassiel shook his head. That's not how it worked. They would end up killing him by nightfall. He clenched his jaw, anger heating him. His blood was his, and no one had a right to take it. *Find a way out.*

An idea came to mind. He placed his heel over the thumb joint of his right hand and kicked down in one swift strike. His thumb popped inward, and he hissed through his clenched teeth at the pain. The shackle slid off. He quickly dislocated his left hand, wincing at the sickening crunch of his ligament. The shackles fell with a dull thud at his feet. He set his thumbs back in place as they healed. Now he had to free his ankles. Those he would probably have to break.

One end of the tarp lifted, and Cassiel hid his hands in his lap. He met Galen's sneer. Behind him, Draven's legs were visible where he stood on a large crate that faced a mass of bodies.

"Stand up," Galen barked. "Try to appear majestic."

Cassiel snorted at the demand. A scowl twisted Galen's face. He lifted a metal baton and hit Cassiel through the bars. The end zapped, and electricity burst in his chest. His body convulsed, lungs scorching. He keeled over, revealing his freed hands and the empty shackles.

"Clever fowl," Galen growled and hit Cassiel again.

He gasped a weak cry as his body arched, electricity searing through him. Galen unlocked the large cage and clambered inside. His boot smashed into Cassiel's jaw. Dirt and blood burst in his mouth. His vision swam, and he was momentarily immobile as Galen shackled him again.

"Try that shite again, and I'll cut off your damn wings myself," Galen snarled. "I'll bleed you dry, hack up your flesh and grind up your bones. Every piece of you will fetch more than your weight in gold."

Malakel's voice slithered in Cassiel's mind. *You are irrelevant. A blight. When you are gone, no one will ever care to remember you.*

But they would remember him. As the Celestial that took away the peace of the Celestial Realms. He would be their eradication.

"There will be nothing left of you once this is over, *Nephilim*."

Cassiel's glare cut to Galen.

"Aye, I know what you are." He cackled. "You may have fooled my brother, but I'm no fool. I heard the stories of half-breed Celestials and their different colored wings. Still, your mixed blood is worth something. I doubt you're the only one left, too. I'll find whatever muck heap the rest of your kind has hidden under, and it'll be the females we take first." Galen sneered in his face. "I'll greatly enjoy making my own flock of Nephilim bastards."

Rage burned through Cassiel. Illustrations of the Decimation flashed in his memories, and the screams of his ancestors filled his head.

"Now get your arse up." He turned to leave.

Cassiel lunged and wrapped the chains around Galen's neck. The startled poacher yelped, dropping his baton as he kicked and jerked like a desperate animal. Cassiel tightened his hold, listening to Glen choke as the life slowly squeezed out of him.

In one last bout of strength, Galen kicked against the cage and threw Cassiel backward with the force. The commotion called the dwarves. They stabbed through the bars with their batons from all sides. The painful zaps seared his limbs, forcing him to let Galen go. He collapsed on his knees, and they continued to shock him until he was writhing on the cage floor.

Galen stumbled to his feet; dark eyes full of wrath. A ring of red and purple marked his neck. He snatched a hatchet from a dwarf.

"Stop, Galen," the dwarf whispered. "Master is about to—"

"Welcome!" They flinched at the boom of Draven's voice. The roar of the market noise fell silent. The lifted section of the tarp exposed the edge of a brick wall and a partial view of Draven standing on a crate, facing the crowd. "You have heard the rumors, and I swear to you they are true!"

Galen jerked his head for the dwarves to leave the cage. He climbed out and remained to guard the door. His hateful glare fixed on Cassiel as his brother's speech continued.

"I have captured the rarest creature that none of you have had the privilege of seeing. Many of you think of it as a myth or as a legend long forgotten, but they exist in this Realm with us. They have not returned to Heaven's Gate, as they led us to believe. Well, I won't keep the suspense going any longer. Ladies and gents, I present to you a real, in the flesh Celestial!"

Galen yanked the tarp off the cage. Cassiel lifted his shackled hands, shielding his face against the sun's glare. He drowned in the deafening cheer that rose from the spectators all around. Once his sight adjusted, he found the cage placed center stage within the Port of Azure Market.

Humans gaped at him in wonder. Rich and poor all gathered together. Some waved their sick children in the air while others held their arms to the Heavens, giving thanks for this sacred gift. Some cried at the sight of him, but most looked hungry to tear him apart. Cassiel's pulse raced, his chest heaving. If it wasn't for the damn shackles, he would have flown into the open skies and vanished behind the clouds.

Draven waved his arms in a grand motion at the cage. "Feast your eyes upon the God of Urn's dark Celestial!"

Galen took the coil of chains from the cage floor and wrenched Cassiel out. His shackled feet stumbled awkwardly onto the stage.

"It's a fake!" someone in the crowd shouted. "He's no Celestial!"

For once, those words were a hope instead of a curse. Cassiel held his breath as a disturbed murmur went through the crowd.

Draven raised his hands to hush them. "Celestials come in all colors. Behold my truth."

Galen jerked on the chains attached to Cassiel's wrists and forced his arms outward. Draven hopped off the crate, and a dwarf popped open the lid. The poacher took out one of the small glass vials nestled within straw and came at Cassiel with a dagger.

He moved back, only to have dwarves circle him with batons.

"Keep still," Galen warned.

Cassiel clenched his teeth as Draven's icy blade sliced across his wrist. Blood poured into the vial held underneath. Before the eyes of everyone watching, the wound seamlessly healed.

Draven stuffed a cork in the vial and grinned at the hushed crowd. "Place your biddings."

The marketplace erupted with shouting voices. In a matter of seconds, the tiny vial of blood sold at an unbelievable price. Draven cut his wrist again and again, filling vial after vial. Cassiel grimaced as the dwarves ripped out handfuls of his feathers and sold them on opposite ends of the stage. His feathers quickly spread like waving black flags among the audience.

People swallowed down his blood like water. They forced it into the mouths of their sick children, leaving crimson rivulets dripping from the corners of their lips. Thousands of crazed faces gawked at him, screaming for more. Cassiel squeezed his eyes shut. He trembled, his body having gone cold. Be it from fear or blood loss, he didn't know.

All he knew was that this spelled the beginning of his end.

CHAPTER 49

Cassiel's uncle once told him he wouldn't realize the value of something until he lost it. It took landing himself in a cage to finally understand. Dizziness swam through his head as more blood left his body. He kept his eyes closed, trying to ignore the slice of the dagger against his skin.

Cassiel. Dyna's voice drifted through his mind like a gentle breeze. He pictured her smile and held on to that image.

He'd not given much value to the fleeting moments he'd spent with her until he realized there would be no more. So he dared to kiss her on the ship without thinking about how she would react. And she'd kissed him back.

It was all she could give to someone dying in place of her, but he was grateful for the last shred of kindness. She couldn't have possibly meant it to be anything but goodbye. The further she ran from the ship, the more his insides stretched, as if she had taken a part of him with her. She had become a balm that softened the jagged edges of his being. But he felt hollow now.

If he could wish for anything at all, it would be to have more time.

Thinking of Dyna, her presence called to him the way it had in Corron. That couldn't be right. He told her to go. Frowning, Cassiel reached out through their connection and sensed Dyna was only a few feet away from him. He opened his eyes and searched for her among the clamoring mass.

What are you doing? Get out of the city!

"How much for the Celestial?"

Cassiel startled at the familiar voice.

"Who said that?" Draven laughed. "No matter. He isn't for sale. Only parts of him."

The crowd hummed with surprise as they looked away from the stage. They parted down the middle to make way for a woman coming forward. Dressed in tight black leather, her dark hair fell straight and short to her chin.

Accompanying her were two slaves in long, charcoal robes with hoods covering their faces. The tallest of the two held the reins to a white horse, pulling along a large cage on wheels. Inside stood the grandest Celestial to ever exist.

He was male, tall, and strapping in layers of muscle, wearing nothing but a loincloth. Pale blond hair fell down the Celestial's back, stark against his bronze skin. His immense golden wings inspired speechless awe from the crowd and the poachers. Cassiel gawked along with the rest of them.

The woman smiled slyly. "I was passing through when I heard someone possessed a Celestial. I have come to offer you a trade."

She snapped her fingers, and her robed slaves opened the cage. They led the calm Celestial by his chains to her side, and the shorter one bowed, placing them in her hands.

"Well?" the woman said to Draven as she caressed the cheek of her golden Celestial.

He didn't recoil from her. He didn't even fight against his bonds, nor look at Cassiel. His green eyes merely fixed on the crowd with a bored expression. How long had they kept him in captivity?

"Where did you find him?" Draven finally asked. "Are there more?"

Her laugh of ridicule rang in the hushed market. "Did you believe yours was the only one?"

The woman led the Celestial up the ramp to the stage and placed the chains in Draven's hands. She went over to inspect Cassiel, walking around him as she thoughtfully tapped her chin. When she had her back to Draven, her lilac gaze met Cassiel's, and she winked.

Lucenna.

She wore glamor to hide her appearance, but he recognized those eyes. Hope made his insides jump. He glanced away, feigning indifference.

"Other than a slave business, I poach Celestials," Lucenna said, lifting Cassiel's wing as she inspected it. "I collect them, you see. As I don't have one with black feathers, I was interested in a trade, but alas, yours is damaged goods."

Draven smirked. "Come off that blather, lass. He's perfect."

"He has bald spots on his wings." Lucenna went to reclaim her chains, but he moved away.

"That's because these idiots ripped out too many feathers." Draven growled at his dwarves, then flashed her a grin. "But he will recover them in due time."

"He's too thin."

"Nothing a good meal won't fix."

Lucenna narrowed her eyes and beckoned for him to return the chains. "Don't take me for a fool. We both know my Celestial is more valuable than yours."

"We can work out a deal." Draven insisted. "You can have him in addition to a thousand silver pieces. I shall pay no more, mind you."

She arched an eyebrow at him. "Silver? He's worth gold."

He grinned sheepishly. "Two thousand gold pieces, then."

"Don't make me laugh."

"Five thousand. Final offer."

"No, brother," Galen whispered to him. "There must be more. We can hunt them ourselves."

"Shut your gob," Draven snapped at him. "Question me again, and what you will get is my ax in your hairy arse. Now get my gold ready."

Lucenna crossed her arms. "I'm not interested."

"Ten thousand pieces!" someone in the crowd called.

"That's ridiculous." The poacher glared at the sea of faces. "Twelve thousand."

She rolled her eyes. "I didn't come to auction my possessions."

"Twenty thousand!" came another offer beyond the stage.

Cassiel suspected the tall slave under the hood was calling out prices. He pursed his lips to keep from smirking. That one must be Rawn, so the other slave was Dyna. He stared at the dainty-hooded figure, knowing without a doubt that it was her.

"Thirty thousand," the poacher growled.

Lucenna filched the chains from his hands and strode away.

"You won't get more than fifty thousand for him."

She kept walking.

"Wait!"

She didn't.

"A hundred thousand gold pieces!" the poacher shouted desperately.

"What?" Galen gawked at him in disbelief. "That is more than half your fortune."

"I can make it back three-fold with her Celestial."

Lucenna paused. Cassiel held his breath, and the audience fell quiet to hear her reply. At the end of the market, Azure Guards shoved their way through the crowd. She noticed them as well.

Lucenna held out the chains of her Celestial. "Deal."

Draven snatched them, and a victorious grin split his scarred face.

Cassiel did his best not to react. He had his freedom!

Lucenna snapped her fingers and her two slaves came forward. The shortest of them took Cassiel's chains, and the other took the key from a dwarf to unchain him. He readily held out his shackled wrists. The key snicked in the keyhole and the chains clanged heavily at his feet. They unlocked the shackles around his ankles, then Dyna took his arm. She raised her head slightly to reveal a smile under the shadow of her hood.

Galen glowered at Lucenna as he thrust a large sack of gold at her.

"Thank you." She snapped her fingers again, and her slaves led Cassiel down the ramp.

He noticed Elric's tall, green form in the crowd, and they locked eyes. The orc made his way to the stage, gripping his hammer in his enormous fists. Cassiel shook his head, signaling that he didn't need help now. Dyna peeked at Elric from beneath her hood, and he halted when he recognized her.

"It was a pleasure doing business with you," Draven called after them.

Lucenna continued ahead to the waiting horse without looking back.

Rawn quickly unlocked the cage strapped to Fair and leaped inside. He motioned for Cassiel and Dyna to hurry in as Lucenna mounted Fair's saddle. But Cassiel stopped. The golden Celestial left on the stage, watched them go. They couldn't leave him there. He was going to say so, but the Celestial met his stare and grinned.

The dwarves plucked a handful of his golden feathers, only for them to disintegrate in their hands. The Celestial's image distorted and faded away until it was Zev left standing. He laughed at Draven's gaping expression.

Galen's head snapped in Cassiel's direction. A gust of wind hit them at that moment, blowing off Dyna's hood.

"Draven, they swindled us!" Galen shouted.

Zev quickly shifted into a wolf and snapped his teeth at the poachers, making them jump back. He leaped off the stage into the crowd.

Draven shoved his men. "Stop them!"

The sky darkened as shadows swept over cobblestone streets, and a wave of gasps and frightened cries rolled through the market. Cassiel looked up, and his breath caught. A flock of female Celestials in golden scale mail armor soared through the sky in a flutter of colorful wings. The sigil of a tree in a mountain peak embossed their breastplates.

The Valkyrie of Hermon Ridge.

Yelrakel flew in the center, a stream of scarlet hair flaring around her shoulders. Her fierce gaze flickered from Cassiel to the poachers, and he saw the rage enter her face. At their leader's war cry, the

Valkyrie whipped out their weapons as one. The sky blazed with white fire, but her sword burned with vivid cerulean flames.

She dived and landed on the stage with a burst of wind. Her gray wings snapped open, and she whipped around, hurtling Draven's dwarves back. One poacher left standing in front of her froze with a vial of divine blood in his shaking hand. Yelrakel him with dark eyes. Her seraph sword swept through the air and slashed clean through him. There was no cry. One moment he was there, the next he burst into a cloud of embers and ash. Nothing left of him but the vial shattering at her feet. Red dripped off the edge of the stage.

Cassiel exhaled a shaky breath. She killed a human. Without hesitation. Without mercy.

Yet her Seraph fire, given only to the Celestials blessed by *Elyōn*, remained.

Yelrakel faced the stunned crowd, and her cold voice carried over the silence, chilling Cassiel to his bones. "You have defiled our prince with your filthy greed. Now this city will *burn*."

The Valkyrie blotted the sun as they descended upon them. The market erupted in chaos. People screamed and scrambled in every direction.

"No!" Cassiel shouted, but his order went ignored.

Blades flashed in steel and fire as they cut down anyone who held a piece of him. Blood rained, and begging cries filled his ears. Bodies became pyres of flame, smoke choking the air as ash scattered through the wind like black snow. He couldn't look away from the massacre.

Death arrived in Azure, and there was no stopping it.

A Valkyrie swiped at Lucenna. The sorceress cast out a wall of water and threw back the female. Fair reared with a wild neigh, racing away with her and only Rawn in the cage.

"Run!" Cassiel grabbed Dyna's hand, and they sprinted after them.

They dodged people and burning heaps as he tried to get her out of there. Screams rang around them. Valkyrie swarmed the skies, their divine swords flaming. He couldn't risk flying without Dyna getting hurt. Azure Guards stormed through the market in a flood of blue. They led people to safety and put out fires, but the Valkyrie rendered any who confronted them to ash. They ran past Draven as he fought against Commissioner Veron, battle-ax against sword.

Cassiel soon lost sight of the others in the mayhem. Dyna's hand gripped his hard, her fear coiling around his racing heart. She screamed his name and yanked on his arm. A hatchet spun past, missing his neck by a fraction. Electricity blasted through his back, and it sent him crashing, taking her with him. He hit the ground, every muscle in his body spasming as he gasped in pain.

"You wretched bitch!" Galen stood over them, his hate-filled eyes pinned on Dyna. "I knew I should have killed you on the boat."

Cassiel pleaded with his body to move, but he was numb. Terror seized him as that hatchet came for Dyna and a cry ripped from his throat. She threw her crossed arms over her head. Galen's hatchet bounced off her with a dull *clang*, the force knocking him back a step. He gaped at her, as did Cassiel.

How?

Galen snarled and raised his hatchet again. A spinning blade struck the weapon out of his hands. They all turned as Von approached. Dressed in all black, riddled with knives, his face chiseled stone.

Galen frowned. "Who are—"

Von leaped into a spin kick. His boot rammed into Galen's jaw and brutally slammed him on the ground. The poacher slumped, head lolling, as he fell unconscious.

Cassiel sat upright as Von faced them, the feeling finally returning to his body. Why did he save them? Von's gaze fixed on Dyna. No, it wasn't to help. Tarn needed her alive.

"Come with me, lass," Von told her. "Don't make me hurt him."

Cassiel snatched the fallen hatchet at the same time she drew her knife and sprang protectively in front of him.

"Try it," Dyna said, the challenge honed in steel.

"Oi! You, there!" Kye and a unit of Azure Guards charged for Von. He cursed and ran in the opposite direction as they chased after him.

Dropping the hatchet, Cassiel grabbed Dyna to inspect her arms. There was no blood. "Are you hurt? What was that?"

She pulled off the heavy cloak to reveal her fae armor and the silver-leafed jacket underneath. "It's enchanted."

"Thank *Elyōn*." He exhaled heavily and pulled her into his embrace. If it wasn't for the jacket, the attack would have killed her.

"Little prince." A Valkyrie towered them, her distinct wings the color of deep wine arching behind her.

She gripped a glaive in her fist, her armor and greaves stained with blood. Vivid blue flames swiveled around the thick blade. Her rich brown eyes, the same color as her skin, looked down at him. Strength oozed from her confident form. She'd braided her black hair in a coronet, exposing a face he had seen a hundred times before.

"Sowmya," Cassiel whispered.

"You must come with us, Your Highness. Lord Jophiel awaits you."

He couldn't go with them, not yet. "The Valkyrie should not be here. Tell Yelrakel I command her to cease this madness and return to Hermon Ridge at once."

"We are under orders, little prince. Orders that not even you can defy."

Cassiel stiffened. For her to say that, the command came beyond his uncle.

Sowmya's gaze flickered to Dyna, and he instinctively held her closer. "Shall I dispose of the human?"

"You will not touch her," he said coolly. "I granted her immunity in *all* Four Realms."

Her eyes widened at his meaning. Before Sowmya could reply, a wide net dropped over her. Azure Guards held the ends and fought to restrain her. With a vicious snarl, Sowmya shoved her glaive through the stomach of a guard and tossed him behind her. His body vanished in a wisp of ash.

"Stand down!" one begged her. "We mean you no harm!"

The guards fought to keep her contained, but Sowmya hacked at the net and would soon be free. Cassiel hauled Dyna to her feet as a black wolf joined them. They sprinted through the market, following Zev toward the alleyway, where Lucenna and Rawn waved at them. Draven and a group of his men were on their heels.

"Pardon me," Dyna said.

Grabbing his wing, her body blazed with light. She threw out a hand behind them, and the air exploded with green fire, casting the poachers back.

Cassiel laughed. "Brilliant."

Dyna flashed him a grin. "I'm glad you should think so."

They reached the alley and jumped into the cage fastened to Fair's saddle.

"Go!" Rawn barked as he leaped inside after them.

Lucenna whipped the reins. Fair galloped away, Zev sprinting alongside them. Cassiel looked out at the end of the alley, the screams growing distant as the market fell out of view.

God of Urn, what happened?

"Your father," Dyna said, probably feeling his shock. "When you didn't arrive in Hermon Ridge ..."

"He ordered my uncle to find me," Cassiel finished.

He didn't expect his father to care enough to risk the Four Realms. At the command, Lord Jophiel would have immediately sent out his Valkyrie. The wanted notices told them exactly where to search.

He pressed his forehead against the bars. Oh, his father would scourge him for this if he didn't exile him first. It would be impossible to hide the existence of Celestials now. The Azure King would surely have something to say about the butchery of his people. This could mean war.

Rawn handed Cassiel his enchanted coat. "Forgive us for not coming sooner."

"I'm grateful you came at all." Cassiel immediately slipped it on, relieved to have his wings out of sight.

Dyna glowered at him. "You gave up your life."

"I did it for you."

She shook her head, closing her eyes as the distant cries reached them. "I am not worth this, Cassiel."

People died because he exposed himself to protect her. This would change everything for his kind, and yet he couldn't bring himself to regret it. Dyna was his bonded, but she meant more to him than that. Whether it was due to their link, or to his role as a Guardian, she'd taken up a central part of his life, and her safety prevailed over all else. Even his own. Although it baffled him, he knew one absolute thing. When it came between her and the world, he would always choose her.

Dyna removed the chain with his mother's ring from her jacket and placed it around his neck. "You have a reason to keep going."

He yanked her into an embrace, holding her close to his heart. She tightened her arms around him, burying her face in his chest. He laid his head over hers and sighed in relief as peace swept over him like a wave. Tendrils of their bond coiled between them and became stronger, as if her presence alone fortified its strength.

"You came back for me."

"Did you truly believe I could live with myself if I left you behind?" Her voice broke. "I'll always come for you, Cassiel. I meant what I said on the ship."

I want to stay. No matter the consequences, I want to stay with you.

There were no words for what that did to him. For most of his life, he had thought his existence didn't matter in the world. That no one would care if he disappeared. For her to say she wanted to stay with him couldn't be right. It had to be a dream, for who could want such a thing?

The cage shook as they raced through the cobblestone streets. Aware of Rawn's presence, he reluctantly let Dyna go. They held onto the bars and watched the streets of the Port of Azure roll past in a blur. It would be the last time they would ever return.

The sorceress headed north, and she didn't slow down. They raced through northern city gates, oddly not manned by any guards. Travelers leaped out of their way as they sped past, eliciting a cloud of dust on the road. The sun lowered in the sky when they finally came to a stop on a soaring cliff miles away.

"Freedom!" Cassiel burst out of the cage onto solid ground. He never thought he would be so overjoyed to stand on grass.

Zev shifted into his human form and laughed. He quickly dressed with clothes Rawn tossed to him. "Did you see the poacher's face when Lucenna dropped the spell? I'll never forget it."

Rawn chuckled as he exited the cage next. "I'm astounded we carried out such a tremendous scheme."

Cassiel took Dyna's hand, helping her down. "How did you plan this?"

"She thought it best to disguise us as poachers to gain Draven's trust," Zev said. "And Lucenna used an illusion spell to turn me into a Celestial." He puffed his chest with pride. "I made a quite handsome one too, didn't I?"

Cassiel smiled and shook his head. "Thank you. I was certain it was the end for me."

"I would not let Draven have you," Dyna said.

Rawn clapped his arm. "My oath to guide and protect extends to you all."

It moved Cassiel that they cared enough to rescue him. They truly were an unexpected, odd group of companions.

"If we had failed at the trade, we had a backup plan." Zev dropped his heavy arm around Cassiel's neck and tousled his hair. "We were going to steal his ship."

"I would have liked to see that."

"Aye, me too."

But Cassiel's smile faded as the sunset cast its light over the sea. Spirals of smoke rose from the center of the city. Ash coated his boots and clothing. This day would mark history, and the consequences would ripple through the Realms.

The Valkyrie had killed humans ruthlessly, without a care for damnation. But if Yelrakel had tainted her soul, why didn't she lose her Seraph fire?

"They're looking for you, aren't they?" Zev asked. "Those females, their wings were..."

Cassiel nodded. "They are the Valkyrie of Hermon Ridge, the Realm of half-breed Celestials."

They all gawked at him, but he was too engulfed by his confusion to react. Had he been damned or not?

"Are they going to force you to return to Hilos?" Dyna asked.

"That must be their intention," he said. "But you have reminded me why I came on this journey. Once they find me again, I will to my uncle explaining my decision."

Lucenna lingered away from them where she stood by Fair's side. What she had done for him today dispelled any doubts he had.

"I should not have called you a witch," Cassiel told her. "I was wrong. Thank you for coming to my aid."

Lucenna gave him a curt nod without looking at him. From her satchel, she took out a small leather purse and took a handful of coins from the sack of Draven's gold tied to Fair's saddle. "This is my portion. The rest I leave to you."

"What do you mean?" Dyna asked.

"I'm leaving. I can no longer travel with you," she said, pocketing the gold.

"What?" Cassiel blurted.

Dyna's eyes widened. "Why?"

"You didn't tell me Tarn was on your tail," Lucenna hissed. "And it led to a bounty on my head. The life of every sorceress in the Magos Empire depends on my survival. Now my father knows where I am. He's coming for me. I need to be far from here before he arrives."

She spun on her heel, heading towards the woods.

"Please don't go." Dyna ran after Lucenna and grabbed her arm. "Forgive me for not telling you about him. I thought you wouldn't come with us if I did."

"You're right. I wouldn't have." Lucenna wrestled herself free. "And for good reason. I didn't spend years hiding from my father to be caught now."

"But he is across the country."

"He has his ways, Dyna. I'm not ready to fight him. The Elite Enforcers were nothing compared to his power."

"You're stronger than you know, even without the Moonstone. Stay with us. We need to stay together."

Lucenna's misty gaze flickered over them and landed on Dyna. Cassiel read the conflict there. She didn't want to leave, but she had already decided. Lucenna was scared, he realized. Her father frightened her enough to run because to her it was the only option. After being alone for so long, she was used to relying solely on herself. He knew exactly what that was like.

"What about the Druid?" Cassiel asked. As much as Lucenna had annoyed him, he didn't mind having her around anymore.

"Clearly, he doesn't want to be found."

"But I know where to find him now." Dyna took her hand. "Please don't leave. You need us."

"I don't need anyone." Lucenna removed her hold. "I'm sorry. Goodbye, Dyna. Be safe."

She headed east for the trees and cast an invisibility spell, disappearing from view.

"Lucenna, wait," Dyna called sadly. "Please don't leave!"

But she was gone.

Zev wrapped an arm around Dyna's slumped shoulders. "She's chosen to make her own way. We have to let her go."

Cassiel shook his head. He hoped Lucenna would be all right out there alone, but he couldn't help but feel they had lost a vital part of their team.

"I'll pray for her safety," Rawn said somberly as he untied Fair's saddle from the cage.

"How do we find the Druid?" Zev asked Dyna.

She sighed and turned away from the forest. "Keena told me he'll be headed for Willows Grove. There is a portal there by which the fae travel."

Cassiel had to question it. "Why would she wait until now to share such significant information?"

Dyna shrugged. "She said it was a secret."

Was that really all it was?

"The grove isn't too far from here," Zev said.

"Then we must make haste lest we encounter the Azure Guard," Rawn said. "Now that bounty hunters seek to capture us, our journey will prove a much more strenuous endeavor. Commander Moreland warned us to avoid the ports. Crossing to Dwarf Shoe by ship is no longer possible."

Cassiel sucked in a breath. "That means we will have to pass through Troll Bridge."

Rawn nodded, looking bleak at the prospect. "I admit I have no experience there. I had no need to cross it before, nor did I dare."

"How dangerous is it?" Zev asked. "Worse than the fjord?"

"Our lives would be at stake, but it may be a risk we have to take to leave Urn's Chip."

"I won't put Dyna in harm's way."

"If there is a safe way to cross, my uncle will know," Cassiel said. "He is the Lord of Hermon Ridge, and he guards the entrance to the isthmus. I could request to have an audience with him."

"We?" Dyna repeated, bouncing on her toes with excitement.

"You have my abiding trust. All of you." Cassiel smiled, allowing the back of his hand to brush hers. "After we find that damn Druid, it would please me to show you the fourth Celestial Realm. Would you care to join me?"

Her emerald eyes shone like jewels. *Oh yes,* her heart seemed to say. *With you, I will go anywhere.*

CHAPTER 50

Von

Von tried not to limp as he walked through Tarn's camp. There was a small bulge on his right thigh where he bandaged his leg beneath his trousers. Dry blood coated the hilts of the knives strapped to the crossed sheaths on his chest. It had been some time since he faced an opponent that was an equal match.

This time around, he'd finally recognized the mercenary's fighting tactics. The dual-blade method was so familiar it was like fighting an echo of the past.

"Who trained you?" Von had asked. He leaned against the alley wall, staunching the blood leaking from his leg.

The mercenary applied pressure to his wounded shoulder. Klyde, Dyna had called him. Lowering his mask, the man's cool blue eyes pinned on Von, exposing a face he sensed he should recognize but didn't.

"Someone no longer alive," Klyde said.

There was something about the harsh stare. This was more than a simple score.

"I get the sense I wronged you somehow," Von said as he pushed off the wall, drawing another knife. "But I don't know you."

A harsh smile curled Klyde's mouth. "That's all right, mate. I know *you*."

Eagon then appeared before Von could question him further. He didn't want to waste time fighting two members of the Skulls at once, so he escaped to search for Dyna. The last thing he expected to see was a flock of female Celestials cutting down people in the city market.

He failed to capture her there too, but one good thing came out of it. The glass vial felt warm in his pocket. He had filched it off a mound of ashes. The vial of divine blood could be beneficial one day. It may be exactly what he needed to gain Yavi's freedom.

As the peak of Tarn's tent came into view, Von pivoted and headed for his tent instead. He should have gone to report to his master first, but he wanted to find his wife. He couldn't go another day without her speaking to him.

Von stepped into his tent and immediately stopped short at the entryway.

Tarn sat at the small table with his muddy black boots resting on top of Von's cot. He wore a long, elegant gray coat with his hands nestled in black leather gloves. Tarn didn't acknowledge him. He played with a knife on the table's surface, the tip of the blade spinning while he held the top of the hilt with a gloved fingertip.

"Master," Von bowed.

"You have returned empty-handed," Tarn said to the knife. "I take it the bounties failed."

"The bounties didn't fail. They were briefly in the hands of the Azure Guard, but there was an occurrence in the city that allowed them to escape. Now they are on the run, and cannot board a ship at any port within the kingdom."

"Where do you think they will run to?" Tarn asked him. By his tone, he already knew the answer.

The Azure Kingdom was a chip in Urn's chalice. If they couldn't board a ship, there was only one other way out.

"Troll Bridge," Von said. A wave of nostalgia went through him. That place was once his home. Although there was nothing left but the memory of the dead, a part of him wanted to see it.

The blade stopped spinning, and the sound of Tarn's leather glove creaked as he squeezed the hilt.

"Troll Bridge..." His wintry blue eyes pinned Von as they frosted over. "I have not set foot there in fifteen years, and I will never do so again."

Von dropped his gaze. "What would you have me do?"

"We will cut them off before they reach the bridge. Elon is already on their tail. He's been watching them since they arrived in the Port of Azure."

Von stiffened. He hadn't known the elf had been in the city, but then he wasn't keeping track of Elon. Now that he thought of it, he hadn't seen Elon since the day before last. Tarn was keeping things from him. To do so meant he was losing favor.

"Elon delivered a rather interesting report," Tarn said as he studied the sharp edge of the knife. "He described the disarray that had occurred in the marketplace once a poacher got his hands on the Nephilim. History has a way of repeating itself, doesn't it? In Corron, you failed to bring me the Maiden, and you've failed me yet again."

Von bowed his head as sweat beaded on his back. "I had her, Master, but the same mercenary from the capital appeared. His interference allowed her to escape." He didn't dare mention his third botched attempt to seize Dyna in the market. "That mercenary is determined to find you and I don't think it's to collect a bounty."

Tarn hardly seemed concerned. "What did he look like?"

"He's young, has dark blond hair, blue eyes, and bearded. Tall and strong, but..." Von frowned, recalling how swiftly he moved. "He fought with the dual-blade technique of Lord Morken. As though he'd trained the mercenary himself."

Which was impossible, because Lord Morken was dead.

Tarn stilled at the mention of his father. He was so motionless Von thought he'd stopped breathing.

"Master?"

"What is the mercenary's name?"

"The Maiden called him Klyde."

Tarn held quiet for a long moment. "Did you kill him?"

"No. I was forced to retreat."

The rigidity left Tarn's shoulders. "What has become of you that you cannot kill your opponents? By the stiffness in your leg, he wounded you."

"It's only a graze—"

Tarn's pale eyes cut to him. "You're losing your touch, Von. Perhaps it's time I make someone else the commander of my Raiders. Elon has proven suitable. He's never disappointed me, not once."

That couldn't happen. Von's position gave him the power to protect Yavi. That priority overshadowed everything, even his empathy to spare Dyna any harm at the hands of Tarn.

"I *will* capture the Maiden for you," he vowed. "I'll leave now to intercept them and bring her to you by dawn."

"No. I have another task for you of equal importance, which will prove your worth to me. Should you squander this opportunity, it will be your last," Tarn said idly, as though he were explaining simple math to a child. An aloof promise of death.

Von dropped to one knee. "I'm at your service, Master."

"Whether your service be of any use begs the question."

"Whatever the task, whatever you desire, I will acquire it for you." The declaration sat like spoiled milk in his stomach.

Without question.

"So you shall. Assemble the spies to set out for Beryl Coast. Bouvier has sent word on the Sacred Scroll he had left to investigate," Tarn started, but Yavi barreled inside the tent.

"Well, did I not say it would happen, Von?" she demanded. "I heard from Novo that you're leaving. That man commands, and you bend—" The rest died on her lips when she noticed the master sitting at their table.

The color drained from her face as cold horror sank into Von's bones.

Tarn rose to his feet.

He would never tolerate such insubordination. Tarn would kill her, or worse. He might whip her until she was nothing but a shredded piece of flesh.

"Hold that insolent tongue lest I cut it out," Von said icily, coming for her. The terror in her eyes made him sick, but he couldn't show that. Tarn was watching.

Yavi recoiled away from him. "F-forgive me."

"Get out of my sight."

She ran out of the tent. He watched her retreating form, resisting the urge to go after her.

"That one has become imprudent, Von." Tarn's mouth thinned as he glanced at their cots and cozy setting within the tent. "You have been too lenient, or should I say comfortable? Softened toward a woman who serves your every need." His icy eyes fell on him like two frozen spheres. "Perhaps I should have her tongue removed, so she may not forget her place."

So *he* may not forget.

It took all Von had to keep his hardened expression. "That would render her useless, Master. What good is a linguist if she cannot speak?"

"Then have her whipped."

"Yes, I'll do it myself." He prayed to the God of Urn that the daze from the Witch's Brew would make Tarn forget about the command.

Satisfied with his harsh reply, Tarn moved on from the subject. "As I was saying, you will assemble the spies to retrieve the scroll. The ruins lay outside of Beryl Cove in the northeast coast of Azure, a fortnight's ride from here."

Only if they rode non-stop. Von didn't expect to go on another expedition while pursuing Dyna. To send him away at such a pivotal time meant this scroll might be the Scroll of the Unending they were searching for.

"I'll go, but before I do, allow me to capture the Maiden. I'll not fail you, Master."

Tarn contemplated him for a moment. "Very well. You and the lieutenants shall accompany me along with another twenty of your best to retrieve her."

Tension coiled around Von's body. This was unusual. Tarn didn't go on any missions. Not since... He glanced at the jagged scar cutting across his master's face. As though Tarn sensed his gaze, he rubbed the discolored skin on his chin.

"Shall I bring Len and Novo?" Von asked.

Tarn's pale blond hair shifted over his forehead as he tilted his head. "Leave them behind. There is no more room for error this time, Von. I want the Maiden and the sorceress alive."

"We will need enchanted bangles to restrain them."

"I'll have it, along with this." Raising his hand, Tarn displayed the leather cuff on his wrist with three amber beads containing black clovers. He had bought it from a witch in their recent trip to Versai for a small fortune.

"What of the others?"

"Kill them." Tarn flung the knife, embedding it on the table's surface. "Starting with the Lycan."

Von realized then it was made of pure silver. Tarn had already thought of the best way to defeat their opponents. To bring his lieutenants meant he was bringing his full force against the Guardians. He wasn't taking any more chances.

"Order the men to break camp. We leave at sundown to follow their trail," Tarn commanded, his cold voice definitive. The temperature dropped in the tent, the air growing thin as his gaze hardened into a sea of ice. "I will have the Maiden, Von. There is no ending this until I do."

Von bowed, and he listened to Tarn's footsteps recede over the crunch of gravel as he left. Once he fell out of view, Von ran to find Yavi. He followed the direction she went, but after passing several tents and faces, she didn't appear.

"Commander Von." Olssen nodded to him as he walked out of the cook's tent with a plate of food.

"Olssen, ready the men to move out," Von said as he hurried past.

"Yes, Commander."

Von entered the cook's tent, but Yavi wasn't there either. Geon worked on chopping turnips rapidly in perfectly even slices. The Minotaur loomed over him like a dark shadow, his stern glower analyzing the boy's technique.

"Not so fast," Sorren growled. "Or you'll lose a thumb and serve it to the men."

"R-right," Geon stuttered, altering the knife's rhythm. He noticed Von and smiled. "Commander, have you come for supper? We're roasting turnips."

"No, I'm searching for Yavi."

"I haven't seen her." Geon lowered his knife, reading Von's expression. "Is something wrong?"

Von shifted on his feet anxiously. "I need to find her."

Sorren nodded in the direction he came. "Try the pond. She was there earlier washing uniforms."

"Thank you," Von said, then ran off again.

He ducked behind tents as he left camp again, not wanting to be seen. Von heard her muffled crying as he got closer. She hid behind a tall wall of reeds and cattail plants. He parted them to find her kneeling by the bank of the pond.

"Yavi." Von slowly approached her, not wanting to startle her further.

The tears on her face were a blow to his heart. A thin layer of sweat covered her ashen complexion. He gathered her stiff body in his arms.

"Forgive me." Von murmured into her hair while rubbing her shaking back. "Forgive me for everything. For making you suffer in this life."

Yavi shoved him off. "At least you acknowledge you're at fault."

"I'm sorry, love. I didn't know what else to do." He reached for her, but she winced away from him. "You have to know I would never do that."

"These are the lengths you're willing to take to protect me, Von. You threaten me, so he doesn't have to." Yavi looked away from him to the pond. "To Tarn and everyone else I am property. But you had never treated me as such until today. For the first time, I finally feel like a slave."

The fact impaled him deep in his chest. He lowered his gaze and bit back a bitter scream. Why must it be this way? He was trapped in the chains of servitude and the holy law. Breaking them would only lead to her destruction, and keeping them would lead to her hatred.

Von saw it growing in her stony expression. She couldn't love him when he couldn't put her first. The fates were cruel. But deep down, he knew it was his fault. He should never have broken the slave edict by marrying Yavi and reaching for more than he was allowed. But good gods, he loved this woman, and the fear of losing her in any way was unfathomable.

"When I saw the knife, I thought we were done for," Yavi said.

"The knife wasn't for me." He withheld a sigh of relief. She was still speaking to him. A kindle of hope sparked that he hadn't lost her yet. "The bounties didn't work in collecting Dyna and her Guardians."

"She got away again?" Relief settled on her features. "No one has ever escaped him this many times before. He must be livid."

Von shook his head. "He is. I expected to be punished for it."

"Your wounds have yet to heal from the last lashing he gave you," Yavi said, finally looking at him again. She noticed the blood soaking through his pant leg. "You're hurt."

"It's only a scratch. Let's return to camp." Von stood and helped Yavi to her feet. She took a couple of stumbling steps before he steadied her. "Are you feeling faint? You don't look well."

"I'm fine. I'm only a little light-headed." Yavi pressed on her stomach and her features pinched with unease. "I think the shock got to me."

Von closed his eyes. "Yavi, I am so sorry."

She took his hand. "I know."

He wasn't foolish enough to believe she forgave him for all he put her through, but he would make it right.

He had to.

They walked hand in hand through the woods towards camp. He took his time so they could have this moment together before they had to return to their roles.

"What is Tarn planning now?" Yavi asked.

"We're leaving tonight to track Dyna. She won't get away from him this time."

Yavi grimaced. "I was hoping he'd never catch her."

"As was I. Keep her company while I'm gone."

She glared at him. "So, it's true. I hate it when Tarn sends you on missions to retrieve Sacred Scrolls." Her wet lashes lowered. "I hope this time it's nothing more than a rumor. I'll not have you kill or force someone away from their family again for that evil man."

Von stopped walking and pulled her into an embrace. Yavi suffered for a long time when he stole her away from her home in the middle of the night. Tarn had sent him to collect her along with her father's Sacred Scrolls so she could translate for him. He hadn't given her a chance to say goodbye to her family. She refused to eat and cried for days. At first, it angered him. He was so frustrated he didn't know what to do with her misery. It took him a while to realize it bothered him because he went through the same when Tarn forced him to leave his home.

"I swear one day I'll free you from this life. Even if it kills me."

Yavi stiffened and stepped back. "We can leave anytime you want. We can flee now. Tarn is distracted and the camp moving. It's our best chance."

It wasn't. If she ran, the spies would track her within hours.

"Please, Von," she begged. "You're free here. On this land, you can walk away from him."

"I have lived my life by the God of Urn's teachings. By his holy law—"

"I know the holy law!" Yavi beat on his chest. "I have read nothing about keeping slaves in the Sacred Scrolls."

"Yavi—" He tried to take her hands, but she pushed him away.

"Why do you refuse to see?" she cried. "Why do you want to live this way?"

"I don't want this life!"

She reared back from his shout, shock crossing her face.

"I don't..." Von turned away with a heaving breath. He closed his eyes as the roar of trolls and the screams rang in his head. "I have no choice. I cannot turn my back on the holy law. Lest the God of Urn damn me."

Again.

"What are you not telling me?"

None other than Tarn knew the truth. There was no one left from their past to know.

"I have seen what happens when you defy the God of Urn. Once was enough. I cannot do so again."

"The life-debt isn't real," Yavi said, coming around to stand in front of him. "It was a lie a few bishops forged a hundred years ago to force orphans and vagrants into serving in the temples. Soon, everyone practiced it because it benefited them. You're free, Von. You have always been free."

Von didn't know what to think. All his life, his parents taught him to regard the God of Urn and to live by his teachings. He had seen the gruesome results when he rebelled against it. How could it all be a lie?

He continued onward. They'd reached the edge of the forest, and the tents became visible through the trees.

"I'm not finished talking about this." Yavi tugged him to a stop. "What do you think would happen if you deserted Tarn?"

Only whence she burns will she be free...

For whatever reason, the Seer had given him a warning. He had to heed it. If being a slave protected Yavi from her fate, then he didn't care how many years he was chained.

Von buried his dejection and smoothed out his expression as he looked at her. "Nothing will happen, for I won't break my vow. Ever. This is the last time we will speak of it."

His tone was cold and firm. The first and only command he'd given her. Yavi's face fell in crushing disappointment, and he felt a divide cut between them. She was going to say more, but then ran to vomit behind a cluster of bushes.

"Yavi." He rubbed her back as she heaved until her stomach emptied. "Are you all right?"

She flicked his hand away and wiped her mouth. "Leave me be. Disputing this with you has made me sick. I'm tired of it."

They had argued over the subject of his servitude for two years, but this was different. His betrayal had formed a crack in their marriage, and his decision fractured it further. He saw it in the way she looked at him with disgust. One day, they would completely break apart, and any love she had for him would vanish.

Yavi walked away, and panic fired through him. Von reached for her, but she slipped through the trees, falling out of reach. Each step speared him as he watched her go. And he couldn't help but feel she was leaving more than the forest behind.

CHAPTER 51

Cassiel

Cassiel's knife cleaved through the air. Dyna mirrored him where she stood in front of him. The blade was a part of her, fused with her hand. With her enchanted armor and silver jacket, she moved with grace. Not flawless and far from perfect, but smooth like the branches of the willow tree behind her, flowing with the wind. They moved in synchronization on the edge of a short crag within Willows Grove. Each step was calculated, every swing measured. Neither of them stopped when a gentle rain fell. Not once did they look away from each other. They were aligned at this moment.

Made one by the edge of a blade.

Something stirred inside of him. The feeling grew as the bond burned in such a way it scorched through every part of his being, seeping into his mind and the depths of his soul. She gasped, and they stopped moving at the same time. Cassiel clutched his chest as his rapid breaths clouded in the air. His heart thudded uncontrollably, the heat inside of him growing so strong it hurt.

Numbness took over his trembling body. Dyna's legs wobbled, and she stumbled. Cassiel reached for her, but she quickly stepped back. He sensed she didn't want to be touched. She must burn the same as him. He retreated further, needing space like he needed air.

They were outside in the brisk weather, yet a heat pressed into him. Dragging a ragged breath in, he closed his eyes. Eventually, his body cooled, and he sighed in relief.

"Cassiel?" she called, his name sounding almost reverent. "What was that?"

He shook his head. Something had happened. Something changed. Again.

Dyna dropped her knife at the same time he did, and he pulled her to him, holding her to his chest. "I feel I should say I'm sorry ..." he murmured. "For many things. For hurting you."

"I'm sorry, too," Dyna said faintly.

They stood still on the edge of Willows Grove, listening to the birds and the trickle of a nearby stream. Rawn and Zev had left an hour ago to scout ahead for the largest willow where Leoake may be. But the Druid had slipped through their fingers too many times that they probably wouldn't find him now.

The brisk wind blew against them, and Cassiel covered her with his wings. He should let go. If Zev found them like this, he may suffer a broken bone, or worse. Dyna's apprehension filtered through the bond. She worried about the same thing, but Cassiel couldn't make himself move yet. He would risk it a little longer.

Even if they were caught, it was about time he accepted what he'd done and took responsibility for it.

"I must speak with Zev," Cassiel said. "He should know the truth."

She stared at him incredulously. "If we tell him, he would probably attempt to strangle you."

"I have no reason to hide. I had no ill intention. If I could find the means to explain, he may understand."

"Yet you didn't think I would understand?" Dyna asked, stepping away. "You lied to me because I'm a stupid human."

He rubbed his forehead. "No."

"Then, why? Because you thought I'd complain? Cry? Because you thought I'd blame you? Or because you wanted nothing to do with a human?"

"You are assuming."

"And you're not explaining." Dyna picked up her bow where it rested on the ground with their belongings. After slipping on her archery gloves and quiver, she loaded the bow with an arrow and moved to the center of the clearing, aiming at a tree twenty yards away. "Why did you lie to me? Are you ashamed of what they would think of you in Hilos?"

Cassiel clenched his jaw. "I already know what they think of me."

He lined up close behind her to pull back her shoulders and lifted her elbow, correcting her form. She released the arrow, and it skimmed the tree trunk. Archery had been more difficult for her to learn, but she was improving.

"Why should any of it matter?" she asked as she reloaded the bow. "Why let that shape who you are?"

"Mind your sight," he instructed. "And you know nothing of what it means to be reviled in Hilos. I withstood their criticism daily. Must I now endure yours?"

"Criticism?"

"Is that not what this is?"

"You're a prince." Dyna made a face as she leveled her eyes with the bowstring. The arrow zipped away and pierced the bottom of the tree with a *thunk*. "What value do you give my opinion? As if you ever cared what I think."

Cassiel glared at her. "Of course, I do."

"Why?"

"Because I care for you," he snapped.

Far more than he should.

Far more than he could bear.

Dyna gaped at him, the bow slipping from her fingers. Heaving a ragged curse under his breath, Cassiel picked up his knife and leaped off the short crag. He landed in the valley below.

"Stop pulling away," she said softly as a wistful pang sank in his chest. "We keep bickering but only because I want to understand. Please speak to me."

He halted in place, obeying her wish. That was how much power she'd unknowingly gained over him. Where his first instinct was to put her first.

"You are right, you know," he grumbled, waving a hand. "I'm a stupid Celestial. You deserve better than some arrogant, stubborn-headed, full-of-himself prince."

Dyna laughed, the sound pulling a small smile to his face. She leaped off the crag, and Cassiel reared back to catch her with a grunt. She was soft, warm, and smelled like sunlight. He held her in his arms as he looked at her, never knowing what to say.

Her full lips curved. "You forgot foolish."

"I think that is a given." He set her down.

Dyna's smile wavered as she sighed. "Why didn't you tell me? I wouldn't have been angry. Perhaps startled, but I wouldn't have held it against you."

Cassiel couldn't bring himself to answer. If he did, it would reveal much more than he cared to show anyone.

Shadows swept through the valley as the rustle of wings snapped his awareness into place. Cassiel hauled Dyna under the thick canopy of a willow tree and lifted a finger to his mouth. Pulling her close, they held quiet. He spied the Valkyrie flying overhead through the branches. Yelrakel led the flock with Sowmya on her flank.

"You don't want them to find you?" Dyna asked, her voice barely a whisper. "I thought we were headed to Hermon Ridge."

"We are, but I would rather make our journey there in due time. I do not wish to explain myself to my uncle quite yet," he said in her ear, his lips grazing her cheek. Dyna's breath hitched.

Cassiel drew away, as was proper, but Dyna clung to his coat. She rested her head on his chest, and he instinctively wrapped her in his wings as her arms slipped around his torso. The warmth of her embrace held him together. Somehow, she'd whittled away those jagged pieces and filled the hollow corners. He shouldn't welcome it. He shouldn't want any of this.

Neither of them moved, even after the Valkyrie were long gone. They stayed beneath the tree in comfortable silence, breathing in the fresh air as a gentle patter of the rain fell. It was a symphony accompanying the rustle of leaves and distant steady chatter of critters in the underbrush. Cassiel looked away from the beauty of the grove to the one beside him.

She was a wonder, this human. If he was being honest, Dyna had saved him as many times as he saved her. Starting from the moment she stumbled onto his path, taking him away from the life that suffocated him. He had gotten used to feeling her emotions. Sensing where she was, and now everything she physically experienced.

They were connected, undeniably so.

But this ... this was different.

"Will you tell me only one thing?" Dyna said. Several emotions crossed her face at once. Hesitation, caution, and something else he was afraid to identify lest it be his imagination. She dropped her gaze, lashes nearly brushing her cheeks. "Does it disgust you to be bonded to a common human?"

Of all the things she could ask, that was the least expected.

Cassiel tentatively wove her silky hair through his fingers. Her eyes lifted, green pools meeting his and holding. "You are a fair many things," he whispered, shifting closer as his gaze dropped to her mouth. "But common is not one of them."

Dyna stilled, and her lips parted in a shallow breath. That small action sent a current through his chest. She affected him the way the sunlight graced the raindrops, casting light over the desolate corners that had long since been abandoned.

But how could he expect her to accept him, given what he was? There was nothing he could offer her as a half-breed but a life of ridicule and scorn. Yet he couldn't help the want she stirred in him. It came with every look and touch, replacing longing where there had once been contempt. Given his arrogance, he'd been taken back by his relief when she kissed him on the ship. But wanting and having were two different things.

Words knotted in his throat, twisting with doubt, and the insults hissed at him from his family. Cassiel dropped his hands, drawing away.

This wasn't meant for him.

"It is not a matter of you being human," he said, though his kind would disagree. "But that it should never have occurred in the first place, least of all by such a careless mistake on my part."

Dyna lowered her head, spilling soft, scarlet locks over her shoulder. Her slender fingers fidgeted with a polished acorn button on the enchanted jacket. "I understand you didn't intend for this to happen, Cassiel. It wasn't ever about that. I had feared that this ... whatever this is, was rooted in a mishap and obligation. We entered each other's lives by chance, but you stayed and protected me, cared for me. Was that also chance ..." Her eyes flickered to her sleeve, layered in silver oak leaves, and they widened. "... or choice?"

He didn't know the answer when it clashed with another constant question lurking in the back of his mind.

Cassiel sighed. "Whatever brought us together, I only wish to give you what you want."

"Aston."

"What?" He blinked, not at all expecting her to answer him with another male's name. It took him a moment to remember the fae from the Phantasmic Moors, who'd put his grubby hands on her.

"Aston!" She gasped and covered her mouth.

"What is it? What is wrong?"

A rustling in the bushes and clopping of hooves had them both leaping to their feet. He swelled with pride at how deftly Dyna whipped out her blade at the same time he did. As much as he would have liked to witness her fight again, it was only Zev and Rawn.

"Come," Lord Norrlen said, smiling. "We found the Druid."

CHAPTER 52

The silvery leaves of the enchanted jacket were soft as velvet beneath the graze of Dyna's fingers. But they had transformed into steel when she needed to defend herself against the poacher. It landed in her hands as if by some strange chance, but it hadn't been chance at all.

That is the question, isn't it? An interesting debate. The fates present us with a path of destiny, but do you reach it because of chance or choice?

She lifted the edges of the jacket, staring at the shimmery surface of the leaves with distinct lobes only found on oak trees.

Leoake, a name meaning oak in a meadow.

Dyna groaned as she remembered the geas on Aston's back. She hadn't paid particular attention to what kind of tree it was, but if she were to look now, she would wager it was an oak tree. Even his alias was of a tree. The Druid had been in front of her from the beginning.

Hiding in plain sight, indeed.

She followed Zev through the grove with Rawn and Cassiel at her back. When they entered a small clearing, she was no longer surprised to find a green-haired fae sitting on a boulder with a small blue fox lying at his feet. Behind him rose an enormous willow. The long swinging branches swayed in the breeze.

"You said your name was Aston," she accused.

He smirked, his gold eyes gleaming with mischief. "I have accumulated many names over the years. Leoake, Aston, *that one*, dastardly Druid. Really, the list is endless."

Cassiel curled his lip. "You can add conniving prat to the list."

"Wait, you have already met?" Zev asked.

"The night at the Moors." She nodded stiffly, glaring at Leoake. "You knew I was searching for the Druid. For *you*. And you led me astray with false—"

Leoake wagged a finger, tsking. "Maiden, I'm called many things, but never a liar. Not once have I told you an untruth. It's impossible for the Folk, as you know."

He was right. He told no lies. She simply missed all the blatant clues.

"Why did Rawn remember you as an old man?" Zev asked. "You look young."

"Why, thank you." Leoake simpered, straightening his elegant brocade jacket. It was patterned with bronze oak leaves and branches. The shiny buttons bore the sigil of a familiar tree. "It's not easy to remain this handsome after living for several centuries. And the answer to your question is simple." He winked at Rawn. "I made it so you saw someone else when we first met."

Rawn rubbed his brow. "Yes, I certainly see that now. What was the purpose of that?"

At the Druid's sly smile, Dyna glowered. "Because he knew we would come looking for him years later."

The rings on Leoake's fingers glinted as he waved nonchalantly. "For every step you make, I have already thought fifty steps ahead."

Dyna narrowed her eyes with a sudden realization. "You sent Princess Keena to me, didn't you?"

His smile widened. "You would have met her, eventually. I made it so you would meet sooner."

"But she didn't seem to know Leoake and Aston were the same person when I described you. Is this an illusion as well?" Dyna asked, motioning at him. "Or does she think you also look like an old man?"

"Don't trouble yourself with that. All you need to know is everything happened as it was meant to."

She clenched her teeth at the vague answer. How far had he manipulated her journey? It could very well have started with Lucenna overhearing a mention of the Druid.

"Nothing was a coincidence, was it? I'm certain you even sent Azulo to me, and it must have been you who put the scale in my boot. Why?"

"To make things more interesting, of course."

She doubted that was the only reason. Leoake presented himself as a humorous flirt, but it was a mask to hide his schemes. He foretold their arrival because *he* was the one who led them there. But the fae didn't go out of their way to help someone unless it benefited them, and their arrival had certainly caused a stir.

Huffing a sharp breath, she said, "You made sure we would come to the Moors, so we could free you of your geas."

He shrugged, neither confirming nor denying, but the amused glint in his gaze was confirmation enough. "It was time to move on."

"You didn't like it there?"

For once, his smile lost its edge. "There are some who aim to control seers. Knowing the future is a powerful weapon to have in your arsenal."

"You don't strike me as someone who would allow himself to be used. How did King Dagden capture you in a geas?"

"Who said I didn't allow it?"

The fae formed a geas through a deal. That meant he had made some sort of agreement with the King of the Wild Fae. Whatever it was, it must have been significant to trade years of his life.

"I take it you know why we're here," she said.

"Of course."

Reaching into her pocket, Dyna held out the tassel of charms with shiny blue scales.

Leoake wrinkled his nose. "And what, pray tell, do I want with such a thing?"

She exchanged a confused look with her friends. "These are grindylow scales."

"Yes, and?"

She stuttered. "Do you not trade your services for something rare and of value? Is that not why you gave one to me before?"

"My dear, the scale wasn't an invitation but merely an incentive to keep you right where I needed you."

Growling a curse, Zev jerked forward, but Rawn held him back. "Let me go. I want to hit him."

"I will hold him for you," Cassiel said, clenching his fists. "We nearly died at the fjord."

Leoake flashed his teeth in a grin. "But you didn't."

Dyna groaned and pressed on her temples. She wanted to be angry, but they had assumed he would want the scales.

Leoake approached as he contemplatively looked her over. "I do trade for what is valuable, clever mortal. For what is not so readily given and not so easily attained. If you want to trade with me, then I will take from you. Maybe years of your life in service or your happiest memory."

"No," Cassiel and Zev rumbled.

The Druid's grin became devious as he curled a hand around the back of her waist and pulled her flush against him. "Then perhaps your first experience with a male."

They yanked her back, snarling curses. A blush heated her face.

"Leoake," Rawn said sharply. "I'm appalled by your impropriety."

He laughed. "I jest, truly."

"I thought your tastes lied elsewhere," Dyna said, thinking of the jilted fae at the Gathering Tree.

"I like a bit of everything." Leoake's admiring gaze roved over Rawn, Zev, and Cassiel, then swept over her. "But I can *see* no matter what I choose, your Guardians will not approve, Maiden. Therefore, my time here is wasted. I'll be on my way."

She supposed it shouldn't surprise her that the Druid knew who they were, given what he was. He gathered his belongings with a jaunty hop and turned to go.

"Princess Keena has invited me to her court," Dyna said, crossing her arms. "I wonder how she would feel when I describe to her in great detail our encounter today, especially how you used her."

He halted mid-step and chuckled nervously. "Hold a moment, let's not be hasty. Forgive me. A friend of the Morphos Court is a friend of mine." He tapped his chin. "Then how about a favor for a favor? I will do this for you, and one day when I need your assistance, you will come."

"Yes," Dyna instantly replied. "Deal."

The shrewd smile that crossed Leoake's face was nothing short of triumphant. She realized too late this was exactly what he wanted, and she had all but recklessly agreed with her thoughtless response. Before she could change her mind, he snatched her wrist. She flinched at the sting on the back of her hand, and it shot up her arm. A swirl of amber light flared between them, then faded as he released her. The others gaped at her in horror.

Cassiel pulled her away from him. "What have you done?"

Zev growled, his eyes flashing.

Rawn stepped in between them. "Undo whatever you have done to Lady Dyna this instant."

"You know I cannot," Leoake said. "We have sealed our agreement with a geas, and the mark will serve as a reminder."

A swirly symbol of an oak tree glowed on Dyna's skin. The canopy of branches spanned her forearm, the trunk coursing to her wrist. Roots curled over her knuckles and looped around each finger like rings. The amber glow pulsed and faded to a light brown mark. She rubbed it but found no indentations. The Druid's magic hummed as it settled into the corners of her being.

A twin symbol marked him in the same spot.

"A favor for a favor to be called upon at any moment," he informed them, clapping his hands. "By this promise, she is bound throughout the known universe until our deal is fulfilled or upon the pain of death."

Leoake trapped her in a geas after all, while not knowing exactly what she'd traded. She would worry about that later.

"I call upon my favor now," Dyna said. "Answer all of my questions."

"You get one."

"Three."

The Druid laughed again. "Agreed."

He sat back on the boulder with a flourish, motioning for her to join him. She kneeled on the grass, and Azulo leaped on her lap.

"Hello, sweet one," she cooed, scratching behind his soft ears. His three trails wagged happily.

Leoake took his time rummaging through his pack, tossing out random items on the ground. A flicker of impatience passed through her mind as Cassiel groused under his breath. He stood guard behind her, the heat of his legs pressing into her back.

"Ah, here it is." Leoake pulled out a black velvet pouch and poured a handful of square chips in his palm that looked like bleached stone. No, she realized, they were bones—each carved with a rune.

"Those are the tools of a soothsayer," Cassiel said. "Are you not a seer?"

"Soothsayer. Druid. Seer. They are all relatively the same in regards to predicting the future. Divination takes too much concentration. Why look into the Time Gate when this works as well?"

"Are you saying you cannot provide divinations? Is it too difficult for you?"

Leoake pursed his mouth. "Do you want answers to your questions or not? I'll divine when I see fit. What you lot mean to ask doesn't require it." He nodded to Dyna. "Speak to the runes, and they will reply. When I toss them in the air, ask your question."

Finally, she would get answers. He threw them in the air and all eyes watched them fall.

Dyna drew a breath. "What did the Seer of Faery Hill divine in my future?"

The runes landed oddly on their side. Neither displaying the front or the back.

"The time runes are a finicky bunch," Leoake said as he gathered them. "They only answer yes or no questions. Now you have two left."

"Wait," Zev growled through his teeth. "You didn't explain that before."

"Three questions, as agreed. I should clarify that I cannot tell you the divination of another seer, only my own. Now carefully consider your next question." The Druid tossed them again without giving her the chance to do so.

"Have I met all my guardians?" she blurted.

Six runes landed faced up.

"Yes."

Fine hairs rose on Dyna's neck, and goosebumps prickled down her arms. Had she met them? When?

"It would be useless to ask when or who." Leoake motioned at the chips of bone nestled in the grass. Energy radiated around them, brushing against her like heat coming off metal. "What is a guardian but a protector?"

Dyna studied the runes. Her father had taught her their many meanings, and his voice came to her then, reading each one. *Uruz* for strength. *Algiz* for protection. *Ansuz* for wisdom. *Gebo* for love. *Tiwaz* for warrior. *Perthro* for destiny.

Six faces surfaced in her mind, and a rush swooped through her to the pit of her stomach.

"All of your Guardians have saved your life in some form or other," the Druid said. "That was always the sign to identify them, and they will continue to shield you, as that is their purpose. They are drawn to you, Maiden. They cannot help but protect you as you cannot help but trust them, for your destinies recognize each other."

Each moment of near death was seen in a new light. Cassiel saved her in Hilos, Zev in Lykos, and Rawn in Elms Nook. It was meant to happen. Emotion swelled in her chest as she thought of the sorceress. Lucenna had saved her in Corron, and Keena saved her life in the Moors. The sixth guardian ... she had a guess who it may be.

Each of them had crossed her path, but half had also left it.

"The moment the Seer divined your future, you were bound together," Leoake said, as if he could hear her thoughts. "You need not search for them, for they will reunite with you again."

That left one thing she needed to worry about now. Dyna paused and looked at the others. They had questions too, but they nodded for her to continue.

"Zev, you said you had something you wanted to ask."

"It's fine, Dyna. Don't worry about me."

"He isn't ready to hear the answer." Leoake leaned back on his hands, crossing a leg over the other. "The Madness already tried to tell him."

Zev's wide yellow eyes pinned on him. What did that mean? Was he speaking to the Madness? Zev hadn't told her that, but he probably wouldn't when it was a sign he was losing himself further. Dyna wanted to ask, to beg him to confide in her as he used to, but he wouldn't look her way.

"Ready?" Leoake asked her.

Far from it.

The future of everyone she cared for weighed on her shoulders. The night of the Third Shadow Winter changed her life. It shoved her onto a path she'd been walking on for years, leading her to a point she could never turn back from. Like a plucked blossom inevitably losing its petals, this moment would seal her future. Whether or not she was ready. But she would hold on to the hope for a life free of fear and darkness. For Lyra, for North Star—and herself.

A breeze swept through the grove, making the branches of the large willow tree sway in a dance to a melody that hummed in her mind. She heard the faint thrum of a harp and the melodious voice of the golden bard from the Moors.

Listen to me, my dearest. Lest ye never return whole...

The shallowest of breaths passed through Dyna's lips and a tremble settled in her chest.

Cassiel and the others shifted closer, enclosing her in a semi-circle. Their presence was a reassuring fortress, meant to keep everything that would harm her at bay. These were her Guardians. Her friends. No matter what happened, they would be by her side every step of the way.

She straightened her back. "I'm ready."

Leoake tossed the runes high in the misty air.

Dyna closed her eyes and drew in a shuddering breath, voicing her hope into the world. "Will I find the Sōl Medallion?"

CHAPTER 53

The runes clattered on the ground by the Druid's feet. Only two faced up. Cassiel hadn't bothered to learn their meanings during his studies, but whatever they meant, it couldn't be good. Both Dyna and the Druid had gone motionless. Even Rawn and Zev looked startled. The fox whined, nuzzling her chin.

"What do they mean?" Cassiel asked in the silence.

"*Eiwaz*," Rawn read, his posture stiffening. "*Nauthiz*."

Zev clenched his fists. "Death and shadow."

Something cold sank heavily in Cassiel's stomach. It fanned his ire, fueled by the suspicion that this was another of the Druid's tricks.

He stepped back and drew *Esh Zayin* free. "Throw them again."

The white flames reflected in Leoake's aloof gaze. "The runes have spoken, dark prince. You cannot change the answer."

"Cassiel." Dyna's hand circled his wrist, and his tension eased with the calm she seeped through him. "It's all right."

The same fiery look of determination he'd seen on her face in his father's study returned. Her resolve mixed with his dread. Everything in him wanted to take her and fly away from the journey she was on, but he sensed nothing would make her turn back.

Dyna continued observing the runes pensively. "If I understand correctly, the runes would face down if the answer was no, or land on their side if the answer was inconclusive."

Leoake nodded.

"Then this is not a no."

"It is not a promising yes, either," Cassiel said, clenching his jaw.

"Runes have more than one meaning," Rawn added as he crouched by Dyna to study them.

"This one." Zev pointed a claw at the rune that had one straight line and two angular dashes on both ends, pointing in opposite directions. "*Eiwaz* primarily means death, but it can also mean life and rebirth."

Cassiel sheathed his sword and strode away, leaving them to formulate some other meaning than the one the runes promised. It only served to lie to themselves. He stopped by the edge of the woodland, looking out at the grove beyond. His lungs drew in the scent of rain and wet earth as he listened to the willow branches rustling in the wind. He needed something solid to keep him calm.

Was Dyna headed for her death? He'd predicted it when she first showed them the map. Apprehension gripped his chest, and he couldn't draw a full breath. Stopping her from going meant he would have to abandon his journey to that island, too. Continuing on this path would lead to his mother, and to the loss of his bonded.

Leoake came to stand beside him. "I take it you're the brooding sort."

The fae were tricksy, and Cassiel didn't trust this one in the least. There was something about those gold eyes that made him uneasy. "I cannot decide if you are good or evil."

"Good. Evil. It's all speculative."

"Which one are you?"

Leoake grinned, the edges of his teeth flashing. "I suppose one could say I'm dastardly wicked."

Cassiel shook his head. "Why are you like this?"

He shrugged. "I have few joys in life."

"And causing unnecessary travail is one of them."

"Precisely." Leoake cocked his head, and a pointed ear with a gold cuff poked out of his hair. "Seers can't help but meddle when we can feel the questions woven through the hearts of those around us and foresee the futures yet to pass."

Cassiel stepped back, feeling exposed. "If you can truly see the future, then tell me, is there another way?"

The Druid's smile sharpened. "If you want answers, you must pay. I don't work for free."

"I will not enter a geas."

"Oh, I know." Leoake eyed his wings. "As I know that isn't all you desire to ask."

Cassiel stopped breathing, a new chill prickling down his arms. Did he want confirmation of what he already suspected?

Leoake plucked a feather. Cassiel cursed and reeled back.

"You would have given it to me eventually after debating for several minutes if knowing the answer to your question would merit breaking Celestial law." He rolled his eyes. "I have no patience for that."

Cassiel gritted his teeth. Unease battled with relief to have the decision made for him, despite every instinct wanting to snatch the feather back. "You have your payment, now answer me. The runes, do they mean Dyna will die?"

"That's the thing about fate. We're not bound to one path but several."

"Speak clearly."

"No future is ever certain. Your every step and decision will affect what happens on that island."

Of course, the all-seeing Druid knew about Mount Ida. But the vague answer, which didn't hold a yes or a no, concerned him the most.

Leoake twirled the feather between his fingers, stroking the glossy surface. "Two more questions."

Since the moment Cassiel heard there was someone out there who had the answers to every secret, he knew what he would ask. But now that he had the chance, the words wedged in his throat.

He had to swallow several times before he could make himself say it. "Is it possible ... to break a Celestial Blood Bond without death?"

The question tasted wrong on his tongue. As the bond convulsed, he wished he could take it back.

Leoake chuckled. "It is, indeed."

Cassiel froze, his mind going blank. His ears rang as if he'd been bashed over the head, a pulse in his temples damning. He thought he might spew. The one absolute thing he'd been told about bonds was that they were perpetual.

"The only way to break a Blood Bond without one of you passing through the Gates is to shear yourself."

Cassiel jerked away, his back spasming painfully. "What?"

Leoake smirked as he ran his finger along the edge of the feather, making it glow. "Blood Bonds are bound to the soul through the divine blood in your veins, which comes from the magic within your wings. Losing them takes away your long life and the power of your blood bound to her. If you wish to be free of the Maiden, then cut off your wings. It's either that or death."

His wings were his most precious possession. They were extensions of him. Created from the skies and the wind, gifted by the Heavens. The only thing that gave him a sliver of freedom. He would never give up his wings, nor would any Celestial. If his ancestors knew, they didn't pass knowledge on to the rest of the Realms. Their wings were the source of their divinity, and the only thing to connect them to any semblance of *Elyōn*.

Without them, they were human.

"Now, I shall answer the question you truly wanted to ask." Leoake's irises stirred like molten gold. The air pulsed with a heavy aura and static crawled on Cassiel's skin. Motioning at where Dyna huddled with the others, The Druid leaned in to croon in his ear, "The string of fate ensnared you both from the moment you met. It's tangled through your hearts and souls, and however much you wish to break free, you cannot, for you know exactly who she is."

Everything in Cassiel went rigid, all of his fears and doubts clashing with the knowledge glowing in the Druid's gaze. They were gilded eyes touched by the God of Time. Their power crippled him, stealing the air from his lungs, constricting around him like a snake.

A slow, roguish grin spread across Leoake's face. "Yes, dark prince. What you feared is *true*. The bond didn't simply tie you together, it merged you mind, body, and soul. But you already knew that, didn't you?"

Truth sliced through his tongue, bleeding denials down his throat. Cassiel's nails dug into his shaking palms as his head whirled. He wanted to call the Druid a liar, to spit out insults for saying such absurd things, but he couldn't. The revelation only cleared the thick fog of unawareness he had hidden behind for so long. He'd ignored how he could find Dyna no matter where she was, ignored that he could feel her pain. Ignored the insatiable, protective—*possessive*— need to keep her safe since he saw her in Hilos.

A deep part of him had always known.

And there was no breaking this type of bond, for it would surely destroy them both.

Leoake laughed as he tucked his prize away. "Your bond was awoken the moment she first touched you."

"On the bridge..." Cassiel mumbled blankly. After he'd caught Dyna out of the sky, she touched his face.

"The *Hyalus*."

"What?" Cassiel blinked, focusing on that. "You are wrong."

Amusement danced across the Druid's face. "I'm never wrong."

In this instance, he was. They hadn't touched by the *Hyalus* tree.

"Cassiel?" Dyna called behind him.

The sound of her voice jolted his pulse. He couldn't face her. Not now. His wings snapped open, and he leaped into the sky, flying away from it all.

CHAPTER 54

Dyna watched Cassiel go, sensing he was avoiding her again. She thought after their conversation he would have stopped doing that. The fox in her arms yipped as he disappeared behind the veil of rain clouds.

She sighed. "What did you say to him?"

Leoake shrugged. "Only the truth."

"And what is that?"

He gave her a sly leer, one that hid secrets, and truths, and knowledge of the world. "That is for him to share, should he so wish."

She shook her head and handed him the enchanted jacket. "Here, this is yours. It took a great deal to return it to you. Though, I have a sense you intended that."

"Ah, thank you." Leoake slipped it into his pack.

"I've been told it's enchanted to turn away any blade."

He winked. "It came to good use, I imagine."

"Why do you have an enchanted jacket?"

"One such as me who has many enemies can't be too careful. It's not a simple spell, but rather useful. I once enchanted armor to do the same and was paid a massive fortune for it, too." Leoake turned away. "Well, if that is all."

That was all she would get? She pursued him across Azure for answers, but there were no right answers anymore. Only endless wrong ones.

"What game are you playing?"

He paused.

"Why lead me on this wild chase, hanging out of reach when you knew how desperately I needed your help? Do you enjoy playing with people's lives?"

"Oh, immensely." Leoake laughed. No shame in it at all. "When you live as long as I do, you learn to find entertainment in the grand scheme of fate."

She narrowed her eyes. "Fate's scheme or yours? You gave me that jacket because you knew I would need it."

"You needed to protect your head, and I made sure you would keep it a little while longer."

A little while longer. His tone was playful, but it left an ominous feeling over her.

"Why?"

"As I said, the fates like to plot and I like to watch how it all weaves together. To predict how each piece fits on the board, and occasionally make a play of my own. It's all quite predictable, but in some rare instances, I'm pleasantly surprised. Your fate is the most entertaining game I have seen in many, many centuries."

Dyna clenched her fists, her head heating. "My life isn't a game."

"And yet it was you who called it that first, clever mortal."

She scowled and raised her chin. "You hide behind your runes and tricks because you're nothing but a charlatan."

Leoake's smile faded, and the angles of his face sharpened.

"Is it not true? You laugh and mock me, patronizing the future I so fear and desperately want to stop while offering nothing useful after binding me in a geas." She was taking a monumental risk of offending the fae, but she was sick and tired of feeling like she was tumbling through life without a solid path. She needed to know if there was any slim chance of defeating the Shadow. "If you're a true seer, then tell me, will I succeed?"

Leoake steepled his long fingers, tapping them together as he studied her. "Very well. Only because I'm intrigued by you and don't wish for you to perish before I attain my favor will I give you what you seek."

He circled her in slow prowling steps, observing her as if everything in her soul was exposed to him. The faint sound of thunder rolled in the distance as light swirled in his gold eyes, making them eerily glow.

"Each of you is on this path for a reason," he said. "Your friends. Your enemies. Those who pass you by. Each has a move to make, a purpose to fulfill." He stopped before her, his gaze radiating vividly with the sight of the future. "You and your Guardians have all come under the same stars by will, and destiny, for this journey is your bonded fate. The pain each of you endured has molded who you are, and the pain yet to come is the cost you must sacrifice to gain that which you most desire. Success is determined by your life, Maiden, for if you don't pay the price, the others will."

She stared at him for a long minute, slowly processing his words. Her decision not to react, not to give any tell on her face held. The longer she purposely stayed quiet, the more awkward it grew. The wind died, and Leoake's glowing eyes dimmed to cool honey. He frowned, his disappointment at her lack of reaction apparent.

She blinked, maintaining the air of unimpressed. "What? No rhyme?"

Leoake scoffed. "I was never considered a poet, and I may have missed the meeting where all seers decided we must rhyme when giving out divinations. Something or other about it being easier to remember."

Dyna doubted she would forget what he had said.

She pressed her trembling fists against her hips. The pain she had endured and pain yet to come. An ultimate sacrifice on her part that would determine if they succeeded.

Fear of the Shadow led her to leave North Star on this mission, and she left knowing there was little chance of surviving the journey. If the cost of destroying the Shadow was her life, then it was a small price to pay. But she would not let others determine her future. For whatever reason, the fates gave her Guardians to keep her alive, be it for their entertainment or some other purpose. If they liked to play games—she would play.

"Will and fate go hand in hand," Leoake said, his tone serious. "You have the power to change your future, but it's what comes at the end of your journey that may prove to be the most arduous."

She wasn't sure if he was giving her advice or a warning.

"Well, I'm bored now. I must be on my way to meddle in the future of another poor soul. Do give Princess Keena my regards." He motioned at Azulo, and the blue fox leaped onto his shoulders.

"I see why they call you the dastardly Druid," Dyna said.

"Indeed." Leoake took her hand and kissed the geas as he bowed, his sardonic smile returning. "Until we meet again, ye fair maid."

Then he strolled for the woods with a cheerful whistle, the tune sounding so familiar it reeled an old memory like the hook on a fishing pole. But it slipped away and sunk back into the depths of her mind before she could grasp it.

"Wait, what do you prefer I call you?" she asked.

"I thought you were a clever mortal," the Druid said as he walked away, repeating the same line he delivered when they met. "You know better than to ask a faerie his name."

Azulo barked at her one last time, then they vanished into the willow trees. Dyna raised her cursed hand in farewell, knowing she would certainly run into *that one* again.

Once they had settled their camp for the evening, Dyna changed out of her leathers and wandered off into the grove. The wet grass clung to the maroon skirts of her dress as she strolled through the trees. She chose the willow she and Cassiel had hidden under with the book of Jökull as an excuse to read, but her mind couldn't focus. Cassiel hadn't returned, and the bond was silent. She leaned against the willow's trunk, watching as the rain gently fell, pattering in the nearby stream. Lush autumn flowers adorned the grove in clusters of yellow, orange, and purples. They were the last of the blooms before the land would be coated in ice come winter.

Dyna sighed as she caressed the sigil of the Ice Phoenix on the cover. How long did it take until Sunnëva and Jökull were no longer at odds? She opened it to the last pages of the story and came to the illustration of two enormous trees. One was white with lush gold leaves, and the other black and barren. She settled against the willow as she read the text on the following page.

The great Ice Phoenix and his queen left behind two seeds. King Jedënkull, a descendant of Jökull, planted them in the garden of Old Tanzanite Keep during the Second Age. The seeds grew into two majestic trees. Any who should eat their fruit would gain the power of the Ice Phoenix over life and death. One was thus named the Tree of the—

Her chest thrummed, the bond signaling Cassiel's approach. The flutter of his wings reached her as he passed over the grove and landed in the clearing. He stood outside the willow's canopy but didn't come any closer. The rain's tempo increased, prattling on the ground. She waited for him to drop his wall, to at least speak, and stop running. But maybe she had been the one to run first.

Dyna lowered the book and stepped out from beneath the branches. He paced beside the willow, his wings twitching restlessly as if he would fly away again at any moment.

"Cassiel."

"I'm trying to understand it," he said, raking a hand through his wet hair. "But I cannot. This cannot be. It should not be. I was never meant to bond with anyone."

"Is this why you avoid me?" she asked, deciding to finally uncover everything. "Because you don't want me?"

Cassiel stopped in place. "Dyna..."

"Please." The rain nearly swallowed her whisper. "Tell me the truth."

Dyna couldn't stand it if he continued to lie to her. She needed to know. He said he cared for her, but was that where it ended? If all they had was friendship, she would accept it and give herself some closure. She would smile for him, even as she broke inside. The wishes for more nights in his arms, for the cradle of his hand, for his gentle touch on her lips, would be a secret kept locked away in a hidden corner of her heart. It would lie beside her other secret—the one of wanting him so much it hurt.

"It would be easy to say I avoid you to unburden you with my presence." Cassiel faced the grove. "But the gods know I'm a coward.

I avoid you so I will not see your despair at what I have done to you. I imprisoned you in this marriage by which I cannot set you free." His voice hardened, even as his deep well of misery leaked into her. "I turn away from you, for that is all I know. That is how I protect myself. Even now, I do not dare see your face. I cannot when I know you want nothing to do with me, for how could you?"

She shook her head. "What do you mean?"

The rain pelted him, dripping from his wings. "You would have me say it? As if it is not clear."

"To me, it isn't."

What could be so wrong with him that she wouldn't want him? But the silence dragged as she waited for Cassiel's answer. If he couldn't say it, then ... maybe he could show her.

Dyna closed her eyes and pictured the wall layered with steel and fire she kept on her end of the bond. Extinguishing the flames, she let her wall fall. She searched for the strand that connected them, and it hummed within her, lighting into a pathway that led to him. Cassiel stiffened, but he didn't resist. His door was made of stone, bared by iron gates, ensnared with thorns. She reached into the bond, tugging and untangling one by one, unbarring the end that he kept so tightly closed.

When she finally got through, he let her crack open his door. So much convulsed inside of him in a tangled web. It took searching and sorting, separating each roiling emotion. And there it was, hidden under the mass of embarrassment and anger—under the equally arduous yearning that made her breath hitch. The reason he had kept the bond from her. He feared what she thought of him, of the disgust she may feel being married to a Nephilim.

Dyna took Cassiel's face, and he allowed her to turn it, at last bringing his silver eyes to meet hers. He looked at her with a broken expression at war with itself. There was so much she wanted, but if she could only have one wish, it would be for him to see himself through her eyes. Inhaling a breath, she opened her heart and showed him everything. Her longing. Her thoughts of him. How beautiful he was. To her, he was as perfect and as wondrous as the stars.

"Why?" he asked, sounding almost angry—but it was his incredulity that swarmed her. His disbelief. He stepped back, and she dropped her hands. "Why me? I deserve your scorn for all I have done. For what I am."

When had she started to care for him so much? There were times when they didn't understand each other and times that they hurt each other. But little by little, they had found a way to slowly show a part of themselves that was vulnerable. Maybe the bond made it impossible to hide how they truly felt sometimes, and at other times, it muddled their communication. Yearning hidden behind worry and confusion. Desire hidden behind anger and frustration.

Honesty was the most difficult when it left them so exposed. Both had fought to hide how they felt, but with each passing day, she had given herself more to him, wanting to break through the stone wall around his heart—by giving him hers.

"Stupid Celestial. I never cared about what you are. None of that ever mattered to me. I was angry that you kept the Blood Bond a secret, but I told you before, nothing you say would ever make me turn my back on you." Her face flushed with warmth as her eyes misted. "I've known since my heart leaped at the first sight of you."

He stood motionless. His stare so intense, her pulse quickened as she laid everything bare. It was those starlit eyes that scattered her thoughts. The breeze ruffled his hair and wings that'd been given the color of the night, lustrous black and deep blue.

"Cassiel, to me, you are everything." Breath trembling, Dyna closed her eyes. "From dawn until dusk, my heart and mind are filled with you. It will always be you."

CHAPTER 55

Cassiel

Never could Cassiel have foreseen himself standing here, with the most beautiful, reckless, impetuous little human. With hair like the rising dawn on the horizon and eyes like spring. A silly, incredible girl who had stumbled into his life by some strange magic, making him wish for another path which he hadn't thought possible. Where he wished to perceive the world through her. Perhaps it would be enough to remain by her side, for he couldn't imagine doing anything else. Both nights he'd held her close had felt so completely and utterly right.

"From the moment I caught you out of the sky, my life changed," Cassiel said, swallowing the lump in his throat. "It was not much of a life. I had grown used to the empty bleakness of it. Of the same colorless days. I did not care for another fate, for what more could there be? Then you came along and made me want more than I ever should. The world is full of things I hate and do not need, but you…" He heaved a breath with the weight of the admission he hadn't allowed himself to see. "I need you."

He needed her like the earth needed the sun. She was the light that cast away all that was dark. If the world could be made right, it was only because he may have found what he needed after all.

"You can't take back what you said, Cassiel Soaraway." Dyna's teary gaze met his, her lips quivering. "Say it again."

He closed his eyes, and his voice caught as he whispered, "You are my dawn."

Her gentle fingers wiped the wetness from his lashes, and relief washed through the bond from both ends. Blood may bond them, but she was choosing him. She *chose* him. Acceptance. Being wanted. It was the most glorious feeling in the world. Well, perhaps the second-best feeling. His eyes fell on her lips, so close and soft, he wanted to feel them again. That yearning had remained with him since that day on the cliff.

He guided her back under the willow tree. The soft rustle of rain trickled like drops of glass from the branches. He slid his hands up her arms, his fingers gliding along the satin sleeves of her maroon dress.

With a gentle nudge from his wings, he drew Dyna closer until they stood mere inches apart. Her scent filled his every thought. The sun streaming in through the branches caught the radiance emitting from her skin. He finally realized it was because she was tied to him. There was so much he wanted to say, but it was as if she already knew. There was nothing he could hide now, and nothing he wanted to keep from her.

He brushed Dyna's damp hair behind her ear and skimmed his fingertips over her collarbones, tracing the scars there, exploring every smooth curve. She shivered in response, and her breath hitched, stealing his with the next rise of his lungs.

Cassiel cupped her cheek and stroked his thumb over her bottom lip. Voice thickening, he asked, "Would it be forward of me to kiss you?"

"Yes," Dyna whispered with a smile. Her bright green eyes held his as her hands settled on his chest, where his rotten heart thrummed. "It would be."

She stood completely still as he skated his fingers along her smooth jaw, gently lifting her chin. With a rush of anticipation, he closed the final distance between them. Ever so slowly, he swept his lips over her cheek until he found the corner of hers. Their noses met, and he paused, checking if she still wanted this. Dyna gripped his jacket, assuring she wasn't going anywhere.

As careful as the first time, Cassiel drew her mouth to his and grazed her full lips. Tentatively teasing. Exploring the soft flesh. Her pulse quickened beneath his fingertips, where his hands curled on her neck. Then his mouth met hers with a brief, gentle press. It sent an electrifying wave through him. But he leaned back and inhaled raggedly, still doubting he could really have this. He was so unworthy of her.

Dyna clamped her arms around his neck and yanked him to her. A surprised exhale rushed out of his nose. He took her supple lips in his, and it was enough to nearly take him to his knees. Every conflict and doubt faded as he wrapped Dyna in his arms and wings, and indulged in what they had denied one another for so long. His mouth moved over hers, memorizing the shape he yearned to learn, tasting the sweetness he'd been starved for. It was a kiss made of sunlight, and wishes, and unyielding impossibilities.

She clung to him with permanence in her grasp, as if afraid he would disappear. Impossible. Cassiel couldn't imagine ever letting go, for one kiss was not enough. It would never be enough. He wanted all of her in every way. Endlessly. And so, he lost himself in each sigh and caress, branding every part of her on his skin. Nothing else existed for him but this.

Kissing her erased the world.

There was a shift, and he shuddered as something fell into place. It filled a vacant hole somewhere in his being, like he had recovered a familiar piece of himself he once lost. The bond blazed, and an ethereal power surged through his mind, weaving through his soul. He was soaring, ascending to a place where Dyna's soul collided with his. It brought a tide of emotion and thought as the deepest parts of her unveiled. It engulfed him. Every part of him was searing as a power wove them seamlessly together in a way that shouldn't have been possible. They were the sun and the night sky meeting in the twilight.

Then he was devouring her mouth with reckless abandon. He pinned her against the willow, and her fingers tangled in his hair as she met him with equal urgency. There was no satiating the need. Her skin was silk beneath his hands, and every caress sparked tingles down his arms. He wanted to touch everything. To feel every dip, swell, and plane. To forget all else until he knew nothing but her.

Yet a nagging thought reminded him there was something else he needed to share before they could go any further.

Cassiel reluctantly made himself break the seal of their lips. He rested his forehead against hers as they tried to catch their breath. Fear swept through their connection. For once, he knew it was his own. A fear that he would lose her after finally having her.

Dyna sighed, feeling his toil. "I ask nothing of you but the truth. Will you promise me only that?"

"The truth is, I want nothing more than to lose myself in these lips." He brushed his thumb over her mouth and her cheeks bloomed pink. "But there is more I must tell you."

She arched an eyebrow. "Another secret? I cannot promise I won't be angry, but if you kiss me like that again, I may forgive you."

A shiver of thrill and angst washed through him.

"Dyna, I think we—" Cassiel swallowed, his throat drying at the thought of explaining. It was best to show her. He gently took her face in his hands as he admired everything about her. *"Ett haor sheli."*

She leaned into his touch, their breaths mingling between their mouths that were mere inches apart. "What does it mean?"

Maybe one day I will tell you, Cassiel said through the bond.

Her eyes grew wide, for she had heard him loud and clear. Then he felt exactly when she realized what it meant. They never had a simple Blood Bond. He should have known from the beginning, from the moment his soul led him to her in Corron.

A tear rolled down her cheek, spilling over his fingers. Her watery smile lit something in his chest, and the bond softly glowed.

Dyna was more than his wife. More than a mate. She was his True Bonded.

Her voice fluttered through his mind. *How?*

There was only one simple answer.

You were made for me and I for you. He grazed her lips in a whisper-soft touch. *My sweet fate.*

CHAPTER 56

Zev

The overcast sky darkened with the evening as the rain fell. A cold gust passed through the surrounding trees, rattling their branches like hollow bones. Zev wished he could feel the bitter wind, but the chill didn't reach him. The heat of his wolf kept it at bay.

The metallic smell of blood drew his attention to Rawn. Vivid red trails leaked from his hands as he worked on skinning a rabbit he'd caught. Crimson drops beaded on the grass by his boots. The sight took him back home, where blood dripped off the walls. It splattered into a pool on the floor, the drips echoing in his head.

"Zev? Zev?"

He blinked at the sound of his name. "Huh?"

"I asked how you preferred the rabbit cooked," Rawn asked.

Zev sighed. "None for me, thank you."

He didn't have an appetite for anything.

"Where is Dyna?" He searched the empty camp. "And Cassiel?"

"I believe Lady Dyna went for a stroll. Prince Cassiel must have accompanied her to gather firewood."

But they had already gathered firewood. Zev rose as he sniffed the air, following her scent toward the willows. Rawn attempted to call him back, but there was a nervousness in that tone that urged Zev onward. He passed through the trees, catching Cassiel's scent mingling with Dyna's before he heard their voices and the tender declarations he refused to acknowledge.

It wasn't until he entered the meadow bathed in the amber glow of the evening sun that he let himself truly perceive what had been occurring behind his back. Dyna and Cassiel stood beneath a willow, kissing like they were the only two people in the world.

At the moment, they may as well be.

When they came up for air, Dyna noticed him first. She pulled away from Cassiel with a gasp, her already flushed cheeks becoming redder. Zev's first instinct was to beat him within an inch of his life. But the prince didn't cower or run as he stormed to them. Cassiel exhaled heavily and faced him with an expression that held no dread of the repercussions. No guilt in this surreptitious moment. No shame of the familiarity in which he held Dyna's waist with hands he had yet to remove.

Zev snarled, and she jumped in between them. "There is no hiding it now, is there, Cassiel? If you think I'll let you get away with it this time, you're sorely mistaken."

"Hit me if it will make you feel better," he said. "I will not apologize."

Zev roared.

Dyna pushed him back. "Stop it! I know it's hard to understand Zev, but we did nothing wrong."

"How can you say that when he has you hiding in the forest?" Zev stabbed a finger in his direction. "When I asked you to protect her, I didn't mean this!"

"First, you must calm down." Cassiel didn't even look embarrassed to be caught.

"Damn you," Zev growled. "And damn me for trusting you."

"He did nothing wrong," Dyna repeated, glancing at Cassiel questioningly. Something silent passed between them, and he nodded. "How could it be wrong when ... when we're bonded?"

Zev blinked, the revelation striking him like a blow to the head.

"What?" the question tumbled from his tongue. "How? *When?*"

Cassiel sighed, dragging a hand down his face. "It happened during the full moon."

The full moon?

"That was a month ago!" Zev bellowed, and they flinched back. "That's how long Dyna was married? How long you both *hid* this from me? I suspected something was happening, but not—" A heavy exhale rushed out as another realization hit him. "This is why she glows."

"I did not mean for it to happen," Cassiel said. "She was dying. I was in a panic and used the only means I had to save her life. But when I healed her, I mistakenly mixed our—"

Zev snatched his throat. There was no thought or reason, only the need to end him. It would be so easy to snap Cassiel's neck. One twitch of his fingers and done, the bond would break, and Dyna would be free of this fraud of a marriage.

Cassiel pulled at his crushing grip and Zev squeezed harder, rendering his face purple. Dyna shouted, her fists bashing against him. He hardly noticed it through his wrath. She was screaming something over and over that he couldn't perceive until he noticed her terrified expression, her mouth gaping as she clutched her neck.

"You're killing him," Dyna wheezed. Her legs gave out, and she fell against his side, sinking to her knees.

Zev released Cassiel and grabbed her limp arms. "Dyna."

They both coughed, sucking in ragged gulps of air.

"We are True Bonded, Zev," Cassiel rasped, rubbing his bruised throat. He shoved him out of the way and gathered her in his arms. "We feel each other's pain. What you do to me, you do to her."

Zev froze. *True ... Bonded ...*

The fury returned threefold, washing out the shock. Only for Dyna's sake could Zev resist thrashing him again. He stood on his feet, his heaving chest rising and falling as he tried to control his wolf.

"If you die, she dies?" Zev growled.

"She would feel as if she had. Breaking a True Bond would shatter her soul, and most have not survived such a pain." Cassiel wore an expression of solemn sincerity, for there was nothing to fight over because Zev had no say in it.

And like that, he was left completely outside of their circle. Of their *pair*. There was no room for three.

Zev marched away, his breath coming in rapidly as anger and anguish hammered through his head. If he didn't leave, he would kill that damn Celestial. He passed by Rawn, who'd been standing by the edge of the trees. The wind muffled their calls as he headed for a nearby knoll covered in yellow and brown leaves. His footsteps crunched over them as he hiked, focusing on his steps, one after the other. Away from them and everything else.

As he reached the top, a breeze filled the sky with hovering leaves. He heaved in gulps of air, needing something to anchor him. The Madness surfaced from the depths of his mind with a cackle, mocking him for losing the last shred of normalcy in his world. Every reason he had for living was gone.

Dyna's scent reached him as her light steps ran up the knoll. "Zev—"

"You lied to me!" Once the accusation was out, it blanketed over them like the rain. "You never hid things from me before, Dyna. I asked if there was something between you two, which you so ardently denied."

She winced. "I didn't lie."

He shook his head at the spike in her heart rate. "You're lying to me now."

"It's complicated. There was noth—" She bit her lip.

Zev knew as well as she did, saying there was nothing between her and Cassiel would be another lie. He had sensed the makings of something, but he thought that's all it had been. Makings. Silly thoughts and the pinning for a handsome prince. Friendship confused for affection. This had gone much farther than the beginnings of infatuation.

"We ... gods, Zev." Dyna covered her face. "There is so much we must explain. That I have yet to fully understand, but we didn't act on it until now."

Zev clenched his jaw. "This cannot be. I won't allow it."

She stared at him. "Why not?"

"Because he's ..."

"He's what?" Her eyes flashed and her hands balled into fists. "Go on. I dare you to say it."

Zev's gut twisted. How could he name Cassiel's half-breed race as a reason to deny his blessing? That wasn't the only reason. With her father gone, it was his duty to protect her wellbeing, and in time—a future he hadn't cared to think about yet—give her hand to another to care for. But not to Cassiel.

The backlash that would occur if he took her to the Realms of Celestials, if this went so much further than either of them was currently prepared for, would be catastrophic. True Bond or not, this couldn't be. They were merely caught in the moment and not realizing what this would mean for them both.

Cassiel was a prince of Hilos, meant to oversee the Realms. To *rule*. The High King would never allow his son to be with a *human*.

"He's a prince," Zev said instead.

"And I'm a peasant with no wealth or prospects," she shot back. "You think I haven't thought of that?"

Zev groaned. "That's not what I meant."

Dyna squeezed her eyes shut, hugging herself. "I know what you're thinking, but I can't help how I feel."

Good gods. There was no hope for it then. Zev saw the truth in her heart in which he no longer had room.

How could this happen? Now, of all times, on *this* journey? When did it have time to happen? Under his nose, it seemed, when he had been taken with his Madness. Zev looked away from her welled eyes to the darkening sky as the rain fell harder. All of him was ready to be washed away beneath it.

"It's not that I don't want you to find love. I do. But is it so wrong to want you to need me a little longer?"

"What do you mean? I'll always need you."

"No, you don't. You're safe with them, protected, and now..." She'd found a mate. Perhaps this was for the best. The final snip on the tie of whatever kept him alive. He shook his head. "I don't have a reason to be here."

Dyna stilled, air passing sharply through her lips. "Zev."

She'd been watching him closely since the incident at the fjord. She had to know he was losing the grasp on his sanity. They'd skirted the issue, but he couldn't ignore it anymore.

"It's been three years to the day since..." Zev closed his eyes as memories tore into him like teeth.

He always remembered the same things. Flashes of blood, broken glass, his mother's screams. Today was the anniversary of his father's death. He didn't need to say it. Dyna already knew. There would be a full moon tonight, and the thought of putting on those wretched chains again made his insides clench.

"I'm so tired, Dyna. Tired of mourning him. Of hating myself for what I did. I want to go where he is and beg him to forgive me."

Dyna's hand slipped over his and gently squeezed his fingers. "I felt that way too when my family died."

She hadn't told him that before.

"I was ashamed of it." Her gaze drifted over the knoll, passing where Rawn and Cassiel lingered in the camp and rested on the Zafiro Mountains in the south toward North Star. "My father died protecting me, yet I was struggling to find a reason to go on. I was drowning, Zev. It was so tempting to let myself sink into the black sea of my grief and guilt, but it wouldn't be fair to their memory to throw it all away. I found my reason to keep going."

And she had. While she had climbed out of the waves, he was nose-deep beneath the surface.

"Do you think it would appease your father if you followed him through Death's Gate?"

Zev hadn't stopped to think about what his father would've wanted for him. He would never know.

"Uncle Belzev was a good man," she said. "He loved you. He believed in you. I know he doesn't harbor ill will for what happened. It's time to let it go."

"Am I to simply forget? Forget the past, the pain, and the chains?" he asked bitterly, repeating what the Madness had said to him once before.

Dyna trembled in the icy rain, sadness creasing her face. "It's not about forgetting. That won't heal you, Zev. You need to forgive yourself."

Forgiveness. That was something he wouldn't ever deserve.

"I can't," he said, his voice cracking.

"Why?"

Curling his fingers, Zev punctured his palms with his claws. "I killed him, Dyna."

Since the day it happened, not once had he voiced the confession aloud. He'd feared the sound and the taste of those words. Each one pierced his chest like claws, burrowing deep. He had killed his father—with his own hands.

"So, you believe you should die as punishment?" Dyna took his arm, her voice shaking as she fought back tears. "What happened that night was a mishap. It wasn't your fault."

"My father was the only one who accepted me, and I tore him to shreds. Nothing will ever change that." Zev gripped his head as the whispering started.

You have nothing left here. Why do you cling on?

He didn't know anymore.

"The Madness is always there, reminding me of what I've done, promising to make me forget. It won't stop. The whispers *never* stop. I'm drowning in the air, Dyna. It's heavy and suffocating, and I can't breathe. I want to forget. If I can't see him, I'd rather forget it all."

"Are you not meant to have happiness?" she asked. "If that's true, then I don't know what to believe in anymore."

"As if it were that easy. No one understands. Do you know how many times I've desired to die? How many times I have thought of ending it?" He pressed a fist over his heart. "I'm screaming inside, and no one can hear it. I've had enough of this life, Dyna. I hate it." His voice broke as his vision blurred. "The rope around my neck tightens every day, slowly strangling me. I beg the God of Urn for forgiveness. To forgive me for everything, for I fear the only way this will end is when I cease to be."

It hurt to live. To breathe. It hurt to exist in a world he didn't fit.

He was alone.

Dyna shook her head, her delicate features crumbling. "Don't say that. Please don't say that."

Zev crouched over his knees and buried his head in his arms, hiding from the desperation in her voice. "What do you want from me?"

"I want you to fight! I want you to fight for yourself as hard as you fight for me."

But what if he had no more fight in him? The Madness was taking over. There was hardly any part of him left. Eventually, he wouldn't be able to suppress the part of him that thirsted to kill on every full moon, that could ravage a pack of wolves and his family without thought. He had no control over the Other, and he never would.

She tugged on his arms. "We can fix this, Zev."

"You cannot fix what is already broken."

He was splintered into thousands of fragments of who he once was. There was no putting that back together.

"I'm finished," he whispered. Why continue clinging on to something he didn't want?

"Fine! Go on, then." Dyna broke into a sob and hit his shoulder. "Go and leave it all behind. But if you die, know that I'll never forgive you."

She stepped away from him as her shuddering cries filled the hill. "I shouldn't have said such a horrible thing. Forgive me. I'm so afraid of losing another brother, and I can't bear it. Please don't leave me, Zev. I can't lose any more family. Stay with me. Please..."

Her pained plea squeezed his heart. It was enough to pull his chin above the dark waters. *Ending your life would not cease the pain. It merely burdens someone else.*

Dumping this on her was unfair. It was his burden to bear, not hers. She was right. He knew she was right. He shouldn't give up because it was easier.

Clenching his teeth, he pressed on his burning eyelids. "I won't leave."

Not yet.

He would make himself get up, grab his cursed chains and shackle himself to a tree. Tomorrow, he would find the will to keep going. He had to.

"Zev." His name was a soft gasp.

"Dyna, I'm sorry—"

"Zev!"

He caught the fear in her voice at the same time he smelled the scent of a new presence. Zev snapped his head up to find a man standing with them in the twilight. His blond hair, so fair it was almost silver, framed his unfeeling, ice-blue eyes. A jagged scar crossed from his temple, over his nose, and to his lip, marring a face he had only seen on wanted posters. Tarn was taller than he had initially thought, body lean and strong. The ends of his long black coat fluttered in the wind.

How had he approached them undetected?

A snarl tore out of Zev, and his sight sharpened with his wolf surfacing. He leaped to his feet. Tarn grabbed Dyna's arm and jerked her to his side.

Zev's claws sharpened, and he bared his teeth as a low growl rumbled deep in his throat. "If you would like to keep your head attached to your body, you will let her go."

Tarn said nothing, his pale gaze piercing.

A hand came around Zev from behind, and he flinched at the sharp touch of silver against his jugular.

"Don't move," a familiar brogue voice said. "Or I'll be forced to harm you."

Zev clenched his jaw against the burn of the knife. He couldn't shift without the risk of the silver poisoning him. The edge lifted slightly, easing the sting. One inhale of breath told him exactly who stood behind him.

Dyna's wide eyes fixed on the man holding the silver knife. "Commander Von." Then she looked at the man gripping her arm, the color draining from her face. "You're Tarn."

He only studied her silently, his expression indifferent and cold. Landing beside them, Cassiel ripped out his sword. The white fire blazed along the blade, emitting waves of incredible heat warping the air.

Rawn aimed his armed bow at Tarn as he came up the hill, his sight lined perfectly with the arrowhead. "Release her at once. Shall you refuse, I will have no choice but to end your life."

Cassiel's face grew murderous when he noticed Von. *"You."*

"This is his master, Tarn Morken," Zev told them without looking away from the silent man. "He's come for her."

Cassiel's furious eyes widened. "Kill him, Rawn!"

The arrow flew. Tarn caught it and snapped the shaft in his grip, tossing it aside. He moved so fast it was *inhuman.*

Fur sprouted along Zev's arms. His wolf was ready to spring.

"Steady." Von held the silver knife close enough to his throat to make him hiss. "Don't make me use it. You'll be dead before you shift."

Rawn loaded another arrow, but a blast of red light tore the bow from his hands. From the balding trees emerged two more—a dark-haired elf in black leather armor and an old mage in dark brown robes flowing around his thin frame. A red crystal glowed from his wooden staff as his power filtered around them, filling the air with static. His slow footsteps clinked with the sound of the brass bangles around his ankles.

That was how these men had ambushed them undetected, Zev realized. With magic.

"Elon," Tarn said, his northern accent empty and cold.

The elf in his company stepped forward as he removed his cloak. Zev recognized him right away.

Elon drew out his sword, the metal soundless as it left the scabbard. "It is a pleasure, Lord Norrlen."

Rawn unsheathed his weapon, boots sliding through the wet grass as he shifted into a stance. "I do not recall having properly met your acquaintance. How is it you know my name?"

"I know of you well. Of your triumphs in war and your skill with a blade."

"You flatter me, sir. I know naught of you," Rawn replied as they circled each other. "To which nation do you pertain?"

"I have no nation," Elon said, and he attacked.

Their blades rang with each strike, glinting across the hill as they fought. Each move was fluid, and swift, a needle's pin away from taking each other's head. Their speed was beyond anything Zev had seen. They moved across the field at a turbulent pace, their moves a perfect match to each other.

Rawn swiped at Elon's chest. The elf leaped back, but he was a hair too slow. The sword sliced through his leathers, and Zev caught the copper scent of blood. A red trickle leaked from the shallow cut.

Elon nodded at his bleeding chest. "I expected no less from Greenwood's General."

Rawn circled him again, matching his pace. "What rank did you hold in the Red Highland army?"

Elon's responding smile was bitter but elated, perhaps to find a formidable challenge. "I will leave that to your assumption."

Their blades clashed again in a dance of ringing metal. This time, Elon used magic. Rawn countered effortlessly, his sword cutting through every spell.

The fight kept Tarn and the mage's rapt attention. Zev caught Cassiel's eye, and his jaw tightened. The prince swung for Tarn with his flaming sword. Zev snatched Von's wrist, twisting it away from his throat. Von dodged the rake of his claws. Steel flashed, and a burst of searing agony stole Zev's next breath.

Confused, he looked down at the silver knife embedded in his gut. Dark blood bloomed around the hilt, soaking through his clothing. He shook violently, his entire body burning like it was engulfed in flames. The pain was unimaginable. It rendered him immobile. His muscles coiled tightly as a ringing filled his ears, muffling all sounds except for the pounding of his heart. Zev's chest heaved for air he couldn't fully receive. His trembling hands took the hilt, but he had no strength to pull it out. He tried to speak, to beg someone to remove the knife. A metallic taste bubbled up this throat, pooling in his mouth.

Pain stealing the last of Zev's might, his knees hit the wet ground. Von's shadow fell over him. His expression tightened with what seemed like regret and he said something, but it was lost to the roaring in Zev's ears. After years of wishing for the end, it had come. And ironically, he wasn't relieved. The Madness fled from his mind, chased away by the fear that gripped him. This was what he wanted, but now that he stood at the precipice of life, he wanted to scream that he wasn't ready yet. That he'd been wrong.

But it was too late.

Within the confines of his soul, he heard the unmistakable sound of Death's Gate at last creaking open for him in welcome.

CHAPTER 57

Everything stopped. Time. Sound. Her heart. The breath in her lungs. It took Dyna's mind a second to comprehend, to make sense of the silver knife embedded in Zev's stomach. Blood spread around it, soaking through his tunic like a bloody sun. Her mouth fell open in a silent cry as black webs spread beneath his ashen skin.

Reality snapped back into place. Everyone was still except for her as she kicked and thrashed against Tarn's iron grip. If she removed the knife, she could save him. She had only minutes to stop the poison, mere minutes. But Tarn wouldn't let her go.

Zev's confused gaze found her. Panting breaths rattled in his chest. A choked whimper caught in her throat as black blood leaked from his eyes like tears. The horrid things she said to him only moments ago echoed back at her. *I didn't mean it.* She didn't mean any of it.

His body keeled—and he fell.

Dyna screamed.

The ear-splitting sound tore through her lungs, a violent, broken cry echoing into the skies for every god to hear. The barrier inside of her splintered. Green light blazed as Essence poured through the cracks, fueled by her sorrow and rage. The feeling swelled, burning through her pores, to every edge of her existence, filling and scorching, demanding to break free.

Green flames erupted out of her. It ripped through the air and wrenched everyone away, throwing them across the hill. As quickly as it appeared, the power vanished. Dyna's legs gave out and she fell in the mud. She gasped for breath, ears ringing and vision briefly blinded.

Dyna forced herself to move, dragging herself on her hands and knees to Zev, repeating his name between breaths like a prayer. Reaching him, she took his face and searched his unfocused eyes. Each painful wheeze for air pulled against his ribs. Black gurgled out of his mouth and trickled from his ears.

Her tears joined with the rain. "Stay with me, Zev. Stay with me."

"Dyna," he rasped.

"It's all right. I'll heal you. I'll fix it."

You cannot fix what is already broken.

Her shaking hands gripped the knife, but she couldn't pull it free. If she did, he would bleed out. Leaving it inside of him kept death at bay while pumping him with poison, searing him from the inside. The stench of burning skin filled her nose. Zev's face spasmed with pain as he coughed up more black blood. Choking on despair, she called on her power to begin the healing, but she had none. It had blown out with that blast. A fresh wave of panic rippled through her. She needed more magic.

"You will be fine," Dyna promised with a shuddering sob.

She whipped around to the others. Tarn and his men slowly righted themselves, stunned by the explosion. Cassiel met her eyes as he jerked up.

"I need you!"

He tore out a handful of feathers and sprang across the distance between them. An arrow zipped from the trees. It pierced through his wing, and she cried out at the sharp pain bursting in her shoulder blade as he hit the ground. Raiders ran out of the forest. Cassiel stumbled to his feet, snapping the arrow free. He withdrew *Esh Zayin* and faced the faction of men dressed in black as they came.

Twenty against one.

It was a repeat of Corron. Her heart squeezed inside of her, but there was only cold calm on Cassiel's face.

The clash of metal met white flame. He slew each one who tried to reach her, moving with swift grace. Bodies lit into bulbs of divine fire and their cries vanished with the scattering of ash, washing away beneath the rain.

None will get past me, he swore.

She shivered at the sensation of feeling him in her mind.

Rawn and Elon resumed their battle, their swords ringing across the clearing. Tarn came for her with the mage flanking his side, and Von approached from the opposite direction. Zev's pulse slowed further beneath her fingers.

Cassiel, hurry!

He twisted, whipping his wings. The gust threw Von and the remaining band of Raiders away, creating an opening. He flew for her, and she reached for the feathers clutched in his fist. A blast of red snatched him from the air and slammed him down. Cassiel's growled curse blared through her mind. She flinched at the potent fury in it.

With a wave of his hand, the mage dragged him to his master's feet.

"Thank you for returning my Maiden," Tarn said.

Cassiel snarled. "She's mine."

Dyna grabbed a fallen Raider's short sword from the grass. It was heavier and more awkward than her knife. Without magic, she had no hope of defeating Tarn, but it didn't matter. She was finished cowering. God of Urn, she would ram the sword straight through that man if he so much as—

The mage flicked his fingers, and a force tore the weapon from her hands. Red mist ensnared her body, carrying her through the air to Tarn. Dyna's heart raced as those pale eyes assessed her. Before she could blink, before she could call on any remnants of magic, he reached for her. She cried out at the bite of icy metal clamping around her throat.

A horrid emptiness sank through her body. The Essence Channels that usually hummed with the faint warmth of her power were now empty. The times she thought a wall had barricaded her was nothing like this. It felt as if he'd trapped all of her Essence inside of a thick iron box and dumped it into a dimension so far out of reach, she would never find it again.

"Rawn!" Cassiel roared. His anger and fear bombarded her as he fought against the vines that held him prisoner on the ground. "Get to Dyna!"

Parrying Elon's next swing, Rawn knocked the sword from his hands, sending it arcing in the air behind them. Elon dove out of the way of his killing blow and ran for the fallen weapon. Rawn dropped his sword and snatched his bow from the grass. He yanked a handful of arrows from the quiver, shooting one after the other in rapid succession. They found their marks, and Raiders toppled around her.

Rawn aimed at Von next. The commander dodged an arrow, and another sliced past his ribs. He tripped, holding his wounded side. Rawn shot another to end his life. Jumping in the way, Elon threw out a shield, but the arrow went right through it and hit his shoulder. Von grabbed the injured elf, dragging him back.

Try to remove it! Cassiel told her.

I can't. Dyna kicked and squirmed in the air, yanking on the brass collar around her neck. It didn't budge. Tarn watched her efforts with mild boredom. She hated the infuriating helplessness. Zev was dying, and she could feel him slipping away.

"Shoot an arrow through his damn eye!" Cassiel shouted.

Rawn loaded his bow and aimed.

"Benton," Tarn calmly called on the mage.

A red detonation struck Rawn. It threw him over the hill, and he crashed on the ground hard. Dyna shrieked his name. Pushing to his feet, a trickle of blood leaked from his temple. Rawn's hard gaze focused on Tarn. She felt the pull of magic as he chanted a word and fire sprouted in his hands. A cyclone of flames ripped through the air, coming right for Tarn. But with a swipe of his hand, the spell evaporated into a swirl of smoke. The cuff on his wrist glowed with amber beads. Gods, he had black clovers.

Switching tactics, Rawn aimed at the mage instead. Benton flung up his staff to shield himself. The distraction released his hold on Dyna, and she dropped to the ground with a grunt. Rawn ran for them, only for a containment dome to slam in place around him. Benton smirked as he banged on it, helplessly trapped.

"These are the Guardians?" Tarn said sharply to Von. "I don't understand why it was so difficult to defeat them."

Von bowed his head. "Forgive me, Master."

The man fixed his cold gaze on Cassiel and picked up *Esh Zayin*. The flames died away. "Where is the sorceress?"

The question elicited a confused scowl on Cassiel's face, and Dyna froze. What did Tarn want with her? If she were here, Lucenna would have wiped them off the face of the earth with a mere snap of her fingers.

"Piss off," Cassiel spat.

Tarn pressed the hot edge against his throat, and Cassiel gritted his teeth as his skin sizzled. Dyna gasped in pain, slapping a hand over her burning neck.

"Stop it! Please don't hurt him!" She latched onto Tarn's arm. "Lucenna isn't here."

Tarn paused when he glanced at her. His expression shifted for a split second before his indifference returned. He tossed her off.

"I have had enough of this," Tarn said to Von as he walked away towards the woods. "Bring the Maiden along with the journal. Kill the rest and drain the Celestial of his blood."

"No!" Dyna cried. "Please!"

Thorns sliced through her palms as she tore at the vines holding Cassiel. More appeared and constricted around his body, strangling him. Von plucked her off, and Elon unsheathed a dagger. The mage pointed his staff at Rawn as the crystal flared vivid red.

"TARN!" Dyna's scream sliced through the air. She faced his retreating back, heaving a gasping sob. "If you kill them, you will regret it!"

"You're not in a position to make threats," he said without stopping.

Dyna smashed her fist into Von's kidney, breaking free. She snatched the opal knife hidden on her calf and backed away before he could grab her.

She brought the edge above the brass collar, and her promise echoed over the hill. "Do it, and I'll cut my throat!"

Tarn halted in place. His icy gaze landed on her.

Cassiel bucked wildly against the roots, shouting for her to stop aloud and through the bond. Rawn beat his fists against the dome. Dyna shivered as she burned with desperation. Leoake's words kept circling in her head.

...if you don't pay the price, the others will.

When she'd left home, this wasn't where she thought she'd be. Facing a different monster who came to take from her. But she wouldn't run anymore. Her fear melted into anger as she looked at Tarn. She may not be a warrior, or a powerful sorceress, but she was *not* weak.

The knife was cool in her steady hand, its cold, sharp edge definitive against her pulse. The value of her life was the only bargaining chip she had, and she was prepared to use it.

No one else would die for her.

"You know the map is enchanted," she told Tarn. "My Essence is the key, and the inscriptions will disappear with my death. Without me, you will *never* get to Mount Ida."

Tarn's pale eyes were frigid. "Where is the journal?"

"I have it, and only I can open it."

Von inched closer, and she backed further away to where no one could reach her in time to stop the knife.

"Don't come near me. I'll do it." Dyna pressed the edge against her skin until a warm trickle leaked down her neck.

"Stop!" Cassiel cried out frantically.

Zev stirred, and his trembling hand reached out to her. Overwhelming shock and relief hit her. He still clung on. He must have caught the scent of her blood.

Her teary eyes flooded. "Zev."

"Show it to me," Tarn ordered in a low tone.

She removed Azeran's journal from her satchel and tossed it at Benton's feet. His hands glowed red as he lifted it, reacting to the power within.

The mage nodded and brought the journal to his master. "It's secured by enchantment."

"Can you open it?"

"Perhaps." Benton shrugged. "But we will need her to reveal the map."

"I'll come with you willingly," Dyna said. "But only if you spare them."

"No, Dyna!" Cassiel bucked, ripping at the vines.

Taking the journal, Tarn's piercing gaze, lined with pale lashes, studied her for a moment. She held her breath.

"Very well," he said after a long pause. "Come with me and I won't kill your Guardians, Dynalya Astron."

A flinch went through her at the coarse sound of her name on his tongue. "I will after I tend to my cousin."

She ran for Zev, but Von seized her waist and snatched the knife out of her hand. He lugged her on his shoulder, heading to his master's side.

"No, wait! Let me help him!"

Tarn turned away for the woods. "That wasn't part of the deal."

"Please." Dyna sobbed, holding out a hand to Zev. "He'll die!"

Von nodded at his two other companions, and they retreated. With a wave of Benton's staff, and the vines detaining Cassiel receded into the ground and the containment dome around Rawn dissipated. He sprinted up the hill.

"You will not take her." Cassiel grasped his sword. Divine fire burst to life.

Elon unsheathed his weapon again while Benton, Von, and the remaining Raiders simply watched.

Rawn reached the top of the hill as Cassiel launched into the air. Elon hurled a knife. It speared his wing, and Dyna's body spasmed at the pain shooting through her. His back hit the ground. The sound of bones snapping swept her in a wave of agony.

Cassiel staggered to his feet, breathing raggedly. His wings hung in irregular angels behind him. Every part of her throbbed with his pain, wild anger hardened his features. *Esh Zayin's* flames crackled in the rain as he faced off with Elon. Divine fire met steel as they fought. Even injured, Elon parried his swings effortlessly. He moved with the nimble speed of the elves that Cassiel couldn't match. Elon's sword slashed across his chest and Dyna cried out at feeling the blade slice through her.

Stumbling back, blood saturated Cassiel's black tunic. The elf delivered a swift kick to his face, throwing him to the ground. The blow reverberated in her skull. She dropped, and Von caught her. Cassiel rose to his feet, spitting out a clot of blood as his wound and wings healed. He lifted his sword and Rawn lined up beside him.

Von sighed. "Stand down."

Cassiel's eyes churned like molten steel in the firelight. "You can cut me a thousand ways. I will never let you have her."

A cold, terrifying rage boiled inside of the bond, sending goosebumps across Dyna's skin. There was nothing in his mind but the impenetrable need to protect his mate.

Esh Zayin blazed.

The cerulean roots seeped through the white, turning the flames brilliant blue. Everyone gawked at the Seraph sword. Cassiel inhaled sharply as his disbelief struck her, followed by a splash of confusion. It quickly receded under a riptide of steely determination.

His grip tightened on the winged hilt, the edges of his face sharpening. "I will protect what is mine," he said, his voice so deathly calm. "Until my last breath."

A ball of emotion flooded Dyna's chest as her vision blurred.

Von set her behind him and took out two knives. "If you wish to die, we will comply."

But Cassiel wouldn't surrender. He would never stop fighting until one of them was dead.

"No." Dyna clung to Von's arm. She shook her head at Rawn pleadingly. "You cannot fight them."

Not without another casualty. Rawn might stop the mage with his enchanted sword, but that would leave Cassiel to face Elon and Von. A fight he would surely lose. If he died, she knew it would destroy her.

Rawn lowered his sword. The sky darkened as the sun dipped on the horizon. Rain pelted down harder, soaking her through.

"Don't follow us," Von said. "I'll not hesitate to kill you if you do."

"The only one dying here is you." Cassiel shot forward, his teeth bared. Rawn threw himself at Cassiel and tackled him to the ground. "What are you doing? Release me!"

"Lady Dyna is right," Rawn said, locking his arms around Cassiel's neck. "This is not a battle to be won. We must yield today."

He reared under him, nearly throwing him off with his wings. "Get off!"

Cassiel, look at me.

He did, enraged and anguished. His fingers clawed through the mud. "No," he said, the single word falling like a shard.

This is the only way.

Do not do this, he pleaded. *I swore to protect you.*

Tears streamed down her face. *Now it's my turn to protect you.*

Von pulled her away, and they walked backward with the others. With each step she took away from him, her body shuddered in protest. Dyna held Cassiel's gaze, conveying much more than could be said aloud. She memorized his face, the color of his eyes, his hair, his voice. If today was the last time they would be together, then she would remember him as he was by the willow.

When they reached the tree line, Cassiel peeled his gaze away from hers to Von. His next words were a quiet, seething promise in the rain. "I will be the darkness behind your steps. The shadow over your head. Wherever you take her, I will follow. If she comes to any harm, I will *burn* everything you hold dear."

Von's hold on her stiffened. He hauled her onto his shoulder, and with his men flanking him, they ran into the trees.

Wait for me. Cassiel's broken thoughts brushed against hers. *There is nowhere he can take you that I will not find you.*

I'll wait for you. She strained to keep him in sight, holding on to the stars shining in his eyes until the forest swallowed them from view. *Always.*

CHAPTER 58

C assiel roared a curse. He punched the ground and his entire
body shook as his pulse thundered in his ears.
"Get *off* me," he said through his teeth.

Rawn sat back. "That man would have killed you if I did not restrain you, Cassiel. We will rescue Lady Dyna. You have my word. Right now, Zev requires our aid."

Cassiel cursed again, and they rushed to Zev's side. His dull eyes, coated in black blood, fluttered open. Cassiel took his hand and searched for a pulse as he listened to his heart. The pulse was feeble, the beats too far in between. His translucent complexion was as pale as ash, veins black beneath his skin. Rawn ripped open Zev's bloody shirt, and he sucked in a sharp breath. The area around the knife was completely black and bubbling as if it was cooking him from within.

"The silver is killing him," Cassiel said. "Pull it out!"

"If I do, the wound will profuse. I'm afraid he may..."

"He will not die today." Cassiel rolled up his sleeves. He took his opal knife and sliced his palm deep, blood gushing freely. "Do it."

Carefully, Rawn removed the knife. Zev spasmed with a weak cry. Cassiel squeezed his hand into a fist above him. Blood cascaded over the wound, coating Zev's abdomen in a gruesome painting. They stared at it, waiting for something to happen, but nothing else had changed. The gash in his stomach continued to bubble.

Rawn touched Zev's wrist and shook his head. "He is faltering,"

"No, he's not." Cassiel cut himself again, deeper this time, and poured the hot red stream over the wound. It merely spilled down his abdomen, mixing with the black sludge. "No. No. It has to work!"

But it wouldn't. He'd killed humans. His power to heal others was gone.

Rawn grasped Zev's hand. "Hold fast, my friend. It is not your time."

Zev's unfocused eyes looked at something past them that they couldn't see. His expression tightened as he mumbled something lost under the downpour. Cassiel leaned in closer so he could catch his fading voice.

"Father, forgive me, please." Black tears leaked down Zev's temples. "I don't want to go."

"Turn away from the Gates, Zev." Cassiel searched his face for some hope that he wouldn't fade, but he long recognized the look of death. "Stay, damn you."

"Please forgive me." His eyes slid closed. "I'm sorry."

Cassiel lowered his head as Zev exhaled his last breath. And it carried off with the rain.

Were the fates watching? Were the Gods of the Seven Gates laughing at him now? What was the point of all of this? They had taken too much from him. Too damn much. He had lost his divinity, his bonded, and now his friend. He'd lost everything that ever mattered.

Cassiel slumped on his heels, letting the rain beat on them where they sat by the body. He pointed his face at the sky, never feeling so lost and alone as he did now. Celestials were descendants of the Heavens, meant to protect life as decreed by *Elyón*. But not him.

Not a dirty half-breed with useless blood.

That hadn't mattered to him when he found Dyna. She had given him a purpose and new meaning, and his friendship with Zev had given him something he never had. They were the Guardians of the Maiden, but they had failed to protect her. He failed.

Releasing a shuddering exhale, Cassiel closed Zev's eyelids and rested a hand on his arm. "May you leave the Mortal Gate with no burden to bind you," he croaked, fighting the burning in his throat. "May you cross Death's Gate with *all* faults forgiven. May you pass through the Time Gate with the wisdom of the age. May you pass through the expanse of the Spatial Gate's wonder. May you pass through Life's Gate as you did at the beginning. May you arrive at Heaven's Gate at the end. May the God of Urn receive your—"

Zev gasped for air.

Cassiel and Rawn gawked as the gash on Zev's stomach stitched itself together, piece by piece, until the rotten flesh healed. The rosy color returned to his complexion, and his green eyes blinked at the storming sky. The rain washed away the black sludge from his face and torso, revealing the flawless skin.

"Am I alive?" Zev rasped.

"God of Urn." Rawn gaped at him incredulously. "You are."

A rush sank through Cassiel's stomach as he stared at his unblemished palms. A rush sank through his stomach. It worked. His blood had never lost its divinity. It simply took longer to heal others. When he'd healed Dyna, it hadn't happened right away either. And his sword ... *Elyōn* had given him Seraph fire. He didn't know why he was chosen to have it, but a layer of his self-doubt and self-loathing stripped away at the revelation that he wasn't damned after all.

"How?" Zev asked.

"Prince Cassiel brought you back."

Zev glanced down at himself then at Cassiel, his mouth parting. "I ... I'm within your debt."

A lump formed in Cassiel's throat at the sound of his voice. He didn't think he would ever hear it again.

"Let us forget about life-debts," he said. "I have lost count of how many times we have saved each other's lives."

Rawn chuckled weakly. "Agreed."

Zev groaned as he sat with their help. He examined his chiseled abdomen, expression contorted with disbelief. Even the old chain scars around it had vanished, leaving a circumference at his center. "It's as if nothing was ever there."

"By the power of divine blood," Rawn said. Both he and Zev looked at Cassiel with a reverence that left him uncomfortable.

He didn't understand what happened. He thought for sure Zev had died. They had heard him take his last breath.

"What did you see?" Cassiel asked. "Did you cross through Death's Gate?"

Zev blinked at the sky with a dazed look on his face. "No."

Now wasn't the time to dwell on it.

Cassiel stood. "We have to go. Tarn took Dyna and the map."

Eyes flashing yellow, fur sprouted along Zev's arms. "I'm truly going to enjoy killing that man."

"He does not possess the map," Rawn told them as he got to his feet. He reached in his cloak and pulled out a rolled up parchment. "Lady Dyna removed it from the journal. After what happened with Lady Lucenna and Commander Von, she thought it best not to leave the map in the one known place we kept it. Since then, I have carried it on my person at all times."

Cassiel smirked. "Clever girl."

"Let's go get her." Zev tore the bloody wet shirt off his back as he shapeshifted into a snarling wolf.

Rawn whistled at Fair, and the white stallion galloped over to him. Zev sprinted into the darkening woods, taking the direction Tarn went. Wings flaring open, Cassiel launched into the sky, and led the search for his wife. He was confident they would find her, for there was one thing Tarn hadn't accounted for. The bond. No matter where that man took Dyna, he would always know where she was.

Cassiel followed the beacon of her soul to the north, letting it guide him. *Dyna, I'm coming—*

An invisible blow struck his chest, and he knew nothing but unbridled agony. It wrenched the air from his lungs, splitting his mouth open in a silent cry. The world skewed on its axis. His wings lost function, and the wind ripped at him as he plummeted back to earth. Crashing through the trees, sharp branches speared his wings, nearly tearing them off his back. Cassiel collided with the ground and his leg snapped. He barely registered the pain of broken bones when another part of him was splintering.

An unbearable torment slashed at the edges of his body, mind, and soul, splitting his sense of self. He couldn't think, move, or even breathe. It was taking from him, taking something deep from inside of him. Cassiel couldn't grasp it. There was no fighting it. He only knew that he was losing something dire to his existence. The unbearable pain grew and grew, the pressure completely crushing him until it severed him clean in half, shattering a core piece of his being into a million pieces.

It felt like death.

When he thought it would annihilate him, the pain suddenly ebbed. There was no solace in it. Only the anguish of loss that left behind a deep hole in his soul where Dyna had once been—where their bond had once been.

Her presence was simply...

Gone.

He couldn't feel her. Their bond had been cleaved away from him, and its absence could only mean one thing.

Dyna was dead.

All reason slipped through the cracks of his rationality like trickles of sand. Then the rest of him broke. His guttural scream tore through the woods, taking the beat of his heart with it.

EPILOGUE

Searing pain slashed through Dyna's body as the bond ripped apart. Agony twisted through her veins, tearing into her soul, splitting it in half down the middle. The half that had been Cassiel's soul, where it had merged with hers, fractured like glass. The shards fell away, leaving behind a vast emptiness. Her bonded was gone. She knew it with certainty at his missing presence inside her. They had hacked him out of her heart.

Someone was screaming.

Dyna writhed on the wet ground, leaves sticking to her skin as she was blinded by tears and pain. The pressure on her chest was too much. It was crushing her. She was trapped her under the entirety of the world, and it threatened to eradicate all that she was. By the burning in her gasping throat, Dyna realized she was the one screaming.

"What is wrong with her?" Tarn's annoyed voice filtered through her cries. "Silence her lest the others hear."

Boots shifted in the mud, accompanied by the soft clink of metal. "They cannot hear her, let alone find her through my spell," the mage replied. "I have veiled her existence in the mortal world. They will never find her."

The spell. Her mind tried to tell her. Her bond wasn't broken. The spell had separated her from Cassiel. He must be alive, but her entire being violently thrashed as she screamed from the loss of him.

"You better be certain, Benton," Tarn said coolly. "Cease her incessant wailing."

Someone rolled Dyna onto her back, and Von's worried face came into view. "What is it, lass? What's wrong?"

As if he cared.

She wanted to hit him, to curse him and spit in his face for what he had done to Zev. But the lost bond was killing her. Dyna's eyes rolled as her throat clamped shut.

"The Maiden is going into shock," another voice said. The elf.

"She isn't wounded, Elon. What caused this?"

"The cause is irrelevant, Commander. If we do not calm her, she will die."

Dyna couldn't breathe. She couldn't remember why she was here, why she was traveling across Urn. She could hardly recall her name through the torment. Dyna clawed at her chest, tearing at her skin. Anything to ease the shattering of her soul.

"Put the Maiden to sleep," Von said.

A glowing red crystal waved over her face, and a mist seeped in her mind, blackening her vision. All else faded with the last thought of Cassiel.

Dyna awoke wrapped in layers of black silk. She was lying on a plush, warm surface. An ache throbbed in her chest and head. Where was she?

It was dark.

Gasping, she jerked up straight. Dyna's hand flew to the heavy brace around her neck, and her breath came in heavy. A candle on the small bedside table provided enough light to distinguish the bed she was in. There were runes burned on the tent walls. From the ceiling hung hundreds of wards, crystals, and paper charms, filling the air with a low hum of power that prickled against her skin.

She met a pair of ice-blue eyes in the dark. Her heart leaped in her throat and a yelp escaped her. Tarn's black clothing blended him well within the shadows. He sat in a chair with his hands loosely linked. As he tilted his head, one corner of his mouth tweaked. The movement was so subtle she hardly noticed it. He was a lot younger than she had first thought.

Every instinct told her to run, but she couldn't move. She had spent weeks evading this man. Now that he was in front of her, every limb locked in place. A draft drew her attention to the tent flaps a few feet away. Thirty paces between her and freedom. She had no magic or weapons. Even if she did, Dyna knew it would be useless against this man. He may harm her for running, but she had to take the chance.

Tarn rose to his feet, and Dyna launched for the exit. With the speed of a snake, he snatched her arm and swung her around. She slammed into his chest. He looked at her with inhumanly vibrant eyes, so pale they were the color of ice. The candlelight shone through the edges of his white-blond hair. It covered half his face, the other half draped in darkness.

"Sit."

At the harsh command, she scurried away from him. Her legs hit the edge of the bed, and she dropped on it. Tarn took a seat at the end. Dyna scooted away, pressing herself against the headboard, wishing she could go through it. Her ragged breaths hung in the dead air between them.

"It's strange," Tarn mused, his cool tone faintly tinged with the Azure accent of the north. He leaned forward, bracing his elbows on his knees. "I have waited years for you, foretold maiden of my future. Now that you're here, I find myself intrigued."

The candlelight shone over the sharp angles of his face and the pale lashes framing irises touched by winter. He had a harsh beauty meant to lull, but the man terrified her. His existence was cold and imposing, hovering with a power she knew could kill her in an instant.

"You waited for me," Dyna repeated, sensing he wanted to talk. She stole glances at her surroundings, searching for something she could use to defend herself. "Yet I knew nothing of you until recently. How do you know that it's I who the Seer foretold would come?"

A muscle in Tarn's jaw flexed as it tightened. He must not have known Von told her about the Seer.

"Many clues were given, and several maidens were brought before me. All of whom proved false. But when I laid eyes on you, I knew there was no mistaking who you are."

There was a sharp cartography divider on the desk beside them, and a fire poker in the brazier near the bed. Both were an equal distance away.

"Are you paying attention, Dynalya?" Tarn's cool hand snatched her ankle in a tight grasp. "Or are you searching for a weapon?"

He yanked her toward him, and a shriek tore from her mouth. He rose on the bed, caging her beneath him. His hands flattened by her head and his knees came around her hips, but he didn't look at her with desire or need. Her heart pounded behind her ribs as he quietly studied her like the phoenix on Draven's ship. Curious. Inquisitive. As though she was something he didn't quite understand, but was moments away from gutting her with his talons if she so much as blinked.

Dyna didn't dare move.

The scent of spiced wine and smoke wafted around him. He reached for her face, and she flinched. With an unexpected gentleness, Tarn weaved his fingers through her hair. He let the locks run through them, watching as they gleamed a fiery red in the candlelight.

"Seek the Maiden with emeralds for sight and tresses of fire," he murmured. "For she holds the key to the Unending thou desires."

A chill crawled over her at the prophetic touch in those words. They must be part of the Seer's foretelling.

"The Unending..." she whispered. "What is that?"

Something told her she should know, but her mind couldn't focus on anything but her pounding heart. Tarn stared at her for a moment, then startled her with a barking laugh. He sat on his heels, and she scrambled back to the headboard.

"You have a map to Mount Ida," he said. "Surely you've heard the tales of its besetting. Captain Ida thieved and plundered, taking all manner of wealth and magic. His greatest feat was stealing the Sacred Scroll of the Unending that contained the secret of never-ending power over life and death."

A small gasp escaped Dyna's lips. The world spun around her again when she remembered the last passage she'd read in Jökull's book. The corner of Tarn's mouth curled at her horror. The smile was mirthless, failing to reach the rest of his face.

"You want ..." Dyna couldn't bring herself to say it.

To have such a thing could mean the end of the world at his hands. He would be invincible. All the powers that be, and all the powers that ever were, could never defeat him.

"Yes," Tarn said, his tone taunting. "The Tree of the Unending."

The floor dropped out from under her, casting her into a void.

Since the moment she had walked out her front door, nothing had been a coincidence. The fates had played with her life, moving her like a piece in a sick game she didn't know the rules of. Each step had taken her to this moment. Tarn had chased her across the kingdom, put a bounty on her head, had Zev killed, and separated her from Cassiel.

All for this.

Behind him hung a dark tapestry with the white crest of a bird in mid-flight. The same one only flown by the royal family.

Something cold plummeted through her. Everything was spinning.

"Who ... who are you?" The question shuddered on her lips.

"Come now. You're smarter than that. You know exactly who I am."

Her eyes squeezed shut, blocking the view of his pale features. Their starkness being the one thing that held the obvious answer from the beginning. She didn't want to look at him when he revealed the secret that would change everything. How did she not see it?

Jökull and Sunnëva Morkhàn.

Tarn *Morken*. Born in Old Tanzanite Keep, where it always snowed. The most wanted man in Azure.

Thus, the king begat a son on a naughty night. Now the prince seeks to put his head on a spike...

Tarn took her chin in his icy fingers and Dyna's eyes flew open to find him inches away. She froze, her vision blurring. Her rapid breaths formed into white clouds between them as the temperature dropped. The candle dimmed further, darkening everything but the gleam in his luminous eyes, like the shadow demon that had once hunted her. Every part of her trembled. This man was a predator, and she had become his prey.

At last, she understood why.

The tent shook as the wind released a haunting howl. A gust billowed through the tent flaps, tossing missives off the desk. It extinguished the candlelight in a puff of smoke—plunging them into a pitch-black abyss. A whimper caught in her throat.

Tarn's chilling voice surfaced from the darkness. "I am a descendant of the Ice Phoenix, Dynalya. And I would have what belongs to me."

The air left her lungs. He wrapped an arm around Dyna's back like a band of steel and drew her close. His cold breath brushed against her cheek as he spoke, at last revealing the hushed declaration that coated her with frost.

"Immortality."

Acknowledgments

They say each book you write gets better than the last, but no one said it would be easier. If they did, I didn't get the memo. Let's be real for a second, and I will admit *Bonded Fate* kicked my butt. It dragged me up a steep mountain of plotting and writing, then shoved me off the top into a terrain of endless edits and rewrites. This book was truly a journey of self-discovery. Not only for the characters, but for me too.

If I didn't have such an incredible squad behind me, *Bonded Fate* might have taken an extra year to get published. That being said, I have so many people to thank for my second book baby being unleashed into the world.

First, always a huge thank you to my husband and my bonded. Michael, thank you for always supporting me, even if it meant dish duty and taking the kids out for the day so I could write. You're my everything.

Second, shout out to my incredible street team, who I call My Sweet Potatoes. You ladies are the dream team. I cannot thank you enough for all your support in getting the word out about my books and for loving on me. Your praise kept me going.

Being an author is a tough gig, and I know I couldn't have done so well alone. I haven't felt alone since I met everyone in the B.R.A Support Group (Book Readers Anonymous). It grew from a group of three book lovers into a club of my closest gal pals who work so hard on their author careers and impress me every damn day.

Special praise to Miranda Lyn for calling me out on my *ish,* and making me laugh at my own mistakes. Thank you for letting me keep you until 2:30 in the morning rambling on about the entire plot of *Bonded Fate* when I was stuck. You inspire me, lady. Don't forget me when you're famous.

Hina Babar, my literary wizard, a.k.a. editor. Thank you for poking holes in my duct taped manuscript and forcing me to make it a hundred times better. You see books and characters like no one else. I'm convinced you have magic. (She is so meticulous that if you found any typos, they're mine.)

Kisses to my amazing betas for reading my feral rough draft and telling me she was pretty. Karley Stafford, my fan club president who was there from the beginning, thank you for thinking I deserved a crown. To me, you'll always be the queen. Devyani, the force of nature, thank you for going above and beyond with critiquing this book and making it shine.

My sweetest potato, a.k.a. Personal Assistant, Veronica Frank. Gurl, you make me laugh every day and your cheerleading got me through the crazy busy times. Thank you for attaching yourself to me and not letting go. Cher Martindill, my adorable helper, you and Veronica kept me sane by taking on everything I couldn't find the time to handle.

And thank you to the ARC Team and bloggers who shouted about my newest book baby to anyone who would listen. I know I couldn't have gotten this far on my own without each of you. I am so incredibly grateful. It always brings tears to my eyes when I think of all of your love. From the bottom of my full heart, THANK YOU.

I am within your debt.

Beck Michaels

Pronunciation Guide

NAMES:
Dynalya/Dyna: Die-nal-yah / Die-nah
Cassiel: Cass-ee-elle
Zev: Zeh-v
Rawn: Ron
Lucenna: Lu-seh-nah
Lucien: Lu-see-en
Keenali: Key-nah-lee
Leoake: Lee-oak
Azulo: Ah-zu-loh
Jökull: Joh-cull
Sunnëva: Sue-neh-vah
Richël: Ree-shell
Yelrakel: Yel-ra-quel
Sowmya: Sao-mya

PLACES:
Mount Ida: Eye-dah
Hilos: He-los
Corron: Core-on
Magos: Mah-goes
Xian Jing: She-an-ging
Saxe Sea: Sah-x
Versai: Ver-sah-i
Morphos: Morr-fos

OTHERS:
Hyalus: Hi-ya-lus
Esh Zayin: Eh-sh Zah-yin
Elyōn: Ehl-yon
Ett haor sheli: Et-ha-or-sheh-lee

A shes of the dead drifted through the air like snow. It hovered around Veron, clinging to the sweat on his skin and uniform. Mounds of charred bodies lined the cobblestone of the market—the only evidence of what had occurred a mere hour ago.

"This has gone far enough, Captain," he said to the female Celestial in golden armor, having heard the others call her by name and rank. "You have killed enough people today. We will take these as our prisoners."

Yelrakel's long red hair stuck to the bloodstains covering her face as her cold grey eyes took in his measure. Veron was the only thing standing between her and the cluster of Azure citizens cowering behind him. He had met all sorts of beings in Urn. Hardly anything ever startled him anymore, but at the moment, his pulse drummed in his veins. The Captain was as striking and intimidating as the rest of the female Celestials in her squadron. Large, powerful wings loomed over their shoulders in every color, their faces and bodies chiseled by some harsh blade.

Everyone heard stories of the Celestials and their history with Azure. But when Veron signed the Accords as a young guard, it never occurred to him that he might see one. The blue flames of Yelrakel's Seraph sword flickered with the wind, their heat so powerful there would be nothing of him left if she struck him. His mind fought with this new reality, but the ardor of divine fire was the only thing proving this encounter was very real.

God of Urn, let me survive this day, Veron prayed as he thought of the one waiting for him at home.

He couldn't die here, not now.

"The Valkyrie do not take prisoners," Yelrakel said in a cool tone, her accent slightly painted with another. "We judge who must pass through the Gates. *Elyōn* will judge where their soul ends."

He failed to stop the market massacre, but he will stop this one.

"Please." Veron held out a placating hand. "I am the Commissioner of the Azure Guard. I will see that our citizens are fairly prosecuted."

"They broke the Accords, Commissioner," Yelrakel said. "There is only one penance for that. Now step aside."

"These people don't have to die." Veron could not stand by and allow them to be slaughtered even with the dire crime they committed.

"They do. For taking what was not theirs and seeing what they should not have seen."

The Valkyrie stepped forward, and the people cried out. They prostrated on their knees, praying and begging for forgiveness. In the panic, a vial slipped from someone's pocket, clinking as it rolled across the ground to the Yelrakel. She met Veron's wide eyes as she crushed it under her foot. Blood splattered, filling the crevices in the cobblestone. The scent wafted through his senses, and it was unlike anything he had ever smelled before. Alluring and powerful, holding the hidden magic to cure any ailment of the world.

Veron gritted his teeth at the waste. Like tossing water to a fire in the middle of a drought.

To humans—to people like him—it was invaluable.

To Celestials, it was sacred. And yet, Yelrakel would instead let it go to waste than allow any human to have it.

There was no mercy on her face. No understanding. Only cruel verdict. Long ago, the Celestials vowed any who dared take divine blood would pay with death. She would kill these people without an ounce of remorse, and it left a chill in his soul. There was a hatred in her gaze, put there by the humans of the past, left to fall on him.

"If you will not move, then I shall cut through you," she said. And he wholeheartedly believed her.

Veron reached for his sword, fear beating in his chest as he thought of his Marla, left to suffer alone in a dark, cold room if he joined the ashes. Nearly every man in his family died protecting Azure, and when he was a young lad with no one to care for, he'd been prepared for that. But now, his mind screamed.

A flash of gold pixie dust and Keena appeared in full size beside him, the torn petals of her pink gown rippling around her. "You will do no such thing," she said in a commanding tone.

"I had asked you to wait in my office, Princess," he muttered under his breath. The iron burns on her dark skin had nearly healed, but she hadn't fully recovered.

She frowned. "Did you really expect me to?"

Yelrakel sneered. "The fae have no business here."

"No, but my father has signed the Accords, as have all the rulers of the courts," Keena said, making her status clear. "I know the laws they entail. The Celestials are within their right to defend themselves from humans, but the danger has passed. There is no reason to continue slaughtering them. Something I know Lord Jophiel would agree with."

At the mention of High King's brother, Veron glanced at the symbol of a tree within a mountain on the breastplates of the Valkyrie—the sigil of Lord Jophiel's House.

Yelrakel's jaw flexed, that hard gaze burning as she observed the fairy for a long moment. The Valkyrie may be powerful, but so was the princess, Veron recalled. In both strength and position. He held quiet, grasping at any hope they could still save lives this day.

Yelrakel sheathed her weapon. "Where is our prince?"

He hid a sigh of relief, releasing the hilt of his sword. "We don't know. The Azure Guards made sure Prince Cassiel would escape, but we didn't follow."

"And the poacher?"

He exchanged a glance with Keena as he cleared his throat. "Unfortunately, Draven Skinner escaped."

Yelrakel's mouth thinned. "He took from our prince. For that, he must die."

Veron wouldn't argue there. The poacher had earned his. "You have my leave do with him what you must."

"I do not require your leave," she snarled.

The brunt of her insolent manner had him clenching his jaw. No one dared to speak to him that way.

"Captain." Another female Celestial with deep red wings and dusky skin approached. Blue fire swiveled around the blade of her glaive. "The Inspector General wishes to speak with you."

Veron internally winced at the mention of his superior—his uncle, outside of professional settings. Corvin Moreland was a tall, willowy man in dark blue robes of status, a grey beard lining his thin face. He stood with his arms folded behind his back, waiting on the other side of the market with his guards. While he had always been a strict man, the Inspector took pride that the Moreland family was responsible for the smooth organization of the city and its safety. Therefore, he tasked Veron with making sure it stayed that way. He greatly disliked inconveniences that required him to leave the courthouse.

This situation went far beyond any inconvenience.

Corvin fixed him with a look that clarified his thoughts on the matter. Veron expected there would be a serious discussion to follow. Yelrakel marched away with the others for the Inspector.

The Azure Guard quickly helped the frightened people stand at Veron's signal, ushering them away to a waiting jail wagon.

"Thank you, princess," Veron said. "You most likely saved their lives and mine."

Keena shook her head at the wrecked market. "I'm sorry I couldn't do more. I fear what may happen next for Azure."

He closed his eyes. The right one was tender from his earlier tussle with Zev. "You and I both."

"Commissioner," Kye called as he came forward with a sack in his arms. Behind him followed two more men carrying a wooden crate. "We confiscated all the vials we could find and the feathers. I have dispatched men to search for anyone else who may have escaped the market."

"Good," Veron said. "Take all of it to my office and have any survivors incarcerated. That is the only safe place for them now."

The blood in the glass vials glistened beneath the window light, seeming to glow with the power they held. Veron felt it from where he stood before the open crate in his silent office.

"I know we must all be thinking it," Keena whispered across from him. "Right?"

Veron clenched his fists, holding back the very thought he had been fighting since she told him there was a Celestial in his city. "We can't."

"Commissioner, it's fate," Kye said. The corporal had guarded the door without being asked, watching him with kind, sad eyes.

Keena nodded. "It has to be."

"It was fate that hundreds of people died in the market today?" Veron asked tightly. "Fate that Tarn killed my father and his calvary of rangers? Fate that his bounties brought a Celestial prince here and may now bring about war for Azure?"

"Veron, we have tried everything to treat Marla's illness," Keena said. "Every healer in the country has come to see her. They failed, and fae medicine failed. If only I had more of the blooms—" She exhaled sharply as she shook her head, reminding him he wasn't the only one with problems.

"Nothing can cure Marla's sickness." A heavy tightness filled his chest, and he felt as if he couldn't fully breathe. It wasn't a soldier's duty to question outcomes, but to strategize and overcome. Yet this ... he couldn't overcome this.

"Celestial blood might," Keena said. "The Druid told me if I followed them, I would find what I was searching for. I thought he meant something else, but when I saw Cassiel in the Moors, I realized he must have meant this."

Kye nodded. "Take it, Commissioner. No one will notice one missing. We haven't cataloged a record yet."

Take it. As if it were that simple. The vials seemed to stare back at him, taunting him with its gift, but he knew the cost. He glanced at the Azure flag hanging in the corner of the office, its symbol of a seven-pointed star matching the one on his badge. Veron never thought there would come a day he would betray everything he stood for.

Kenna took his arms and made him look at her. "If we don't do this, she will die."

"I've lived my life by the law, and if I should defy it, I will lose her and my life with it," Veron said, but the justification felt empty. A parallel to what his life would become when Marla left this world. Everything he strived for, everything he did for her, would be for nothing.

Kenna's yellow butterfly wings twitched, expelling a flutter of gold dust into the room. "No harm will come to either of you. Should this come to light, I will take the blame."

He'd held up the law all of his life and honored his King and country. But the moment he saw the Celestial Prince chained up on stage, his blood spilling for those begging for it, the need and desperation hidden behind his armor of duty had penetrated through.

"Princess, that is my burden alone." Veron picked up a vial, turning the dark red contents glimmering inside as fear wove through his new hope. "Should taking this step lead to my hanging, know that I go willingly."

Keena lowered her head.

"Kye, go so you may deny all accountability," Veron commanded. "I cannot have you involved in this illegal matter."

"Of course, sir. Good luck to you." Kye saluted and quickly left the room, but as soon as the door shut, they heard him say aloud, "Evening, Inspector General."

Keena snatched the vial from Veron's hand. In a swirl of pixie dust, she shrunk in size and zipped away to the bookshelves, ducking behind a pile of scrolls and stacked books.

Corvin's voice boomed in the hallway. "Move aside, Corporal."

The door slammed open, banging against the wall, and he entered with Captain Yelrakel and the other female who'd spoken to her in the market. They now wore enchanted cloaks over their armor that hid their wings, but their presence filled the space in the office.

"We have come for His Highness's blood," Yelrakel said coolly.

"Is this all of it?" his uncle asked, nodding to the crate. The wily man hardly reached their shoulders.

"Yes, sir." Veron nodded. "My men have confiscated everything they could find."

Nothing about him gave away the lie, but he felt it prickle over every inch of his skin. This sealed his fate. He was a criminal in guard clothing.

A hypocrite.

How many others had broken the law out of desperation as he was doing now?

"If I find you have lied to me, there will be nothing left of you. Not even bones," Yelrakel said, a dark promise lacing her words. She picked up the heavy crate with no effort. "Show us to the roof."

"Right away." Corvin motioned for them to follow.

The Captain paused and said to Veron, "As for the survivors, you may keep them locked away. Our High King will be here shortly to deal with them."

Veron's jaw tightened. Was the High King coming to eradicate those remaining who witnessed their secret? With Celestial history and after what the Valkyrie did in the market, they clearly would kill to protect the Realms.

He followed them into the hallway, glimpsing a flash of yellow slip out of the broken office window. They took the stairs to the roof. The bitter wind blew against them as they set down the crate. Once again, Veron felt the heat of divine fire when Yelrakel drew her sword. She touched it to the crate, and petals of blue flame wrapped around the crate.

The Valkyrie watched it burn in silence until all that remained were embers and ash. A fate he would share if they ever found out the truth. Without another word, they removed their cloaks, and their graceful wings carried them into the sky. They flew away, heading north as they disappeared behind the veil of clouds.

Inspector Corvin grunted and turned to Veron. "A word, Commissioner."

"Of course, sir." He braced himself, expecting to be demoted as punishment for what befell the city—or worse. But he came to find his position now had little value to him.

"This is a grave matter, as you know. I have informed the King of what occurred today, and the King of Hilos is on his way. Azure is a peaceful kingdom. We have no interest in war." The Inspector crossed his arms behind his back as they looked out at the city. Smoke rose from the rooftops in the distance. "We cannot afford to offend the Celestials any further. Therefore, I will conduct a thorough investigation with the remaining survivors and guards. I have called upon a local mage to aid us in the questioning to be sure we have confiscated all divine blood and feathers and apprehended everyone who bore witness to the market massacre."

Veron stiffened, his pulse quickening. "A mage, sir? Is that necessary? The men are loyal to the crown."

"No one will be exempt from the truth spell questioning."

Veron folded his arms behind his back, spinning his marital ring around his finger as everything in him went cold. His mind raced with a hundred thoughts, and all concluded the same thing. They needed to run. "I understand, sir. When will you begin?"

"We begin now."

"Now?"

"Have somewhere to be, Commissioner?" His uncle's calculative gaze met his.

At first, Veron kept his expression schooled, but Corvin was a sharp man who would see through a lie. He searched for the truth in every investigation, and it was the only thing that would save Veron now.

"My wife, she is—" His voice caught, the painful words too hard to speak. He'd never been close with his uncle, so the hesitation and embarrassment of sharing something so raw and personal were all too real. His vision blurred with the pain he hid since he learned of Marla's illness. All of it now left bear on his face. "The Herb Master said she doesn't have much time left. Any day now … I wish to be there when she…"

For the first time, his uncle's expression softened. "Right, of course. You may be dismissed. Go home. See to your wife and give her my best. I know I haven't said so, but I am sorry this happened, Veron. No one deserves such a disease, least of all Marla. To be born with such a poor set of lungs..." Corvin cleared his throat. "Return first thing in the morning for your questioning."

"Thank you, sir." Veron saluted and turned away, burying his elation.

This gave them time.

Keena will have already left ahead with the precious cargo, so he made his way out of the building to the stables. He mounted his horse and wasted no time riding out of the city.

The canter of hooves beat in his head with every memory of Marla. When they met. When they fell in love. When she fell ill. It beat with every worry and fear of what would happen to her next. Not what he would do without her, but what she would do without him if they were caught.

Veron whipped the reins. Soon the buildings gave way to cottage homes and fallow fields. The cobblestone road eventually became dirt. He followed it as he had many times before, and his mansion on sprawling green lands came into view.

Laurie was already waiting by the door when he pulled up. His stable hand took the reins as Veron dismounted and rushed up the stairs.

"Welcome home, my lord." Laurie bowed her head but could not hide the worry creasing within the wrinkles of her soft face.

"My wife?"

"She rests," Laurie said carefully, but it was what she always said instead of "she looks worse." He always knew what she meant.

He rushed inside. "I will see her."

"You have guests in the drawing-room, my lord. Princess Keenali from the Morphos arrived with her—"

Keena stepped out and gave him a curtsy in greeting. The guardsmen were behind her.

"Parden our intrusion, Lord Moreland," the princess said, playing her part perfectly. "I thought I should come visit the Lady of the house, but perhaps I should come another time."

"Nonsense," Veron said before Laurie could agree. "Come, I'm sure Marla would be happy to see you. Laurie, tend to the guardsmen. Serve them food and drink in the dining hall. Under no circumstances are you to disturb me."

"Yes, my lord." The old housekeeper frowned and left to do as ordered.

Exchanging a look with Keena, they rushed up the stairs inside to the second floor. Their footsteps were muffled as they practically ran down the blue runner of their long hallway to his chambers. The room was dark, with heavy drapes covering the tall windows. Warmth came from the fire, crackling in the fireplace in the far corner.

Marla slept in the massive four-poster bed, nearly swallowed by the silk comforters.

Once so bright with warmth and life, her face was now gaunt, face sunken in. Cheekbones stretched against her sickly complexion, hair long golden hair now ashy and wiry on the pillows. But still beautiful. To him, she always would be.

He sat on the edge of the bed and brushed his wife's hair away from her face. "Wake up, love."

Lashes fluttering open, Marla's blue eyes found his. "Veron?" she rasped sleepily. Her loving smile grew with a new joy when she spotted Keena on her other side. "My pretty pixie. You came."

"Sorry I haven't come sooner," Keena said softly.

"How lovely it is to see you. Thank you for bringing my dear friend, love." Every word Marla spoke cost her, her lungs wheezing with each weak breath.

It hurt to hear. He swallowed several times, struggling to find the right words.

I'm sorry. I love you. Forgive me.

It wasn't his fault she fell ill, but it felt as if it was all the same. He always had a solution for every battle he came across, but not this one. Not until today.

Marla reached out to him, and Veron carefully took her soft, frail hand in his. Her skin was thin, her fingers so delicate and bony.

Absent was her glow. The warmth and joy that had brought light to his dull existence. The life slowly draining from her was being drained from him, as well.

"I know how much you have missed her," he said.

"Dearly." A frown crossed her face as she took in Keena's appearance. "But look at the state of you, Keena. What happened?"

"Nothing you should fret over." Keena said.

"You should have told us you were in the city," Marla fussed. "You know we would have provided a safe place for you and your guardsmen to stay—"

A fit of violent coughs interrupted her. Veron held her through it, feeling as her body heaved against his. He pretended not to notice when she discreetly wiped her mouth with a handkerchief and hid it beneath the blanket.

But he saw the red stains. Keena did too.

"I didn't wish to be a burden," the fairy said, her voice wobbling.

Marla searched her face knowingly. Her sad smile was used to the pity and acknowledgment of what little life she had left. "You are never a burden. Now no tears. Only smiles. Come sit and tell me about the adventures you have been up to."

Keen released a shaky breath and glanced at Veron, giving him the chance to change his mind. But a part of him had decided what he would do the moment he saw divine blood. There was no going back now.

He nodded. "She has brought you a gift."

The princess removed the vial from the folds of her torn gown.

"You did?" Marla's eyes sparked a little brighter, and she struggled to sit. Veron quickly helped prop her up against the pillows. "What is it? Another one of your lovely perfumes?"

"Something else." Keena turned the vial in her hands. "It's ... medicine."

Marla sighed. "Keena, sweetheart, I know you wish to help, but there's no cure. And it's all right. I had a good life."

Too short of a life. Human lives were but a blink in the life of the fae, but this was simply unfair. It wasn't right.

"This is a rare medicine, Mar." He caressed her delicate cheek. "Don't ask me what's inside, but please trust me when I say it will heal you."

For once in his life, Veron wanted to be selfish. This disease stole their time together, but if Celestial blood would return their future, he didn't care about the repercussions anymore.

Marla's brows furrowed. "Veron…"

"Please take it," he told her, clutching her hand. The desperation and anguish he tried so hard to hide bubbled out of his throat. "I tried to be strong enough to lose you, but I'm not. I can't do it."

"All right," Marla said softly and wiped the tears that spilled down his face. "All right, I'll take it."

He could tell she was only humoring him. She'd already given up on herself, and he hated that.

Removing the cork, Keena passed the vial to him, and he helped Marla drink. She sipped the thick liquid, repeatedly blinking in confusion and awe.

"What is this? It almost tasted like—"

"Finish it." He tipped the end, making her swallow every drop.

She sat there in bewilderment, her eyelids falling heavy. Her body sagged back into the pillows. "What … what did you give me, Veron? It was unlike any medicine I've had before. It was sweet and heavenly, almost like…" Marla licked her bloodied lips, completely perplexed. "Magic."

Veron took the vial and tossed it into the fireplace. Marla frowned questioningly. Keena shook her head and put a finger to her lips. The room fell absolutely still until every shard of broken glass melted.

"How are you feeling?" he finally asked, surveying Marla. But for all of his fears, for the first time in a very long time, there was color in her cheeks.

Marla inhaled a breath, and her eyes widened when she did so without trouble. She inhaled again, laying a hand on her chest. "God of Urn. I can…" Her eyes watered as she stared at him. "I can breathe, Veron. The pain is gone. I can breathe."

Veron pulled her into his arms as he buried his face in the crook of her throat and broke down. Every emotion he held back: anger, sadness, panic, hope, joy, relief. It all swelled in his body as he released each one. She cried with him, and he gave thanks for every rise and fall of her lungs. He had his wife back.

Marla sniffled, caressing his hair. "Veron, what's going on? What did you give me? For a moment, I thought it was blood."

Veron wiped his face, quickly composing himself as he rose to his feet. Taking Marla's hands in his, he pressed his mouth over her fingers. "It was a miracle in a bottle, but one you must tell no one."

"I don't understand."

"I cannot explain. Not here." He kissed her forehead, then her lips. "Everything I do is for you."

They may have saved her life, but Veron couldn't bring himself to confess he may have condemned his.

But worry crossed Marla's features as she searched his. "What do you mean? Darling, what's the matter?"

"We have to leave Azure." Veron glanced at Keena, and she nodded sadly. She knew giving Marla divine blood meant they could no longer stay in Azure. He went to the wardrobe and began pulling out clothing. "Get dressed, love. We're leaving. Now."

"Veron?" Marla called, rising from bed. "What's happening? You're scaring me."

"He will explain later," Keena said, helping pull a dress over her chemise and patting down her hair. "But right now, you must go. No time for questions."

"What? But—"

Keena slipped shoes on Marla's feet. "Quickly now."

Within minutes, Veron had their bags packed. They rushed Marla down the stairs, promising to answer her questions when it was safe. The foyer was empty. Laughter and the clink of silverware leaked from another hall, the servants preoccupied with tending to the guardsmen.

"Where will you go?" Keena asked Veron at the front door.

"I have family in the United Crown."

"Good."

The United Crown was halfway across the country and safely out of Azure's jurisdiction. A distant cousin owed him a favor. It was time Veron called it in.

"Gold?" Keena asked next.

"I have enough." It was too late to go to the bank.

"Avoid the ports. Take the portal in Willows Grove. You know the tree." Keena hugged them both. "Well then, I suppose this is goodbye for now."

Tears streamed down Marla's face. "Will we ever see each other again, pretty pixie?"

"Of course, we will. Now, no more crying." Keena kissed Marla's cheek, fighting tears herself. "Fate has given you a second chance. Live a long and happy life."

Veron unpinned his Azure badge off his lapel and set it on a table by the door, surprised to feel relieved to be free of its weight. Marla's hand slipped into his, and he and kissed her temple. Not one part of him regretted what he'd done. Perhaps some guilt for dishonoring the Moreland name. But not regret.

He glanced out one of the mansion's windows at the smoky sky in the distance. "The prince must regret ever stepping foot in my city, but I am so grateful he did," Veron said, thinking of Cassiel. "I wish I had the opportunity to thank him."

Keena smiled as she reached for the door. "Maybe one day you will."

Character Art

Come along as I share with you the last three pieces of completed artwork of the gang back in 2006, when the story was still titled *Relic Hunters* and intended to be a graphic novel.

This is Lord Rawn Norrlen and Princess Keenali. Rawn, as most of you know, was inspired by Legolas (I might have had a little crush on him back in the day). There is just something about that bow and gentle personality. I loved the *Lord of the Rings* movie trilogy and it was a major influence for the *Guardians of the Maiden* series.

Keena went through the most change. I noticed all my Guardians were white, and this didn't sit well with me, especially as someone who loves to see representation. The world of Urn has races and creatures of all backgrounds and colors. That should show in the main cast as well. So the strongest Guardian became a POC character.

And this is my Klyde! He easily ties with Cassiel as one of my favorite characters. His funny personality balances out his ruthlessness and he always keeps those around him on his toes. He went through some minor changes, like longer hair and a beard that covers up that scar, his weapons ect. But overall, he is the same Klyde from fifteen years ago.

And here we have Cassiel and Dyna (she had short hair back then). I have this drawing framed in my office because it's near and dear to my heart. I simply had to recreate this scene in *Bonded Fate* as a shout out to the past and where the story all began.

While I may not draw anymore, the characters still come to life in the work of others. If you would like to see your *Guardians of the Maiden* fan art in future limited editions, please send a copy to **beck@beckmichaels.com**

Thank you for joining the Guardians on their journey!

The adventure continues in...

SHATTERED SOULS

GUARDIANS OF THE MAIDEN: BOOK 3

Keep reading for a sneak peek snippet

Are you aware of what that does to you? Dyna wanted to ask. *Of the toll it takes?*

But she kept still, pretending to be asleep as she peered through her lashes and watched Tarn swallow the enchanted wine to the dregs. With the layer of perspiration on his face and clothes, his labored breathing, it was clear he knew what it was doing to him other than keeping sleep at bay.

He had a camp of men at his service, yet he didn't trust them enough to leave himself unguarded. Which only proved that instilling fear didn't inspire loyalty—

Tarn unbuttoned his shirt, and the fabric slipped away. Dyna's next breath caught in her lungs.

It wasn't his partial nakedness that stalled her thoughts, not even the rigid muscles of his tall frame. It was the many horrifying scars over nearly every inch of him, as if some creature had chewed him up and spat him out. He cursed under his breath, pressing on his forehead as he turned away to rummage in his trunk, giving her view of the deep scars that lacerated through his back. Not made by teeth ... but with a whip. Violence was embedded in each one so deeply, as if delivered with fury and hate. Somehow more terrible than all the rest.

Tarn slipped on a clean tunic, the scars vanishing from her brief view. But she'd seen enough to know that sort of thing left a mark on more than the body. It had a way of resurfacing again and again. She would know.

"You don't drink Witch's Brew to avoid vulnerability," Dyna whispered.

Tarn stiffened, and his cold, pale blue eyes met hers over his shoulder. The tent chilled at the warning in his gaze not to speak aloud what she'd discovered, but the words fell from her lips.

"You're afraid to dream."

About the Author

BECK MICHAELS is the American author of the enchanting young adult novel *Divine Blood*, the first book in the epic fantasy series *The Guardians of the Maiden*. Beck lives in Indiana with her husband and two children, where she spends her time reading and daydreaming of stories in faraway lands.

WWW.BECKMICHAELS.COM

PLUMA
PRESS

Made in the USA
Middletown, DE
06 January 2022

57939227R00328